THE EVIL SEED

THE EVIL SEED

Joanne Harris

WINDSOR

PARAGON

First published 1992
by Warner Books
This Large Print edition published 2009
by BBC Audiobooks Ltd by arrangement with
Transworld Publishers Ltd

Hardcover   ISBN: 978 1 408 42965 5
Softcover   ISBN: 978 1 408 42966 2

British Library Cataloguing in Publication Data available

Printed and bound in Great Britain by
CPI Antony Rowe, Chippenham and Eastbourne

Acknowledgements

Many thanks to all those who contributed to bringing this book back from the dead. To my editor Francesca Liversidge, to Lucie Jordan and Lucy Pinney, to Holly Macdonald who did the artwork. To my heroic agent Peter Robinson, to Jennifer and Penny Luithlen and, as always, to the book reps, book sellers and enthusiasts who work so tirelessly to keep my books on the shelves. Thanks also to the many readers who persisted in asking for the reissue of this book. It wouldn't be here without you.

Author's Note

There are dangers in trying to dig up the past. There must be rewards as well, I daresay, but as a child it was always the dangers that appealed most to my imagination: the curse of the pharaoh's tomb, the artefacts removed, in the face of ancient warnings, from the ruined Mayan temple, bringing catastrophe in their wake; the lost city guarded by the ghosts of the dead. Perhaps, then, it was inevitable that this book, written so many years ago that I had thought it safely buried, should haunt me so persistently, clamouring for release, just as so many of my more avid and curious readers have clamoured for its re-publication.

A little background, then. First, let me say that it was never my intention to bury this book. Time does that pretty well on its own; and I was twenty-three when I wrote it. That makes this seed a good twenty years old, and when it was first planted, I had no idea of what it might one day blossom into.

I was a trainee teacher a few years out of Cambridge, living with my boyfriend (later to become my husband) in a mining village near Barnsley. We had seven cats, no central heating, no real furniture except for a bed, a drum kit and a couple of MFI bookcases, and my computer was an unwieldy thing with only five hundred bytes of RAM, which had an unpleasant mind of its own and a definite tendency to sulk. The neighbours referred to us as *Them Hippies* because I had decorated our walls with psychedelic murals, painted in acrylics and oils on to the Anaglypta. I made the patchwork curtains myself, as well as re-grouting the bathroom. My study was an upstairs bedroom, a kind of eyrie from which I could see the whole village: terrace houses, cobbled streets, back yards, distant fields. It always seemed to be foggy. I drove an ancient, bad-tempered Vauxhall Viva called Christine (after the Stephen King novel), which broke down on a weekly basis. Looking back now, I don't even know how I found the courage to write. It was freezing cold in my study; I had a little gas heater that threw out toxic fumes, and some multicoloured fingerless gloves. Maybe I thought it was romantic. My previous attempt at a novel, *Witchlight*, had been rejected by numerous publishers. I believe my pig-headed, awkward side (which is still the strongest part of me) took this as a kind of challenge. In any case, I began writing *The Evil Seed*—what my mother came to call *That Terrible Book*—and the idea slowly gained momentum, was galvanized into a kind of life and finally attracted the attention of a reader employed by a literary agency, which ultimately took me on.

Of course, I had no idea of what I was doing. I had no experience of the literary world, no contacts, no friends in the business. I had never studied creative writing, or even joined a writers' group. I didn't have a long-term plan; I didn't expect to make money. I was simply playing *Can You?*—that game that all storytellers play, following the skein of cherry-coloured twist along the crooked path through the woods to find out where it leads them.

For me, it was Cambridge—partly because I knew the place, and it seemed like the ideal setting for the kind of ghost story I wanted to write. I'd had the idea originally when I was just a student. On a visit to Grantchester, I happened to look in the cemetery and saw an interesting gravestone, bearing the inscription: *Something inside me remembers and will not forget.* That phrase, and the odd open-door shape of the monument, sparked off the beginnings of this story. My plot was ambitious; my style experimental. I was still too young to have quite found my voice, and so I wrote in two voices: one, that of a middle-aged man, Daniel Holmes, the other as a more conventional third-person narrator. I headed all the chapters, *One* and *Two* alternately, to distinguish between the two time frames; one being the present day, the other being just after the Second World War. I made it a story about vampires without ever using the word itself; a ghost story without a ghost; a horror story in which the mundane turns out to be more unsettling than any mythology. But it wasn't just a horror tale. It was also about seduction; about lost friendship, about art and madness and love and betrayal. I chose quite an ambitious structure—rather too ambitious for a horror novel. But I didn't think of what I was writing as genre fiction at all. I was trying to recreate the atmosphere of a nineteenth-century Gothic novel in a modern environment and a literary style. My publishers wanted the next Anne Rice. I should have known *that* would cause trouble.

The book came out some years later, under a somewhat gruesome black jacket. I'd wanted to call it *Remember*, but had been persuaded to change the name because my editor felt that it sounded too much like a romance. I never felt sure of the new name. Still, there's nothing to beat the feeling of seeing your first book in print. I used to lurk in bookshops, trying to spot someone buying my book, occasionally removing copies from the horror section and putting them into literature.

It *wasn't* literature, of course. It was a piece of fairly juvenile writing from someone who yet had to find her own style. At best, it was a heroic failure. At worst, it was pretentious and over-written. For a long time I resisted the demands of my readers to see it back in print—out of superstition, perhaps; my version of the mummy's curse. But given the chance to revisit this particular ruined temple, I have found it strangely rewarding. Heroic failure though it may be, I'm still rather fond of this first book of mine, in spite of all the time that has elapsed and in spite of the way my style has evolved. There's something in there that still resonates, something I had thought dead and buried, but which has come quite readily back to life. I'm not sure what my readers will make of it. Students of creative writing may use it as a means of charting the progress of one author over twenty years of trial and error. Others will just read the story for what it is, and, hopefully, may enjoy it.

The editor in me has made a few changes—only a few, I promise you—the story remains completely intact, but I couldn't resist brushing away some of the cobwebs that have gathered in the passageways. Even so, you should read the inscription over the door before you decide to follow me in. It's written in Latin (or maybe in hieroglyphics). It reads, roughly translated:

Caution—May Contain Vampires.
There. You can come in now.
Don't say I didn't warn you.

PART ONE

The Beggar Maid

Introduction

Larger than life, face and hands startlingly pale in a canvas as dark and narrow as a coffin, eyes fathomless as the Underworld and lips touched with blood, Proserpine seems to watch some object beyond the canvas in a mournful reverie. She holds the orb of the pomegranate, forgotten, against her breast, its golden perfection marred by the slash of crimson which bisects it, indicating that she has eaten, and thereby forfeited her soul. Doomed to remain for half the year in the Underworld, she broods, watching for the reflections of the far-away sun which flicker on the ivy-crusted walls.

Or so we are led to believe.

But she is a woman of many faces, this Queen of the Underworld; therein lies her power and her glamour. Pale as incense she stands, and the square of light which frames her face does not touch her skin; she shines with her own lambency, her pose weary as the ages, yet filled with the strength of her invulnerability. Her eyes never meet yours, and yet they never cease to fix a certain point just beyond your left shoulder; some other man, perhaps, doomed to the terrible bliss of her love, some other chosen man. The fruit she holds is red as her lips, red as a heart at its centre. And who knows what appetites, what ecstasies lie within that crimson flesh? What unearthly delights wait in those seeds to be born?

From *The Blessed Damozel*, Daniel Holmes

Prologue

There's rosemary, that's for remembrance;
pray you, love, remember.

Hamlet, 4.5

When I was a child, I had a lot of toys; my parents were rich and could afford them, I suppose, even in those days, but the one which I always remembered was the train. Not a clockwork train, or even one of those which you can pull behind you, but the real thing, speeding through countryside of its own, trailing a plume of white steam behind it, racing faster and faster towards a destination which always seemed to elude it. It was a spinning-top, painted red on the bottom half and made of a kind of clear celluloid on top, beneath which a whole world glowed and spun like a jewel, little hedges and houses and the edge of a painted circle of sky so clean and blue that it nearly hurt you to look at it too long. But best of all when you pumped the little handle ('always be careful with that handle, Danny, never spin your top too hard'), the train would come puffing bravely into view, like a dragon trapped under glass and shrunk by magic to minuscule size; coming slowly at first, then faster and faster until houses and trees blurred into nothingness around it, the whine of the top lost in the triumphant scream of the engine-whistle, as if the little train were singing with the fierce joy of being so nearly there.

Mother, of course, said that to spin the top too hard might break it (and I always took care, just in

5

case that might be true). But I think I believed, even then, that one day, if I was careless, if I let my attention wander even for a moment, then the train might finally reach its mysterious, impossible destination like a snake eating itself, tail first, and come bursting, monstrous, into the real world, all fires blazing, steel throwing sparks into the quiet of the playroom, to come for me in revenge at its long imprisonment. And maybe some of my pleasure was knowing that I had it trapped, that it could never escape because I was too careful, and that I could watch it when I liked. Its sky, its hedges, its mad race through the world were all mine, to set into motion when I liked, to stop when I liked, because I was careful, because I was clever.

But then again, maybe not. I don't recall being a fanciful child. I was certainly not morbid. Rosemary did that to me—did it to all of us, I suppose. She made us all into children again, looming over us like the wicked witch in the gingerbread house, ourselves little gingerbread men running around in circles, like little trains under celluloid as she watched and smiled and pumped the handle to set her wheels in motion.

My mind is wandering; a bad sign, like the lines around my eyes and the thin patch at the top of my head. There again, Rosemary's doing. When the priest said, 'Dust to dust', I looked up and thought I saw her again, just for a moment, leaning against the hawthorn tree with a smile in her eyes. If she had looked at me, I think I would have screamed. But she looked at Robert instead.

Robert was white, his face hollow and haunted beneath his hat, but not because he saw her. I was the only one who saw her, and only for a moment;

6

a change in the light, a movement, and I would probably have missed her. But I didn't. I saw her. And that, more than anything, is why I am writing to you now, to you, to my future beyond the grave, to tell you about myself and Robert and Rosemary . . . yes, Rosemary. Because she still remembers, you see. Rosemary remembers.

One

It was a beautiful day, crisp and autumn-clear, the ground bright with leaves, and the sky as round and as blue as the sky beneath which the little train had raced so many years ago. There were not many people: myself, Robert, a handful of others, all in black, their faces a blur in the sunlight. Only Robert's stands out in my memory, pale and caricatured by grief. It hurt me to look at him.

'White flowers only', had said the advertisement in the *Cambridge News* and that day there were hundreds of them: lilies and roses and great shaggy overblown chrysanthemums, lining the grave and the grassy path and crowning the coffin as it was lowered into the ground. Their scent was overwhelming, but the dark smell from the grave was stronger, and as the priest spoke the final words of the service I backed away from that open hole as a man retreats from the side of a cliff, feeling wretched for my friend but also strangely light-headed. Maybe it was the flowers.

He had chosen a lovely plot for her: right at the back of the churchyard, up against the wall, beneath the combined branches of a hawthorn tree and a shady yew. The death-tree stood arm-in-arm with the life-tree, their bright berries seeming to mock the grief of the mourner, as if they had been in league with the sweetness of the day to bedeck themselves in their most joyful colours to celebrate her passing. It would be beautiful in summer, I thought to myself, shady and green and silent. This year, the hemlock and the tall weeds had been

9

cleared away for the funeral but they would grow back.

Grow back.

The thought disturbed me in some way, but I could not think why. Let them grow, after all, let them invade that quiet place, overgrow the grave and the stone and the memory of Rosemary for ever; let flowers grow from her blind eyes. If only this could be the end, I thought. If only she could be forgotten. But Robert would remember, of course. After all, he loved her.

*   *   *

It was in the spring of 1947 when Rosemary first entered our lives. I was passing the weir at Magdalene Bridge, on my way to meet Robert at a tea-shop before we went to the library. I was twenty-five, a graduate student at the university; I was writing a doctorate paper on the Pre-Raphaelites (a much-maligned school of painting at the time, which I hoped to bring back into fashion). I existed in a world of books and absolutes; which suited my withdrawn, and somewhat obsessive personality. The stones and cobbles of Cambridge rested quiet, as they had done for centuries, an ideal backdrop for my studies and a retreat for myself from the bewildering advances of the modern world. I lived in the past and was happy there.

I had one good friend, a very nice lodging by Grantchester way and a comfortable allowance from my father, which supplemented my grant from the faculty. I had always assumed that when my doctorate was finished I would join the university as a full-time lecturer perhaps staying on at Pembroke, where my tutor, Doctor Shakeshafte, had always had high hopes for me. My life was all planned out as neatly and precisely as the gardens and lawns of Cambridge, and it never occurred to me to question the plan, or to hope for something more.

On that particular day, with the bright morning sun reflecting great panels of gold from the mullioned windows of Magdalene College, I was feeling on top of the world. As I quickened my step on the bridge, I was just beginning to sing to myself when I heard a sound below me and stopped.

I sometimes wonder what would have happened if I had ignored the sound, if I had run across the bridge for dear life without looking back, but there was no question of that of course. She had it all too well planned out. You see, it was the sound, unmistakably, of something falling into the river.

It was spring, and the Cam was at its highest. The weir rushed and snarled less than a hundred yards away, and anyone who fell in at that point was likely to be caught in the sluice and drowned. That was why punting was forbidden beyond the bridge; not that anyone would have been fool enough to try it. For a moment I was still, squinting over the parapet for the log or the broken punt or the piece of floating debris which must have caused the sound; then I saw her, a pale blur of a face over some kind of a pale dress ballooning out around her, hollows for eyes, every feature a blur, as if she were already a ghost.

'Hey!' I called, and I saw her head tilt into the rushing water like a tired child's into a pillow. No

11

call, no wave, nothing. For an instant, I thought I'd imagined her, so unreal was the apparition. Then the realization hit me that this was no accident, no dream, but some poor desperate woman half a minute from muddy death, with only me to save her. And so I came running, as she knew I would, stripping off coat and jacket and shoes as I ran along the bank, my glasses slipping from my nose, panting and shouting; 'Wait! Hey! Miss! Young lady!' without drawing even a glance from her. I jumped in close to the bank, a few yards downstream from her as she drifted slowly towards me, bracing myself for the shock of the cold water. My bare feet touched mud at the bed of the river, but at least I was not out of my depth. I reached for her. My hands brushed her dress and clenched like a vice. The flimsy fabric ripped, but by then I had a good grip on the girl, who seemed to be only half-conscious, and with all my strength I held on to her as I tried to fight my way back to the bridge. I don't know how long it took me, or how I managed to do it; I was never a man of action, but I suppose that in those days I had youth and ignorance on my side, and somehow I managed to use the uneven brick shoring of the river-bank to pull us both towards safe, still water. I hauled her out first and myself after her and for a while I had to lie on the bank, my breath coming in great, tearing gasps and my nose bleeding a little. She was lying as I had left her, her head thrown back and her arms flung wide, but her eyelids fluttered and her breathing was regular. My first thought was that she must be cold, and I retrieved my coat, the first in a line of garments discarded along the river-bank, and wrapped it clumsily around her shoulders, somehow embarrassed to touch her now that she was out of immediate danger, as if she might be angry at my familiarity.

My second thought, quite simply, was amazement at how lovely she was.

There was no lack of beautiful women in Cambridge in those days; you saw them at parties or at the theatre or at balls, walking arm-in-arm with their young men in the gardens or punting on the Cam. But this one, as soon as I saw her, seemed from another century. She was slim, and translucent, like very fine china, pale and tragic and delicate. Her cheekbones were high, her lips full, her features small and childlike. Her hair, I guessed, would be red when dry. But her beauty was not really any of these things. It was lambent, ardent, arrogant, as if it had looked upon ugliness only to become still more beautiful. She was one of those women, I knew it then, who are at their most lovely in rags; maybe King Cophetua had thought that too, the first time he looked upon the beggar maid. Then her eyes opened, a deep grey, almost lavender, blank at first, then fixing on my face with a wildness which wrenched at my heart.

'I'm not dead?' she whispered.

'No, you're not,' I said, foolishly. 'Everything will be all right.'

Well, of course, I didn't know it then. I said it simply to comfort her. But things were far from being all right. That day, or ever again.

Two

The tabby jumped on to Alice's knee, as if to remind her that she had been sitting in that chair doing nothing for nearly half an hour and that it might be time to do some work. Sighing, she kissed Cat's furry head before she put her down on the floor.

Cat mewed and rolled over to play, paws frantically kicking the air. Alice grinned and glanced at her sketch-pad, which showed the lively outline of a sleeping cat, firm pencil strokes for the body and paws, details half filled-in with brown ink.

Not a bad one, that, she thought, especially as it took no less than a miracle to get Cat to keep still for even a minute. But it wasn't real work; it had been six months since she had painted anything worthwhile, and it was time to begin in earnest again. Last year she had had quite a successful exhibition at Kettle's Yard which had resulted in a nice fat contract to illustrate a series of children's folk tales, but since then, the ideas seemed to have run temporarily dry and it didn't look as if she was going to have very much to exhibit this year. Well, that was how things went, thought Alice. Her pictures—the good ones—took time and thought, and the ideas either came or they didn't. There was no point worrying about all that now; it would only slow things down even more. She glanced at the three official-looking envelopes tacked to her notice-board (even at a distance, she could read the flowery 'Red Rose' logo across one of them), and sighed. That was where the money came from, she thought drily. The magazines. The teen romances. They were the reason she wasn't still sharing a flat with two other students at the rough end of Mill Road and claiming income support. A sudden wave of fierce resentment washed over her at the thought, and she stood up abruptly to face the window. Was this what she was reduced to doing? Illustrations for pulp romances? She deserved so much better than that. *Celtic Tales* had been her first really exciting project since her 'Spirit of Adventure' exhibition at Kettle's Yard, and after that . . . Alice shrugged. Forget it, she told herself. There was no point sitting indoors feeling resentful.

She pulled on a sweatshirt over her jeans, then slipped on a pair of old, scuffed trainers. She tacked the half-finished sketch on to the notice-board, ran her fingers through her short brown hair in lieu of a comb, and, thus ready to face the world, stepped out into the sunny street. The warmth and the combined scents of wallflowers and magnolia hit her with a sudden wave of well-being, and she took a deep breath of the pleasant air.

It occurred to her that it had been some time since she had walked into Cambridge. Strange, thought Alice. When she and Joe had been students there, they had always liked the town centre with its shops and little galleries and its cobbled streets under the linden trees. Still, that was all a long time ago. Better not to think of Joe. Better not to remember him too clearly, not to imagine him standing beside her, squinting into the shop windows with his hands in his pockets.

15

Better not to remember him at all.

Suddenly, she felt depressed. It was thinking about Joe, she told herself. That and the heat and the Cambridge crowds with their cameras and their college scarves and their brittle camaraderie.

Her favourite tea-shop was just round the corner, and there she found a window-seat, began to order Earl Grey, and ended up, unaccountably, ordering hot chocolate with cream and a large slice of fudge cake instead. Something in Alice responded well to chocolate.

The Copper Kettle was a good place. As a student, Alice had spent hours there, drinking Earl Grey or hot chocolate with cream, watching the flow of people in a pleasant, timeless daydream. Sitting in the same window watching the same street with the smell of chocolate and old leather in the smoky air, Alice looked down King's Parade, the Senate House reflecting the sunlight from its clean white stones, King's warm golden façade, and to her far left, the red brick walls of St Catherine's glowing behind its tall railings. The light in Cambridge was different to anywhere else Alice had ever seen; warm, sleepy, golden light, shifting like a Dali landscape over the floating spires, the sleeping gardens. Such a beautiful town, thought Alice, a town of illusions, ghosts and dreams. Even the students seemed vacant, somehow, for all their animated talk, as if in spite of everything they knew themselves to be transient, nothing but the dreams of those old and half-awakened stones.

Watching the students now, Alice felt old. She remembered herself, slimmer then and with long, untamed hair, wearing cut-off jeans and baggy

16

pullovers, Indian skirts and beads. Riding her bicycle in the rain. Sneaking over the gates at night. Sleeping with Joe in his narrow bed. She tried to remember. Had they felt it then, she thought, that sense of destiny? The brevity of their time rushing past? That terrible awareness of death?

Alice closed her eyes, uneasy, and tried to think of nothing at all.

Suddenly, in the muted hubbub of the crowded tea-shop, she recognized a voice and her eyes snapped open in surprise, something tightening like a wire inside her heart, in spite of herself. She knew that voice well, with its northern accent, and remembered sitting there in the Copper Kettle listening to Joe talking to her about his many enthusiasms: Jaco Pastorius and Roy Harper, and how Marxism was going to change the world . . .

She looked round, wondering whether she had imagined it. She had not seen him for three years, not since he had moved out. Ridiculous that she should still feel that sorry little jump of the heart. Ridiculous that she should look round, furtively, as if it were him. And if it were, then so what? He'd probably be with some girl.

She had almost persuaded herself that she had been wrong, that it had not been his voice at all, when she finally caught sight of him. He was sitting at a table in a corner of the room, his familiar face bent at a familiar angle which denoted attentiveness, a cigarette cupped in one hand, shoulders bent, hair falling messily over a narrow face, round wire glasses over piercing blue eyes. So he had started smoking again, thought Alice, remembering the smell of his cigarettes, how it

17

used to get everywhere, in his clothes, in his hair.

Her heart sank. He was not alone. There was a girl with him and, though much of her face was in shadow, Alice could guess at a small, graceful frame, the curve of a perfect collar-bone beneath a sheaf of bright-red hair. Well, what did she expect, she thought? So what if he had found someone else? Surely, after all this time—

She caught the sound of his voice again as she pushed back her chair to go, and the wire in her heart twisted again.

She could not distinguish actual words, but the tone was enough. Smoke from his cigarette obscured his face, giving his features a disturbing transparency, but in the semi-darkness she could guess his smile.

A memory, long-stored in Alice's mind, flipped over like a dead leaf. Suddenly the busy little tea-shop was nowhere near crowded enough and, trying not to catch his eye, Alice fled into the sunlight, tight-lipped and hating herself for caring, but caring anyway. Impelled by an anger she dared not admit she quickened her pace, making her way out of the town, so that more than an hour later she found that without meaning to she had walked as far as Grantchester. Alice was barely even surprised. Walking was her way of dealing with stress. In the weeks and months following the break-up with Joe, Alice had done a great deal of walking. She slowed down and looked around.

There was a church in front of her. A little round tower rising up from the trees. It was not a place Alice knew well, in spite of visits to Grantchester—but now the little church drew her, and the shady trees looked inviting. The grass in

18

front was neatly cut, the graves well-kept and orderly. Around the church and its grounds stood a curving, solid-looking old wall. A little path twisted here and there between headstones and monuments, touching this one and that one, gently, like a friend. Alice followed the path a little way, reading the gravestones. Some of them were even older than she expected: under a tree she found one dated 1690, though most of the others seemed more recent. On reaching the other side of the church, Alice found the path leading her into the second churchyard, even more enclosed than the first, shaded by cedars and apple trees. A squirrel skittered across the path and over the ivy-covered wall. Alice followed it. At the end of the path there was an arch, with a door set into the arch, half-open, looking on to a third graveyard; a more modern one, sheltered from the road by the same wall and still half-empty.

It happens sometimes that people are led by chance to where they need to be; at other times, events touch each other like threads in a woven fabric, one picture overlapping another, the rough binding at the back of the tapestry joined together so that heroine bleeds on to villain, sea and sky merge in uneasy union, clean edges break up and become strange and disquieting boundaries to the other side. Whichever way she tried to look at it afterwards, Alice was sure that it was there that it all began, that from the moment she set eyes on that door, all her movements were accountable, all her thoughts a completion of something much greater, much older than she. The Tailor of Gloucester in Beatrix Potter's little book nearly lost everything for the sake of a single twist of cherry-coloured silk; for want of a thread a whole embroidered coat and waistcoat, fit for the mayor, could not be finished. And looking back at events later, when the pattern of things began at last to emerge, Alice always imagined, in her mind's eye, the long strand of silk leading to that little wooden door, leading her on to the other side of the picture, where no rules applied, and where something was about to awaken.

Of course, at the time she had no such thoughts. They came later, with Ginny and Joe. Only a sense of peace and a quiet pleasure in the still warm air as she pushed the door and went into the hidden churchyard. The graves there were beautifully tended, planted with shrubs and flowering trees. A couple of the headstones were crooked, half hidden in the undergrowth, but there was no sense of desolation about the place, only an air of dignity, as of tired old people sitting down in the grass. A couple of the graves were marked with flowers, planted perhaps by some relative; yes, it was a good place. Two trees stood at the very back of the garden, a hawthorn in bloom, and a dark yew in stark contrast, shadowing a grave half hidden by vegetation. She wondered whose grave it was, overgrown with long, ripe weeds, so beautifully and almost self-consciously framed by the two trees.

She took a closer look, and saw that there was no headstone, or visible name, but from its elegance she thought that it was probably a woman's grave. A simple sculpture topped the slab. A gate, half open, allowed to swing loosely on its hinges, with an inscription on the outside:

Something inside me remembers and will not forget.

Experimentally, Alice pulled at the clinging ivy, trying to dislodge it. The roots were long, but dry, and they came free easily enough, leaving pale scars in the decaying stone, but the inscription began to appear, faintly at the foot of the slab. It was more modern than the state of the grave might have suggested, and read:

Rosemary Virginia Ashley
August 1948

Alice searched for some other detail: whether Rosemary had been married, what she died of, who the lover or husband had been who had promised never to forget, but there was nothing more to see. She covered up the inscription, once more replacing the ivy where she had found it. It would be somehow wrong, she felt, to leave the grave exposed, like a wound.

Her mind was wandering as she replaced the last of the trailing ivy, and, for a moment, she did not even notice the thin piece of metal which brushed her fingers from beneath the leaves. At first, she thought it was the ring-pull from a Coke can; it was light, and had the same uneven sharpness at the edges. There was a hole in one end, as if it had once been attached to something, and there was moss clinging to one surface, but even then, Alice could read the inscription:

Rosemary
For Remembrance

21

Alice felt her heart beat faster. Surely this could be no coincidence. This tag had been hers, Rosemary's, placed on her grave when she was buried. Maybe tied on to some wreath or plant. Somehow, just finding that little piece of metal made everything all the more real, all the more sad. She wondered for a moment whether to throw the tag back on to the grave, then she shrugged and hid it in her pocket, without really thinking what she was doing, without considering the implications; just as the cat had hidden the final twist of cherry-coloured silk from the Tailor of Gloucester.

*　　　　*　　　　*

As soon as she got home, Alice made a cup of tea, took it to her workroom (a table, a stool, an easel, a window facing north, a record player and a messy stack of albums), dragged a thick watercolour pad out of an overflowing cupboard and began to draw. The idea had come to her full-blown, had followed her home from Grantchester, had refused to let her be, and now it was growing, line by line, light and precise on the paper, gaining a depth as the lines grew thicker, gaining shadow, sunlight, greenery.

A girl's figure, thin-shouldered, but with a pure half-profile half-hidden in a tumbling mass of hair, barefoot and dressed in a long white robe. She was sitting on the ground, hugging her knees, her head tilted away from the viewer at an odd, childish angle. Around her, long grass, flowers and weeds; in the background, two half-defined trees and a sketched-in figure, possibly male, stooping slightly

22

under the tree branches. Alice stepped back a pace to look at the finished sketch and smiled, liking it. It was deliberately Pre-Raphaelite in composition: the ordered disorder of the undergrowth contrasting with the quiescence of the girl, shrouded in her mystery, watching the river with that curious intentness, while the ill-defined figure in the background watched or waited.

She took a gulp of cold tea and began to think about colour. Then she put a record on to the turntable and deftly began to ink in the colours. A splash of reflection in the water . . . the girl's dress undefined—she could airbrush that in later—the hair a single bright spray of colour among the muted greens and greys. Yes, quite good, Alice thought. But then again, she often did in the heat of creativity. Tomorrow might reveal it to be nothing special, after all. And yet it gave her a feeling she hadn't had for a long time.

The light dimmed. She turned on the lights and carried on working. Side one of the record played twice before she noticed and turned it over, the other side three times. She heard a mewing at her door, indicating that the cats should be fed; she heard the telephone and ignored it. Acrylics replaced inks; she carefully painted on and peeled off masking gum while airbrushing the triangle of sky, the water, the girl's dress; replaced her thin acrylic brush for an even thinner one, adding detail to the leaves, the grass, the texture of the girl's hair; then she stepped back, dropped her brushes, and stared.

There was no doubt about it; it was good. Just simple enough to reproduce beautifully as a poster or the cover of a book, classic enough to hang in an airy gallery, peaceful enough to grace a church altar. Never had inks and acrylic produced such pure colours for her before; never had Alice managed a composition which had had quite the same intensity. You *had* to look at it; even Alice found herself speculating about who the girl was, what she was doing, wondering who the figure in the background might be.

She looked at the picture for a long time before she took the brush again and signed it. Then, after a moment's hesitation, in her delicate, precise calligraphy, she wrote the name of the picture underneath her own:

Remembrance: The Madness of Ophelia

By now she was exhausted; looking at her watch, she realized with something of a shock that it was almost ten o'clock, and that she had worked through half the afternoon and most of the evening, but it was a good exhaustion, as if working had cleansed her of all her worries and negative thoughts. Already, her mind was racing. Maybe, after such a long time without painting anything worthwhile, she had hit a new lode of creation within herself; maybe there would be more Ophelia paintings, maybe a whole series of them which would be exhibited at Kettle's Yard that summer. The new ideas spun like carnival wheels and, ravenously hungry all of a sudden, she made herself a late snack, fed the cats, went to bed and slept like the dead for the rest of the night.

One

I never thought to come back to her grave. For the three months after her funeral I deliberately stayed clear of Grantchester, as if, by my very presence, I might fill that place with unquiet ghosts. If she rested easy, then so much the better but, thought I, I would not be the one to watch over her rest. In the nervous and despondent state in which her passing had left me, I saw her often; or thought I did. A girl in black, profile slightly averted, stepping into a cab. A girl in the rain, face hidden beneath a dark umbrella. Once, a girl walking by the river, red hair fiery-bright beneath a pale scarf. No, I was not haunted, but she mocked me, touching every part of my life with her delicate, spidery hand, walking with me wherever I went.

Or so I thought. I think I fell ill; the doctor told me that overwork and overworry had led to a poverty of the blood, prescribed a rich diet with plenty of wine, advised me to stop working for a week or two. I made my own secret diagnosis, took the doctor's advice concerning the wine a little too literally, contracted pneumonia and nearly died.

When I resumed interest in life a couple of months later (my landlady had nursed me lovingly throughout my illness in a sweet half-life free from troubles or disturbing realities), it was already too late. Robert had been dead for more than two weeks, buried in the same churchyard as Rosemary while I slept and tossed and whined, thinking of myself as usual, when he needed me most. Not that the act really surprised me, when I came to think about it; the moment I saw her watching him the day of the funeral, I should have guessed that that was what she had in mind. Her smile was possessive, protective, indulgent, horribly knowing. In the same way does the Blessed Damozel in Rossetti's painting look down upon her tormented, stricken lover; patiently, silently, with the hint of a smile. I could never look at that picture afterwards without a shudder, for though I could never see any physical resemblance to Rosemary in it, there was something—something in the smile, perhaps, or maybe simply the witchlike outsizedness of the blessed lady in comparison to her doomed lover— that reminded me too sharply of her. I wrote a book, fifteen years later, a rewriting of my dissertation paper on the Pre-Raphaelites, in which I examined Rossetti's fascination for beautiful witchlike women; I dedicated it on paper to my college art lecturer, but I knew that I wrote it for Rosemary, to Rosemary, about Rosemary. I called it *The Blessed Damozel*. I believe it still sells.

It took me five days of guilt and self-loathing before I went to Robert's graveside. By that time the wreaths and ribbons had been removed, and all that was left was the little mound of earth and some shrubs in a stone trough at the foot of the grave. Small green plants, no flowers. There was a label on the thin stem of one of the shrubs, one of those metal tags you see on the stems of prize rose bushes at garden shows, and I flipped it over to read it.

Rosemary
For Remembrance

26

I think I kept my calm well enough then, despite the first onrush of panic which threatened to overwhelm me. I had already seen too much to be terrified by a cheap practical joke. I already knew she was there. It would take more than that to hurt me—in fact, I foolishly thought that with Robert gone, I had nothing else to fear. She was gone, I said to myself, gone, buried, forgotten. I laid my little bunch of mistletoe and holly at the head of the grave and turned to go.

Poor Robert.

Suddenly, I felt her there, her presence filling the churchyard. Her hate, and with it, amusement. The scent of rosemary wafted up from the little row of shrubs in front of me, warmed by the slanting winter sun, sweet and oddly nostalgic, the scent of country kitchens, of drawers filled with clean white linen, of country girls combing rosemary oil through their long hair. I was absolutely convinced that if I were to look up I would see her there, watching me from beneath her heavy eyelids, face pale, her tragic mouth curling in something not quite like a smile . . . I was so convinced that she was there that when I raised my eyes I actually saw her standing in the shade of the hawthorn tree, then she was only a jumble of light and shade on the bare path, where a patch of brown and frozen weeds nodded almost imperceptibly over a gravestone I had never noticed before.

For a moment I stared stupidly. It was a simple enough idea: a flat stone set into the mossy ground with a small cast-iron sculpture rising above it, maybe two feet high. A frame, like a door-frame, with a kind of crest on the top, within which stood what looked to me like a little door or gate, set against the frame with hinges. As I looked, a gust of wind pushed against the little gate and it blew open with a tiny sound, then clicked shut as the wind released it. At the head of the grave was a shallow stone trough, in which a few small green shrubs nodded and whispered.

Of course. This must be her grave; this the remembrance Robert had spoken of. His idea. I don't know why I approached it then; I should have known that it would do me no good. It may be that I wanted to know what had been in my friend's mind before his suicide, as if my penance before Rosemary's grave might help his tortured soul to rest. Maybe I felt some stirring of guilt. Because I killed her, you know, or at least, I did the best I could. Or maybe I went for the same reason that the young girl looks into Bluebeard's chamber, for the same reason that the two children go to the gingerbread house, or that the boy lets the genie out of the bottle . . .

I read the inscription, of course. After all, that was why it was there.

Something inside me remembers and will not forget.
Rosemary Virginia Ashley
August 1948

Something inside me remembers . . . I came there often after that, not able to help myself, fascinated and repelled and terrified all at once. *Something inside me remembers* . . . Only I really understood those words. Everyone else took it as a message from Robert, proof of his love for his dead wife.

28

But I knew Robert better than that. He may have been weak, but he was not maudlin. He may have died a little when Rosemary was buried, but he would not have laid his heart open like that for lovers to gawp at as they took their romantic walks in Grantchester churchyard. He was a practical man, and practical men are the ones who suffer the most from love, when it comes their way. And whatever the evidence, I know he didn't kill himself. That was a message to me from her. A defiant cry from beyond the grave. She isn't dead, and she wants me to know it. She has all the time in the world. And she still remembers.

But I'm not afraid. I'm safe. I still have my final trick to play, the last card which will keep me safe. And do you know what my last card is? It's you, friend. You don't believe me? You will. As you read this diary you'll hate me, despise me, but you won't disbelieve me. It's all right, you don't have to do it all at once; put the book away in a drawer, forget it for a while, for years if you like, but you'll come back. I know you will. You'll have to come back sooner or later, because she's here. She's waiting for you. Just as she was waiting for me. So be careful.

When the time comes, much may depend upon which way I turn you.

Two

All that day Alice had been restless. Now she nibbled her way through a packet of biscuits, turned the television on. A black-and-white film, a chat-show, a Russian cartoon . . . she turned it off.

She made some tea, sat down, let the tea go cold, poured it down the sink, put on a record, played it twice without hearing it, took it off.

Then she reached for the letter from her contact at Red Rose and tried to re-awaken her interest in the illustrator's job they had offered her. It was a fairly easy one—six line-drawings and a book jacket for a teen romance called *Heartbreak High*. It should have been easy, Alice thought; and yet she had wasted most of the day filling the waste-basket with half-finished sketches, until finally she admitted to herself that it was seeing that girl with Joe that had done it, hearing his voice so unexpectedly.

Not that it mattered now of course. It was over. End of topic.

And yet tonight, it felt lonely. Just for tonight, it might be good to hear the phone ring. A fleeting query from her subconscious (*something inside me remembers* . . .); but who *would* remember her if she disappeared tomorrow? Her mother, keeping the faith for her vanished ones two hundred miles away? Her contact at Red Rose? The only friends she had had were also Joe's friends; she had lost them when she lost Joe. And while times had been good, she had not felt the need for anyone outside him. Damn. A sudden rage at herself overpowered Alice. Why couldn't she let it go? Part of it was seeing that gravestone, the inexplicable sense of *envy* for the dead girl whose lover would not forget.

She considered ringing up her mother in Leeds, the only person outside her work from whom she ever received phone calls, then she shrugged and sat down again. No. It would be nice to hear her mother's voice, but ringing her would simply open the doorway to all the usual reproaches and criticisms and enquiries: 'When are you going to come and visit us?' 'Have you got a job yet?' (As if what Alice was doing for a living were some kind of a hobby in preparation for 'real work'.) 'Are you sure you're looking after yourself?'

Poor Mother, thought Alice, Mother who had grown harder and sharper with the years after the cancer finally got Dad, Mother whose sweetness had become buried under all the extra flesh she had put on since turning fifty, and who always spoke in the same careful code, never quite saying what she meant, perhaps never quite finding the words.

She had been bright once: black-and-white photographs showed a dark, narrow-waisted girl with a lovely smile, arm-in-arm with the handsome young man Dad had been before he lost his hair so early. She had been romantic enough to call her little girl Alice after Alice in Wonderland. 'Because,' she said, 'you had just the same kind of wide astonished eyes.' But now she was a disappointed fat woman, coarsened and faded not by grief but by the constant erosion of joyless days passing; and the worst of it was that, some day, Alice was terribly afraid that she might look into the mirror and see her mother's face staring out at her.

Alice sighed and looked at the clock. Half past ten. She supposed she ought to go to bed soon, but didn't feel tired. She reached across to the bookshelf, chose a paperback at random, hoping to put herself to sleep by reading a few pages.

31

There might be some leftover chocolate ice-cream in the ice-box, she thought; she couldn't remember. She went to the fridge to check, thinking vaguely that she was eating too much nowadays and that she ought to try and cut down. She suppressed the image of her mother, sitting in the lounge in their old house soon after Dad died, eating packets of prawn cocktail crisps with a blank-eyed, ferocious energy.

Bottles clinked inside the fridge door, and the four cats materialized, seemingly from nowhere, to investigate the promise of milk. Alice felt the warm, wriggling bodies around her legs and felt herself relax a little.

Rogue memories of Joe. Joe in the upstairs bedroom practising endless riffs on his guitar, frightening the cats. Joe frowning over a pile of manuscript paper and an overflowing ashtray. Joe at the head of a peace demonstration carrying a big banner with 'Bum the Bomb'. Joe arguing with a policeman, Alice tugging at his arm. Joe rolling a joint one-handed, Joe frowning over one of Alice's paintings, saying: 'The lines are too weak. It doesn't stand out at a distance.'

Alice: 'It's perfectly all right, you Philistine. It's supposed to look ethereal, like a Rackham.'

Alice sneaking back to her studio later that night to change the picture and sharpen the lines.

Joe playing in his first band, blind drunk, but never a wrong note.

The binges; making love on an unmade bed with dozens of wine bottles and chocolate wrappers and pizza boxes piled up on the floor. The quarrels, screaming at each other in Joe's music-room as Alice found success and Joe didn't. His jealousy, his sudden flashes of bitterness at everything: the band which never managed to get a contract, never having enough money, never having been given a chance. As they grew older, watching the students come and go, knowing that the whole world belonged to *them*, and finally having to accept that he was ten years older and that a new generation had sprung up beneath him. Youngsters who were strong and smart and who knew exactly where they were going. People who wore the right clothes. Who went to see the right bands. And with that realization came a kind of helplessness and a kind of anger, against the kids, the government, all the bloodsuckers who were killing him by degrees.

Alice smiled, remembering. If only he had known how to stay friends. If only he hadn't been so afraid.

Still, her choice was made now. The regrets were few. She checked the ice-box. The chocolate ice-cream was there after all. That would help a lot, she thought.

Suddenly, the phone rang, and Alice knew that it was Joe.

'Alice?' his voice was breathless, so that she had difficulty placing it. Then the memory locked into place with a jolt, like changing gears on an old bicycle.

'Joe! How are you?' She fought for control; seeing him, then thinking about him, and now hearing his voice on the phone gave her a strange sensation, something like dizziness, as if a long-stopped wheel had begun to turn.

'I'm fine.' His voice was slightly unsteady, as it sometimes was when he was particularly excited or angry; Alice, straining over the poor line, could

33

not tell which.

'Still playing the blues?' she asked, stalling for time and automatically slipping into the old pattern of their conversations, that light, brittle humour which masked so much intensity.

'That's me, the mean guitar machine.'

A pause.

'What about you, Al? I saw your book. It was pretty good. Kids' stuff, but still . . . I always knew you'd make it, you know. And I saw your exhibition. You'll be at the RA next time I look.' He gave a little laugh which tugged at her heart. 'I see you still have that trouble with outlines, though.'

'Flattery gets you anywhere, Joe.'

'Me, I've got a new band. We call ourselves Fiddle the Dole. We've been going for near to a year, now. Electric folk, covers and original songs. We play the Wheatsheaf every Saturday. You should come to listen to us some day. We're good.' A pause. 'So how're you doing?'

'Fine, Joe. Yes, I'm—'

'Jess told me about— Are you OK—'

'You talked to my mother?' said Alice. 'When?'

'Hey, relax. I met her by accident. We were playing the university in Leeds. She said you'd been ill. She was just trying to find out how you were.'

'I wasn't ill,' said Alice flatly. 'I just went out of circulation for a while.'

'Well, I'm back here to stay now,' went on Joe. 'I've got a flat on Maid's Causeway, I told the landlady I was a grad student and she believed me. She's deaf as a post, and lets the band practise in her cellar. She says she likes Irish music because

34

she's a lapsed Catholic. Just as long as she doesn't listen to any of the lyrics.'

Alice smiled in spite of herself. 'That bad, eh?' she asked.

He made a non-committal sound. 'Could be better,' he admitted. 'Still, we manage all right on income support, and once we start playing the colleges, you never know, we might begin to get a core of discerning followers. You know, the kind that throw full cans at you instead of empty ones.'

'Joe . . .' said Alice carefully. 'It's late. Why are you phoning me now? It's been over three years—'

'Does there have to be a reason?' His voice was almost aggressive now. 'You always did try to find hidden meanings in everything. Why don't you loosen up a bit? I felt like catching up, that's all. Maybe we could go for a walk, have a pizza, anything. You might even want to see me play.'

The anger, if it had been there at all, was gone from Joe's voice now, and the idea suddenly seemed not just possible, but attractive. A pause, during which Alice looked out of the window at the magnolia nodding in the orange street-light. Then Joe went on in a strange tight voice: 'So how're you doing these days, Al? You've not gone and married the boy next door?'

'*You* were the boy next door,' she said. 'And you? Have you found the L-word yet? Does she play the cello? You always fantasized about a girl who could play the cello.'

'No, she doesn't play the cello,' said Joe, with a low laugh. 'But . . .' Underneath the light tone Alice thought she could hear anxiety. 'I met her quite by accident. You'd never have expected to see her there, in a dive like the Sluice . . . you know

35

the place? They drink the beer, then they eat the glass. Anyway, there was this girl there, sitting right at the front, all by herself, watching me all the time. Did you ever hear of anyone going to see a gig and watching the bass player all the time? The lead singer, yes. That's the pretty one with the long blond hair and that kind of fetching undernourished look. But me? I mean, who am I? I went to the bar to get a beer and she watched me all the way there as well. It made me feel weird. As if she could see right through me. So I kept looking away, right? Thinking, pretty soon she'll get bored and move off. But she never did. And so I took another look at her, and then I went in for a closer look. And she was waiting, as if she knew. The rest, as they say, is history.'

Alice was silent, taking it in. She was beginning to feel she understood. This phone call, after all this time . . . A complex feeling overwhelmed her; something a little like regret, but mostly like relief.

'Good for you,' she said at last, realizing that she meant it.

'Do you mean that?'

'Of course I do. Friends, Joe, remember?'

His answering laugh was a little unsteady, and she could tell that he was moved.

'God, I'm relieved!'

'So am I. Now I don't have to spend my life looking over my shoulder expecting to see you in pursuit.'

Good laughter together. Alice held the moment to her, that warmth, knowing that in some way for Joe it was an exorcism of her, of their wild and bad years, of what he still thought of as her rejection of him. She felt a sudden rush of unpossessive, uncomplicated love for him, sad Joe hiding his isolation behind a wall of facetiousness, Joe who only needed to be needed and wanted and clung to before he could blossom. She hoped that this girl would be the right one for him now, hoped that she would like electric folk music, would want babies and marriage and all the things which Joe had wanted, and Alice had given up in the name of her freedom.

Something cold and hard and lonely inside her melted and disappeared, and the relief she felt was like a blessing.

'So,' said Alice. 'What's she like?'

'Well—' he began. 'She's different. Different from everybody else. She likes Virginia Woolf and Egyptian art and chamber music . . . would you believe that I could fall for a girl who likes chamber music? She looks a bit like Kate Bush, and . . . I suppose I'd better translate that into aesthetic terms you can relate to. You're so square you probably don't get this technical stuff.'

'Watch it,' warned Alice.

'Well, she has kind of Rossetti-ish hair, and a kind of Burne-Jones-ish face . . .'

'She sounds like a woman of many parts. I suppose she has a William Morris beard?' said Alice with a grin.

'Well, why don't you find out for yourself? You'll have to meet her; that's mostly why I phoned in the first place.'

'Oh,' said Alice. 'Sure, OK.'

Joe seemed to sense her reluctance.

'I mean it, Al,' he said firmly. 'I'd really like you two to be friends.'

For a moment, Alice hesitated, choked by a

sudden poignant regret. Then, with an effort, she shrugged it off, almost in control again.

'I'd love to meet her, Joe,' she said. 'And I'd love to see you again, too. I've lost touch with too many old friends to let this one pass me by.' She tried to stop her voice from breaking. 'How about meeting you both in town? Or maybe I could come and hear your band. Does . . .' she paused. 'Joe, you mutt, you never even told me her name.'

Joe laughed.

'Didn't I? Hey, you can't expect me to think of everything. It's Virginia, Virginia Mae Ashley, but everyone just calls her Ginny. She says Virginia Mae's too much of a mouthful for someone like her. Do you still like pizza? We could go for a pizza somewhere if you like. The band doesn't play again till Tuesday, but we could go out, see a film. How does that sound?'

'That sounds fine.'

'What about you? You sound a bit down. You OK?'

'Of course I am. I'm just a bit tired. It's late, you know.'

'Yes . . . ah . . . I'll get off in a minute. Let you get some sleep. There's just one more thing, but the fact of it is that . . . I'm in a bit of a quandary here, and normally, you know I wouldn't ask you, but . . . well . . . Ginny's new to Cambridge, and she doesn't have very much money . . . I wondered if you'd mind putting her up?'

'Joe—'

'Tell me if I'm out of line,' he went on, 'but it would only be for a day or two. I can't offer her a place in my digs because the landlady wouldn't allow it. We're looking for a flat or something, but

38

you know how hard it is to get something decent in Cambridge at this time of year, when all the good places have been snapped up by the students or the tourists. It would only be for a little while, maybe just a few days, while we find somewhere else, and failing that, I've got a friend who lives in Grantchester who's going off to the States on Friday, and he says we can use his house as a stopgap, so even if the worst comes to the worst it would only be till the end of the week.' He stopped. 'Alice? What do you think?'

Alice sighed inwardly.

'I suppose it'll be all right,' she said, as he had known she would. 'Where is she staying now?'

'Nowhere yet,' replied Joe. 'She's just come out of Fulbourn.'

'Fulbourn?'

'They've offered to put her up for a while, but I hate the idea of her having to stay in that rotten place any longer than she has to. Just looking round there's enough to give anyone terminal depression.'

'Oh, no. Are you serious?' You never really knew with Joe; years earlier, when they had been good friends, before intimacy had come to take their friendship away, Alice would have been able to say: 'Fulbourn? Well, she must be a nutcase if she sees anything in you,' but here, the link between them was still too distant, still too fraught with bad memories, to allow more than a momentary easing of the tension.

'You mean . . . Was she a patient?'

Joe tutted. 'Honestly, I knew how you'd react. There's nothing wrong with it, you know, one person in three has a breakdown at some time or

39

other. Your mother told me that you were pretty close to it yourself, when you went through that bad patch of yours, so don't try to make it sound as if she—'

'Don't be silly. That wasn't what I meant. What I meant was . . .' Searching for the right words. 'How is she?'

Joe's answer sounded a little cold; Alice wondered whether she had overstepped the mark. After all, what claim on Joe's private life could she have now?

'It's not that I don't want to tell you, Al,' he said, 'but after all, it's Ginny's private life we're talking about here. I don't think I should have the right to tell people about her private life without asking her first, and I'm not sure how much she wants people to know about what happened to her. I only told you about Fulbourn so that you'd know to be careful of what you say and how you talk to her. She's still very vulnerable, you know.'

So am I, thought Alice, but let it pass.

'Al? You don't mind, do you?'

Alice said: 'I don't mind.'

'Good.' The relief in his voice was apparent. 'Besides, she's fine. You'd never think her life had been touched by so much crap. She's only eighteen, you know, she's got everything to live for. You'll love her, Al. Everyone loves her.'

He broke off for a moment, laughed quietly to himself. 'I think this is it, Al. You know, the L-word. It's funny, isn't it? I never used to think that I'd feel this way; I thought that there was only room in my life for the music, playing and grafting and getting bottled off stage, and all in the hope that the graft would pay off. And in a funny way, it

40

has. If I hadn't played the Sluice, I wouldn't have met Ginny. God knows what she was doing in the Sluice in the first place. But ever since then she's been bringing me luck. Everything's been looking up for me.'

Alice was silent for a long time. She hated the idea. More than hated it. Not because she loved Joe any more, but because it was all wrong. It wasn't like Joe to talk like this. Joe only cared for himself and his music and his ambitions; Joe was charming, likeable, amusing, but underneath, he was unscrupulously selfish. He didn't put himself out for anyone, didn't really consider what other people might be feeling . . . he was usually too much involved with his own enthusiasms. And he never mentioned what he called the L-word—she had thought he never would.

But Joe was a friend . . . had been, anyway, and she had behaved badly, as she always did when a good friendship went the bad way into intimacy. Maybe this was her chance to make up for that. And more than that, she was conscious of a desire to see him again, to talk to him, to remake their old, comfortable companionship. When he had laughed with her, laughed with the good laughter of old times recalled and recaptured, she had felt warmed, and had known that it was the friendship she missed coming back, and that she would do what she could to keep it, even if it meant putting up Joe's girl. She gave an unwilling laugh.

'Sounds good to me,' she said. 'Who knows? Maybe I'll like having her here. I can even put you up too, if you like. I'd be glad to have you both.'

As she spoke the words, they were almost true. The last of the old resentment melted, and Alice

41

felt an easy warmth for this girl Ginny, whom she had never met. It was so good to feel the rift beginning to close at last, as if the sourness and emptiness had been there all this time, half-felt but in disguise, touching everything with cold . . . Alice realized that Joe was talking.

'We could meet at your place, if that's all right,' he was saying. 'We'll have tea or something, then we'll go and have a pizza, or see a film, or both. Does that sound good?'

'That's fine.'

Alice must have hesitated for an instant, because Joe picked up on it at once.

'Hey, Alice? Are you sure?'

Alice made her voice light. 'I'll look forward to it, Joe. Keep playing those blues, hey?'

'Hang in there. I'll be round at about six. I tell you, things are going to be just great. You won't be disappointed.'

One

I don't suppose there was anything I could have done to avert what she had planned. As I said, she was very clever, and she knew my failings only too well. When I hauled her, dripping, into the cab with my coat flung protectively around her shoulders, myself only half-dressed, with my shoes and hat and tie still abandoned by the edge of the Cam, she must have smiled to herself, as such creatures may. She must have smiled through her lavender eyes as I hastened to revive her with my little flask of brandy, panting around her like an eager dog. There was nowhere to take her except to Grantchester and my landlady's house, nothing to do but to take her in (she was shivering now and could walk shakily from the cab to the door of the house), to explain as best I could and to watch helplessly as she was whisked away upstairs by a concerned and clucking Mrs Brown to an unknowable and half-defined realm of hot water and soft pillows. Lucky that she was such a kind, easy-going old soul. Other, more suspicious landladies might have treated my strange visitor with less consideration; but Mrs Brown was by far the best woman in my long and varied experience. She provided sympathy, attention, and tea—her all-purpose cure-all—then left Rosemary in the best bedroom, threatened me with the direst consequences if I were to disturb the young lady, and retired to her business, supremely unruffled, as if I brought half-drowned ladies to the house every day of the week. Bless her.

Left on her own in the best spare room, her bright hair washed, and wearing one of Mrs Brown's starched linen nightdresses, how Rosemary must have laughed. Laughed at the foolishness of it all: at our kindness, our misplaced sympathy; my hopeful adoration. I couldn't stop thinking about her.

I spent the rest of that day in a haze. I did not dare leave the house in case some new development arose; in case the girl disappeared. Her face haunted me. The memory of her silent floating on the water filled me with poetic thoughts. I spent the long enchanted hours lying in my room, reliving those dreamlike instants again and again, my ears tuned to the slightest sound from that secret, silent room in which she slept, my heart bursting with a kind of music. Mrs Brown came and went with cheerful, concerned efficiency. A vase of early cherry-blossom found its way into the sleeping girl's room, then a number of patchwork cushions; then, at about half past four, a tray of tea and biscuits. At five Mrs Brown announced that the young lady might like to get up and have some hot soup; and at six I found myself sitting at the dinner table, shaking with anticipation, staring at the extra place set by my landlady, my head feverish and my hands clenched out of sight in my lap.

I was love-lorn, I suppose; what young man would not have been? She had stepped out of a fairy tale for me, a white Ophelia borne from nowhere on a muddy wave and a whisper of morning. The threat of scandal, the riot of speculation which might have arisen later from the society of which I was a part did not even enter my mind; for me, Rosemary might have been new-born there and then, like Venus from the wave. And it was with these thoughts in mind that I waited for my first glimpse of her, half afraid to look, as if I might see some hitherto unsuspected flaw in her perfection. I need not have worried. A quick mothlike sound on the stairs, a clip of high heels, and suddenly, she was there, her features, blurred by the movement of light and shade in the passageway, coming into abrupt relief as she stopped in front of the window. Her hair was a nimbus of flame in the sunlight, her figure trim and childishly slight. Her face was pale, her eyes lost and haunted, but even then she was the most beautiful woman I had ever seen. Even then. Even now.

She looked at me silently for a while, then turned slantways against the sunshine, so that I caught the flutter from her hooded eyes. Her hair was so bright that it threw coppery reflections on to a cheekbone, the curve of her neck.

'To be alive,' she said quietly, turning to me again, her voice hoarse and sweet, like scratched silver. 'What little difference between being alive and not. Don't you think?' I think I just stared at her, not knowing what to say, not thinking.

'To be alive,' she repeated, 'such a brief mystery, too short to understand. The thing to have is power. Power is everything and lasts for ever.'

There I had it; the creed of Rosemary Ashley, but, like a fool, I just gaped, offered pity where none was needed, impulsively stretched out my hand towards her (the sunlight bled it white), and said: 'Don't talk. Try to eat something. You're among friends now.'

Her strange gaze fixed me for an instant.

'Friends,' she said, almost blankly.

'I pulled you out of the river,' I said, trying not to sound too pleased with myself. 'Believe me, miss. I'm your friend now, if you'll have me—if you'll trust me. The river isn't any answer . . . Whatever it is . . . not that.'

I think that somewhere in my mind there might have been a suspicion of something tawdry; some slinking tale of seduction and abandonment, but whatever it was, was banished as soon as I looked into her eyes. She was innocent. I could have sworn she was; staked my life on it, as, in a way, I suppose I did. It shone through her like a searchlight. Innocence. Or so I thought.

Later I learned to know her better. It was not innocence which streamed from every part of her, piercing her transparent skin and shining from her lilac eyes.

I think it was power.

Three

He closed his book and went to the window again. It was raining now; the light from the street fell in great corrugated sheets against the thick glass of the window and bounced from the windowsill with a sound like shrapnel. It was half past two in the morning, and still she did not come.

He went to the drinks cabinet and poured himself a whisky. He didn't really like the stuff, though he would never have admitted it to anyone, but it was what *she* drank, whisky, no ice; and he was still too much in love and wanted to drink it for her sake, as if the taste could somehow bring her closer to him. He swallowed, made an involuntary face, then downed the whole glassful, slamming the glass back on to the table in front of him in a way he imagined might have impressed *her*, if she had been there to see him.

But she did not come. Where was she? A movement from outside caught his eye, and he squinted through the window again; was that a figure in the courtyard below, the gleam of a plastic mackintosh in the lamplight? He fumbled with the catch of the window, pushed it open, regardless of the rain pouring in.

'Over here!' he shouted through the crashing of the overflow pipe, and the figure halted, looked up. He caught a brief glimpse of her face above the shiny black collar, saw her nod, and the familiar thrill always occasioned by her presence overcame him again, a starburst of adrenalin which began somewhere in the region of his stomach and expanded in thin, prickly lines towards the palms of his hands and the soles of his feet; a delight which was partly compounded of lust and wonder and a kind of fearful *insignificance*. Making love to her never changed her. She renewed her chastity like the moon, every time; only he was defiled.

Her footsteps sounded on the stairs. He poured himself another glass of whisky and drank half of it at once, afraid she might see his trembling hands. She was not kind, his lady; she knew his weaknesses and laughed at them. Sometimes, in his moments of lucidity, he wondered why he needed her so, knowing as he did that all she had ever offered him were the joys of fear and humiliation and the dark exhilaration of the fairground, rank with the scent of sweat and the beast which was himself. She had no love for him. They had nothing in common, never talked like friends. And yet, her step on the landing, quick and light as a cat's, set his pulses racing, his head spinning, and he ran to open the door as eager as a schoolboy.

So slim, so frail; even now she never ceased to amaze him, that so much perversity could be contained in such a thin white vessel. She stood before him in the semi-darkness, sensing his feelings, mocking him. She was wearing the black plastic raincoat, tightly belted at the waist, the

47

collar turned up to frame her face. She had pushed back her hood, and the thick curls of her pale red hair spilled out on to her shoulders. Her mouth was very red; he felt dizzy with his proximity to her, felt as if he were falling towards that mouth, saw the lips part very slightly to allow him to fall . . . She untied the belt of her raincoat, shrugged it open; dropped the coat on to the floor of the landing where it lay in a pool of rain, smiled. She was naked under the raincoat, her body opalescent in the reflected light from the street-lamps, her hair a wild cascade, her eyes, her lips, the tips of her breasts, the dark delta of her pubic hair like holes in that pallid body, holes from which cables of mystic night winched him closer and closer to her, powerless in the face of her irresistible attraction.

'Not here . . .' he mumbled. 'Never know . . . the porter . . . the others . . .'

He stooped to pick up her raincoat; caught the scent of chypre and rain from her body, caught a dizzying glimpse of waterdrops on a slim thigh, and stumbled in his eagerness. She gave a low laugh of contempt.

'My little gentleman,' she murmured. 'So much concern . . .'

She stepped lightly into the room, shedding her low shoes at the door, as graceful and as unconcerned of her nakedness as if she had been fully clothed. He shut the door hastily; not even lust could blind him to the possible consequences if she were seen; he did have his position to maintain after all; he had to be discreet. He hung up her raincoat by the sink, where the water could drip without harming the carpet, turned, almost

48

afraid now that everything was ready.

She was sitting in his armchair, legs crossed, hands clenched wantonly in her hair, and smiling. Despite himself, he began to tremble, and he turned away to hide the movement.

'Drink?' His mouth was dry as he topped up his own glass.

'Whisky, no ice,' she said, and as he poured, he was suddenly certain that she was laughing at him, knowing that hers were the strings which set him dancing, that with her, *he* was always the whore.

'There,' he said, handing her the glass, thankful that his hands had stopped trembling.

She drank the filthy, oily stuff as if it were water, in quick little gulps, the thin reed of her throat moving up and down like a swan's. Another of her tricks, he thought. Didn't he know them all by now?

She was only a woman, almost a child; he had picked her up out of the gutter; she had been half-dead with starvation, half-poisoned with cheap gin and forbidden drugs. He had settled her in a nice little apartment where nobody would ask any questions . . . he had spent more than half his generous study grant on her, on her clothes, her lodging, her pills and powders, her doctors and therapists . . . had asked nothing more of her than this, this little comfort. Damn it, he thought: he *loved* her. She should have belonged to him body and soul.

'Are you brave enough yet?' Her voice roused him out of his reverie. 'You stink of whisky. Have you managed to drown your bourgeois scruples?'

He cringed.

'There's no harm in a little drink,' he said,

hating the weak note of defensiveness in his voice. 'You're partial enough to it yourself.'

She laughed.

'You don't think I could bear you to touch me otherwise?'

'Damn you, you've a wicked tongue.'

'That's why you want me,' she said, stretching out on the chair like a cat. 'You like to be punished. I know you intellectuals. I've had enough of them in my time, you know.'

'Your time!'

'Don't raise your voice,' she said. 'Remember the porter, the others.'

'Damn them!' he snapped. 'How old are you anyway? Seventeen?' He tried to laugh.

'Older than I look,' she replied. 'Old enough to know all about your kind. You're such victims, all of you.' There was venom behind the mockery.

'Be quiet.'

'Certainly. That's what you pay me for, isn't it? Do you want me to scream when I come?'

'Be quiet!' He grabbed her by the wrist, pulled her from the chair. Her small bones moved under her skin, and he knew he was hurting her, but still she seemed to be smiling. Whatever he did, she was still always in control. He held her wrists high above her head, pushed her towards the bed, flung her down with a brutality which both satisfied him and wrenched at his heart. Despite that, she landed gracefully, like a cat; in fact, if he thought about it, he had never seen her do anything without that natural grace; it was one of her obscure ways of taunting him.

'Oh, God . . .' he breathed her name. 'I'm sorry . . . I . . . I love you so much. Please . . .'

50

The plea died on his lips. She could do as she liked, this child, could annihilate or exhilarate him at a whim; hers was the power of fairy tale, that gypsy sensuality which transcends reason. Her fathomless eyes were tunnels of rain. The light caught the curve of her neck, a perfect collar-bone, the white dune of a breast. Her beauty was more than bone-deep, it was eternal, white as the moon. She opened her arms, and he fell towards her with a long, soundless cry of joy.

She moved underneath him like a dancer, unconcerned by his touch, but pushed onwards by some strange unguessed-at lust of her own. Her lips moved over his face, his shoulder. Her cool hands found his neck. A rictus seized him, half-pleasure, half-pain, like biting into an unripe fruit ... He felt her lips on his throat. He felt her teeth on him, small and sharp, her hands holding him firmly down.

'Ouch! Stop it!' His hands were off her body and his legs thrashed with the violence of his reaction, but still she did not let him go. Close against his flesh he felt her breath as she laughed. Then, with a sudden *crunch*, she bit. Blood rushed out as his head lolled; blood soaked the front of his shirt, blood rushed down the side of the girl's face and dripped from the stray damp strands of her hair. He tried to scream, tried to move, but the pain, the movement, the sensation of her cool body against his, all these were at the end of a dark tunnel of feeling, receding to a pinpoint of light and heat in the icy dark. He tried her name; it burst in a bubble of blood and ran down the side of his shoulder, but he did not feel it. He was alone in the tunnel falling further and further away ... and

51

not unwilling to fall, either; in fact, very glad to escape from the memory, mercifully fading already, of that last *crunch* which tore him open like a peach, and the muffled, wet bubbling sound of the girl's laughter against him.

* * *

When—some time later—she had sated her appetite, the girl wiped her face fastidiously on the dead man's handkerchief. She always washed after meals.

Two

It was nearly dark by the time they arrived, and the street-lamps were lit on Gwydir Street. Alice, watching upstairs, saw them coming long before they knocked at her door, and she had time to cast a final glance at her immaculate living-room, to tweak a cushion here, to straighten a picture there, before she let them in. She was as nervous as if she were on her first date; she had dressed with more than usual care. Maybe something inside her wanted Ginny to know she had a rival.

Surely not. Alice shrugged. She hoped she was not so primitive. But all the same, as the knock came she took a moment to straighten her hair in front of the mirror and put up her chin defiantly.

Friends, she thought furiously to herself. That was all. It had to be all. It had been she who decided they would be better off living apart. She had no more hold over him, could not hope to gain any now. So just enjoy it, she thought, as she went to open the door. Enjoy it if you can.

Joe stood at the door, flowers in his hands: white roses wrapped in clear, crinkly cellophane paper. The scent, and the moment, engulfed her.

'Hello Joe,' she said softly, and smiled.

'Long time,' he answered with a grin, and raised his fist to his shoulder in a kind of salute. Then he looked over his shoulder, almost furtively, and the moment was lost as a figure emerged from the shadows, a crescent of fiery hair, an arc of light following the line of a prominent collar-bone, the rest black with shadow.

'Hey, Alice . . .'

His voice was slightly unsteady, like that of a child.

'Alice . . . this is Ginny.'

The girl stepped out into the light.

Alice supposed that she made all the right noises; thanks for the flowers, invitations to come in, to sit down; polite commonplaces. But all the time, she was covertly looking at Ginny, taking in every little detail; every line, every hair etched into her remembrance in sharp little razor cuts of precision.

Imagination was nothing, she thought to herself.

She had imagined that she would not be a prey to jealousy, that she would not be primitive, and yet she had discovered within herself such depths of jealousy and . . . yes, almost *hatred* that she even frightened herself. She could feel the hairs on the back of her neck rising.

The girl was pretty enough, she thought. Slight, without being too small, supple as a birch wand, light as a dancer, in a wide-skirted dress which reached almost to her ankles. Her red hair was rather short, artlessly pushed back from her face and her eyes were an unusual shade of lavender filled with lights and reflections. But her beauty was more than an accumulation of features. It was somehow abstract, ethereal.

There had been a picture on Alice's bedroom wall in her student days, an indifferent reproduction of a Rossetti watercolour entitled *The First Madness of Ophelia*. It showed the doomed girl, wreathed in flowers, crowned in flowers, long hair loose, pale features a blur of dark eyes and open mouth as she sang, heedless of her friends' concern, sang her sorrow and her madness, childlike in her self-possession. What had Joe said? That she had had a breakdown? That she had spent time in a mental ward? Alice could believe it. Ginny had that same look, reproduced in black-and-white on that half-forgotten poster. Her beauty was an abyss, an insanity all of its own.

For a moment Alice seemed to see herself through Ginny's eyes, as that cool, appraising stare flicked over her; she saw herself as she knew she must seem before that little island of teenage self-possession. Over-tall, her eyes too small behind those wire frames, features too heavy, inelegant. She saw her own graceless movements, as she watched herself making coffee for them. She saw Joe watching her, making no comment, but noticing the weight she had put on in three years, the fine tracery of new lines around her eyes. And the worst of it was that Joe hadn't changed at all; if he had, if she had been able to detect a hint of grey in his hair, new wrinkles around his mouth, extra flab on his thin arms, she might have felt more reconciled to her own imperfections, but she detected nothing. The same smile, the same endearing squint through the glasses, the same thin-as-a-rake body and slightly stooped shoulders. A half-expected jolt as she realized that even now she felt the same attraction.

Alice spent the rest of the evening in a haze of jumbled emotions. Places and faces passed without really registering: a pizza restaurant somewhere in the upper Backs, eating, for once without appetite, with the same dogged concentration she had seen in her mother; a path by the river, a bridge. A crescent moon throwing frosty shadows on to the grass and the river. A weir, looking down into the black night water, watching neon reflections in the scum.

She ate, drank, made conversation, without effort, without thinking. Joe sparkled; Ginny turning towards him smiling shyly, watching him. A late-night film at the cinema which Alice did not really see. Waiters. Usherettes. A student giving out leaflets. Ginny's eyes reflecting light from the screens. Joe buying chocolate, his eyes bright . . . Joe happy, unsuspecting, his arm around Ginny's shoulders, looking down at her with that intent look that Alice knew to be short-sightedness. Ginny smiling passively, her voice the barest whisper, like a child's, glancing at Joe before she spoke, as if he somehow held the key to her words. Soundless pictures, their lips moving without meaning, their colours as random and exciting as a magic-lantern show. Themselves a part of the play, coloured shadows on a flat screen.

And only Ginny's face through it all, watching

her as if through glass, slightly distorted, the bones of her face seeming to change shape; here like the face of a woman looking into a fishbowl, there one eye magnifying suddenly, mouth twisting into curling, sneering shapes. Ginny's face, and the beginnings of obsession.

For a moment, Alice had been so absorbed that she could not remember where she was. Colours rushed in upon her, jumbled sounds filled the soundless world. A face rushed towards her through fathoms of water . . . then normality, as if nothing had ever been different, as if the dark carousel she had ridden through all that evening had finally tired of her, thrown her back in disgust, while the fair continued, on some other dimension, maybe just across the water.

The face was Joe's.

'Thank you,' he said, his hand brushing hers, raising the hairs on her wrist.

'It's really good to see you again. We should have done this a long time ago, but I expect I was too immature, or too bloody arrogant to suggest it.'

'That's fine,' answered Alice mechanically. 'I had a great time.'

'I knew you would.' His voice was warm. 'I'm so glad you and Ginny got to know each other. I knew she'd like you, and I really hoped you'd like her.' He lowered his voice slightly, glancing back at Ginny to make sure she did not hear him. 'She needs someone like you, you know. This evening has really done her a world of good; maybe you don't realize it, because you don't know her very well yet, but I can tell how much she likes you.'

Alice nodded, feeling helpless. Already the

violence of her previous emotions seemed to hold the logic of certain dreams, which appear to make sense at the time of dreaming, but afterwards dissolve back into the incomprehensible code of the subconscious from which they are born. She looked back at Ginny, who was sitting in a chair by the fire, and tried to recapture that certainty, that awareness of something malicious, something morally tainted . . . She rubbed her eyes with the back of her hand.

'Do you want a drink?' she said, her feelings under control again.

Ginny shrugged, with a vague, sweet smile.

'Why not?' said Joe. 'What have you got?'

'Tea and coffee.'

'Tea? Coffee?'

'Cold beers in the fridge. It's the best I can do.' Alice smiled.

'That's better,' Joe said, and went into the kitchen.

'One for you?' he called to Ginny, but she only shook her head, nervously twisting the flimsy fabric of her dress with long, pale fingers.

Alice was irritated. Perhaps it was the utterly passive, dependent persona Ginny adopted which grated on her nerves. It was the way she looked to Joe for every little thing; it was the modest lowering of her eyelids when she was not looking at him. Somehow Ginny, despite her shyness, made her very uneasy. She tried to overcome it, speaking to the girl directly for the first time that evening.

'Are you new to Cambridge?' she said, determined to elicit some response.

Ginny looked up, her strange eyes like cracked

mirrors. Alice saw herself trapped there in reflection.

'I used to know it, a long time ago.'

'It never changes much, does it?'

Silently, Ginny shook her head.

'What do you like best? The Backs? The colleges?'

Ginny smiled.

'The graveyards. And the river of course,' she said.

Alice muttered some reply, already feeling exhausted. Joe, however, did not seem to see anything amiss; but he had been drinking cheerfully for most of the evening already, and Alice had not expected him to notice the tension. He came back from the kitchen carrying a six-pack of beer and some glasses, but ended up drinking out of the cans, as usual.

'Hey, Al,' he said, between gulps, 'I see you still have old Cat. I'm sure she remembers me. When I went to the fridge she came right up to me and started rubbing my leg with her nose. How's that for memory? I always liked that cat. Even when she shat in my shoes.'

'I think she just knows there's food in the fridge.'

'Oh.' For a minute he was crestfallen, then, as a new idea came to him, he brightened again.

'Tomorrow we're playing the Corn Exchange. Big-time stuff. Benefit gig with three more bands. You'll enjoy it. Ginny wants to hear us, too. Perhaps you two could come together; Gin's a bit nervous of being there on her own.'

Ginny gave a little nod, Alice gave a strained smile.

'I'd love to come. What sort of thing did you tell me you were playing?'

Alice knew that any reference to his precious band was enough to keep Joe talking for the whole evening. She knew that he would be satisfied as long as she smiled and nodded and looked interested; and for the moment, she was too drained to attempt any other conversation. Besides, there was Ginny; and her very presence inhibited Alice in some inexplicable way. This feeling was so intense that she answered Joe almost at random as he spoke, which earned her, despite his self-absorption, a speculative glance.

'You're very quiet,' he said, laughing. 'Has age mellowed you at last, or am I just boring you witless? You always used to have plenty to say for yourself in the old days.'

Alice flicked a glance at Ginny.

'And you always used to say that women talked far too much.'

He grinned. 'They do.'

'Do you stand for this sort of thing, Ginny?' said Alice, forcing herself to include the quiet girl in their conversation.

'She doesn't have to,' said Joe, opening another can one-handed, 'she's the most restful female I know.'

'Don't be taken in,' said Alice. 'Beneath that charming exterior there's a first-class chauvinist pig.'

Ginny gave a little, secret smile, raising her eyes to Alice's, then dropped them again. She murmured something in a feathery voice, which Alice did not hear; but Joe gave a low laugh. Alice assumed that she had managed to counterfeit enthusiasm well enough to deceive him, anyway.

'I'll have to go now, I'm afraid,' he said, with a quick glance at his watch. 'I'll be here in the morning as soon as I can. I have a practice at ten, and we've got another at about three, but I'm sure I'll be able to find time to take you both out to lunch.'

Alice smiled automatically, grasping at the moment, understanding at last what this was leading to: soon he would be gone, and she would be alone with Ginny.

'Coffee before you go?' she asked, half in despair, because he was draining the last can of beer, because he had his coat on, because he was half-way to the door . . .

'I'd really better be going, Al. It's getting late. But thanks, goodbye.'

'Goodbye,' said Alice forlornly to the door as he stepped out into the night. 'Oh, Joe . . .'

But Joe had already gone, the orange of the streetlight making a strange, garish figure of him as he moved rapidly down the street.

'Goodnight,' said Alice lamely; she couldn't remember what she had wanted to say to him anyway. She turned, and there was Ginny, waiting politely beside the stairs, that little, knowing smile on her face, her eyes in a band of shadow so dark that it might have been a mask. Alice tried to smile back, shook her heavy head, took two steps towards the kitchen.

'Ginny, would you like a drink?' she offered, with an effort.

'That's very kind,' Ginny said. Her voice was soft but clear, with an undertone of mockery, her accent light and untraceable. 'But do you mind if I go upstairs and change? I'll feel much more comfortable.'

'Of course!' Alice's smile felt better now, more sincere. Maybe it was Joe's absence which did it. 'I'm afraid it's a bit makeshift upstairs, but it was the best I could do at short notice. You can put your clothes in the wardrobe, if you like, and if there's anything you need, just give me a shout.'

'Thank you. I'll be fine.'

'OK. Take your time.'

Ginny did not reply, but Alice heard her going upstairs.

It occurred to her then, with a sudden jolt, that the girl was shy and a long way from home, and she felt ashamed of the extent of her antipathy. It was probably *her* fault that Ginny had been unresponsive; she supposed she had been rude. She should have tried to include the girl and make her talk.

Mentally berating herself for the failure of her good intentions, she determined to give Ginny a chance, to be friends with her, and felt better at once, having made the decision. She put the kettle on, set out two cups, smiled, and brought out a tin of biscuits as well. As she began to set the biscuits out on a dish, she even began to hum.

One

I dreamed of her again tonight; why mention it, I wonder, when it happens every night, every night without failing, each time in some new and monstrous clothing, my dreams bloated like poison fruit? Why write it, when her face looks out from the page at me, when her delicate hands close on mine as I hold the pen? Oh, Rosemary.

Her presence is like a perfume in the air, her voice, a whistle to the winds. Last night I dreamed of her. All in grey, she was, with flowers in her hands and her long red hair loose to the winds, singing to herself as she walked along the riverside where the hemlock was growing tall, and I thought to myself: here is a lady lost, in danger. So I stood up and walked through the graveyard towards her; I stumbled over a stone in my haste and she turned and saw me. I don't think she spoke, but, as she turned, I saw that she was holding something in one hand, a little round glass something, like a marble, and she held it out towards me, and smiled. The wind whistled through the little round thing as she held it, a strange, mournful sound, and as I stretched out my hand to receive it, I saw my own face staring out at me, long and distorted in the glass surface, mouth open in an impossibly wide, moaning scream. As I looked, the marble seemed to grow bigger and bigger, until I could see trees and houses through its convex surface, houses and bushes and a road, and a railway line winding its way through a wood . . . Suddenly, I was afraid. I looked around. Nothing.

Nothing but the rails, the trees, the whistle of the engine far away. I looked up at the sky. And then I understood. She was there, had been there all the time, looking down, her hair drifting out, her eyes great tunnels of death, bigger than the world. And outside the world, in the strange fisheye she inhabited, there was nothing but darkness. No sky but the blue painted inside of the spinning-top, no sun but her eyes, no moon but the round pink imprints of her thumbs against the glass. And I knew that sometime or other, she would remember the handle, the red wooden handle which turns the world . . . and where would I be then? Spinning, spinning, there in the dark for ever, at her pleasure, beneath her watchful eyes? My blessed Damozel.

Suddenly, I was jolted from my thoughts by a sound: a slow, deep, groaning and creaking sound, impossibly huge, from the very engines of the earth, as if some ancient underground forge had been opened anew. A scraping music accompanied it, like the world's oldest and most decrepit roundabout. The music's pace quickened, became a fairground tune, loud and brash, laboriously out of key. The light had changed; shadows lay over most of the land, hiding the trees and bushes from sight, except in a few cases, where a sudden spray of light (green, pink, electric blue) outlined a stump here, a protruding branch there, into lurid, swaying relief. Branches? Why had I thought of branches? As the top began to spin faster, the music to play more rhythmically, I held on to the first solid object I could grasp. In the semi-darkness, I could feel a hard, rippled surface, a jingle of bells, the harshness of a horsehair mane . . . What could be more natural, on a fairground roundabout, than a roundabout horse? I closed my eyes (the roundabout was spinning very quickly now, the horse leaping up and down), but there was no way I could let go of the only solid object in my world, and I held on with my eyes closed until I began to feel a little better, a little more steady, and I dared to open them a crack.

It was light again, not the brightness and clarity of daylight, but a garish kind of fairground light, vulgar, and spectral at the same time. And in the brightness, I could see that I was not the only rider on Rosemary's carousel. There were other horses, red and white and black and blue, bells at their saddles, long manes flying in the wind, glass eyes wild and red nostrils flaring. Robert was there too, knuckles white against the reins, coat flapping behind him like wings. I called his name, hoping that he would hear me against the deafening music . . . and he turned his face towards me.

He was dead, poor Robert. His face was pale, clown-coloured, and his lips were faintly blue. His eyes were turned upwards to the whites. As I cried out in horror and pity, the roundabout lurched, and his head lolled away from me on its broken neck. Then, I saw that all the horses had a rider; a dead rider. Men, women, some I recognized, some total strangers. Some grinned at me as we rode alongside each other; a masked woman blew me a kiss which smelt of carrion. Others slumped over slit throats and broken backs; one rode backwards, head bent completely round, like a doll's. Then a thought overtook me with cold terror as I rode. I had seen all my roundabout companions save one. One.

A coldness at my back, like a sudden draught. A sudden, gassy reek, like putrid vegetables. A kind of touch, horribly intimate, at my shoulder. Turning was an unbearable effort, like walking underwater. Another touch, at my face.

Cold.

I began to struggle, vainly trying to avert the predestined. I believe I thrashed my legs, as if in a pointless attempt to outride my pursuer. I tried to turn again. And this time, I succeeded.

My scream was lost in a redoubled burst of the music; my terror ripe as fermented plums. She was masked, only the mouth and the tip of her nose visible from beneath the velvet, but I knew who it was. Ophelia, ten days after her drowning, the stench of the river still on her, mixed with another stench, darker. The slime of the Cam in her hair, her limbs hunched and misshapen, bloated beneath her white dress. I had once owned a Japanese print, showing the six stages of decomposition of the corpse of a young girl left out on a mountainside; I had found it gruesome, but fascinating, to see how the corpse, in her jewellery, her white burial-robes, had changed, had swollen, then shrunk . . .

'I am a maid at your window . . .' she croaked at me, and I screamed again, scrabbling at the flanks of my horse, pushing myself backwards with my fingernails, burning the palms of my hands, leaving shreds of my skin on the polished wood, my sanity leaving me in great, sparkling bursts of light, like fireworks (and for a moment, I could *see* them, brighter than any fairground illuminations) as she began to creep towards me.

'A maid at your window . . .' she went on, relentlessly, 'to be your Valentine . . .' Then her hands met around my neck, soft and cold, her mouth opened, sending a great cloud of that dark, graveyard reek towards me, and I fell towards her open mouth, all will gone, all feeling gone, into the tunnel of blackness which was Rosemary, where even screams become meaningless.

Two

'How do you take your coffee, Ginny?' Alice broke off in mid-sentence. The cup she was carrying wobbled, but did not fall.

'Thank you,' said Ginny softly, 'but I don't think I'll have coffee after all. I think I'm going out for a while.'

'Oh . . . ? Oh yes, of course.'

Alice was so stunned by Ginny's transformation that she was unable to say anything, but her mind raced uselessly on. Was that really Ginny there? She would hardly have recognized her, she thought, and it was not only her clothes which had changed, but her whole self, sloughed off to reveal something closer to the bone. She had taken off the powder-blue dress which had given her such a medieval look. She had aerosol-sprayed a band of black lacquer across her eyes, like a mask, and her red hair had been made to stand up around her face like quills. She was wearing faded jeans (a long tear positioned high on each leg to reveal white skin), and a T-shirt with the sleeves torn off which sported the picture of a grinning skull and a flowery DEATH logo. Her boots were of purple suede, laced up to mid-thigh, and the spiked heels had left little indentations in the pile of Alice's living-room carpet, little gaps, like airholes for something which might be living under there. She looked even younger than before, vulnerable, somehow, in that lurid adolescent's garb, still wrenchingly beautiful, but wiser somehow. Older.

Her eyes danced, a roller-coaster of troubling, multicoloured lights.

'There's a fair,' she said, brightly. Even the voice had changed, adopting, instead of the whisper of a shy child, the slightly nasal, ungrateful intonations of the adolescent girl.

'Yes?' said Alice.

'On Parker's Piece. It's only eleven. It won't be shutting down till midnight. It won't take me long to get there.'

Her eyes were a band of fractured light behind the spray-paint, glimmering dangerously. She seemed entirely unconscious of the effect she had created.

'So when will you be back?' said Alice rather coldly.

Ginny shrugged.

'Not very long. I'm meeting some friends . . . don't bother to wait up, will you?'

'I'll leave the door open.'

'Thank you.'

Her hand was on the door-handle. Suddenly, Alice felt an abrupt rushing of emotion; anger, anxiety and reaction against all the things she had been made to feel during the evening. She reached impulsively for the girl's arm; held it. The skin felt cool and smooth.

'Ginny?'

'Yes, what is it?' The note of mockery was there again, almost . . . almost as if she knew what was in Alice's thoughts better than she did herself.

'Joe . . . You like him, don't you?'

Ginny faced her for a second, then she ticked her head to one side, like a doll. Behind the grey of her eyes, the fairground lights cavorted.

'Joe?' she said in a birdlike voice. 'Who's Joe?'

Then the door opened, and she walked off into

the night.

Alice paused at the door for a moment, her emotions a mixture of anger, shame, and an odd feeling of not *fear*, precisely, but unease.

She could not resist the temptation to peep through the slats of the blinds out into the street. Not a brief, casual look, such as she might have taken by accident, but a good, long, calculating stare. She knew what she was looking for, and that thought made her *really* uneasy; it was hard to admit, but she was looking for a glimpse of those friends; some shred of proof to justify her feeling that Ginny would be bad for Joe, that she would be somehow *wrong*. She turned away from the window in disgust, but not before she had seen what she expected, what she had hoped for. The man was standing beneath a lamp-post, face turned away from the house, but his silhouette was outlined sharply in the bright orange light, and Alice saw him well enough. He was tall, long hair drawn back in a pony-tail, long greatcoat with a turned-up collar, motorcycle boots with chains on the back which winked at Alice from the shadows. As she watched, Alice saw Ginny half-run towards him, her steps light as a dancer's despite those preposterous boots, and tuck her hand confidingly under his arm. He half-turned towards her, spoke, touched her shoulder with a strangely intimate gesture, laughed. Alice heard the faint echo of Ginny's answering laugh, ringing tinnily in the deserted street. She clenched her teeth. No, she didn't like Joe's Ginny, or her friends either; there was something disturbing about that man in the greatcoat, something more than arrogant about the set of his shoulders, the gaudy winking of the metal on the instep of his boots, the protective way his arm went around Ginny's shoulders, almost hiding her from sight. For an instant, Alice wondered if the girl would be safe with him.

And then, she turned away from the window, her cheeks flushing, for impossible though she knew it to be, it had seemed to her during that instant that the man had turned, too far away for her to see his face, and had stared at the house. Only for a moment, mind you, and there was no way, thought Alice, no way at all that he could have seen her, let alone known that she was watching him, but all the same . . . she was sure he had *known* she was there, that his eyes had sought her out as she hid behind the blinds . . . that he had seen her and, seeing her, had smiled.

*   *   *

Alice turned on to her left side and tried to blank out her mind. Tried to sleep. Images filled the darkness of her closed eyelids, images, faces, voices, glimpses of her paintings and unformed ideas for others. A snatch of music throbbed somewhere on the fringes of sleep, a rhythm and a lyric:

One day you see a strange little girl look at you
One day you see a strange little girl feeling blue
She'd run to the town one day
*   leaving home and her country fair*
Just beware when you're there
Strange little girl . . .

Alice shook her head on the hot pillow, shifted

position again.

Damn.

She flicked on the bedside lamp with abrupt impatience, reached for a book. Maybe half an hour's reading would do it. Her hand paused on the paperback's cover, reached out again, paused. Froze. There it was again, a sound, like whispering. Voices. Alice sat up in bed, alert to any sound, then relaxed. It's nothing, she thought. It's just Ginny back from the fair. For an instant, there was nothing; then the whispering began again, soft and unpleasantly intimate, coming from Ginny's room.

Ginny's friends of that evening?

The thought appalled Alice; the memory of Ginny's appearance, her dreamlike conversation, the way she and her unknown friend had disappeared into the dark without a sound . . . these things all convinced Alice that there was something wrong going on, and, knowing that, there was nothing, absolutely *nothing*, she repeated inwardly, which was going to persuade her to get out of bed and interfere. Who Ginny invited back was none of her business. She certainly wasn't going to make a fool of herself by going to find out. After all, it might even be Joe. She would make sure Ginny and her belongings were out of the house by the end of that week, without fail, and then she would be free of her. The voices came again, more than two, maybe three or four. Alice knew she would have recognized Joe's voice if she had heard it.

Almost angrily, she turned her head on the pillow and tried to ignore the whispering. A snatch of music, half imagined:

70

One day you see a strange little girl look at you
One day you see a strange little girl feeling blue
Strange little girl . . .

Dammit. Why couldn't she leave it alone? It wasn't any of her business. She wasn't going to interfere.

Her train of thought stopped abruptly as she realized that, despite everything, she had thrown back the covers and had got up. Worse still, she recognized within herself a feeling that she *was* going to interfere, that she was not going to be happy until she had left the safety of her bedroom and had sneaked a look into Ginny's room, just to know, she told herself, just to see. She pulled on her jeans and a T-shirt, careful of the occasionally creaking boards, padded to the door in her bare feet. Still the stealthy, almost mocking undertone of the voices, at the edge of sound, elusive and tantalizing. A soft *Shhhhhhh* as the door opened over the thick pile of the carpet, then the steps, each one an endless held-breath-long over the landing, muscles aching and the carpet sinking into the soles of her feet like pine-needles as Alice edged her way along the impossible distance of the landing towards Ginny's room. Under Ginny's door, a spray of light. As she came closer, the voices blossomed in the darkness, huge and formless as flowers of smoke. Their sense eluded her, the sounds amplified by the straining of her ears into booming, giddying syllables. Here and there, a word found its way into her comprehension, menacing and full of secret meanings.

71

A man's voice: '*She . . . when she sleeps . . . the picture . . . know . . . think she . . . the picture . . .*'

Another: '*Some quiet place . . .*'

Ginny's voice, above the rest and more audible, its vagueness gone. With her friends, Ginny's voice was clear and commanding:

'Be quiet. I don't want to run the risk of him suspecting. It was a mistake . . .' (The voice blurred again as she turned away from the door.) 'Give me time. I remember everything now.'

Alice felt her head spinning with the strain of standing there, channels of blackness all around her. A sudden, idiotic desire to laugh seized her, and she chuckled nervously to herself in the shadows.

What had she expected? Black magic? Green men from Mars? Nervous laughter choked her, and she began to feel ridiculous as well as afraid. So what if Ginny was entertaining? Most likely all they were doing was smoking joints or something, where they knew they wouldn't be interrupted. It was really no business of hers. Joe could and would look after himself. Alice didn't want to know. Footsteps on the other side of the door, a voice, clear with proximity.

'Enough talk . . . too much time wasted . . . waited . . . long time . . . find it . . . do what . . . should have been done . . . ready . . . find it and get rid of it . . . not safe for it to still be there . . . one day someone . . . might know who . . .'

Ginny's voice, crisp and carrying: 'No need to worry. Poor Daniel is already dead and done for. He just doesn't know it yet.'

And then the door opened.

From the crack behind the hinges of the

72

darkened bathroom Alice saw the flowering of light across the stair carpet, saw the three figures cross the lighted stretch, saw shapes: a wedge of light on an upturned cheekbone, a flare of red and purple from the braiding on someone's coat, a cold spark from the chain on a motorcycle boot . . . then the light snapped off abruptly, and their steps were only subtle shiftings in the darkness, their whispering the sound of dust against dust.

'Mustn't wake her . . . door latched . . . simple enough . . . sleeps like the dead . . .' (Laughter, light as cobwebs.) '. . . Back before light . . . child's play . . .'

'Suspects . . . remember . . . picture . . . find it and get rid . . .'

Down the stairs . . . *Shh* . . . *Shh* . . . *Shh* . . . *Shh* . . . as the skirts of a long greatcoat brushed the carpet. Alice opened the door of the bathroom a crack wider. There was no light. Somewhere a little beyond the stairwell she detected, or thought she detected, the tiny gleam of a street-lamp through drawn curtains. The door opened wider. Her feet made tiny sounds against the floor, but she took careful steps, avoiding the squeaky board, holding on to the banister to stabilize her own descent into the well. A ripple of sound pushed its way into the blackness towards her; she heard the click of the latch. A bar of light extended into the dark house, probed, flickered and finally withdrew.

Alice was alone again.

Her steps were light; she ran downstairs in the darkness, parted the curtains an inch . . . they were already half-way down the street, figures long as shadows, steps even and purposeful. Alice's foot bumped into her shoes as she moved back from

73

the window. Without thinking anything, she slipped them on. The latch almost drew itself.

Click.

The door closed behind Alice and she set off after them into the orange-lit silence.

She kept well hidden; her shoes were soft, her clothes, accidentally chosen, were dark. She knew the streets and kept to the shadows; alleys and archways were plentiful. The night air was still and cold; here and there the pavements twinkled with a light frost; Alice's breath spiralled away behind her . . . her steps were easy and elastic. She crossed the town; deserted streets, the colleges blank carnival masks with the occasional winking eye at a late-night student's window. Gradually she left the town behind. The road grew narrower and darker, the buildings few. They crossed the river, twice, crossed a road, waded through a field of green corn. Alice waited until the others had crossed the field before she began to make her own way across it; the delay left them far ahead of her, but she was virtually certain of where they were going; this was the short road across the fields to Grantchester. She knew this way by day; by night the path was loaded with signs and portents, the sky was bright with hidden moonlight, the clouds huge. In darkness it dwarfed the ground more efficiently than it ever did by day. Alice felt unease, but accepted it, dreamlike, and broke into a half-run to catch up with the three shadows, the ground flying beneath her like a magic carpet. She did not feel tired or impatient, only thrilled with the chase, the hairs on her arms electric with cold and anticipation. The snatch of song still played inside her, matching the rhythm of her padding feet:

Strange little girl, where are you going?
Strange little girl, where are you going?
Do you know where you could be going?

Grantchester crouched at the end of the road, the squat little tower of the church with its stubby spire black against the luminous sky. The three figures were almost upon it. Then, at the gate, they slackened their pace. A voice, clear and almost careless, reached Alice from further down the road. Its message was inaudible, but the speaker was unexcited, unafraid.

There was only a tiny spark of sound, metal against metal, as he leaped up on to the spiked gate, then down to the other side. A second figure followed suit, then the third, with equal ease. A languid word spoken; laughter. The figures were at one with the dark; the church swallowed them up. By now Alice was trembling. This was no student prank, no joke; this they had done before, maybe many times. The thought of black magic did not seem so laughable now. But still she followed them, fascinated and appalled, her mind spinning its own mandala of fear and foreboding, until she stood in front of the gate. She surveyed the church for a moment, somehow disliking its cold face, its mean little windows. The gate was not too high; not higher than the college gate which Alice used to climb on sly Cambridge nights. But it was locked.

She wondered why a churchyard should have to be locked; remembered, or half-remembered, Joe telling her (on the way back from some nocturnal escapade, her hand in the pocket of his overcoat), his voice warm and humorous.

'Beats me why they lock them. The way I see it, no one wants to get in, and no one's likely to be wanting to get out!'

The memory was a sad ghost in the still cold night, its warmth evaporated into pale nostalgia. And the joke seemed sinister now; the thought of people trying to escape chilled her. She touched the wooden bars of the gate; rot had bubbled through the paint, grains of it clinging to her fingers. Beyond the gate was the Darkside, the other side of the looking-glass. She longed to know what lay beyond, but was afraid to leave the safety of the road; yet, dreamlike, she knew that she would cross over whether she wanted to or not. She pulled herself up, the world shifting perspective abruptly as she did so; the darkness made her feel seventy feet high, hovering above a chasm of blackness. She tilted, feeling carefully for the wood beneath her . . . swung her leg over the top.

She found them under cover of night, and hid behind a monument to see what they were doing; but the wall of the third churchyard shadowed them, and she could see only jumbled shapes, shadowplay without meaning, hear their voices in broken snatches, hear the sound of metal against stone, of metal against earth . . . of digging.

The red-haired figure was Ginny, she could see that much, could hear her voice, higher and clearer than the others, could occasionally glimpse her dancer's body moving among the graves. Another figure was tall, had long hair in a pony-tail, metal on the instep of his boots. The third was fair, androgynous; Alice could see no face.

'. . . somewhere close by . . . has to be here . . . had no time . . . anywhere else . . . find it, even if I have to . . . dig him up . . . sure . . . know it . . .'

She waited there for a long time, listening to the sound of the digging, then the sound of wood against metal, metal against metal. Whatever it was, they seemed to have found it; Alice could tell by their voices. More sounds, a tearing of paper, a sound of metal scraping . . . footsteps. Alice could feel them in her teeth. She crouched against the monument, the throbbing of her eardrum echoing in the cold stone, as the footsteps passed and died away. After a while she got up.

Her eyes were accustomed to the darkness, and she could see quite well; the hammering fear had left her for the moment, to be replaced by a strange, transparent calm. She took two steps nearer to the patch of shadow she now knew to be an open grave; one step nearer and stopped. There was a hole in front of her, not deep, but magnified by the strange night-time perspective, and in front of it, the slab of carved stone had been shifted, laid neatly by the side of the grave. A thought struck her; she had been here before. She recognized the corner of the churchyard, the yew tree and the hawthorn . . . caught sight, as she spun round, of the place she had seen earlier, when it was light, the grave with the little gate. (*Something inside me remembers . . .*)

The gate was open now, a line of moonlight touching the frame, and for a sudden, panic-stricken moment, Alice thought she could see something on the other side, something waiting to get out. Then it moved, pushed, no doubt by a gust of wind, moved and swung back on its hinges with

77

a little sound of rusty metal, as if some tiny, invisible child were swinging on it. Alice could feel no wind, but the gate swung again, more violently this time, open, shut, open . . . shut . . . open . . . the squeaking voice had three notes, two falling, one rising, like the song of a marsh bird: *Ti-ri-weeee . . . tiriweeeeeee.* Alice watched it, eyes wide, mouth wide, stomach falling away within her into a great cauldron of panic, the song of the marsh bird following her, its three sad, limping notes forlorn as snowflakes in a dark well, and throughout, the gate continued its dance, open, closed . . . open.

*　　　*　　　*

She wondered why she did not scream.

Two

Alice awoke with a sudden start, the last image of a terrible dream in her mind, and, for a moment, she wondered where she was. She ached all over; her neck was stiff, her legs curled awkwardly underneath her body, her clothes clammy against her skin.

'Ginny?'

She shook her head to clear it and sat up. What on earth had she been doing? Working? It certainly seemed that way; it had happened to her before to fall asleep in her workroom, but never to wake up with no memory at all of how she had got there. She remembered. What? A dream? She supposed it must have been, a dream of uncommonly vivid detail. She remembered getting up. But there was her painting, propped up on the easel and covered with a piece of muslin so that the dust would not dry on it, where she had, presumably, left it.

So why was it that she had no recollection of any picture, any picture at all? There was nothing but that damned dream in her aching head, nothing but that and a half-dispelled foreboding, spinning its mandala of fear into her mind. She wondered, with a now-familiar paranoia, whether Ginny had drugged her. She stood up, shaking the pins and needles out of her legs, fumbled an aspirin out of a brown bottle, swallowed it with a crunch and a grimace, shook out two more.

She remembered the outing with Joe, remembered going to bed, remembered, was that the dream? She could not seem to remember going to the workroom, could not remember the painting.

The painting!

Surely if she saw it again, it would trigger some memory, some fragment of that lost time; surely. She paused, hand poised over the sheet; through the thin cloth she could see green, grey, the palette, still smeared with acrylics, a half-filled water pot containing green water . . . Suddenly, she was not at all sure she wanted to see what was behind the muslin cloth. But the compulsion was too great . . . that, and perhaps she still could not quite believe in that familiar easel, laden with unfamiliar memories, the paint hardly dry.

She lifted the cloth. A blaze of chaotic colour met her eyes, colour which merged form and motion, symmetry and abandon in a composition of perfect completeness. It was her work, all right, her style, and yet the memory eluded her. Her signature in the corner; there. Her pointed calligraphy at the edge of the work, indicating the name of the picture. And what a picture! A river, a water's-edge spiral of grass and wildflowers, roots trailing surrealistically down into the limpid grey water, the willow tree, seen dizzyingly from above, a half-reflection mirrored shakily in the river; green, a tunnel of green with a white figure at the end of it, a white lady dimly glimpsed in the green and the water . . . Alice drew nearer. The perspective shifted, and she realized that she was looking at the figure from above, from above the surface of the water, while the white lady lay below. The water and the partial reflection from the tree obscured her image; only the face, by some trick of refracted light, was clearly visible: a pale oval, greenish in the shade of the leaves, open eyes and mouth dark beneath the water, red hair darkened to almost-black under the surface, while above the surface it regained its brightness in patches, like floating weed, lurid against the still grey river. The features were clear, still not clear enough for Alice to be sure, and yet, she was sure; they were Ginny's. And name of the painting was:

Repentance: The Drowning of Ophelia

Alice stared at it for a long time, this troubling thing from the country of dreams; for it was both like and unlike any work she had ever done. The colours were hers—there was paint on her hands, ingrained into her fingernails—the detail was hers, the tricks of the light. It was the same size as her

80

work of the preceding evening, the impression of space and clarity was the same, the details swiftly and surely etched in acrylics over the luminous tints of the inks, God, it must have taken her hours! She had never in her life worked so swiftly. The suspicion of drugs came back, more plausibly this time, frightening yet reassuring. Easier to believe that she had been fed some hallucinogen than to accept the dreams, the blank in her memory—the picture itself. Unable to keep away, she looked more closely. Yes, there was something else there, behind the light, something more disturbing still than the fact that Alice did not remember the slightest detail of how or when she had painted it; an impression of—she could not quite put a name to it, but it haunted her. Something in the strange perspective, deceiving the spectator into thinking that it was *she* who was underwater, she who was drowning, the roots of the willow tree reaching down towards her, the figure of the woman some above-world fancy, split into a million facets of refracted light, face smiling down in to the water, hair trailing towards her . . .

Alice pulled away, fascinated. The illusion of movement was intense. Even as she looked, she seemed to feel the pull of the undertow, the circular movement of the composition dragging her down and around . . . Had she really done that? Looking again, the unease changing slowly to awe and delight, she realized that it was the best thing she had ever done, even better than the other *Ophelia*. And Alice, looking into her canvas, seemed to see the vortex of her subconscious spinning further and further downwards, and each level was like a new and undiscovered world, turning its own axis, kaleidoscope-changing in a continuous loop of shadow and counter-shadow; and as she watched, the movement caught her and drew her closer and closer, and without even knowing it, she began to laugh.

Whatever the spell was, the phone broke it, its clear trill startling in the empty house, and Alice jumped nervously. A sudden, dream-memory returned (darkness, a smell of age and earth, figures leaping and dancing around an open grave), then faded as she rose to her feet. When she reached the phone, however, it had already stopped ringing. Alice looked at her watch. It was already past ten.

Ginny!

Still shaking off the memories of the previous night Alice made her way slowly into the kitchen and put on the kettle. Davy Crockett was sitting on the fridge, and he jumped down as soon as he saw Alice, yowling and winding his long furry body round her legs.

'Just a minute, Dave . . .' murmured Alice. 'Just let me see if Ginny's awake.'

She ran quietly up the stairs, paused to open the window on the landing, then went to knock softly on Ginny's door.

'Ginny? Are you up?' she called gently.

No answer.

'Ginny?' Louder, this time.

Still no answer. Alice, glancing at the clock on the landing, saw that it was nearly ten fifteen.

'Ginny, are you awake?' She tried the handle experimentally; the door opened, and Alice peered into the bedroom.

The window was open, the curtains pulled back,

allowing the fresh morning air and a faint scent of wallflowers into the pretty room. The bed was made, the pillows plump and cool, the primrose coverlet in place; Alice found herself admiring her guest's neatness. Suddenly, she felt suspicious. She tweaked the coverlet away to examine the sheet . . . it was as she had thought.

The bed had not been slept in at all. The nightdress on the bedside table had not even been unfolded. She yanked open the wardrobe. A few dresses hung there, a pullover was neatly folded over two blouses . . . shoes at the bottom. And right at the back, scrunched up in a bundle, she found those torn jeans, the T-shirt, the purple boots Ginny had been wearing, spattered with mud. Feeling somehow guilty, Alice pulled the things out. With them came a few other odds and ends: some muddy trainers; a shiny raincoat; black leather bike jacket; another T-shirt; some cheap jewellery; a heavy belt with a grinning face for a buckle; earrings in the shape of skulls; an upside-down cross on a chain. The kind of lurid, harmless clothes Alice associated with the bands of kids who prowled the shopping centre at night, pushed as far into the back of the wardrobe as they would go. And underneath the lot, a plastic bag containing two syringes, one almost new, the other so worn that the tip had begun to take on a frayed and feathered look. So that was it, Alice thought. The syringes explained everything.

But Alice was concerned for Joe, Joe who was so trusting and so naive. Joe who had no idea that the little girl he had fallen for in such a big way had gone off as soon as he had been out of the house (in the company of someone she seemed to be fairly intimate with, despite her lack of friends), and had stayed out all night.

It all made sense to Alice now, even the meeting with the 'friends' . . . Ginny had gone out because she wanted to find someone to score from, that was all. *And the dreams? Just dreams, she told herself. Just dreams.*

Alice felt oddly reassured. That was something she could understand, a weakness in Ginny which was wholly explicable, and which revealed the girl's real insecurity. Alice began to feel herself warming again towards the girl, so lovely in her borrowed clothes. She felt she had been insensitive, had seen calculation where there was only uncertainty, had shown hostility where she should have offered comfort and understanding. And now Ginny had gone.

Putting the anger aside, Alice went downstairs and stroked the tortoiseshell cat, which was sitting on the fridge, poured milk for the others, cut herself some bread and put it under the grill to toast. The cat jumped on to the side of the cooker, meowed and sniffed the toast with interest.

Alice picked the cat up and cuddled her, feeling cat-fur in her nostrils and cat-whiskers in her face. Through the window the sky looked grey; not a day for going out of doors, she thought, and she went to the door, picked up the paper which was still lying on the doormat, and settled down to read it while the bread toasted. She usually only read the *Cambridge News* for the cinema programme and the plays, and would in normal circumstances not even have noticed the first page, if she had not recognized the picture. Under a picture of a middle-aged man, and the headline LECTURER

84

DIES IN RENTED ROOM SEX SCANDAL, a photograph caught her eye. At first, she did not realize where she knew the place from. The photograph was dark and rather blurry; the short paragraph had obviously been a hasty addition, but she did recognize the picture.

That wall, that gate, the side of the church there at the left, the outline of one pointed window along the side of the dark wall . . . it was Grantchester church, the photograph taken just alongside the gate which led into the churchyard.

A fleeting memory crossed her mind again (a girl dancing alongside an open grave . . . the sound of digging . . . mud . . . metal . . . wood), then faded. The article was short and simple; the information therein minimal, but disturbing.

GRANTCHESTER VANDALS WRECK CEMETERY

Vandals broke into the grounds of Grantchester churchyard late last night, causing damage to the church, which was disfigured by graffiti, and to some of the graves.

Police are investigating the damage, which is reported to be 'quite extensive', but are not prepared to give details at present.

The Revd Martin Holmes (45), present vicar of Grantchester, describes the vandalism as 'a petty and cruel attack on our community', and lays the blame on 'student pranksters'. He has denied the allegations of witnesses that the churchyard has been used in the past by practitioners of black magic.

Alice re-read the article, the half-memory growing stronger and stronger. The dream? Had it been a dream? She remembered the sound of metal against wood, metal against stone. She remembered hiding in shadows, crossing the field of green wheat. Remembered mud on her shoes . . . She lifted her head, saw her trainers on the doormat, caked to the laces with graveyard mud . . .

And remembered everything.

One

Sometimes I wonder how much of my life has been dreams, or the dreams of dreams. Maybe I will wake to the teeth of my fantasy in my throat, or maybe I will simply float away on a river of ether like Wynken, Blynken and Nod. My nice young doctor came again today and frowned over my veins. He, too, has teeth which bring dreams. I asked him to stop the dreams, but he just smiled. For a minute, I thought he was Rosemary.

Ah yes. Rosemary. We never go far from her, do we? Still, I've written my story now; I don't flatter myself that she doesn't know about it, but I think I've hit on a way to keep her at bay for a while. Don't you know? Yes, I thought you did. That should keep me safe, don't you think? Because she'll be coming soon, I know that. Coming to bring me back, like Elaine and the others. But I'll not go to her. No. Better the dark. Better the dark.

One more glass of whisky against the dreams.

What did I write last night? I meant to tell you

about Robert, and of how he was ensnared, but instead I find that in a whole evening I wrote nothing but my dreams, as if I did not have enough of them already, as if I needed to multiply the madnesses which assail me in every part of my life. I go to Grantchester still, you know; they let me go, because they think it does me good. Not to see her (I see her every night), but to make sure that she is still there. If she came back, I would know it. I know I would. But she is powerless to hurt. She is laid to rest at last. But sometimes I see her, feel her, deep in the dark earth, moving. Maybe she sucks life from her shroud, like the witches of old. But I have faith. Faith is the answer. I tell myself that when she comes to me: I look the other way and pray.

All I need is Faith.

Maybe it was Faith which saved me then; I know that I was infatuated by her, bewitched by her every movement. Do not blame me; I was a fool, but she was so lovely! She was a prism, a sunbeam, a dancing bolt of lightning. I remember that first meal I spent with her; the sunlight like needfire in her hair, motes of light and dust circling her face like an aura. I was shy at first: staring tongue-tied at her over my untouched supper, she eating delicately, cat-like in little, precise bites, her teeth leaving tiny, even indentations in the piece of bread by her plate, the small sounds of her spoon against Mrs Brown's best china plate magnified, like an eye through a lens, in the troubled air. I did not think to speak; I think I stared, foolishly smiling, unaware that she too was watching me from beneath her demure eyelashes, that she was *seeing* everything through the veil of her mockery.

Nothing escaped her. Not Robert. Not I.

I'm sure she spoke first; over a dish of fruit, piled high. Apples, peaches, oranges . . . some parts of Cambridge had stayed almost untouched by the rationing; I think Mrs Brown prided herself on the way she supplied her 'young men' with the kind of food they would have found difficult to find even in the best restaurants. I reached for the dish to offer it to Rosemary just as she reached for it herself . . . my hand slipped clumsily and brushed hers. I drew it away, blushing with a muttered apology. Her hand was cool, like a child's.

'Oh, excuse me, miss . . .' I stammered.

Rosemary gave me a shy smile.

'You don't even know my name, do you?' she said.

My confusion increased. I mumbled something totally unintelligible.

'It's Rosemary,' she said. 'For remembrance, you know.'

'It's a beautiful name,' I said foolishly.

'And yours?' she said. 'I know I can't even begin to thank you for what you did, but at least tell me your name.' Her smile lit up the room again with its brightness. 'Maybe it should be Lancelot,' she said, with a touch of mockery. 'Or maybe Galahad.'

I was not an accomplished flirt; in fact, I was uniformly dull. I shook my head.

'No, Holmes. Daniel Holmes.' I wrestled with my shyness again for a moment. 'I'm so glad. I mean . . .'

'Rosemary. Please call me Rosemary.'

'Rosem . . . rose . . .' I gave a nervous laugh.

'And I am feeling better,' she continued.

88

'Thanks to you, Daniel. How brave you must be, to tackle the complete unknown like that, to leap in the river after me . . . And you don't know me at all, do you? I could be anyone. Anything.'

'I don't care,' I said, braver now. 'You're marvellous, like a poem—'

Her arms across her breast she laid;
She was more fair than words can say;
Barefooted came the beggar maid
Before the king Cophetua.

'A poet!' cried Rosemary, clapping her hands.

'No, no,' I blushed. 'That was Tennyson.'

She smiled, more sadly now, it seemed to me. She turned her face away into the sunlight, a rogue sunbeam lighting up the transparency of one of her irises into a crescent of brightness.

'I can hardly believe it now,' she said softly. 'That I wanted to die, I mean. But it's only a reprieve, you know. One day there will be no Daniel Holmes to save me and make me feel whole again; there will only be the river, waiting its time. Soon, I'll have to leave, and you'll forget me.'

'Forget you?' I gasped.

'Nothing lasts for ever,' said Rosemary. 'I had friends, Daniel. I thought they were good friends. But now, I'm alone, and there is a coldness inside me which can never be melted. You called me the beggar maid; perhaps I am that, for ever on the fringes of things, for ever alone.'

'But—'

'I have a face,' said Rosemary. 'Was that what you were going to say? A beautiful face? I wish I didn't!' She closed her eyes; the tragic mouth thinned, her fists clenched in her lap. I longed to touch her, to comfort her, but I did not dare, so inviolate was her air of tragedy. I will never forget what she made me feel, that passionate rush of pity and love. I felt the tears spring to my eyes: I make no apologies. She was a superb actress.

'My parents were poor,' she said. 'I don't blame them for that, or for wanting me to use my face to help them. They didn't understand. They thought that it would be easy, with my face, to find the kind of husband who could look after me and them, there are lots of nice young men in Cambridge, they said.'

'You don't have to tell me,' I said. 'None of it matters, Rosemary!'

'I want to tell you,' she insisted. 'I want you to know, even if it means you despise me afterwards. I want you to try and understand. I found a job in a pub.' She shuddered. 'It was hot, and noisy; sometimes I worked very late, and I was afraid to walk home at night. I lived in a little flat in the town centre; it was too far to go back to my parents' house in Peterborough every day. My landlady was suspicious of me—jealous, perhaps, of my face. Sometimes, men would follow me home. I never let them in!'

She stared at me, her lavender eyes intense and passionate.

'Understand, Daniel, I never did!'

I nodded. You would have believed her too.

'Then, one day, I met, well, even now, I dare not tell you his name. It doesn't matter; it may not even have been his name. He said he was a professor at one of the colleges. He was handsome, intelligent and, I thought, kind. As

90

soon as he saw me, he said he fell in love with me, told me that it was wrong for me to be working in that place, said that all he wanted was to look after me. I was suspicious at first, but he seemed sincere. He broke down my defences with kindness and consideration, led me to think that he wanted to marry me. He never said so, but . . .' Here, she broke off, and passed her hands over her eyes.

'Weeks passed. He was kind. He held my hand when we walked in the park, he took me to the theatre. One day he took me to London in his car . . . but never to his house. I didn't mind. I knew that if he married me, his family would be shocked. I waited, patiently, blinded by my happiness. Then, one day, I saw him as I was carrying some shopping home from the market. I saw him and called his name in the street. He turned around . . . and I saw that he had a lady on his arm.'

She stopped, her eyes brimming, and impulsively, I took her hand.

'I heard the young lady say: "Who is that woman?"'

'He turned away without a word, and he said . . . God, I can still hear it now! "Nobody, darling."'

'Nobody! That's who I am, despite my pretty face. Not good enough to earn the respect of a good man. The beggar maid! You couldn't have put it better, Daniel. My dear Daniel.'

I tried to comfort her, but she went on.

'No! I want you to hear the whole. I suppose I knew then that all hope was gone, but I couldn't bear it to be ended like that. I watched for him on every street; waited in vain for him to call and explain everything . . . I think I was still desperate enough to want to believe any lie, just as long as it could be like it was before . . . but he never came. I could not bear to work in the pub again; so I did sewing work for my landlady . . . earning just enough to keep myself alive. That woman was glad, I know it. She knew that something had happened . . . you cannot begin to believe the scornful words she heaped upon me . . . hints . . . comments . . . but I was afraid to leave. I was afraid that no one else would agree to house a single woman on her own. I drank . . . alone in my room at night . . . I drank gin, like the lowest of sluts. I hated it, but it would appease the loneliness and the despair a little. Then, one day, I saw him again, coming out of the theatre with some friends. I was afraid to speak to him, I was shabby, maybe I had been drinking, I can't remember. I followed him home. I waited at the door until the friends had left, I don't know how long. A long time, I think. Then I knocked.

'He didn't come to the door straightaway; I was beginning to be afraid that he would not come at all . . . then I saw him, through the glass of the door. He opened it . . . looked at me for a moment. His eyes were cold.

' "I'm sorry," he said. "I don't know you." And he closed the door on me. I waited there for a long time, cold . . . despairing, until I saw the dawn beginning to rise. I had been there all night. I never understood why he had changed so much, and not knowing was worse than anything else. When I came back to my flat, my things were waiting for me on the doorstep, neatly packed into a bag and a suitcase. I am sure it must have given her pleasure to do that . . . to handle and gloat over all my possessions . . . to write that little note

I found pinned to the door. What it said, I don't think I could tell even you, Daniel; though I was innocent, it shamed me to the core, made me dirty. And so, I went to the river. And somewhere, there must have been a little pity left in the world, because you came. You came.'

And then, she did cry—long, hitching, tearing sobs which bruised my heart—her face in her hands, like a little girl. I put my arm around her, mumbled sorry, sincere, adolescent words of comfort to her . . . felt that jerk of the heart which I never felt before or since as I held her; that moment of epiphany when she looked up at me and smiled.

No, I could never have blamed Robert, even if he had not been my friend, for taking her from me. Rosemary was the wedge which drove friend from friend, drove the honest man to crime, the good man to murder. In his place, no doubt I would have done the same, and sometimes my blood runs cold to think how easily our roles could have reversed. It could have been me, there in Grantchester churchyard. Maybe it will be yet.

PART TWO

The Blessed Damozel

Two

The Reverend Holmes was a small, thin, rather insignificant-looking man, the lovely stained-glass window of the nave behind him bleeding all colour from his oddly childish features; but the pale eyes behind the magnifying lenses of wire-framed glasses were shrewd and bright with humour. His eyebrows were thick and very dark, giving him an earnest, rather faraway look, and at the moment they were drawn together in a frown which managed only to convey bewilderment. His voice was that of a much older man, or a man who is so much involved in his own little circle of events that the comings and goings of the world simply pass him by, and he spoke slowly, with much hesitation, his voice the cultured, gentle, slightly bleating voice of the country priest.

'Ahh . . . Well,' he said, shaking his head, 'I can't really say any more about it than, ahh, you know. Just a prank, albeit a nasty one, just one of those student tricks. Though I fail to see any humour at all in the, ahh, digging up of graves and the vandalizing of a church. I'd rather see it as a prank, my dear.'

'But what happened?' insisted Alice, trying to curb her impatience.

'No one knows,' said the Reverend. 'Just another of those incidents . . . rather nasty, though, and a bit of a shock for me, actually.'

He lowered his voice and turned to her conspiratorially. 'I think it's . . . ahh . . . a personal *dig* against me ahh . . . no pun intended, you know,' he said.

Alice looked suitably interested, though privately she was beginning to think that she must have been crazy to look up this man in the first place. What she thought she remembered had never happened; what she had seen in the paper had been a coincidence, nothing more.

Martin Holmes beckoned her closer.

'One of the graves which was tampered with, I knew. It was my uncle's.' He paused for a moment. 'We're an old family, miss, er?'

'Alice Farrell.'

'Ahh . . . yes. An old family, as I was saying; Cambridgeshire born and bred, though I have not actually lived here very long myself. It could be that, ahh, rancour still exists, old grudges, you know the kind of thing.'

Alice glanced at her watch. The Reverend Holmes did not notice, but continued his halting, gentle narrative with the air of a man who has found a captive audience.

'I . . . ahh . . . can't say I was a, ahh, a *popular* choice as vicar of this parish. There were, let us say, ahh, factions, who found me unsuitable. There was a bit of an upset in the family long ago, ahh, insanity, you know, that sort of thing. I suppose they remembered it still. Long memories, Cambridgeshire folk. Maybe some of the young ones thought it was funny to dig up the grave of my poor Uncle Dan to tease me with it.'

Alice looked sympathetic.

'Mad as a hatter, poor chap,' said Martin Holmes with a shake of his head. 'Died in some kind of a home . . . hanged himself, so I've been told. Not that I knew him at all . . . ahh . . . can't remember him too well. Uncle Dan kept himself to himself. Remember seeing him once, with my father, when I was a boy . . . he tried to give me a shilling, but Father wouldn't let him. Father told me afterwards that he talked endless nonsense about *devils* . . . and monsters. Monsters!' he repeated, and laughed.

Alice looked at her watch.

'Well . . .' she said, 'if there's nothing else . . .'

'Nothing else?' said the Reverend. 'No . . . except that they were fooled, of course. Poor old Uncle Dan.'

'Fooled?'

'Well, he's not there, of course,' said the Reverend Holmes simply. 'Whoever dug him up didn't find a thing. There's nothing in that coffin except a box and a few oddments.'

Catching sight of Alice's astonished face (she now had no desire to go away), he turned an apologetic smile towards her.

'I said he was mad as a hatter,' he said.

'Well, where is he?'

The Reverend laughed again, very softly.

'He's here,' he said, 'right here in the church. They ahh . . . *cremated* him, you know, then they put him in the east wall, behind a plaque. It was all in his will, you know, and, ahh, my father felt obliged to carry out his last wishes, even though he was so peculiar.' He paused again. 'Funny,' he mused, 'it looks as if he may have been right in hiding away.'

'Why?' (I can't believe I'm hearing all this, thought Alice desperately, can't believe I'm still here *listening* to all this . . .)

'Because that's what he was afraid of all that

time,' explained the priest, patiently. 'Being dug up.' He shrugged. 'Kept on spouting a lot of . . . ahh . . . nonsense about . . . being *dug up*, don't you know, and ahh . . . used in some kind of, ahh . . . Though why it happened now, after all these years, beats me. Poor old fellow.' He turned to Alice.

'Look there,' he said.

Alice couldn't see anything.

'*There*,' insisted the Reverend. 'Just at the end of my finger. Can you see a little brass plaque?'

Alice moved forwards, squinted, moved forwards again. Yes, she could see it, set into the wall about eight inches above the ground. The plaque was very small, about twelve inches by ten, and it was drab with oxidization. She peered at it to read the inscription, traced the words with her fingers with a growing feeling of unease. It said, in very plain letters, cut deep into the thick metal:

KEEP ME SAFE

That was all. No name, no date, nothing. For a moment, she wondered whether the priest had not invented the whole thing as an excuse to keep her there talking. '*Keep me safe*'? What kind of an inscription was that? She had not even known that it was legal to hide a body in the wall of a church like that. She examined the plaque again, rubbed it with the tip of her finger, not liking the dirt which came off on to her hand.

'That's where he is,' chirped the Reverend Holmes. 'Just his ashes, of course, and his papers, ahh. He was a writer, you know, in the . . . ahh . . . old days. Quite famous too, in his way. Had his manuscript buried with him. I always wondered what was in it.'

Alice ignored him. Behind the half-inch or inch of plaque and the three-inch wall behind it, there was a mystery. A story as immediate and as poignant as the one behind that little metal door on which was engraved:

Something inside me remembers and will not forget.

She jerked away from the plaque as if she had been stung. The Reverend Holmes was standing above her, an expression of slight concern on his good-natured face.

'Are you all right?'

Alice nodded. What had she been doing? For a moment there, she had been somewhere else, had almost *seen*, almost *known* something of tremendous, dizzying importance . . . Not for the first time in these few days, she wondered if she was quite sane. Surely, there had been a man . . . a scent of the circus in the air . . . an altered light. And more than that, a strong compulsion to pull back the plaque, loosen the stones . . . to *find*, to *see* . . .

'I'm fine,' she said. 'This is very interesting. I really had no idea.' The sentences were meaningless in her mouth, but sufficed to give her the courage to ask the question she wanted to ask.

'Tell me . . .' she said, 'do you know a girl called Virginia Ashley? Red-haired girl . . . slim, very pretty? She has a friend, a dark man with a ponytail . . . black trenchcoat. Have you seen them near here?'

The Reverend Holmes thought about it for a moment.

101

'I don't think so,' he said at last. 'Not that that means much, you know . . . my memory isn't what it should be . . . especially . . . ah . . . faces . . . but I might . . . Redhead, did you say? No. But I'll certainly look out for her if she's a friend of yours. What was the name again?'

'No, it's all right,' said Alice. 'It's nothing. I just thought you might know her. I really do have to go now. Thank you so much. Thank you.'

And on that, she turned and left the church, almost running through the churchyard, even though most of the mess had by now been cleared up: only a toppled gravestone remained and some meaningless scrawlings in red spray-paint. The sunlight was bright in the lane outside, the walk across the fields to Cambridge so different from the walk of her dream that Alice began to feel better. No, it could not have happened. Even the trail of footprints across the cornfield (three tracks together and a fourth, winding cautiously round the outside in the shadows) might have been someone else's.

And while Alice made her way along the Backs towards the town, a figure walked softly into the church, came in through the vestry door and hesitated at the entrance to the nave, the light from the stained-glass window throwing multicoloured reflections on to her bright hair. For a moment, she watched the priest standing by the altar in silence, then she came towards him with hardly a sound, her ballet shoes barely a whisper of leather against the stone as she ran, cat-like, to the altar. As she passed it, the sanctuary light went out, but the priest did not notice.

One

Robert was my oldest friend; my best and only true friend. He was two years older than I; that made him twenty-seven, but to me he was so much more mature and aware that he seemed to move in an entirely different sphere. He had been in the war (I myself had been judged unfit for service because of my poor eyesight), and had been sent home from Alamein after taking a volley of shrapnel in his leg; now he walked with a limp, which in my eyes gave him even greater sophistication. I would have given anything to be like him, to be handsome and popular, to have followed him to the war and to have been a hero. He was everything I admired and wanted to emulate. He was taller than I was, loose-limbed and naturally at ease in the slightly overlarge suits and overcoats he tended to affect, with brown hair falling carelessly over eyes which were clear and humorous. He was studying English literature, the course he had been obliged to give up at the beginning of the war, and had already nurtured in me a passion for Keats and Rossetti and Swinburne. He smoked foul-smelling cigarettes, spent hours in crowded coffee-shops, drank cup after cup of black coffee and talked incessantly about literature. I had read some of his writings, and they were youthful, incisive, sometimes gently self-mocking. There was never any doubt in my mind then that his work would some day be published; I followed his progress with pride and admiration, but no envy. That came later, with Rosemary.

I would no more have hidden recent events from Robert than forgotten to breathe. Of course I told him. I told him everything in those days, he accepting this proof of my admiration of him as if it were his due, and with the kind of half-contemptuous indulgence he might have shown to a younger brother. I never resented this, feeling privileged that he should choose my company over that of so many others, and with him I shared my passions and my enthusiasms and even my dreams, which for days had been filled with Rosemary.

I found him in his usual place, drinking coffee and reading a book. I must have looked a sorry sight; I had not slept that night at all, my suit was crumpled, my eyes watery and my hair uncombed. Besides that, I had the beginnings of a streaming cold from jumping into the river; my throat was sore and my limbs ached. I told you I was no man of action. He grinned easily at me as I came in, stubbing out his cigarette in the marble ashtray in front of him. He put down the book he was reading (Morris's *News from Nowhere*) and beckoned the waitress to fetch another pot of coffee and a cup.

'Have you read this?' he demanded, waving the book vaguely in my direction. 'Marvellous. Did you know . . .' His brow creased slightly as he took in my crumpled appearance. 'What happened to you?' he queried, with some amusement. 'You look like a mad inventor. Have you been out on the tiles again, or are you simply cultivating a kind of Byronic disarray?'

I swallowed, trying to tame the hair which was falling over my eyes.

'I thought you had to give a class this morning,'

continued Robert. 'Aren't you late?' He looked at his watch. 'It's past nine.'

I shook my head, flinging my hat on the table. 'I cancelled it.'

'How very dashing of you,' he said. 'Go on then, don't keep me in suspense. I suppose whatever it is is something terribly exciting to make you skip classes. You're always so enviably precise.' And he sighed, a kind of self-mocking dramatic sigh you might have expected from Keats or Beardsley. He was laughing at me again, gently making fun of me, but underneath that I could tell that he was really puzzled, perhaps a little worried. Robert's veneer of sophistication was really rather thin, despite appearances; what others often mistook for pretentiousness was in reality nothing but protective coloration. I think retrospectively that he was an insecure man. Propelled from the hermetic atmosphere of public school and Cambridge into a traumatic, though mercifully brief, period of combat, he had returned to Cambridge to escape from ugliness in whatever way he could; he had retreated into the close circle of the Cambridge intellectuals, going to lectures, staying up late to talk about art and poetry in smoky coffee-shops. To him it was all escapism, and while his doting father was willing to encourage and finance his study, Robert was happy to remain the eternal student, gravitating towards ever more intellectual pursuits, shielded from pain and the unwanted complexity of adult relationships. Young as I was then, I saw only the carefree, handsome exterior; later, with Rosemary, I saw my friend stripped bare, but at the beginning he was my strength, my buffer against a cruel world. He encouraged me in my work, talked to me, tolerated me; my gratitude was such that at that time I would willingly have died for him.

My story must have sounded garbled to him; I remember his smile, his hand coming down soothingly on my shoulder.

'Steady down, old fellow,' he said. 'I don't know about you, but I'm never at my best first thing in the morning.'

I accepted his offer of coffee, tried to stop my hands from trembling around the china cup, began again. I think I was more coherent then; he listened to me, a faint crease between his brows, the cup held in the palm of one hand, a cigarette in the other, its smoke idling unhindered towards the ceiling. Once or twice he asked a question, nodded; I stumbled forward in my narrative, trying vainly to put words to what I felt, the words cleaving to my tongue as I spoke. When I had stopped speaking, I drank deeply from my cup, blew my nose and waited, watching him over my glasses, half-contorted with fear lest he should laugh at me, for he did sometimes hurt me with his mockery, although he never meant to. Maybe he saw the fear in my eyes, because he paused, almost appraisingly, as if deciding whether to treat my story seriously or to take it as a joke. He took a drag at his cigarette, blew the smoke out of the corner of his mouth and frowned.

'Seems like a funny kind of business to me,' he said, pouring himself another cup of coffee. 'I wonder if you're not landing yourself in trouble somehow.'

I shook my head violently. 'Oh, no! If only you'd *seen* her, Robert, you'd know that isn't true. I know how odd it sounds, but . . . oh, confound it! There's no way I can put it into words. She's a miracle, Rob, a dream come true. She's from another age.'

Robert cast me a humorous look.

'She certainly seems to have taken you back to the age of chivalry,' he said.

'Oh, please be serious!' I said. 'If only you had seen her.'

'I doubt whether it would have made any difference,' he said lazily, 'I think I'm immune to women. They never seem to have any conversation other than themselves and their clothes and other women. I know your experience isn't vast, but believe me, after you've known a few . . .'

His eyes twinkled, and I knew he was making fun of me; that languid tone was not the real Robert, but the man behind the many affectations was an elusive character, and I had not encountered him often.

'However, I admit to some curiosity,' he said, 'I have not yet encountered the perfect woman, and I would very much like to see her.'

I sighed with relief, clapped Robert on the back and managed to spill a cup of coffee in my enthusiasm. I felt like a schoolboy who has just been complimented by a sixth-form hero.

'Good man!' I cried. 'We'll see her now. Shall we? You won't be disappointed, Rob. You'll love her, you really will. You won't be disappointed.'

As it happened, I was right; he did love her, and he was not disappointed. Cold enough comfort that offers me, even though I could not be expected to know—how could I have known? I am blameless, I know that, but the knowledge does not stop my ultimate guilt, or obliterate the memory of the youthful joy I felt that day, as I happily led my friend across the river to his destruction.

Two

Well, thought Alice, that line of enquiry had only led to a baffling dead end. The Reverend Holmes had certainly never seen Ginny or her friends, nor had anything he told Alice seemed to corroborate her dream. She was still inclined to think that Ginny had gone out with friends to buy or sell drugs and what Alice herself had experienced had simply been an isolated incident of memory loss caused by exhaustion or the beginnings of some virus. Fair enough. It sounded convincing. But there was still the mystery of Ginny to solve; still Alice's resolution to befriend the girl and try to give her what help she could; and to do that, she needed to know more about her. Joe? She remembered his chilly response to her earlier questions on the phone, and doubted that he would be of any help. Who, then?

Alice pondered the question for a moment, frowning, then her face cleared. Reaching for the directory, she flicked quickly through the medical section, allowing her fingers to come to rest on the letter F.

*   *   *

'Hello? My name is Alice Farrell. I wonder if you

could give me a few details on a former patient of yours.'

'Please wait a moment.' The receptionist's voice was cool and competent. 'I'll put you through to the doctor on duty.'

Alice waited for a few minutes, while the hospital's hold system piped would-be soothing music through the earpiece. Then she heard the tone change, and a man's voice, dry and faintly irritable, answered.

'Yes? Menezies speaking.'

Alice repeated what she had told reception.

'Why the enquiry?' the doctor asked. 'Are you professionally interested?'

'Not exactly.'

'Well, in that case, I'm very busy.'

'Just a few details, please. This girl is going to be staying with me for a few days, and I'm a little worried about her mental condition.'

'Then make an appointment for her. All cases are treated as confidential here. I don't discuss my patients.'

'I don't need confidential details,' began Alice, 'I just need to know if a girl called Virginia Ashley was a patient here, and whether she is likely to need special help—'

'Look,' snapped the doctor. 'There are dozens of doctors in this hospital. I don't know the case at all. Obviously someone else treated her. If you'll just wait a moment, I'll tell you the name of the colleague who dealt with her case, and you can contact him.'

And he slammed the receiver back on to hold.

Alice waited again. After a much longer time, the receiver was lifted, and she heard the man's voice again, more distant this time, as if the line had suddenly worsened.

'Ms Farrell?'

'Yes?'

'Miss Ashley was admitted to Fulbourn last Christmas on a short-term basis. That's all the information I'm able to give.'

'Can I talk to the doctor in charge of her case?' said Alice.

'I'm sorry; that's impossible.'

'Could you give me the name of the doctor?'

'Look, I'm afraid there is no way you can talk to Doctor Pryce,' said Dr Menezies. 'My colleague died last week. The funeral was yesterday.'

One

She was gone when we got to the house, and I knew a dreadful instant of panic, certain that she had never been real, that I had imagined her, and that like the snow-child, she had simply dissolved into air and water at the first rays of the sun. Mrs Brown was out, and I remember calling through the house, every room throwing back the sound of her absence in my face, every breath a new emptiness. I must have been more ill than I thought, for my head raged with fever, but none of that registered. All I could think was, she was gone. She was gone, and the one person I could trust with my mystery, my only friend, the only one who could understand, was looking at me with a mischievous expression, as if he did not believe me.

'Look, there's her bed,' I cried, the crumpled coverlet in my hands. 'The pillow she rested on. There'll be hair on it. Let me see. Look! The cup she drank from, her flowers!'

'Come on, old man,' said Robert, gently. 'Don't take it so badly. Like as not she's just stepped out for a walk.' He patted my shoulder, and I flinched away.

'She was here a minute ago, I swear—'

'Have a drink, there's a good chap. Sit down.'

He pushed me gently into one of Mrs Brown's soft leather armchairs, pressed a glass of sherry into my hand. My arm jerked violently; some of the sherry spilled. Patiently, he took the glass from me and refilled it. I drank, shuddered, drained the glass and closed my eyes. I have no way of explaining the power Rosemary had managed to gain over me, nor the despair which played in me, like the monotonous whirring of a toy train in a child's spinning-top. She was gone, she was gone, she was gone, she was gone . . . Fragments of poetry entered my brain like flying glass, images like pieces of a torn canvas, tantalizing . . . the curve of a collar-bone here, the light on her hair, the turn of her mouth . . . I tried to get up from my chair, slipped. The world tilted.

'Daniel!' Robert's voice was sharp. 'Are you all right? Hey, Danny! Danny!'

A tremor in the earth as I fell.

Spangled darkness all around.

A voice, light as an aspen leaf, crystallizing in ether: 'Is anything wrong?'

A brief glimpse of a figure standing in the doorway, head and shoulders etched in copper.

'Where's Daniel? Who are you?' A voice made

111

shrill by controlled hysteria.

Robert's voice, 'So you're Rosemary.'

Then, in the darkness, a vision of wheels. Turning.

Two

Joe's band were on the stage setting up. Joe waved and grinned at Alice as she came in, then returned to the business in hand, oddly competent in his chosen element, positioning speakers and amps and coiling cables with speed and economy of movement. Ginny was not yet there.

Alice made her way to the bar and ordered a drink, seating herself at a table by the side of the stage, where she would be able to see and hear everything. Little by little, the room began to fill up with all the variegated night-lifers of Cambridge, rubbing together in neon and shadow. Alice stood up and looked around; Ginny was still not there.

The first band played, and the crowd settled down to listen, some talking quite softly amongst themselves as they stood at the bar, most of them drifting to the music. Somebody near the back lit a couple of joints, and soon the room was permeated by the scent. Alice ordered another drink as the group left and Joe's band took their place; she even took a stroll around the hall to see if she could find Ginny, but without success. She had just returned to her place by the stage when Ginny appeared—a slight, hesitant figure in a pale dress—and Alice beckoned to her to come and sit with her. The girl acknowledged her gesture with a nod, but made no movement to come across.

The lights dimmed, and the band went into the introduction to a slow, traditional song Alice knew well; it was a favourite of Joe's, 'The Dalesman's Litany'. Joe had come to the front to sing, his bass around his neck, a single spotlight on his face. His voice was stronger than Alice remembered it, the northern accent still in evidence, but more mellow. She liked the change.

It's hard when folks can't find their work
Where they've been bred and born . . .

She reached the back of the hall, where a few latecomers were standing, holding cans. She scanned the darkness for Ginny. The spotlight was off now, the quiet mood of the music highlighted by soft green and blue filters which lit the faces of the audience with a drowned underwater glow.

When I was young I always thought
I'd bide 'midst roots and corn . . .

Ginny was waiting at the other side of the crowd; Alice could see her drowned-girl's face, the livid dress, her hair black in the stage lights, eyes supernaturally huge.

But I've been forced to work in town
And here's my litany . . .

For an instant Ginny looked at her; and perhaps it was the light, but it seemed to Alice that her tragic mouth curled in a rictus of such complex

113

malevolence that it transfigured her entirely, illuminating her from within with a ghastly radiance, like radioactivity.

From Hull and Halifax and hell
Good Lord deliver me . . .

Then the expression was gone, and there was only Ginny, with her air of blank and almost simple-minded sweetness as she watched the stage. But whatever Alice had seen or imagined, it was enough to kill any desire to be near her; she lingered at the fringes of the audience, still holding her drink, and was it her imagination again, or had the atmosphere suddenly changed? Had that group of people standing by the door been there all the time? Had there been that subtle charge trembling at the edges of the hall?

The band had gone into a solo instrumental, the violin stretching, almost unbearably, through the registers, groaning and shrieking. It was too much for Alice. She felt stifled, drowning, spread-eagled in the cross-currents coming from the crowd and the stage. Instinctively, she began to move towards the door, where there was some room to breathe and to stand away from the audience. A few others must have had the same idea, for there was a little group of people watching the stage from the doorway: a girl with hair almost to her knees, outlined in neon from the EXIT sign, a youth with dyed red hair and a bird tattoo on his face, a blonde girl, her head laid confidingly on the red-haired lad's shoulder, a man in a dark greatcoat, face in shadow.

Alice felt the hairs on her bare arms rise. The

114

stance was familiar, arrogant and relaxed . . . so were the lights reflected from the metal tip of a motorcycle boot.

So what? she thought, half angrily, taking another step towards the door. There were dozens of men who looked like that. There was no reason to be so sure that it was Ginny's friend of the night before. No reason to remember her dream, to suddenly feel the sting of sweat under her arms, in her throat. Another step . . . and suddenly their eyes were upon her, and the blonde lifted her head from the shoulder of her red-haired companion. But it wasn't a girl. It was a young boy, spectrally fair, beautiful, disturbing. The redhead grinned at Alice, showing a gold tooth, beckoned . . . and Alice suddenly knew without doubt that behind their beauty was something corrupt. She pulled away, rejoined the crowd, and tried to concentrate on the music. But the spell was broken. Only the watchers behind her remained, thrilling the nape of her neck. The spectators around her seemed restless too, like a herd which scents the predator.

She glanced to her left and saw Ginny, closer now, almost by the door. As she watched, the group closed around her, protectively. Ginny lit a cigarette; the sweet smell of cannabis reached Alice across the hall over the hot reek of sweat and lager.

A voice behind her, raised angrily. A ripple ran through the audience, a shiver, like anticipation. She turned, saw an older man approach the little group of watchers at the door. She could not hear what he was saying, but saw his face, briefly, swollen with anger. He did not look strong, not beautiful with the beauty of these strange savage ones; he was balding, hiding the fact beneath a leather hat, long wispy hair trailing out from the back. To Alice he looked oddly vulnerable, half-drowned in the lights and his desperate rage. She heard no words, but saw the tall man smile, speak. Ginny stared, blankly. The man gestured wildly, turned, was engulfed into the crowd. Alice did not see the fight break out, but she saw the repercussions. First, a depression in the rising tide of people; a dimple of bowed heads. It exploded outwards, ripples moving towards the outside. Someone fell. The music faltered but did not stop; a woman screamed, the sound a flight of birds in the dark. A voice from the stage, its message through the PA lost in a squeal of feedback. She looked to the door; they were still there, untouchable, blank, but she could feel the power coming from them, the attraction and the amusement. She moved towards them, irresistibly, the crowd already beginning to push at her back. She saw a man fall in the crowd, shockingly close, saw another strike out, almost aimlessly, at a woman, who stumbled into the wall. The music stopped. Some instrument began to feed back on a high, unbearable frequency.

As if at a signal, the voice of the crowd was raised, ululating in a toneless music of its own. As Alice reached the door someone screamed. Someone threw a full glass at the stage. The glass exploded under the lights like fireworks. Someone shoved her hard in the small of the back and she was sent flying uncontrollably towards the man at the door. She felt his arms around her, holding her upright against the crowd's undertow. He whispered something in her ear, something low

116

and intimate. He smelt sweet, almost sugary, like candy-floss. His hands were cold, his breath cool against her face. For an interminable second, Alice was absurdly convinced that he was going to kiss her, and that in that moment she would die, but the knowledge was something abstract, someone else's voice heard from under water. She was aware that she was about to pass out and tried to speak, but could not form words. She tilted helplessly into the rushing silence.

It was only a minute later, when she was safely outside, stretched out on the damp grass, looking up into the concerned face of a medic, that she remembered what the man had whispered in her ear.

The word was *chosen.*

One

I was ill with fever for a long time; long enough for Rosemary to do her work, and more. For near to a fortnight I was ravaged by fever and by dreams of such potency that they left me gasping for a breath of reality, and while I raved and sweated out my fever I betrayed my friend Robert for the first time, leaving him alone with Rosemary. When I recovered it was too late.

My first inkling of it was when Mrs Brown came to give me my broth. I remembered her doing so at intervals during my illness, but in my mind she became confused with many people, and I had not yet been able to speak lucidly to her. But that day, I was feeling weak but clear-headed, and my first

117

thought was of Rosemary.

'Where is she?' I asked Mrs Brown, between two mouthfuls of broth. 'Is she all right? She hasn't been ill?'

'Now, now,' scolded Mrs Brown. 'Plenty of time for that later, my lad.'

'Please!' I begged. 'Is she still here? You didn't send her away?'

'Mr Robert's found her somewhere to live, so don't you fret,' answered Mrs Brown.

That was the moment when I began to suspect what had gone on in those two weeks. But she would tell me nothing; all she cared about was to see me well again; as for the rest, that could wait until I was better prepared for it.

Robert did not come to see me; I assumed that Mrs Brown had told him that I must not be disturbed, and did not worry, but I missed Rosemary desperately, and I was anxious that she might attract criticism from Robert for her unwitting part in my illness. And so I continued to fret until the day the doctor told me I could leave my bed, and then I dressed, ignoring all protests from Mrs Brown that it was raining, that I was still not well; with my battered hat on my head and a crumpled woollen cravat around my sore throat I went off in search of my friend. He was not in his usual place; not in any of his usual places, and his lodging was shut. I tried all the coffee-shops, all the bars; I tried his tutors, who told me that they had not seen him for nearly a fortnight, and at last, I began to suspect that there was something wrong. Not that my suspicions were anywhere near the truth, but as I dragged my weariness and my anxiety through the drizzle and the greyness of the unchanging Cambridge streets I began to feel a sense of foreboding.

The mirage of Rosemary followed me everywhere; it was she I saw when a girl in a yellow scarf pushed past me through a gateway, she I saw sheltering under a bridge, she the face looking through a streaming window. And then, I really saw her. Walking with Robert down King's Parade. Robert had his arm on hers, and was holding his umbrella over her, looking down at her so that I could see his profile; a smile on his aquiline countenance. She was wearing a raincoat several sizes too big, the large cuffs turned over her small hands, her hair tucked into the side of the collar so that I could see the white nape of her neck. I called, but the rain snatched away my words. I ran towards the two of them, splashing clumsily through the puddles, then I stopped. Rosemary turned towards Robert, her hands on the lapels of his coat. Then he kissed her, lightly, with the intimacy of long acquaintance. I froze, then he kissed her again, his arms tight around her, the umbrella slipping from his hand.

The world slipped with it.

I was close enough now to see the drops fall on to Rosemary's raincoat. I stood there, speechless. Oh, Rosemary.

And then she turned, and looked right at me. I'm sure she did; she looked at me, and for a moment her eyes held me, the colour of rain . . . and I read humour there, and a cold contempt, and something like triumph. Oh, she knew, she knew all right; she knew I was watching, and all my thoughts and jealousies, all my life, she saw without pity and dismissed. She had Robert, and she had me, and knowing that, she turned away with him into the Cambridge rain, taking my innocence with her.

Two

Alice went home feeling sick and exhausted. After the scene in the Corn Exchange, she had found Joe in confrontation with a police officer who was trying to persuade him to come to the station to give evidence. At the far side of a little group of stragglers and police, she could see him in the bright lights, shaking his head, turning away. The policeman tried to catch him by the arm; Joe shook him off abruptly. Another policeman, sensing trouble, took a step towards him, a fairground figure in the revolving lights of the departing ambulance.

Damn.

Alice knew Joe's relationship with the police of old; he had a habit of picking quarrels at demonstrations, and had been taken in on several occasions, although Alice knew that he had never really meant to cause trouble. She supposed she would have to intervene before Joe hit someone, or got hit himself, and she ran out of the Corn Exchange doorway towards the little knot of people which had gathered around the cars. A dozen or so were standing around, though there was no sign of Ginny's friends.

Joe turned when he heard her voice.

'Thank God. Is Ginny with you?'

Alice shook her head.

'Shit! Where the hell did she go? Where was she standing?'

'Relax, Joe. She was right at the back of the hall, with some friends. She must have got out right away, and gone off with them. Don't worry.'

'What do you mean?' His anger focused on Alice. 'What friends? She doesn't have friends.'

'She did tonight,' said Alice, with a glance at the policeman. 'Look . . . she's probably gone home, and I'll find her waiting for me on the doorstep. There's really no reason to worry about her. I'm sure she can look after herself.'

Joe didn't look convinced. His mouth tightened in a stubborn expression.

'I'll take you home in the van,' he said, then, turning to the policeman, continued. 'So you see, I can't help you. I didn't see anything, anyway. I was on stage. The first I knew of it was when someone started throwing bottles. Sorry. OK?'

'I'll have to ask you to come with me, sir,' answered the policeman (politely enough, though his patience seemed to be wearing thin). 'It won't be for long, but—'

'Dammit, what's with you? I told you . . .' Joe took a deep breath and, with an effort, brought himself under control.

'I'll phone you to check that Ginny got back,' he told Alice.

Alice gave him a quick smile.

'Fine. And keep your temper, hey?'

'I'm OK.'

She hoped he was.

*   *   *

121

The first thing she did when she got home was to make a pot of tea. The cats were imperious, demanding their food, and she opened a tin for them and mixed the fish with bread. There were biscuits in the cupboard, and she opened a packet and ate them, without hunger or pleasure, between swallows of tea until she began to feel the aftermath of the night's events subside. Ginny hadn't been waiting on the doorstep, but then again, Alice hadn't for a minute imagined she would. Very likely she was still with her friends, the friends Joe didn't know about. Alice found that she didn't care. In fact, she thought as she sipped from her mug, the less she knew about Ginny the better. It was none of her business.

She put down the empty mug, reached out to switch on the gas fire beside her armchair . . . sat up. Just for a second, she imagined a movement out there in the night—a figure shifting into the darkness. She stood up. Nothing. It was probably her own reflection in the window. She reached up to pull down the blind . . . and hesitated. There it was again, that movement, part-furtive, part-mocking. Inviting her out to investigate.

Cautiously, Alice looked out, and saw two figures standing under the street-lamp. At once, Alice flinched back towards the kitchen, switching off the overhead light. Fear stapled her tongue to her mouth.

It was the man from the Corn Exchange. He was still wearing his greatcoat, collar turned up so that a wing of it hid part of his face. Alice could see long hair, tied loosely back and spilling over the collar below a pale, angular face with deep shadows at the eyes and cheekbones. He seemed to be looking straight at her, but she knew now that it was only an optical illusion caused by the shadowplay. His companion was the blond boy, and she could see his face clearly. He was thin and bony, with that graceful angularity peculiar to adolescent boys. Alice took him to be no older than sixteen, and his face, beneath a shock of bleached blond hair, was disturbingly feminine. Under a black leather bike jacket, Alice glimpsed a white T-shirt with the slogan DEATH OR GLORY printed on it, and was reminded of Ginny. He turned to the taller man, said something. The tall man shrugged, without taking his eyes from the window. The boy shivered, looked at the sky, pulled his jacket tighter. Maybe they were cold, thought Alice.

On the tail of that thought came another, at the same time compulsive and terrifying: Why not ask them in? That way she would find out who they were and their exact relationship to Ginny. Maybe she would find out what Ginny was hiding. She hesitated for a moment, then flipped on the light and opened the door. Light flooded out, on to the doorstep so that she could hardly see the two figures as they merged into the shadows.

'Excuse me,' she said to the darkness, 'are you waiting for Ginny? I'm fairly sure she'll be back soon; I thought she might have been with you. You're welcome to come in here and wait for her, if you like.'

For a moment, there was no answer, and Alice had the peculiar sensation that she was calling down a tunnel, with only the echoes of her own voice to answer her. Then two faces turned towards her from the dark.

'We're friends of Virginia.' It was the tall man; his voice was quiet and cultured, unexpectedly so, given his bohemian appearance. As he stepped closer to the light, Alice noticed that he was older than she had first thought; the fine-boned face was lined, giving it a hard look, and the long hair was touched with grey.

'Do come in,' urged Alice. 'Wait for her in the warm. I'll make you coffee if you like.'

The door was wide, but the stranger made no move to go in. The boy stepped through the gate, lingered at the fringes of the light. There was a silence, rather too long for comfort, and Alice began to feel a little embarrassed. A little frightened. She shook herself. What possible harm could come to her here, in the light? In her own house? Cat poked her head through the door to see what was going on, then hissed furiously and fled back in.

Alice smiled, uneasily.

The blond boy grinned, exposing slightly uneven teeth.

'Do come in,' said Alice, once more. 'It's getting really cold out here.'

At once, as if they had only been waiting to be asked a third time, Ginny's two friends came through the door into Alice's living-room, bringing a draught in with them.

'Pleased to meet you. I'm Alice,' she said. 'Are you old friends of Ginny's?'

'My name is Java,' said the tall man with a smile. 'My young companion is Rafe. Yes, we're old friends.' He smiled at the blond boy. 'Very old friends.'

'You're a painter,' he said. He looked at her. He

124

nodded at the painting she had tacked to the cork noticeboard. 'She looks like Virginia.'

Alice was slightly startled. 'Maybe it's the hair,' she said.

He smiled. 'Maybe it is,' he said.

*　　　*　　　*

Alice heaved a sigh of relief when they left, then locked the door and drew the curtains. Even then she knew she would follow them, drawn to them, just as she had been before. She waited a moment for them to leave before letting herself out through the back door, keeping to the shadows, never moving closer than a hundred yards to the two garish neon-lit figures as they half-ran down the narrow streets, casting long arcs of shadow in their wake. Alice was conscious of the scuffling of her shoes on the pavements, of the sounds of her clothes as she brushed walls and archways, but Rafe and Java were utterly silent, never exchanging a word or slackening the pace of their eerie night walk. Breathless and furtive, Alice followed.

The town centre was empty; windows and doorways were dark blind eyes. A couple of tramps waited on benches by the side of the market square, occasionally dipping into a brown paper bag which contained a bottle of cider and watching the night with incurious eyes. This was their time, the people of the night, when the colleges had locked their gates and the pubs closed their doors and the security men patrolled the shopping precinct to evict the undesirables. That was when the old men came out of hiding, silent, hunched in their tattered overcoats and fingerless gloves.

Alice hardly noticed them, but their eyes were on her. For a moment she stopped to catch her breath, and as she was about to set off again, she became aware of a presence at her elbow and she turned to see who it was. An old tramp, scrubbily bearded and muffled in a dirty pink scarf, a woollen hat on his greyish-white hair, and carrying the inevitable brown paper bag, had hesitantly moved to her side. Both arms were clamped around the precious bag, and he was watching her intently.

'Excuse me?' he said.

'I'm sorry,' said Alice. 'I don't have any money.'

For a moment she thought he was going to say more. His mouth worked, and his rheumy eyes fixed hers with a wild kind of hope.

Then he turned away again, and once more Alice resumed her pursuit of the two men as they made their way to the Grantchester road.

Alice was not certain what she had expected: another visit to the church, perhaps, but Java and Rafe did not stay on the road for long. Instead they turned towards the river about a mile before they reached the village, leading Alice down a dark section of street bordered by derelict terraces. There were no street-lamps, and Alice soon lost the two men from view, feeling her way in the darkness along the empty houses. From time to time she caught sight of Rafe's pale hair or a spark from one of Java's steel-capped boots in front of her, but apart from that she was blind. Sweat plastered her hair to her face, and there was a tightness in her throat. A snatch of music began to play, inconsequentially, in her mind:

126

Strange little girl, where are you going?
Strange little girl, where are you going?

Suddenly she heard a sound, shockingly near, and froze. She had come much closer than she had intended in the dark, and she was almost on them. A door opened, metal sparked against metal, and the flame of a cigarette lighter blossomed, bright, in the darkness. Instinctively Alice drew back; Rafe was standing at an open door, one foot on the step, and Java was holding the lighter, a cigarette between his teeth, hands cupped around the flame. A nimbus of light surrounded his head. He looked up as Alice shrank back towards the wall, and although the shadows seemed impenetrable, smiled directly at her.

'Alice,' he said. 'Won't you come in?'

For an instant, her mind was a total blank. She took a step backwards, and almost fell in her haste to get away. Java's quiet voice halted her; she imagined his inhuman gaze drawing her back like a fish on a hook.

'You have come such a long way,' he said. 'Perhaps you would like a drink before you go? Besides, Virginia is here.'

At Ginny's name Alice turned feeling suddenly foolish. Surely no harm could come to her no more than a mile from the town. Besides, if Ginny was here . . . She shifted her gaze to the door, where Rafe was still standing, a tiny smile touching his lips. If she backed out now, she thought, she might as well give up trying to find out anything else about Ginny or what had happened in Grantchester. She had dared to come this far—

surely she could stay a while.

'Do come in,' said Java. For a second time Alice was conscious of an undeniable attraction to him, an almost unbearable awareness of the beauty of the man, of the flawlessness of his angular features, an admiration of the grace with which he stood, that poetry of movement indicating that here was a creature entirely self-possessed, content to be himself and prey to none of the anxieties and insecurities of normal people. He radiated a glamour which was almost irresistible. Alice found herself smiling in response, and before she even knew it she was through the door and in the house.

By the cigarette lighter's hesitant flame Alice found that she had entered a lobby, where a number of stained and yellowed cards still bore the names of former residents. Beyond that a narrow staircase led to the upper floor. Rafe led the way with the light, and Java followed behind in silence. They passed several doors until they reached the right one; Rafe opened it and went in. Alice looked round. A spirit lamp lit the room casting monstrous shadows against the walls. The room itself was filthy, with wooden boxes covered in blankets to serve as seats, and the remains of several meals littering the floor. A table stood in the centre, with newspapers to cover it, and a dozen or so empty bottles winking green and white in the lamplight. There was a smell of mould and dust, and a sweet under-smell, like incense. Ginny was sitting on an old sofa in the corner of the room, legs crossed, face turned up towards Alice with a peculiar insolence.

'So it's you,' she said without interest. 'Is Joe here?'

Alice shook her head. 'He was looking for you. He was worried.'

Ginny shrugged. 'So you came to find me. How nice. Now what do you want?'

'To learn, of course. To know what we do in here.' Java laughed lightly, touching the nape of Alice's neck with thrilling, icy fingers. Rafe came a step closer, a cross-shaped earring dangling hypnotically . . . the sense of unreality was so overwhelming that Alice even forgot to feel afraid.

'I . . .' She realized that she had no idea what to say; feeling eerily light-headed, she gave a low laugh. A hand came up, with dreamlike slowness, to wipe her damp forehead; for a moment the arc of its motion seemed to fill the world. Java's arm crept round her waist, cold and intimate, and she caught another breath of the sweet circus smell which clung to him. She must be very tired, she thought for a second, she was sure her eyes had closed of their own accord. Her head tilted back like a sleepy child's, her eyes beginning to close again . . .

A voice jerked her back to reality.

'Not here!' said Ginny sharply. 'Don't you two have any sense?'

Alice started, aware for the first time that she had been half asleep in Java's arms, her face almost touching his.

'Soft,' he whispered against her hair, not releasing his grip.

Ginny sprang up from her reclining position on the couch.

'I *said* not here.'

Alice felt Java stiffen against her, but his voice was still coaxing, seductive.

'Wait for me.' He released Alice; still disorientated, she allowed herself to be propelled towards the little door at her back. Before she knew it she had been pushed through, the door shut after her. Voices drifted towards her through the wood.

Whatever glamour had possessed her in the other room left her abruptly as soon as she was alone. A fear which was not only a fear of the dark came crashing down upon her. She tried the door, but it had been locked. She considered shouting to the others, but shivered at the very thought. Claustrophobia overwhelmed her momentarily and she flailed out at the encroaching dark; then, forcing herself to be calm, she began to feel along the walls to gauge the size and shape of the room.

It was barely larger than a cupboard; maybe six by eight feet, that was all, and she guessed from the tiles along one side that it had once been a bathroom. All fittings were now gone, however, and the only furniture was a stool by the door. In the half-minute in which she had been in the room her eyes had had time to accustom themselves partially to the darkness, and she could just distinguish a thin silver scratch of light around the door-frame, etching a narrow line of brightness on to the tiles. And beside that she imagined she could see a patch of shadow which was darker than the rest—something like a hole in the wall.

In a second she was on her hands and knees, exploring the hole; the bath had been ripped out of the wall, which itself was only plasterboard, and the wall was broken right the way to the other side. If only she could get her head and shoulders through . . . she thought she might. If the hole was only a little bit wider . . . On impulse she picked up the stool and jabbed at the rotten plaster. Something gave with a crumbling sound, and the air was suddenly filled with mouldering dust. She jabbed again. A voice from the other side of the door:

'Alice?'

Another voice, unintelligible but commanding. Alice needed only that. Head first she dived for the hole and pushed her way through the damp plasterboard, eyes watering, face caked with dust. She grabbed a piece of loose wood and used it to clear away the debris before her as she emerged into blackness. She took two reckless steps and half-fell down the stairs; grabbing hold of the banister, she used it to guide her as she limped, at an agonizingly slow pace, down the stairs and into the street. Once she heard voices quite close behind her, bolted in panic, and almost fell, but somehow she reached the ground floor in spite of her panic, and within a minute was racing down the Grantchester road, mouth dry, her heart a drum, her shadow a demon at her tail. She did not slacken her pace, her feet skimming the pavements as she fled back to her safe, warm house, slamming the door behind her. Only then did she allow herself the luxury of exhaustion; and later, as she sat in front of the fire trying to analyse what had happened she felt that slow, certain terror come upon her again, not the primitive terror she had felt in the dark of the derelict house, or the superstitious fear of the beautiful strangers who were Ginny's friends, but something far older and heavier. Her cheeks burned as if with the imprint of Java's touch, and as she looked at herself in the

131

bathroom mirror she noticed that she was flushed and feverish-looking, with a strangeness in her eyes. She splashed cold water on her burning cheeks, then undressed and showered quickly, scrubbing her body with a kind of fervent anger which temporarily blocked the fear. But even as she scrubbed and splashed she remained conscious of that persistent feeling, a strange, unfocused *desire* . . . But for what? She did not know.

One

Dreams again; more dreams. She walks them like a general walking a battlefield of her own making, the screams of the dying a hymn to her glory and her pride. Sometimes I try to write, sometimes I just drink gin and sit in the light. My books tell me many things, but never how to combat her, how to destroy her and her satellites. I am alone, as I was from the beginning. My walls are lined with books and pictures; her face stares out from every one, her names are written everywhere. I know her now; know her now for what she is.

Her face looks out from Grimm's fairy tales, from Dante, from Shakespeare and the Apocrypha, from all countries and times when she has walked and fed, been feared and loved. I pray for deliverance, but hear only the howling of the pit below me, my words dead Latin in my withered mouth, the crucifix turning to blood on my lips. God is not home today. He walks with Rosemary.

*   *   *

It was a long time before I saw her again, after I came across them that time in the rain. Robert avoided me, as I avoided him, ashamed maybe of his betrayal, but more likely too much ensnared by Rosemary to care about old friends. I plunged back into *The Blessed Damozel*, little knowing the truth of what I wrote, and time passed. Summer came and went in a blink, wet and cheerless, and I huddled in my cold room, cut-off gloves on my numb hands, and tried to lose myself in my work. I visited galleries, libraries, the Ashmolean Museum in Oxford where so many of Rossetti's lovely pencil drawings are exhibited, the Fitzwilliam Museum in Cambridge where his *Girl at a Lattice* and his *Mary Magdalene* and Millais' *Bridesmaid* all lie hidden in basement archives. Rosemary's face blurred into wistful regret, fused with the beauty of those other women, and though I did not forget her (who would?), there were times when I wondered whether she had not been a dream; and I made up for my longing with hours of unceasing work.

I wrote hundreds of pages on technique, learning how the Pre-Raphaelites created their luminous effects by painting only with pure colours on a wet white background, or how Rossetti used red and green lead for flesh tones, knowing that he used impermanent colours which would fade and be lost with time, but not caring, as if the creation of beauty alone interested him. Perhaps he too was afraid of immortality. I studied their models— those strange tragic enchantresses: Lizzie Siddall and Jane Morris and Maria Zambaco—until I knew every aspect of their faces and histories.

133

They were artists in their own right, most of them, fascinating and untouchable, serene and troubling. They peopled my fantasies, walking my dreams with Rosemary. I explored their influences, the poets they loved, Mallory and Tennyson and Keats. I re-read Grimm's fairy tales, Greek and Roman mythology, explored the dark side of the fantasy world from which they came, discovered the works of Jung, adapting all that I read to my newly emerging theories. I lost touch with most of my friends, cancelled many of my classes, made myself a virtual recluse in my lodging, saw the first version of *The Blessed Damozel* almost finished with midwinter . . . worked on. I earned extra money by writing articles for the university art publications, things more of fiction than fact; lurid, self-indulgent works which now had little to do with technique and everything to do with a kind of Gothic craving for the sensations which my austere and scholarly life denied me. I interspersed my descriptions and essays with fairy stories which grew ever blacker and stranger as the year bled into the next, and I kept writing, throughout those months which led up to her death in August and Robert's in the winter of 1948. I existed in limbo until the spring, and although time had for the most part ceased to have any great meaning for me, it must have been a year after I first pulled Rosemary from the river that I found myself there again, early in the morning, on my way to my favourite gallery, my overcoat tightly drawn across my shoulders, my nose red and watery with the cold I had dragged with me almost constantly since the winter, eyes streaming behind lenses which seemed to have become even thicker and heavier as time passed. A stray thought escaped my memory, insubstantial as the steam which puffed from my nostrils; a girl in white, pale face, dark eyes, dark open mouth . . . and for a moment, I almost thought I saw her, just a little further down the river, saw the curve of a bare arm, took a clump of weed to be the tangle of her hair . . . I blinked and wiped the lenses of my glasses with a clumsy one-handed movement.

There *was* something there, caught in the rubbish at the head of the weir; a bundle of rags, perhaps, or a floating log . . . The similarity to that day in April threw the hallucination into sharp, surreal perspective, and I actually *saw* the limp body with eyesight far too sharp to be my own, saw a drifting arm, the line of a neck lolling gently into the dark water . . .

It was too much; I had to see.

I jumped down on to the river-bank (there were punts moored there, but no one had used them since July), lowered myself gingerly on to the muddy tow-path, hobbled down to the water. The weir was bloated to overwhelming size, and the stink from it was palpable; it was the smell of slime and mud, salt and decay, and all the rubbish of summer dragged beneath the water by the undertow to dark and muddy oblivion. And as I squinted at the pale bundle caught in the rushing greenish flow, I saw her; no mistaking the shape of the arm, the movement of the hair, the clothes . . .

'Rosemary?' I whispered.

But it was not Rosemary. The woman I had found by Magdalene Bridge was old; the hair was greying, wispy, the arm which had caught my attention by its whiteness was short and sturdy, even in death, the trunk stiff and twice as thick as Rosemary's slender figure. That the woman was dead could not be doubted; the exposed flesh was like lime, greenish-white and bloodless, the clothes half torn from the body, allowing a glimpse of a leg and some dirty underwear. I felt a sudden ache of pity for the poor woman, pitilessly exposed by death in all the harsh light of an April morning; pity, not horror. In a way, I was glad I found her; that one stab of pity I felt for her then was the only caring thought given to her in her strange and loveless passing. Later, with the police, came the horror and the disgust, but then I could almost have imagined her as Ophelia, trapped by the weeds in her muddy dignity, face still and pale, turned downwards to fathom the depths of the secret Cam. And there my imaginings ceased abruptly. For a sudden, perverse twitch of the living water loosened the weeds which held her, and the body rolled bonelessly over like a tired old whore, and I saw her.

Only for an instant; the moment after, I was on my knees in the long wet grass, coughing and retching, slime drooling from my mouth, my glasses slipping from a face which was suddenly, despite the chill, slick with sweat. I told you I was no hero; I vomited until my throat was tight, and all the while my skin was hot and my hands were shaking with terror . . . not that she would rise after me and touch me, poor woman (though the time would come when I was ready to believe in such things), but that the thing which had fed upon her might.

I never saw her face.

That, at least, will never be there to haunt my

dreams; for that I am grateful. But as for the rest of her pitiful violated body . . . the thought of it, so long ago, blots out the horror of a war in the space of a memory. There was no blood. Only ropes of intestine and bone and a dreadful black-lined hole which had been her chest cavity, and was mostly empty. Oh yes, something had fed.

I wiped my mouth gingerly on a handful of the coarse, gritty grass of the river-bank, and stood up, legs weak and head spinning. I shouted: 'Help! Police!'; began to stumble and slide my way back along the muddy bank towards the bridge. There was a man standing on the bridge, looking my way; a tall man, slightly hunched, collar turned up against the damp. He did not walk away, but seemed to wait for me, his very presence a comfort to my shock and fear. Tears of gratitude filled my eyes; I reached out towards him.

'Thank God!' I cried fervently. 'There's a body there by the weir.' I stumbled towards him, one knee printed with mud as I fell, tears in my eyes. Through their mist, the man seemed vaguely familiar. For an instant, I felt his eyes meet mine, though the expression on his face was still unclear. A tiny sound escaped his lips, a white hand twitched and withdrew into the pocket of his coat . . . then, with a single movement, he turned away and ran, in long, jerky strides, away from me, away from the bridge, and disappeared through a gateway out of my sight.

I must have cried out loud, because, just then, a group of students rounded the corner, laughing and talking, and in an instant I was surrounded by friendly, sympathetic faces, hands touching mine, arms around my shoulders.

Their cries of: 'Make room!' and 'Give him air!' surrounded me.

I tried to smile, to breathe normally, to tell my story, to stop the dreadful palsy in my arms and legs. Slowly, the tilted world righted itself. One of the boys ran to the police station, bringing back with him two constables and an ambulance. I refused to get into the ambulance but accepted a drink of brandy. I began to feel better. I told my story three times, once to the students who had helped me, once to the policemen, once again to the hard-faced young inspector with a surprisingly gentle voice who interviewed me at the station and gave me a cup of tea. I did not mind telling the story; every time I did it seemed to remove it a little further into the realm of fiction. Over the teacup, looking into the grey eyes of Inspector Turner and comforted by the sympathy in his voice, I felt almost a hero. I had been in the war, yes, but now it was over.

'What made you think there might have been a body there, Mr Holmes?' asked Turner softly. 'The two men I sent out tell me there was nothing to be seen from the bridge, and . . . you tell me yourself that your eyesight is not good.'

'I know,' I replied. 'I can't explain it.' I told him some of the events of the previous spring, about Rosemary and how I had pulled her out of the river, and he nodded, as if he understood.

'I see,' he said. 'And did you recognize the deceased?' I shuddered, but this time it was a controlled reaction, and my tea did not spill.

'I didn't see her face,' I said in a low voice. 'When she . . . turned over . . . I was sick.'

Turner smiled narrowly.

'Don't be ashamed of that, Mr Holmes,' he said briskly. 'I've seen more corpses than you have, and this one is enough to make any man wish he hadn't had any breakfast.' He paused and closed his little book.

'That's it for now, you'll be glad to know,' he said. 'Are you going to be all right to go home now, Mr Holmes?'

'I think so, thank you, Inspector.' I smiled, hesitated, fumbled with the buttons on my coat for a moment, then asked the question he had known I would ask all along.

'Are you treating this case as a . . . I mean . . . do you think it's murder?'

The Inspector sighed and appeared to contemplate my question.

'I don't know,' he said. 'Do you?' And for that moment, I felt as if he were asking me a serious question, as an equal, as if he thought I really might be able to tell him something.

'Well . . . maybe a marauding animal . . .' I suggested, feeling foolish.

The Inspector cocked an eyebrow.

'Maybe,' he said mildly.

'What sort of *person* would do that to someone?' I asked, helplessly.

Turner shook his head and sprang his last question.

'Are you sure you've told me everything you saw?' he asked, and his grey eyes were cold in the middle of his smile.

'Of course . . . at least . . . I think so,' I stammered. 'Why? I'm not a suspect, am I?'

'No.' The Inspector's denial was offhand, almost disinterested. 'There can be no suspect until there has been a murder, and that will be for the pathologist to decide.'

'Oh.' The syllable sounded lame, and I immediately began to *feel* suspect, guilt spilling unbidden into my mind. 'I see.'

I looked at Turner's smile, and a secret chill crept up from my feet and raised the prickly hairs on my thighs. I am not good at lies, and I think the Inspector knew that I had not told him everything, but this thing was too much, too secret for me to hand it to him just yet. Besides, I hardly believed it myself, and I had to know before I acted, before I decided what to do.

Because, you see, the man I had seen on the bridge, the man I had called out to, and who had run away with the abrupt graceless movements of total panic, the man whose eyes had touched mine in a second of horror and understanding . . . I had known him.

It was Robert.

One

What I had seen of my friend Robert plagued my mind for some time before I gained enough courage to do what I did. I remembered his grey face and the way he had looked at me before he ran away—not the look of a sane man—and I was afraid. When I eventually went in search of him, it was as much for my own peace of mind as it was out of concern for Robert, for I had brushed with horrible death, and I was certain that my old friend had somehow the key to the secret, whatever it

140

was.

The *Cambridge News* had published an article on what they called the 'Body in the Weir' case, describing how I had found the woman, 'as yet unnamed' but presumed to be 'a missing person'. Apparently the pathologist's inquiry had been inconclusive over the cause of death, but had uncovered the fact that the injuries I had seen on the body, which the newspapers had euphemistically termed 'a massive internal insult' had been inflicted after death. No one knew at the time of printing whether it had been murder or not. Except, perhaps, Robert.

It took me some time to locate him, for since we had lost touch with each other, he had moved from his lodging and had left no forwarding address. I contacted his college, but his tutors were as bewildered as I; they had not seen him or spoken to him regularly for weeks. At last, after another three days of fruitless enquiry, I was directed to an unwholesome cellar-bar at the end of Mill Road, where, my informant told me, the drink was cheap, 'If you're not particular about the company'; and there I found Robert, alone at a table with a bottle of wine. The change which had been wrought in him even in those few days was horrific. His hair was unkempt and had grown too long, and he had not shaved. He was wearing no tie, and his suit looked crumpled, as if it had been slept in, maybe more than once. His eyes were red-rimmed, like a drunkard's, his face drawn, his cheekbones too prominent in his sunken face. He gave me one brief, incurious glance and poured himself another glass of wine, propped up on his elbows on the greasy table like an old man.

141

I sat down beside him, saying nothing, but my mind boiled over with questions. He drank again, the smell of the cheap red wine overpowering in that small, close place, but even then, not managing entirely to camouflage the under-smells of sweat and dirt of the cellar.

After a while, he spoke.

'What d'you want?' His voice was only slightly slurred by alcohol, but his tone was expressionless.

'Oh, Robert . . .' I think my voice was unsteady; I felt close to tears at seeing him like this, in this place. 'What are you doing to yourself? Why didn't you come to see me if you had any trouble? Why hide away in this awful place like . . .' My voice failed me, and I laid a hand on his arm, more to steady myself than to comfort him. Robert had always been my touchstone in times of trouble, he had always been stable, carefree, happy. What could have changed him so much?

The answer leapt unbidden to my mind . . . in fact, it had never been very far from my thoughts anyway.

'Rosemary . . .' I whispered. 'Is it something to do with Rosemary?'

The reaction was immediate.

'No!' he snapped. 'Nothing. Nothing! Leave her out of it. It's me. My business. Leave me alone.' His voice was a bitter, self-pitying whine. The facetious and affected Robert I had known had coarsened, his nerves stripped raw, and with the terrible underlying current of weakness, of helplessness one can sometimes see in drug addicts or mental patients, that sense of abyss. For a moment I was disorientated, everything I had thought solid and permanent in my world dissolving around me.

'But I'm your friend . . .' I protested. 'If you're ill, need help, I can always—'

'*I don't need help!*' His retort was so loud that the coarse woman behind the bar glanced his way, wondering, perhaps, whether he was going to cause trouble. Robert saw her reaction and lowered his voice, but his eyes were still overbright and hostile, and there was venom in his voice.

'I don't need help,' he repeated. 'I'm very happy with Rosemary. In fact, I've asked her to marry me.' He paused. 'And she said she would,' he added, as if to dispel any doubt I might have as to the authenticity of his story.

'Oh,' I said in a small voice. 'Marry you? Congratulations, I, really. When?' His announcement had taken the wind out of my sails to such an extent that I could hardly string two words together without stammering.

Robert saw my confusion and made an effort to speak normally again.

'Rosemary thinks . . . in August. That will give us plenty of time.' He tried to smile; the result would have been a good approximation if the eyes had not been so blank. 'I don't know what bee you've got in your bonnet about me, old man, but there's really no need, as you can see. I would have called, of course, but I've been very busy, you know, with Rosemary and the preparations for the wedding and so—family to contact—not much time . . .'

'You look ill,' I said, lamely.

'A few too many late nights. A little attack of *Weltschmerz*. You caught me on a bad day, what else can I tell you? Rosemary was busy tonight; I

143

went out a-roving on my own and ended up on the edge of Lethe.' His tone was deliberately flippant; the fact that he was trying hard to deceive me frightened me even more than when he had snapped at me. I looked at my friend and saw a total stranger, bright psychopathic eyes behind the carnival-mask. A sudden pain in my heart as I realized that I had never known him at all.

'I saw you on the bridge, Robert. You ran away, but I recognized you.'

'What bridge?'

I told my story, beginning with my finding of the body, then how I had seen him and called for help. His reaction was frankly incredulous, touched with the old half-good-natured contempt of the old days.

'It wasn't me, Dan,' he said. 'You're really off on the wrong track here.'

'I'm certain it was! You were wearing the same coat . . . you looked at me, for heaven's sake!'

For the first time that evening, my friend looked me straight in the eye, and put his hand on my arm.

'Look, old man,' he said, not unreasonably. 'If it had been me, and you had called me for help, do you really think I would have run away?' I shook my head helplessly. 'What's more,' he went on, 'you say yourself that you'd had a shock. And I know what bad eyes you've got. You were feeling rocky, you saw a man in a coat like mine, shouted to him . . . your imagination did the rest. No wonder the poor devil ran away.' He tried the smile again; this time, I was almost convinced.

'And as for being ill,' he said, 'you don't look so good yourself. Too much worry, old chap. Now

144

take yourself home and get some rest, and stop fretting. I'll call round one of these days, and we'll go out and have a drink. Just like the old days. Right?'

I nodded.

'Just like the old days. See you later, Dan. Now push off, that's a good chap, and come to see me when I'm more sociable.' And at that he turned to pour himself another drink, leaving me feeling isolated and rejected. Helplessly, I went up the cellar stairs and out into the fresh air, thinking furiously to myself. There was something wrong, I *knew* there was something wrong, and none of his arguments could change that, but why did I think he had lied to me? Why would he have *needed* to lie to me?

Rosemary. Everything came back to Rosemary. She was the root of it; she was the one who had changed him and taken him from me. Maybe she could give me an answer; maybe she could explain. I halted at the top of Mill Road, the germ of an idea forming in my mind.

Then I went back to the cellar.

A few words with the female behind the bar were enough to obtain what I needed to know; she remembered Rosemary, though not by name, of course. She had seen her with Robert often enough, yes, and she knew where she lived, described a row of shabby apartments outside the town and overlooking the river. I looked at my watch; it was just past ten o'clock. Maybe, if I was lucky, I would catch her before she went to bed.

I quickened my pace, trying to tell myself that it was only the unaccustomed exercise which made my heart beat faster, and it was only twenty past

145

ten when I came to the row of apartments, a long terrace which had once been lodgings for one of the colleges, and was now privately owned. The building was mostly dark, but here and there a light shone, tinted red or blue or purple with the colour of the curtains, and at the base of each staircase there was a lighted porch for the letter-boxes bearing the name of each resident.

I tried six staircases before I found the plaque which said ASHLEY 2; then I made my way up the stairs to apartment 2. I knocked, but no one answered. I knocked again, straining my ears, but no one came, and there was no light under the door. Rosemary was out. I looked at my watch and frowned; it was twenty-five to eleven already; rather late for a young woman to be out on her own. But maybe she was not on her own. I thought about that for a while. Had she found another waitressing job, or a job behind a bar?

Had she found another man?

I wondered if I had not hit the nail on the head. The fact that Rosemary was in love with someone else might possibly account for Robert's despondent, almost aggressive mood. It would explain why Robert had been less than eager to see me: maybe he thought I still harboured some resentment against him for having taken Rosemary from me. I resolutely pushed the episode at the bridge from my mind; that had been explained already. I went down the stairs again, intrigued, but with a certain satisfaction that I had solved the mystery. Poor Robert. No wonder he had snapped my head off when I asked him about Rosemary. The first time he had ever taken a real interest in a woman, had even gone as far as to propose marriage to her. Not that I hadn't suspected something of the kind before this, in view of her disloyalty towards myself. I was pondering this as I happened to halt at the window of the first landing, and a movement from outside caught my eye. There was no reason for me to believe that it was Rosemary; and yet, with an obscure certainty, I knew. Maybe there was something about the way she moved, the way she held her head, though how I could have been sure, how I could still have been so poignantly aware, even after all this time, of her every gesture, even half-glimpsed through a first-floor window, I cannot say. Maybe it was simply that Rosemary, once seen, however briefly, was not so easily forgotten.

I wasted no time in trying to distinguish her features through the blurry glass; instead I ran as fast as I could down the staircase, steadying myself with my hands as I crashed against the wall on the landing and again, in the porch. I tore out of the front door and into the night, her name on my lips, my face flushed, my cry wasted on the cold air. She was gone.

I ran down the road after her, searched every side-street, every porch, every archway. I ran back on my tracks and tried the back of the building, the alley where the dustbins were kept in neat rows; nothing. Rosemary had vanished.

Cursing, I even went back to the dingy cellar in which I had met Robert, but by now it was closing down, and Robert was gone, too.

I went back to Rosemary's apartment then, and I waited for her to come home; I waited for a long time, but she never came.

From that night, when I waited outside

Rosemary's door, I felt outcast from my life and from the lives of ordinary people. It was then that I began to dream again; dreams of Rosemary, overpowering in their imagery, and the more I dreamed, the more my dreams became reality and my life spun meaninglessly away around me, like water down a drain. I dreamed of her every night in longing and a transfixed kind of fear . . . she was the witch of my secret desires, my Blessed Damozel, her hair the blood-red veil through which I beheld my dreams. I was sick with renewed longing for her, sick with guilt and worry for my friend Robert. I forgot to eat, forgot to work, spent my days in idle and morbid contemplation of my bewitchment. I sat in coffee-shops, hoping for a glimpse of her, as if seeing her again would solve everything, while around me the summer blossomed, and Cambridge grew heavy and restless with the coming of it. There must have been something in the air of the place even then, for the papers were full of reports of crimes, thefts and assaults, and the continuation of the police investigation on the 'Body in the Weir' case (now being treated as murder and coupled with warnings to the public to stay away from the river, or any isolated place at night), but I hardly noticed them, moving through life as I did without a ripple.

Twice I caught sight of her, once from afar, alone, and once with Robert. They stopped when I greeted them; Rosemary looked pale and ill, her face robbed of all colour in the strong sunlight, but she was still beautiful, her pale lavender eyes fathomless in her angular face, her bright hair tied strictly back beneath a dark-green scarf. Robert, to my astonishment, looked rested and well, with no

148

sign of the haunted, hunted look I had noticed in him before, and he responded to my cautious enquiry with good temper and a friendliness which reminded me strongly of our earlier friendship and of the old days, before Rosemary. She, however, said little; she had been unwell recently and had had to stay in bed; nothing but a touch of influenza, Robert assured me, but he knew that she was not yet in the best of health; she was delicate, she was too thin, and she needed rest.

Robert was almost possessive with me; he talked incessantly while Rosemary said virtually nothing and I mouthed platitudes. I had never felt as remote from him as I did then; he was a minor character in the chequered background of my existence, bled dry of individuality. His facility for talk, which I had once admired, was revealed to me to be the light, pretentious banter of the dilettante; I saw no real intelligence behind his charm, felt ashamed that once I had almost worshipped this man with the unquestioning awe of a high school freshman. What I felt then was the first step in Rosemary's domination of me; I began for the first time to envy my friend.

I watched the pair of them go with mixed feelings; but uppermost in my mind was the fact that they were to be married in August, and that if I was to act, I had better act quickly. You see, I had wrestled with my conscience for long enough; I was infatuated, and maybe I fancied that Rosemary was not as happy as she might have been with Robert. Clutching at straws, I imagined her forced into an unwelcome marriage with a man I had seen to be disturbed and unstable; I fancied her falling ill with worry, pining, maybe, for the

149

man who had saved her from the river, and who now seemed too busy to pay any attention to her. I behaved, in fact, like the moonstruck young fool I was. The truth was too simple to be obvious to me: it had been a novelty for me to play the part of the hero; it was a feeling I wanted to experience again.

And so one night, maybe two weeks later—it must have been near the end of May—I went back there, to the place where she lived, and since then I have lived in hell, reality passing me by in a bright, remote flow, myself a shadow among shadows. I see monsters everywhere and know that they are real, for she has made a monster of me too, in allowing me to know what should have remained unknown, and she mocks me, as well she might, knowing that for all my knowledge I am helpless. No one will believe me, no one will touch me. She remains inviolate.

I sought her out of my own accord, at dark of night and after having imbibed more courage than was good for me, hoping, perhaps, to find her alone. I had built her up so high in my fancy that I believed that on a single word from me she would abandon Robert and come to me unquestioning. I believed it so desperately that as I came to her door, my face slick with sweat, my glasses slipping down my nose, and my heart fluttering like a bird's with something other than the steep climb up the stairs, her absence hit me like a blow. The door was locked, all the lights out. I hammered on the door; no answer.

My disappointment was too much for me to bear; I sank down on the dark landing beside her door. I could not have moved if I had tried, and I knew that if I left the place, I would never have the courage to come there again. Some part of me must have known that it was all folly, that I had betrayed my friend and made myself ridiculous, but I refused to admit it then, and I waited, curled up against the door-jamb, eyes closed. As I waited, despite the discomfort of my position, I must have gone to sleep.

It was dark, as I said, and I waited for a long time between sleep and wakefulness. Once I was aware, in the haze of my drowsiness, of someone passing me by, stealthily; once I heard clear voices from another world come to me from the stairwell. I do not know how long I waited. The dark pressed upon me, I smelt dust and floor polish and turpentine, and maybe I dreamed. I hoped I dreamed.

In my dream I awoke to darkness; even the lamp at the bottom of the stairwell had been put out, and the night was cold. I shifted on the wooden floor, pulled my coat further around my shoulders and tried to think. Maybe I already regretted having come in search of Rosemary; maybe I was afraid of whatever it was which had brought me to her door; in either case, the white heat of my ardour had cooled, and at last I considered going home.

Shaking the stiffness from my cramped limbs, I stood up, feeling foolish. I had failed in everything: as a friend, as a scholar, as a lover. Since I had pulled Rosemary from the river, everything I had ever cared about had fallen apart; and what had I done? I had fallen apart too, slowly, like an old scarecrow, and crawled here to die in front of her door, in front of her ridicule. What on earth had I hoped to achieve? Spleen filled me. Suddenly my anger changed direction, and Rosemary was its target, Rosemary with her lovely face and her strange ways, Rosemary who had been gone all night, Rosemary who was going to marry another man, Rosemary who had brought me here, somehow, and, in a blaze of irrational anger, I turned towards the door and threw myself at it with all my strength. Well, I was not a strong man; I was short of sight and short of breath, so I can only surmise that the reason the door opened then was that it had been unlocked while I slept. Whatever the reason, it burst open and I catapulted into the room, coming to land against an armchair at the far side of the chamber. My glasses fell off as I stumbled, and it took me half a minute or so to find them again in the unfamiliar place, so that it was some time before I was in a fit state to look around.

The small room was dimly lit by a lamp draped with a green silk scarf, and there were a number of items of furniture neatly positioned around it: two chairs with embroidered cushions, a dressing-table, on which rested bottles and boxes and toiletries, a bed, pictures on the walls, a fur rug on the floor. There was a strange smell in the air, too sweet, like incense, which made my head spin. I remember this now, but, at the time, very little registered in my mind but the two men sitting by the door, one on a chair, the other slumped on the floor, both looking at me with an amused, but savage intensity.

My first reaction was horror; I had come to the wrong room. I backed away in desperate embarrassment.

'Excuse me—wrong room, sorry . . .' but before

152

I reached the door, which was still standing open behind me, another thought struck me, so forcibly that I stopped again and stared at the strange tableau upon which I had just entered.

Firstly, the young man on the floor was ill. Not just ill, but frighteningly so, his face livid even for that greenish light, his eyes and mouth gaping holes in his face. What was more, he looked hurt; a thin dark trickle of blood embroidered the side of his mouth, disappearing down the side of his throat and into the collar of his shirt. As I stared at him, I realized that he was just a boy, still in his teens, his ragged hair as fair as flax; and from the exhausted way in which he was lying on the ground, he looked to me to be close to unconsciousness. The other man was older, maybe between forty and fifty; black hair allowed to grow long, a dark, heavy coat, features which were at the same time sharp and disturbingly feminine. He too was pale, almost sick-looking, with the consumptive look of one who has exhausted himself with debauchery; and although I judged him to be considerably older than myself, he exhaled something much younger than I had ever been, some primal radiance which transfigured him. As I watched, he covered the boy over, protectively, with his arm, and watched me without a word.

Maybe it was this gesture which led me to believe that he had hit the boy; maybe I took it for defensiveness—you must remember that I was still as close to being drunk as I ever got, and in those days it took considerably less alcohol to do that than it does today—but I took a step forwards.

'What's going on?' I asked. 'Who are you?'

'Friends,' said the dark man softly.

'Whose friends?' I demanded, my voice a little too shrill.

'Well, Rosemary's, of course,' he replied. He paused for a moment. 'And you, of course, are Daniel Holmes.'

I was rather taken-aback at that.

'How do you know me?'

'We know all Rosemary's friends,' said the dark man with a slow smile. 'Don't we, Rafe?' And he smiled down at the flax-haired boy, reaching down to brush his face with one long white finger. The boy did not answer, but turned slightly towards me, and I caught a glimpse of long lashes shadowing a high cheekbone; he too looked oddly androgynous, and in that position he reminded me suddenly, sharply of Rosemary. I wondered for a moment if he could be her brother. I took another step towards them.

'What are you doing here?' I asked. 'And where's Rosemary?'

'Rosemary? She'll be here soon. We're here to see her.' He gave a short laugh, as if what he had said amused him.

It may be difficult for you, in your different time and with your different morals, to understand fully the sense of outrage I felt then, hearing his casual words. Sometimes I find it difficult myself to remember what it was like to be young and principled.

'Rosemary is going to be married in August,' I said coldly. 'I don't think that she should be entertaining *friends* in her rooms at this time of night. Does she know you're here?' The dark man shrugged as if it was not important. I glanced again

154

at the figure collapsed on the floor.

'Is that boy sick? Is he hurt?'

'No.'

His insolent tone nettled me.

'He looks sick,' I said, 'and he's bleeding. If you don't tell me what's going on now, I'll report you to the police. That boy should be at home in bed. And you, you shouldn't be here in Rosemary's room without her knowledge!'

His tone was flat, almost bored. 'Rafe's all right. He's been drinking, and he's not used to the stuff yet.' Idly, with a long, pale index finger, he wiped the trickle of blood from Rafe's cheek, then, without taking his green eyes from mine, licked the blood from his hand. The gesture was somehow more explicit than any pornography, and I felt myself flushing angrily.

'A boy that age shouldn't be drinking at all!' I cried, partly to hide my sense of unease, and I stepped closer to the boy he called Rafe.

'Look. Wake up. Where do you live? I can take you home, if you like. Are you all right?' I cast a smouldering glance in the direction of the dark man, only to see that he was smiling again.

Rafe said nothing, but gave a faint moan, and turned his head away petulantly, like a sick child.

'Where do you live?' I took hold of his shoulder; it felt very cold beneath his thin shirt. Another thought struck me.

'What were you taking?' I questioned urgently. 'What was it? What were you drinking?'

It seemed to me that the boy's breathing was shallow; that his face was too pale, his skin too cold.

'For God's sake, what was it?' I almost

155

screamed. 'Can't you see he's dying?'

But before the other man could say anything to answer or to refute my question, the half-open door swung open, and in she came, the Blessed Damozel, her glorious hair loose over her shoulders, slim as a switch in a long dress of black muslin which swirled around her ankles like smoke. She ignored me totally, and turned to the dark man.

'Java, who let him in? I told you admit no one, especially not Daniel. Why did you let him come?'

The man said something unidentifiable. Rosemary shook her damp curls impatiently.

'Can't you think of anything else?'

Then she turned towards me again.

'Poor Daniel,' she said, and, believe me, her smile was everything a man could dream of, loving and tender and sweet as an angel's.

'Poor, stupid Daniel.'

And before I could say another word, she had opened the bathroom door behind me and pushed me in. I was taken off-balance; my glasses slipped, I reached to steady myself, shouted uselessly as I saw her slam the door in my face, fumbled for the door-handle, found the door jammed from the outside, slipped again, dropped my glasses on the floor (I heard them rattle against the tiles), fumbled for the light switch, and with one thing and another adding to my own panic and confusion, it was a full two minutes before I found the light and realized exactly what it was that was in the room with me.

It was in the bath. It was naked, what was left of it, and the white enamel was smeared darkly with its drying blood, fingerprints and handprints and

156

long formless stains where it had been pulled to and fro in the bathtub, as if by the greedy hands of children. It was entirely dismembered; the limbs separated from the trunk like the hams of a slaughtered pig, repulsive in its whiteness, its bloodiness, its headless anonymity . . . for the corpse was headless, the severed neck black and white with blood and bone. And the ewer beside the sink was filled to the brim with a dark sticky liquid . . . And I realized the source of the blood I had seen around the mouth of the boy called Rafe, and I understood which grisly wine he had drunk. An awful panic bloomed in me. I tried to scream, tried to think, fell, spinning, turning, away from the light, into nothing.

PART THREE

Death and the Maiden

One

Maybe I dreamed it all: on the dark days when I no longer know man from beast I sometimes wonder whether I dreamed it all. I seek my answers at the bottom of my glass, but too many are the days when I look there for comfort and see nothing but the beast grinning at me from under the surface with death in his eyes. I cannot complain overmuch; they are good to me here, at least, as good as I can expect from these people who cannot see the demon in their midst.

Kind nurses in clean white uniforms come and go; some spare a moment of their time for the poor old drunkard in room 9, and last Tuesday one of them—no more than a child, on her way to a meeting with her young man, no doubt—brought me a gardenia from her hair and put it in a glass at the side of my bed. You can't imagine how precious that gardenia was to me, how soft and fresh and scented, like a breath of sanity in the dark circle of my world. For a whole evening I was filled with a new hope, a certainty that I was not alone, that if I managed to wait out the dawn, with the new light I might at last glimpse God. But when the night came, and the shadows crawled from out of the corners of my room to squat around my bed like hungry demons, I broke and reached for my bottle again to find sleep in its bitter quenching, and, as I slept, I dreamed again.

*   *   *

161

I awoke from a drugged, animal sleep with the reek of the circus in my nostrils, and I felt as if I had been buried alive.

For a moment, I could remember nothing, then as the memory of what I had seen returned, I gave a cry and scrabbled to my knees in the dark. I was blind; I could feel stones and earth beneath my hands, could feel beads of graveyard sweat on my face, could smell dirt and blood and cheap whisky. I had no idea where I was.

I waited for an instant for the world to stabilize, then I began to crawl. I was not in a side-street, that was for certain; my rapidly clearing vision could by now discern a dim pattern of light and shade on the uneven ground, and what I took to be the light of a street-lamp was shining through a crack in the darkness somewhere to my right. It looked as if I was in some kind of building. A shack, I thought as I crawled, or a derelict farmhouse; maybe an animal shelter. I had probably staggered there in my drunken stupor to shelter from the cold, and had collapsed there out of sight. I must have been very drunk; only that could explain the dreadful clarity of my nightmares, the horrors which had arisen from the pit of my subconscious to plague my rational mind. I touched the wall at my left, hoping to pull myself to my feet, but the stone was sweaty and loathsome to touch, and I shrank away as if from dead flesh. The light was nearer now, and by its glow I could see the outline of a doorway, a pile of stones or rubble on one side, a slick, moist wall at the entrance. Beyond the doorway I could just see a gate of some kind . . . spiked metal railings with an ornamental cast-iron design . . . and with a sick jolt which brought the remnant of the sour whisky I had ingested churning up the narrow channel of my throat in a bilious flood, I realized where this place was, realized, as I then thought, the source of my nightmares.

It was a crypt.

As soon as this realization came to me, I was able to see a dozen hitherto unnoticed details: the light of the church window outside, the rows of plaques in the damp wall where the coffins had been slotted like drawers, the remains of a wreath hanging on the railings like a trophy. Maybe I gave a little moan. It was not so much the fact of finding myself here which frightened me, than the fear of insanity. Why had I come to this place? Why had my subconscious formulated such fantasies about Rosemary and her friends? Was I still so shocked by my discovery of the body in the river that I must needs subject myself to still more of the same? I stumbled towards the entrance of the crypt, quite sober now, though my stomach roiled, fell over a stone, half-fell to one knee, put out my hands to steady myself, slipped . . .

My hands met something soft and wet, cold as mud, but as I looked down I saw that it was not mud. No mud could have that rainbow gleam, that horrible, yielding softness . . . And as I looked down, still, unable to scream or to look away or even to move, entombed for ever in the hellish timelessness of that moment, I understood that if this was reality, then I had not dreamed, had not been drunk, had not been at the mercy of my own subconsciousness, but of something deadlier by far. Maybe I had known already; maybe I had fled the truth.

163

But now, with the truth twelve inches from my face, I could hardly deny it. For it was the body I had seen in Rosemary's bathroom, dismembered, bloody, headless, and I was kneeling above it, embracing it with both hands, my arms buried up to the elbows in the meat of its shattered ribcage, like a washerwoman over her tub.

Two

Curiosity, and something more, had impelled her to go back into Ginny's room. It was nearly three in the morning; the girl had not yet returned, and Alice, in spite of her fatigue, could not bear the thought of sleep. What was wrong with her? she thought. She pushed open the bedroom door, flipped the light on, looked inside. The bed was still untouched, the room as neat and impersonal as if it had never been inhabited. Alice went straight to the wardrobe and opened it, throwing Ginny's clothes on to the bed with a kind of fury. Damn you, she thought wildly. There was a secret there, she knew it, and she also knew she had to find it, find it or choke on her terrified, suppressed rage. Discarded clothes flew around her as she searched; a couple of syringes, and some ampoules were scrutinized for a moment, then tossed aside. Nothing. Alice almost wept in frustration. She was *sure* there was something to be found, certain with the irrational, compulsive knowledge of dreams. As she began to replace the clothes where she had found them, folding jumpers and hanging up dresses, her eye caught the squarish outline of

164

Ginny's suitcase half-hidden under the bed. She pounced on it, pulling it out and snapping it open with a cry of triumph. Inside the case, roughly wrapped in old newspapers, was a box.

It was about the size of a church Bible, and it was of some kind of hard wood, bound with metal. There was a handle with which to carry it, and though the wood was scratched from being dragged out of the hole in which it had been placed, it was still easy to read the inscription on the lid:

KEEP ME SAFE

It took Alice a few moments to remember where she had seen that inscription, but when it came the realization was like a redoubling of her terror. The trap closed upon her.

The lock was secure; it was the wood which finally gave way, the metal coming away from the box like cardboard as she prised it open. For a moment, Alice paused.

What was a box, if not an opening into the unknown, a doorway into a world of secrets? Alice was quite sure that she had had enough secrets for the moment, enough of doors. What she really wanted was to be able to forget all the events of the past few days, to lie comfortably in bed and go to sleep, with all the secrets back where they belonged.

But it was too late; she had already taken the box into the workroom where she could not be disturbed. She had broken the lock; even if she did not look inside, Ginny would know Alice had spied on her. She had declared war; she knew it. She

165

could not go back.

She flipped back the lid, looked for the first time into the box, and fell headfirst into Looking-Glass Land.

Her first reaction was amazement; her first incoherent thought: *My God! It's a Rossetti!* Trembling, she reached into the box, drew out a manuscript—and pictures. Delight flooded her, as she spread the pictures out over the floor of her workroom, eyes flitting from one to the others as if she were unsure which one to study first.

They were beautiful, but they were not Rossettis.

There were maybe twenty of them, watercolours, pen-and-inks, chalk studies, all under twenty by fifteen inches square, edges ragged as if they had been carelessly trimmed with a paper-knife, the thick, creamy paper yellowed with age. They were old, old and lovely, all studies of women, no, of one woman. Head-and-shoulders portraits, full-length portraits in different poses, nudes, elegantly draped over a couch, lush in glowing blue velvet, delicately pencilled, leaning against a wall holding a musical instrument, studies of eyes, lips, hair . . . eyes closed, toying with a strand of hair, head thrown back, head angled forwards . . . It was some time before Alice was even able to look at them properly, even longer before her mind began to work normally again. Her next rational thought was: 'The old devil. He had no right to immure these in Grantchester chapel. They must be worth a fortune.' She picked up a picture at random; a delicate pastel in shades of brown and red. Her first reaction had not been so stupid; it did look like a Rossetti, although looking at it more closely, she could see that it lacked the overemphasized lips of a Rossetti. It showed the head and shoulders of a young woman, head bent at a strange and slightly menacing angle, as if looking back at someone. The hair was luxuriant, painstakingly textured in differing shades of red, and pushed to one side so as to expose a rounded and perfect expanse of bare shoulder. It was dated 1869, and monogrammed in precise, interwoven letters: W.H.C.

The monogram meant nothing to Alice, though the style and the date did; she flipped the drawing over, but apart from a rough sketch on the other side of the picture, could see no more clues there. She reached for another drawing, a pencil, touched with brown ink around the eyes and lips. Again, the monogram. Again, a date, this time 1868. The pictures were a puzzle to Alice. First, they looked genuine: they were clearly finished works of the first order, Pre-Raphaelite in origin, though not signed with the initials of any Victorian painter she knew of. There was some Rossetti there, some Burne-Jones, some Waterhouse, and yet the pictures were none of these; there was a strength in the lines of those compositions, a power in the features beside which Rossetti's pale and wilting damsels and Burne-Jones's angelic but weak-featured ladies of legend seemed slightly ridiculous. These pictures were something different. From sheet after sheet of the thick yellow paper, her eyes stared out at Alice, taunting, aloof, enticing, and faintly familiar, in the way that all really classic works of art can appear . . .

167

Familiar.

Alice was jolted out of her reverie by a thought which was as ludicrous as it was terrifying; of *course* that face was familiar! She had drawn it herself, that same face, the wide eyes, the lips which were a curving mockery of their own sensuality . . . She reached for her file of artwork, fumbled for the string which closed it . . . tugged. Papers spilled out, faces which were all the same face, hallucinatingly similar, images laid upon images like reflections along a hall of mirrors, a hall which reflected not only images, but time. She looked at the pictures for a long while, her gaze moving from her own portraits to the ones marked W.H.C., and back, searching vainly for logic. And though there was no logic to be found there, the facts still stared out at her from the pages which a dead man had thought important enough to hide for ever in a church wall, and her growing certainty was a little like hysteria, a little like insanity.

For the pictures of Ginny and those of an unknown Victorian model, no doubt long since buried, looked very like twins.

One

How long I knelt there in the dust, myself and the corpse in an embrace as intimate and unholy as ever was shared between monster and prey, I cannot tell you. The last of the whisky had faded like mist into the cold pre-dawn, leaving an emptiness in me where for a timeless time my sanity flickered, assailed by monstrous shadows.

Maybe I wept. I could not move; I was at the end of all movement, all hope. I had seen what no man should ever see, and, mockingly, scornfully, they had let me live, knowing that I could be no danger to them; knowing that they had made a monster and a fugitive out of me, they had let me live. Maybe it pleased them to. It would have been very easy for me, at that moment, to crawl back into the crypt, like a snail into its shell, into the comforting dark, and hide; my despair was more than I could stomach, and the darkness beckoned, womblike, promising oblivion. I was so close to accepting what it offered . . . I stood, my arms gloved in blood almost to the shoulders, stumbled, began to turn away from the light . . .

Then I remembered Robert.

The thought was like a shower of cold water. I gasped, clapped my hands to my mouth, felt cold blood smear across my lips. In all my fear and self-pity, I had forgotten Robert, my friend. Robert who was going to marry Rosemary.

Rosemary. The name alone brought me out in a cold sweat. Everything was centred around Rosemary, my Blessed Damozel. Even then, I did not begin fully to understand what she was; there were no words, no thoughts in my world for that. Already, as I began to slide out of my catatonia, I had begun to rationalize, to think in terms of *crime*, of police (I hastily put out of mind that thin trickle of blood at the side of the fair-haired boy's mouth), for I liked to think of myself as a rational man; I could *believe* in murder. The rest I chose to ignore. So I closed my eyes to the truth again and began to sift the evidence for what was acceptable to me. She was a murderess. Her friends had probably committed the actual deed, but the fact that the body had been in her apartment proved that she was as guilty as they were. Maybe they were all three of them insane . . . only an insane man could bring himself to drink blood . . . if the boy *had* been drinking blood. I chose to believe my frenzied imagination had created that. They had been panic-stricken when I had walked in on them; they had been afraid to kill me, and instead had dumped me in the churchyard, with the body, hoping, perhaps, that I would be discovered unconscious and reeking of alcohol, the next morning, and accused of the crime. It made sense.

By this time, my panic had grown cold; my mind had begun to function again, and coolly I surveyed my situation. It would not do to be caught. No one, on seeing me, could fail to suspect me of the murder; I was up to my armpits in blood; there was blood on my face, my knees where I had knelt on the bloody floor, my clothes were torn and filthy, and I suspected there was a wild light in my eyes, born of having seen too much.

I stepped over the body and made my way to the gate of the crypt; I had wasted too much valuable time, and I could see the beginnings of a pale grey dawn on the horizon. The rest of the sky was dark; I judged it to be about four o'clock in the morning, but even that was too late for me to pass unseen in the streets of Cambridge. It would take only one person . . . a milkman, perhaps, on his way to work, to see me. I ran my hands through my hair, pushed my glasses up the bridge of my nose, tried to clean the smeared lenses with a hand I had wiped on my trouser leg, and carefully, with newfound stealth, I made my way out of the churchyard and down

170

towards the Grantchester road. I followed a line parallel to the road, keeping low in the fields, dodging behind trees, occasionally crawling on my stomach through thin vegetation to avoid being seen. Only once did I see someone, and even then they were so far away that I could not make out whether they were men or women, walking slowly in a group of three or four down the road, but although I knew I had not been spotted, terror nailed me to the ground, my tongue cleaving to the roof of my mouth, and I cowered in the ditch for a full ten minutes before I gained enough courage to go on.

It took me almost an hour to reach my house, and by that time a red dawn was blazing, the mullioned windows reflecting blood as the sun came up. Spurred by panic, I ran for the door, grasped for the keys in my pocket, fumbled the key into the lock. One endless moment of terror as the key jammed, then the door was open, and I hauled myself in, as a drowning man hauls himself aboard a lifeboat. Two, four, six, eight stairs, and I was in my room, gasping for breath, the air thick as blood in my lungs, panic still tearing, mindlessly, at my throat.

For a nightmare instant I caught sight of my reflection in the mirror and I almost screamed. Then, coming closer, I recognized myself behind the deathmask of blood, my hair on end, blood smearing the lenses of my glasses, a long scratch across my forehead, broken bruises on my neck. Only my eyes were sane, very bright behind my thick lenses. Looking into my own eyes in the dark, lead-marked mirror, I knew I was no monster.

Methodically, I stripped off all my clothes and

put them in the fireplace. With paper and wood, I lit the fire, and as I burned every scrap of evidence that I had ever been in that crypt, I washed very carefully, using Mrs Brown's antiquated bathtub, a pitcher and cold water, washing my glasses too, so that not a smear or speck of blood remained. Then I washed the tub and the pitcher, stirred the ashes of the fire with the poker, dressed in fresh clothes, and with a damp cloth painstakingly wiped the door-knob, the banisters, the inside and outside door-handles and the keys, before deciding that I had done all I could, and that none of Rosemary's grim work could be traced back to me.

A glance at the hall clock told me that it was now a quarter to six in the morning; I could hear sounds from the kitchen, where Mrs Brown was making breakfast for herself (she always was an early riser, although I never tended to get up much before nine), and I crept upstairs again before she could come out and speak to me. After everything I had been through, I felt drained and exhausted, and all I wanted to do was lie down, sleep, and try to forget. I locked my door, undressed, fastened my curtains so that no light could enter and trouble my sleep, then, with a long sigh of total exhaustion, I crawled between the cool lavender-scented sheets into oblivion.

A tapping on my door awoke me, and I sat up in bed, my eyes crusted and sore, my head aching. The tapping continued.

'Are you all right?' It was Mrs Brown. 'Don't you want any breakfast?'

'What time is it?' I asked, both hands on my head as if to still its ache. My eyes felt gravelly and hot.

'Near ten. Would you like a cup of tea?'

I shook my head.

'No. I . . . I don't feel very well. I need some sleep. Let me sleep, Mrs Brown. Don't wake me up.'

Clucking noises from behind the door. 'Come back too late last night, did we? Well, if you do want a bite to eat later, just give me a call, won't you?'

'Thanks.'

I heard her footsteps recede, and I crawled under the covers again, thankful of the darkness. The sheets were no longer cool and fresh, but clung saltily to my sweating body. I rolled over, trying to find a cool spot, instinctively shielding my face from the glow of the window. I wished the curtains were darker, for their deep crimson allowed the sunlight to cast a coloured nimbus of light around the window which hurt my tired and sensitive eyes. My throat, too, felt swollen and sore, my face puffy. I pulled the covers over my face as far as they would go, and in the cryptlike, uneasy darkness, I slept again. And this time, as I slept, I dreamed.

I was in the crypt again; damp, clinging darkness all around me, the smell of grave-earth in my nostrils and grave-sweat at my fingertips, and I was hungry. My hunger was a coiling sickness at the pit of my cavernous stomach, a spinning delirium in the echoing chambers of my brain, worse than panic, more demanding than the sexual urge, more overwhelming than drug withdrawal. My eardrums boomed with it, my tongue was dry with it; I was weak. I turned towards the light at the end of the chamber and winced away, though the thin

173

filaments of daylight which showed they were weak indeed. Hunger drove me on. I left the cool, comforting darkness, put one hand on the gate, stopped. Beside one of the graves knelt a figure, a young girl, her back turned to me, a shawl wrapped round her thin shoulders. Tendrils of light hair had escaped the confines of the headscarf to flutter around her face.

The hunger hit me like a sledgehammer; I staggered. My lips were dry; despite myself, I licked them. The palms of my hands were slick; I rubbed them on my trousers and came a little closer. The girl was praying; she did not turn as I came to stand behind her, did not move as I reached out my hand, almost close enough to touch her face. Her warmth was palpable; the thin ribbon of the exposed nape of her neck between the shawl and the headscarf was pale, almost translucent. I could see the delicate tracery of her veins beneath the skin, living deltas in an alien landscape. I reached for her; spun her round, imagined her head thrown back, eyes wide, mouth open ready to scream . . . and saw none of those things.

She was smiling, arms open to receive me, lavender eyes huge in a pale, delicate face, beautiful eyes in which I read a hunger akin to my own. It was Rosemary.

I hesitated, knowing in my dream no fear, only hunger. I had caught her by the wrist; I allowed my gaze to travel down her bare arm, down the sensual river of her veins.

'Daniel.' Her voice was breathy, erotic. My own caught in mid-breath as I looked at her. Never, never, had I seen anyone as beautiful. She smiled

174

again, lifted a small hand to press it against my cheek.

'What's happening to me?' I spoke almost to myself, but my eyes were lost deep in hers.

'Love me,' she whispered. Her hand was warm on my mouth. I caught a sudden, exhilarating scent from her skin; lavender, sweetness, and warm, quick blood.

'My God!' I cried out incoherently, her wrist against my mouth. My arms were around her, her hair in my face, her thin bones so light against my embrace, the pounding of her blood against my lips . . .

'Love me.' With a sudden wrench, I twisted her hand towards my mouth; her skin was smooth, salty beneath my tongue. I bit deeply into the flesh; it was yielding, like the skin of a fruit, then the blood came, clean and salt. I gagged on it in my eagerness, fumbled against the wound, licked abjectly. Blood trickled down the side of my mouth, awakening a memory . . . though of what, I could not quite remember. The sides of the incision had a faintly metallic taste, were slightly uneven, and I pushed my tongue between them to feel the pulse of the rushing blood, my breath ragged and laboured in an excess of delight and greed. I remember the taste of her. The pattern of every line and vein on that wrist. Could I have dreamed it? Am I insane? The blood was power, was life . . . I lapped it deliriously, fearfully, aware that at any moment she might choose to withdraw her favours and leave me to hunger and hopelessness again.

And as I fed, I looked up into her pure, fathomless eyes.

And the stars in her hair were seven.

                    *   *   *

Restlessly I dreamed and whimpered for hours between my damp and fevered sheets, and she walked my dreams in glory. It seems strange, now that I live my life in the midst of such dreams, to remember how new and how terrifying it was to me then, to enter the crypt of my subconscious. I was racked with lust and horror; my limbs were water, my head pulsed with migraine. I don't remember Mrs Brown knocking on my door again, though I expect she must have heard me cry out in my sleep, and twice I was just able to drag myself to the sink in time to retch a darkish slime into the porcelain basin . . . at that time, I took it for bile. The scratches on my face hurt wretchedly; touching them with the numbed tips of my fingers, I realized that they had become great raised welts, reaching from my forehead, across one cheek and right down my neck though I had been protected to some extent by my shirt. There were marks like needle-tracks on the inner part of my wrists, half explaining my disorientation and my nightmares. They must have drugged me. My throat was swollen, and I wondered whether one of Rosemary's cronies had tried to strangle me, but I was too weak and too feverish to examine the damage any further.

It was near dark when I awoke completely; I looked at my watch, and was astounded to see that it was half past seven. Never in my life, even after all-night parties, had I slept away a whole day, and I flung back the sheets and stood up, feeling more

176

refreshed, but still rather sick and light-headed. I put on my dressing-gown and went to the bathroom, where I switched on the light, washed my face, took two aspirin, and looked at myself in the mirror.

I could not have said that I looked well; I was pale, and my eyes were bloodshot and bright with fever. I am not the kind of man who looks at all attractive when he is unshaven; I simply looked dirty, and the scratch down my face was an ugly weal, beaded with pus. The bruises on my throat were visible now as fingerprints: four roundish points, each with a crescent of broken skin where the nail had penetrated the flesh, and on the other side of the throat, below the jugular vein, a broader, less defined bruise where the thumb had been. A little way above that was an incision I had not previously noticed, a crescent-shaped wound, some three inches long, slightly raised. I frowned at myself in the mirror. That was not the mark of fingernails, nor had it been accidental. It had been deliberately placed. But why? And how? By the size and shape of the mark, the slight irregularity of the incision, it almost looked like the mark of—I shook my aching head irritably. I had had too many nightmares. What possible reason would anyone have? And yet, they did look very like the marks of teeth. Angry with myself and my fancies, I deliberately turned away. Those scratches would have to be disinfected, otherwise I would have more than bad dreams to worry about. I found a bottle of iodine, and, standing in front of the mirror, dabbed at my face and neck until all the cuts and scratches were covered. That was better. Now for something to eat, for I still felt weak and dizzy, and I realized that I had eaten nothing since the previous morning. I went to my room to change, and stopped as I noticed a screw of paper tacked to my door. I had been in such a hurry that I had not seen it before, and I took it (correctly, as it happened) to be a note from Mrs Brown.

Dear Mr Daniel,
I have had to Pop out for a While to Visit my Sister, I will be Back this Evening. I am Sorry you are not Yourself today. Should you be Wanting a Bite to eat I have left a Pot of Tea on the Hob and a Nice Piece of Cod in the Oven for your Supper. And help Yourself to Anything in the Larder.
Yours Sincerely,
V. Brown

I smiled. That meant I had the house to myself for the evening, and I was glad of it; I would have no awkward questions to answer, for Mrs Brown was as protective as she was good-hearted, and I sometimes found her affection rather overpowering. I did not bother to dress, knowing that I was alone in the house, and I made my way down to the kitchen. There was food left for me in the oven, as promised, and tea on the hob, and I settled myself down at the kitchen table to eat. I had hardly eaten more than a mouthful, however, before the sickness came upon me again; my head swam, my stomach roiled, and I pushed the plate away unfinished. I drank two glasses of water in rapid succession, fighting off nausea, and remained for a few moments in front of the fire, shivering with fever. The events of the previous night had taken more from me than I had suspected. I reached my hands towards the fire, and began for the first time since the beginning of my nightmare to review the situation logically. I prided myself on being a logical man, a man of learning, and my natural pragmatism had begun, with the help of a bath and a long sleep, to return to me. This I must emphasize; I was not neurotic, nor am I yet; all conclusions I have since reached are based on my own experiences and research. Even then, dragging myself from a vortex of horrors, I began to view the situation objectively.

My first thought was a profound gratitude at being alive at all. I had obviously witnessed something which incriminated Rosemary and her band of murderers to the hilt; they had tried to be rid of me, and in some way had bungled it. Perhaps they had intended me to be accused of the crime; perhaps after having tried to throttle and drug me, they had abandoned me for dead. It was clearly a police matter, as much for my own sake as for Robert's (I refused to believe that he had in any way been involved in the affair), and I racked my brains for the best way to handle the situation.

By now, the murderers would have disposed of the evidence; the body, I knew, was hidden in the churchyard, and would no doubt be found sooner or later. Rosemary, in her apartment, would be unassailable. Rafe and Java . . . they were my only chance of being believed, and I had no idea of who they were or where to find them. I myself—well, there was no doubt that even as a police informant I might be suspect; I had already been strategically placed to discover one corpse, and the

179

circumstances in which I had found myself this time might easily be seen to be suspicious. I shrank from placing myself in a situation where it would be Rosemary's word against my own . . . where would it end?

My head had begun to ache again with the effort of concentrating. I knew that this was by no means the first violent death to hit Cambridge in the past few months. Could Rosemary somehow be implicated in the death of the woman in the weir? Or was my evidence circumstantial, and Rosemary innocent?

I wanted to believe it. Remembering her face, the sweetness of her features, the innocence which shone through her eyes, I wanted it, for I loved her, have maybe never ceased to love her, and I wanted to believe it with all my heart. My brain began to formulate wild and attractive hypotheses. She was innocent: a pawn of Java and Rafe, somehow in their power. They had hypnotized her. They had drugged her, too. They were somehow blackmailing her. From my earlier suspicion and horror of her, my delusions led me to believe that she was the persecuted one, that she needed my help, that my fearsome nightmares were only the product of jealousy and the trauma of what I had seen the previous night. I told you, Rosemary made children of all of us.

Contact the police? I dared not, as much for fear of incriminating Rosemary as myself; could I expect them to fail to suspect her? The newspapers had by now revealed that Scotland Yard had been called in to investigate the 'Body in the Weir' case; I expected to be contacted for questioning again at any time. The last thing I wanted was to draw the attention of the investigators towards myself, or towards Rosemary. I saw that I would have to act on my own, and as quickly as possible. I went back to my room, dressed in a plain, dark suit, a light overcoat and my hat, returned to the kitchen, and lingered over the drawer of knives. Finally I chose a small carving-knife, sharp, but small enough to hide in my sleeve, and set off out, feeling slightly ridiculous, but excited too. I suppose that for a man of action, to set out into the night with murder on his mind and a lady for the rescuing would have been no great thing; but I was no man of action.

My watch told me it was close on eight o'clock; the day had been hot, and had given way to a sultry, cloudy evening. I was still shivering, however, and glad of my overcoat, though most of the people I encountered were more lightly dressed than I was. My step was purposeful, my left arm stiff from the pressure of the knife; I knew where I was going. Where? To her apartment, of course, but in stealth, this time, forewarned and careful. I had walked about half the way to the town centre when the first cramps hit me; one moment they were sudden but bearable, like a stitch in my side, the next they had me doubled up beside the road, almost on my knees, cold sweat running down my face, my jaw locked in agony. The road was not a busy one; no one came to help me. I sank to my knees by the roadside, hardly even able to breathe, to wait it out. A breath, drawn out an eternity-long, acid in my belly, my lungs . . . another breath. The pain ebbed, ceased. Carefully, I stood up, afraid to move too quickly

181

lest the pain came on again. I straightened, took several deep breaths.

Satisfied that the cramps, whatever had caused them, were indeed over, I began to walk again, with more care, down the deserted road. I had hardly gone more than a hundred yards, however, when the cramps hit me once more, flooring me immediately this time, paralysing. The world spun around me like a carnival ride, I retched agonizingly, spat blackness on to the road. Maybe I cried out; maybe I imagined it. My glasses slipped on to the grass, I fumbled for them, touched only grass, tried to stand, slipped, fell to my side. I think I suspected I was having a heart attack, and with both hands clasped to my chest I managed to crawl on to the road, where a street-lamp threw uncertain fragments of light in an ellipse around me. Then, I fainted.

When I regained consciousness (not, I believe, more than a few minutes after), the pain was gone, and the street was still deserted. I stood up carefully, felt no hint of a cramp, straightened up to my full height. I brushed my clothes, feeling rather foolish now that my malaise was over. I was inclined to disbelieve the whole thing and put it down to my lack of food, or perhaps the after-effects of whatever poison they had injected into me, for now I felt quite recovered, indeed, I had the beginnings of a healthy appetite. I found my glasses, wiped them and put them on, immediately feeling better. I brushed my hat, replaced it on my head and set off on my way again, feeling distinctly hungry now, and wondering whether I should not stop somewhere on the way to Rosemary's apartment for a bite to eat. It would not do for me to pass out while I was there. A group of students, strangers to me, passed me as I joined the main road into Cambridge; I caught the sound of laughter as they went by, a merry call of: 'Good evening!'

Maybe they had surprised me; I started as I heard the voice and my steps wavered again. I was suddenly, acutely conscious of the cold, of the sickness in the pit of my stomach. I felt dizzy once more, raised my hand to touch the brim of my hat in greeting, and paused in mid-gesture, my smile faltering on my lips. The hunger was suddenly very acute. They passed me, still chattering; only one young fellow looked at me askance as he went by, wondering, perhaps, if I were drunk. He was the closest to me of the group; the lamplight reflecting from his broad, ruddy face as he loomed out at me from the darkness. For an instant, my sense of perspective was distorted; his young face seemed to rush towards mine like something grotesque seen through a fishbowl, and I backed away; his vapid blue eyes, his broad laughing mouth, the beads of sweat in the enlarged pores of his shaven cheeks horribly magnified in my mind's eye. The sudden heat of him was overwhelming; I could *smell* him, ripe as a parcel of meat in the night, the scent of his hair-cream only an accompaniment to the primal throb of his young blood. Before I knew it, I had reached out a hand to touch him . . . but the party was gone, laughing into the night, and I was left to stand beneath the lamp-post, shaking and appalled at my thoughts. Surely, I had not been thinking . . . ? I cursed under my breath and went on my way. My experiences of the past twenty-four hours were giving me delusions. I walked on, and the hunger stalked me, whetted, as I resumed the hunt.

Two

Alice painted swiftly, precisely, thinking over the facts as she had read them in Daniel Holmes's journal.

The facts. They loomed overhead like apocalyptic birds, spiralling out of the dim past with their message of destruction. It was tempting to go beyond the facts, to imagine all kinds of rare and disturbing things, but Alice frowned at her canvas, her deft fingers handling airbrush and paintbrush and masking gum and thinner as her mind went over and over what she had read in compelling, primal rhythms of thought.

She painted absently, unconsciously, her hands moving deftly and quickly, her mind elsewhere. She supposed that she had planned what she was going to do; had made preliminary sketches, had mixed paints and wiped brushes, but hours later as she looked at the canvas, she saw it with the eyes of a stranger. It was not that she had not looked at it before, but as she had been working on it, she had only ever seen details: a hand here, a patch of vegetation, a square of sky; she had seen only effects of pigment and form. Now she saw a work of art, utterly individual, compelling her to *look* at it. She took a step backwards, looked calmly at the canvas for a long time, and listened to the deceptive beating of her heart as everything swung slowly into place with the inevitability of a pendulum.

A riverside scene again, perhaps even the same place: Alice recognized the little twist in the river-bank, the overhanging vegetation, the pale reflections of the trees in the dark water. Again, everything was rendered in painstaking detail, somehow clearer than reality, cleaner in shape and with its own lambency. Two figures stood in the foreground, one facing Alice on the far side of the river-bank, though with his face turned down towards the water, the other seen in profile, standing up to his knees in the river, trousers rolled up to reveal thin, pallid legs, comically foreshortened by the refraction of the light from the river's surface.

Both were young men, dressed rather formally in suits with broad lapels; the one with the glasses, facing Alice, was wearing a hat. Alice could not quite read their expressions, but there was something in the way both of them were standing, something *strained*, as if by curiosity, but at the same time holding back from the object which floated between them in the river. Alice squinted to see it, then as she realized what she had painted, she gave an involuntary grimace. God! What on earth had possessed her?

The canvas was small; the figure should have been mercifully indistinct, but was not. On the contrary, as she approached it, it seemed to move sharply into focus, so that she saw it in far more detail than she would have liked. It was partly submerged; she could distinguish its pallid bulk just below the surface, resting bonelessly on the greenish water; could imagine the lazy movement of the ripples around it. But she could see its face,

185

turned towards her, saw it and recognized it, despite the discoloration and the bloating, recognized the mass of red hair which pooled around it; and as she peered closer, Alice thought (no, she knew) she saw the expression on that ruined face. The eyes piggy with swelling, the mouth open to reveal a black hole framed with yellow and carnivorous teeth . . . the expression was triumph, morbidly out of place on the face of that corpse, no, not even triumph; it was *rapture*.

Alice was mesmerized; it seemed that the closer she looked, the more detail she saw; she imagined every twig, every blade of grass to contain infinities of divergences, though whether this delusion came from the picture or her own subconscious, she never knew. Maybe the picture was her way of dealing with ideas her rational mind was at first incapable of accepting; while her conscious mind struggled to make sense of what she had read in Daniel's papers, her subconscious was sifting the information and drawing (literally, it seemed) its own conclusions.

Alice had somehow believed it all along.

In some ways, it was a relief to accept this; believe in the irrational, she thought inconsequentially, and anything becomes possible; even in Looking-Glass Land there were rules, if you only knew where to look. She studied the picture further, paying especial attention to the two figures standing by the water; it seemed to her that at least one of them, the one with the hat, should be familiar. There was something about the way he was standing, the slight stoop of his shoulders, the light reflecting from the lenses of his glasses . . .

Joe.

Joe and Daniel?

Daniel and Joe.

And as the last important piece of the puzzle slammed into place like a door on to the world of reason, Alice picked up her paintbrush one last time, and added the name of the picture to the bottom of the canvas, without thinking, knowing that the act was as inevitable as all the other acts which had led up to this one moment.

Poor Daniel, she thought, and wrote, in neat precise capitals:

RETRIBUTION: THE CHOSEN OF OPHELIA

One

I walked in nightmare along that road, the hunger at my heels all the time. The brain of which I was so unjustly proud was filled with unaccustomed turmoil; the scent of blood was in my nostrils, and though I fought my growing certainties, I weakened in the face of that hunger, weakened as any normal man would.

I have always thought of myself as a Christian; I did not lie or steal, and if I had lustful thoughts I hid them well; my sins were the little sins of a man very like other men; my thoughts never touched either despair or the sublime. Suddenly, in the space of a night and a day, everything was different. I would never be like other men again, and the knowledge was like damnation inside me. How can I convey to you the depths of my horror then, the first time I looked at myself and saw the beast under the skin? Later, when I had looked upon such things too often to be broken, I was able to view what happened dispassionately, almost scientifically, but there were many mirrors and icons to be broken before then, many forbidden pages to be turned. So I walked, and I hungered, and I kept my face in shadow so that the passers-by could not recognize the murder in my eyes.

Murder.

The word meant nothing to me as I walked blindly through the streets, my hands in my pockets to hide their trembling. It was a pit, spiralling downwards into never-never-never, huge as destiny. Just a word, superimposed like a photographic negative over everything I saw, bigger than God. Believe me, I fought it as long as I could, but it was insidious, twisting and turning in my mind, hallucinating, casting kaleidoscope images into the painful grid of my reason. For seconds at a time I was apart from reality, spinning, hunger riding my brain like a child on a fairground helter-skelter; several times I ducked into side-streets or shady archways and retched, pain digging sharp fingers under my ribs. And all that I endured, ultimately, for nothing. Strange, that I should still feel pride at not giving in immediately. Grant me that much humanity, that I did not give in at once.

I never made it to Rosemary's apartment—I did not expect to—though I did get as far as the river. The streets were not as crowded as I had feared, and though groups of students congregated outside the public houses, I was not obliged to touch them or go too near. I was glad of that; the very smell of them made my head spin. A couple of policemen passed me; I was conscious of a wary glance flicked in my direction. Paranoid, I quickened my step, imagining that they had seen something of my altered condition. My hands were shaking. As I came to Magdalene Bridge (the irony was not lost to me), I suffered a particularly violent spasm which left me breathless and trembling, and I managed to climb down on to the banking, and from there, under the bridge itself, where it was dark and cool, and, I thought, I would be able to rest without being seen and questioned.

I settled myself on a narrow ledge in the shadow of the bridge. The air was cold and sweaty, the underside of the bridge green with mould, but at least I felt safer there. Someone passed above my head; I felt the heat of their footsteps, imagined I saw it, like a torch shining through thick cloth, a faint glimmer on the water, closed my eyes. Only a few moments, I deluded myself, just a few minutes' rest, and I would be myself again. All I needed was the coolness of the water, the moist silence of stone to still what was raging inside me. I waited.

'Daniel.'

My eyes snapped open, my hands raised automatically to steady my glasses. For a moment I thought the voice came from the water, and I felt a stab of superstitious dread; it was her, the dead lady, her ribcage torn open like a sack of laundry and her eyes staring accusingly at me. Maybe there was worse; maybe the wreckage of her face would show a wide, desperate smile, and her arms would be open to receive me . . .

'Danny.'

I turned so suddenly that I nearly fell off the

ledge.

'I'm so glad I found you, Danny.'

It was Rafe.

For a moment, the essential meaning of his presence eluded me and I simply stared at him. He was crouching on the ledge, barely two or three feet away from me, and a ray of light, freakishly reflected from the water, fell on to his face. I had thought him beautiful before when I had seen him in Rosemary's apartment; beautiful in a disturbing way; now he was spectral, ethereally fair, his pale eyes at the same time innocent and corrupt. I was beyond fear; my terror of what I had already begun to discover within myself was enough to eclipse any fear a normal man might have had at being alone with a vicious murderer.

'My God,' I whispered, 'what have you done to me? What did you give me?'

Rafe smiled.

'Don't worry, Danny. Everybody's like that at first. You'll get over it soon enough.'

'Over what?' I began to raise my voice. 'What have I become?' I reached over and grabbed him by the front of his coat; shook him. Rafe just smiled.

'Soon you'll be one of us,' he said. 'That's what you wanted, isn't it? To be one of us?'

I shook my head.

'Yes, you did,' chided Rafe. 'Isn't that what everybody wants? To belong to someone? You belong to us now; you don't like it now, because you are not used to the idea yet, but you will. You'll live for ever, Danny. You'll be more than a man; and Danny, the things you'll *know*! Everybody wants that, believe me.'

'What did you give me?'

'You know.'

The fact that I did know, and more than I wanted, made me see red. I pulled the boy towards me and hit him hard across the mouth.

'You bastard! I don't know *any*thing! All I know is that you're murderers, all of you . . . God help me, and you're poisoning me. You're poisoning me and I feel. I want.' My voice soared above its normal register, shrill with panic; hearing myself so badly out of control frightened me even more, and I loosened my grip on the boy, pushed him away. 'I don't know anything.'

There was a thin trickle of blood running out of the left side of Rafe's mouth; still smiling, he wiped the blood with the ball of his thumb, then, very delicately, licked it away.

'You know.'

I slumped against the side of the bridge. His pale eyes pinned me to the stone, his smile was more than I could bear. I began to weep quietly into my hands, the tears falling through my fingers like lost worlds. I wanted to die.

Rafe watched me for a long time, then he stood up. His head was ringed with light from the reflections on the water; he looked like an angel. I was panic-stricken at the thought that he was about to go away, and I clutched, convulsively, at the skirt of his coat.

'Don't leave me.'

'Then come with me. If you dare.'

'Stay with me. Help me.'

Rafe nodded.

'That's why I'm here. That's why they sent me.'

'Who sent you?'

191

'The others. Rosemary. You belong to all of us now, Danny. You have nothing to be afraid of now, I promise you. From now on, you will be feared, as we are feared. You're one of us.'

'But what are you?' I asked, still clutching at him like a lost child.

Rafe flung up his head and laughed—and suddenly my heart was filled with admiration and love for him, for the savage freedom of that gesture. For an instant, I wanted nothing more than to be like that, free and beautiful and cruel and young—unchained from the shackles of the sordid world. I wanted to be a law unto myself; yes, I wanted to belong to him and to his kind for ever, to run with them, feed with them, to be for ever blessed.

God forgive me, I wanted that.

He smiled at me, and I basked in reflected glory.

'We're the masters, Danny,' he said softly. 'The chosen ones. The lords of creation. The predators.'

I shuddered with a cold joy. I was a child again, eagerly waiting on the brink of the longest and most exhilarating fairground ride of my life; I could smell popcorn and candy-floss and the dull, hot under-smell of the animal-house.

'Oh, yes,' I murmured, hardly even aware that I had spoken.

'Oh, yes.'

One

Black night had fallen, and I ran with the night. In the shadows we ran, Rafe and I, and as we went through the town, following secret channels through which he led me, the others joined us silently, Java and Rosemary and others whose names I knew without having to ask them: Elaine with her long matted hair and huge eyes; Anton, seven years old, his hand tucked trustingly into hers in a parody of real childhood; Zach with red hair like Rosemary's and a bird tattoo on his face. *My* people, I thought with a whirling pride, *my* people, and, God help me, I loved them that night, loved the feel and the scent of them and the throb of the hunger which was our friend and only ally. Most of all I loved Rosemary, loved the ripple of her hair on her shoulders, the turn of her head, the whiteness of her bare legs beneath the black raincoat. I walked in dreams, and, forgive me, I felt ecstasy, I felt *joy*, and that's what I miss most, now she is gone, and the joy buried in the earth of Grantchester churchyard, never to blossom again.

Try to understand: I was born a lonely child among adults with their own problems to live with; I grew into a lonely man. I immersed myself in study in the hope of bringing order to my life. I surrounded myself with art to satisfy my need for sensuality.

What child has never craved the company of others, the wild thrill of the pack, that feeling of running for ever? I saw myself as we ran: the lonely boy constantly left out and teased, the clever boy seeking in books the friendships he failed to find elsewhere. I am sorry, but believe me when I say that despite everything, I felt joy. I think I would have felt it even without the substance Rafe had injected into my arm before we set off; no drugs could entirely explain the euphoria, the fulfilment I experienced. The train inside the bubble of my spinning-top had broken free at last, and I rode it in one glorious night, bearing down upon my destiny with cries of triumph.

I no longer questioned anything; the glamour of the night was enough for me, and I followed the pack down alleys, under dark archways, across bridges and back across the river until we came to the poorer part of town. Once or twice a passer-by caught sight of us; we answered his stares with cat-calls and whoops. Java was carrying a knife. Light from the street-lamps slickered off its blade like mercury, but I was not afraid; the hunger was like the most powerful of drugs in my system, a strong, compelling music in the soundbox of my skull. Tribal rhythms drove me on. How long we travelled I do not know; I suspect it was not long, but it might have been for ever. Like Peter Pan, I felt as if I were walking on magic dust, effortlessly; and I know the others felt the same. Elaine was singing softly, her voice a thin lost warble in the shadows. Only Rosemary was untouched; utterly serene, she led the way towards the place she had chosen, and the hunger pushed us from behind like a strong wind.

It was a place I knew slightly: a run-down public house with a reputation for cheap drink and illicit hours. Even then, I thought that it must surely be closing, for it seemed deserted, and the light from the windows was yellow and drab. But the others looked so sure of themselves that I followed, afraid to hesitate, fumbling in my pockets for money. Even then, you see, I had not really understood. Maybe I still suspected that I might be dreaming; whatever the reason, I fumbled for money in my pockets, as if I were planning nothing more serious than an evening out drinking with my friends. It might have been ridiculous if it had not been so horrible.

Rosemary led the way in; the door was open, and I found myself standing in a grimy tap-room, where two people, a man and a woman, were clearing glasses and bottles from the bar. There was sawdust on the floor of the room, a pall of greasy smoke in the air; mingled under-smells of mould, wine and vomit.

The man was wiping the bar with a damp cloth; he did not even look up when we came in.

'We're shut,' he said brusquely. 'Eve! Lock that door before anyone else turns up.' The woman he had addressed as Eve stood up from mopping the floor, a cigarette hanging from her mouth. I had a moment to notice that she was young, and might even have been pretty in different circumstances; as it was, she looked sullen and drab, a dirty cloth tying back hair of a cheap, metallic blonde.

'You heard,' she said, without removing the cigarette. 'We're shut. Sorry.'

There was a short silence; I saw Java glance at Rafe, saw Anton take a step forwards, pulling away from Elaine.

The young woman stared at him.

'An' what's more, that kid ought to be home in

195

bed,' she said. 'Don't you know what time it is?'

I shifted uneasily, remembering, perhaps, my own words, rather too similar for comfort, when I had spoken to Rafe and Java a short twenty-four hours previously.

No one moved for a moment or two, then Rosemary stepped forwards.

'We won't be very long,' she said.

Eve ignored her. 'I'm locking up.' She began to move towards the door.

Java stepped to one side to bar her way.

'What're you doing?' she said, an edge of fear lending animation to the flat voice.

Java ignored her.

'Tony!' This time the edge of fear was unmistakable, and the man who was mopping the bar looked up for the first time. His eyes met Java's.

What happened then I could never quite recall; the unreality of it all washed over me like a breaker, tipping the world sideways, and when it stabilized a few moments later it was over. I think that it was then that Java drew out his knife; no, the knife *sprang* from the palm of his hand like an animal, and with one liquid movement it touched the woman's throat. A touch was all it took; she gave a cry of surprise, then the blood flowered down the front of her blouse. She clutched at the wound, eyes getting rounder and rounder; the blood sprayed. Java had never ceased to look into the eyes of the man at the bar. I don't remember who went for the man first. I think it might have been Zach and Elaine. Anton was groping for the body of the woman; blood sprayed his face, and I saw the look of *hunger* there, the bright gleam of greed in his eyes, older and more corrupt than any child's eyes have a right to be; but the hunger was on me then, terrifying and uncontrollable, and before I knew what I was doing, I had pushed the child out of the way and was feeding myself. Blood starred the lenses of my glasses; the world swam in shades of red. I fed messily, without any other thought than appeasing the blood-god within me, biting at the flesh of the woman's throat, feeling her shudder beneath me. Anton whimpered like a puppy, trying to push past me again, clawing at the body with his little hands; somehow we both fed. As I rolled over, drugged and sated, I saw the man at the bar—at least, what they had left of him. They had ripped him apart, from belly to throat. Elaine had found the till and was stuffing coins and banknotes into her pockets. Java had found the bottles of oil for the stove and was splashing the floor and furniture with it. Rosemary was cleaning the blood from Rafe's face with her tongue, a mist of tiny droplets sprayed across her eyes like a mask. She looked up and smiled at me.

'We are the chosen ones,' she said. 'That's what we are. And I chose you. Remember that, and be loyal to me. Be mine, Daniel.'

Two

Alice managed to get to sleep at about six that morning. Ginny knocked on the door at half past five and went straight to her room without a word; Alice let her go with a guilty quickening of the heart as she thought of the box she had stolen. Her vision was scrambled from too long trying to decipher Daniel Holmes's crabbed, neurotic handwriting, and her head felt terribly heavy. Perhaps after a couple of hours' sleep she might be able to see things in a better perspective. Perhaps she might wake up and find that all the events of that night had been a dream.

She awoke at eight o'clock, pulled on her robe and tiptoed down to her workroom. For a long time she looked calmly at the box and the picture she had painted. She knew that it was a false calm, but she welcomed it all the same, allowing her perception of the situation to shift again, like sand, into a new pattern.

She would have to confront Ginny, she decided; maybe the girl would admit everything as soon as Alice told her what she already knew. Perhaps Ginny needed help.

She looked at her watch: twenty past eight. Joe would be coming round soon, she imagined. She would have to talk to Ginny before he arrived.

*　　　　*　　　　*

'Tea, Ginny?' That was better. Her voice was steady now, her smile confident.

Ginny was sitting by the fire, still barefoot, but wearing jeans and a dark jumper which highlighted her bright hair. She shook her head.

'You look ill.'

'I didn't sleep much. I was too busy thinking about last night.'

Ginny looked at her blankly.

'You can tell me,' Alice went on. 'I know more about it than you think. I know you're in trouble,

198

and I don't think you know how to handle it.'

Ginny just looked at her silently, giving no indication she even understood.

'Rafe and Java,' said Alice, coming closer. 'Do they live in that old house?'

Ginny shrugged.

'Don't you know?'

She shook her head.

'But they are your friends.'

'Sometimes.' Ginny had begun to rock gently in her chair, her eyes distant, like those of a child. Alice took her hand.

'Ginny. Look at me.' The lavender-grey eyes fixed on hers, sweet and empty, as if the soul behind them were simply a blank, with no more life in it than a mirror.

'I found the syringes in your cupboard. I saw you go out with Java. Is he selling dope? And what else is he doing? At the church . . . what was he doing there?'

Ginny simply stared at her.

'Ginny. You have to tell someone. You have to get help before you become too involved. If it was only drugs they were involved with it might be OK to keep quiet, but I was there in Grantchester that night. I saw you digging in the churchyard. And what about the box in your suitcase? I know where that came from. It was in the wall of the church, marked with a brass plaque. Why did they take it, Ginny? What are they doing it all for?'

But Ginny had withdrawn again. And half an hour later, when Joe knocked on the door, Ginny was still sitting there, looking into the fire and rocking gently to herself, like a cursed princess in a fairy tale.

One

I suppose they think I'm safe here; safe from myself and my delusions. I have a nurse to bring me a soothing drink of camomile tea when I go to sleep; I much prefer whisky, but they tell me it excites me. On sunny days I am allowed to go for a walk around the grounds, but I prefer to stay in the library. Sometimes my doctor comes to keep me company; I beat him at chess. I like him, inasmuch as I like anyone here, and I talk to him, though I am certain he does not believe me. My proof, the books and the pictures, mean nothing to him. His concern is with my mind, though I tell him that only my soul is worth saving now. A young man, Doctor Pryce, young and strong and filled with laughter, like Robert before he met Rosemary.

He tries to help. He even brings me books, all the ones I ask for; he shakes his head and grins and says: 'They'd have my neck for this if they knew I was encouraging you.' But he brings them: Frazer and Crowley and Ahikar from the Apocrypha, even the writers of fiction, Lovecraft and Poe and the modern ones, whose names I forget, book titles emblazoned in red foil on cheap black paperback covers. All those whom I thought might have met Rosemary in one or another of her aspects, kindred spirits who might somehow give me a clue as to how to escape her, though I never find what I am looking for. He sits quietly with me as I search; sometimes I read him passages from works in Latin and French and German. I do not read Romanian, which is a pity, as many of the texts I need are not publicly available in translation. I send money to the local university, so that impoverished and unquestioning students can do the work for me, but it is a slow and impatient business. The young man nods and seems to listen; sometimes I find myself wanting to warn him. All your knowledge, I want to tell him, is nothing in the face of *her* knowledge, her hunger. If she were to look at you, you would become what I became, with all your intellect and your certainties. Because Rosemary remembers. Remembers and waits.

My research is fruitless, I know; there is no way to stop her. I tried once; maybe she was careless. It took her thirty years to return; by now she will have been reborn. Maybe by the time you read these pages, she will be full-grown. All I know is that I will be dead; maybe by my own hands, maybe by hers. She will never allow me to interfere again.

The young man is logical; he tries to use my research to prove me wrong. How can she be a vampire, he says, when the medieval accounts of vampirism in Romania do not correspond in the least with what you believe you know of her?

No factual or folkloric source describes a creature such as you have described.

No name fits her, I tell him; in the same way, all names do. All I know is that she is old, as old as the corruption from which she came, though at the same time monstrously young. She is something which transcends legend, as God transcends childish superstitions of loaves and fishes. I suppose that Jung would have called her an evil anima; you see, I can speak in your language too, I can use your arguments better than you yourself, but that cannot exorcise the demoness who rides my dreams. The image of blood which transcends all my visions of her sickens and excites me, as I suppose you would say my conception of my own sexuality appalls me.

I am a man who prides himself on intellect and rational thinking; inconceivable, that there should be such thoughts beyond my consciousness; repressed, they only grow, like mould in a crypt. The part of myself I cannot accept takes on a different identity. I call the entity Rosemary. I imagine that it is she who is responsible for the darkness within myself. I make it into a werewolf fantasy, of murder and feeding by night, of blood, mystic river of the subconscious; Rosemary the vampire, irresistible and lethal . . . I substitute the kiss she gives me for an act of aggression, a bite (is not every sexual act an act of aggression, and am I not inherently afraid of women?) which makes me into an imitation of herself. Part of me wants it— to be wanted, loved, aggressed—the other part fears it, disassociates itself once more, and distorts my natural desire for a beautiful woman into something perverse, monstrous, even to the point of deluding myself into believing that I was guilty of the most bestial of atrocities.

You see, I tell him, I speak your language. A guilt complex involving my basic fear of women, perhaps a latent homosexual tendency emerging on the event of the tragic death of my best friend . . . and here we have all the classic elements of a neurosis.

He smiles doubtfully; he has heard me speak in this fashion before. The first time, he was elated; could it be that at last I was showing some proof of recovery? He has heard me speak; he is puzzled at the apparent coherency of my arguments, my apparent sanity in all areas except one.

She is not a neurosis.

She is neither vampire nor werewolf but a real entity. Fragments of her walk the pages of books, but her reality is something more real even than that; she is an infection of the soul, no human being, but something older and more archetypal than the most familiar of Jung's figures. I call her the Blessed Damozel.

*   *   *

They took me home, you know, after that night at the bar; it would never have done to have left me on my own. The police would have found me half an hour later, still screaming as the café burned; as it was, they found nobody, and the others half-dragged me, almost catatonic with the shock of what we had done, to Rosemary's hideout. It was a disused warehouse, half burnt to the ground in a fire several years previously, and damp, but it was an excellent place to hide. She took me in hand; I remember her hands around my neck, her breath on my cheek as she held the beaker of hot whisky to my lips; I gagged, drank, spluttered, but managed to keep down the drink.

'Don't worry,' she told me, her hair hanging down towards me, almost touching my face. 'The worst is nearly over. You'll feel ill for a while, you'll have a fever, and bright light will hurt your eyes, but it will be over in a week or two. Drink some more.'

I swallowed. I struggled to raise myself to my

elbows, and looked round. Rafe and Java were sitting together in a corner, their backs turned to me. I could hear the sibilances of their conversation, light as cobwebs on the still air. Zach was asleep already, hunched beneath a pile of sacking and blankets, his face turned at an odd and somehow touchingly youthful angle into his folded arms.

Elaine was nursing Anton, rocking and singing a little meaningless song.

'Be still,' admonished Rosemary. 'Everything will be all right.'

But I could not be still.

'What happened? Did I? Did we . . . What happened?'

'We are the chosen ones,' she said. 'We do what we have to do. Don't worry; you'll get used to it; all the others did.'

With a lunge and a wrench, I sat up. I was caught between laughter and mounting hysteria.

'What do you mean? You're telling me I'm a *vampire*? Like Dracula?' I thrashed at the beaker of whisky and knocked it out of her hand. I made a grab for her, meaning to shake her. I saw Java make a sudden movement in the corner, caught the flick of a glance from his cold eyes, and knew he was ready to intervene if I showed any sign of violence. The laughter welled up in me again.

'Vampires!' I hooted.

Rosemary looked at me with a cold, sad calm.

'No one mentioned that name but yourself,' she said. 'There are no vampires. But we are different, as you are different now. We have certain privileges. And we must feed. You know we must.'

I shook my head.

'No! I don't want, I mean. I don't want to be chosen.'

'Neither did Moses,' said Rosemary. 'You'll get used to it, I told you. The rest of them are like cattle to us. Do you ask cattle whether they want to be eaten? In the Bible it says that God gave us dominion over all the other beasts of the field; and Danny, *they* are the beasts of the field. When you get used to this idea, you'll realize what a chance we've given you, no, not to live for ever, but to live more, and experience more, learn more than any other man you know. I've given you life.'

'You've made me a monster,' I said.

Rosemary looked angry. 'There are no monsters. I have given you power, and with power comes new appetite. I have not changed you into a vampire; your appetites come from *you*, not me. Your subconscious knows what you need a lot better than you do. And it compensates, allowing you to transfer feelings of guilt on to me.'

She smiled. 'You'll adjust soon enough. Soon you will wonder why on earth you had to make such a fuss about it all. But it's only natural, after all. Later, I will begin to teach you.'

I suppose you have seen her pictures. You know how lovely she was, and maybe you can understand how easily I was subjugated. To me, bloodstained and half-drunk and crushed beneath the dictates of religion and morality, she looked like a thing out of legend, and the cup she offered me was *freedom*, no less, freedom from everything, from my lonely life, from the law, from my God and my conscience and the consequences of my actions. From then onwards, I would be free to take whatever I wanted from life, and there would be no one to stop me. Suddenly I wanted that freedom so badly that I was overwhelmed with panic that she might withdraw her offer, and I reached out for her like a beggar.

'Teach me now,' I said.

*   *   *

What Rosemary taught me that day, on a pile of old sacks and blankets in a dusty, disused warehouse with the sunlight strung out like skeins of silk across the broken rafters, I try not to remember. Enough to say that she was sweet and soft, her hair smelt of lavender and I loved her with a frenzy of which I would never have imagined myself capable. It was true then, that my altered state brought new appetites, and I sated them fully in the endlessness of Rosemary until there was nothing of me left. They had all loved her, that I knew instinctively: Zach and Rafe and Java and Elaine and Anton (seven years old, going on fifty), and that somehow made it all the more liberating and marvellous. Rosemary was the vial of eternal life; we had all drunk deep, and she had given us grace.

Maybe you find me ridiculous, maybe even blasphemous. Try to understand. I am not writing this for my own glory, or even to salvage my conscience, but to warn you. I am inventing nothing; I write only what I felt. This is Rosemary; this she can be again.

It is proof of the enchantment she laid on me that it was only as I was ready to leave that I remembered Robert. I froze, the sensation of epiphany falling from me in an instant of shock.

'My God!'

Rosemary turned to look at me; she was sitting on a pile of rubbish in the doorway, all fire and ivory in the sunlight.

'Where does Robert fit into this?' The coldness grew; I began to recognize it as guilt. 'Does he know, is he?'

Rosemary arched her back and stretched.

'No, he isn't chosen.' Her voice was faintly contemptuous.

'You mean he doesn't know?' I said. 'But he's going to marry you.'

She laughed. 'I know it's hard for you, because you still haven't outgrown your quaint notions of loyalty, but you must, you know. Someone who is chosen must put aside all loyalties to the cattle; they are misplaced loyalties, unworthy of you. I have my own uses for Robert, but he has no part in our plans.'

'But—' I said.

'When you are truly one of us, I will tell you why I need Robert,' said Rosemary, with her serene smile. 'Until then, Danny, know your true loyalties, and be satisfied with them.' I wanted to say more, but dared not. I had displeased her, I knew, by mentioning my friend, and by then, I was too much hers to risk doing so again. I took my leave of her, without arranging another time to meet. ('You'll know when I need you,' she had told me, and I had to be satisfied with that.) And with my hat pulled hard over my eyes and my coat buttoned to the neck, I began the long walk home over the fields.

Two

Joe was wearing the same clothes he had worn for the concert the previous night, and he looked crumpled and tired, his mouth drawn down and his eyes swollen. As Alice opened the door he was lighting a cigarette, hands cupped round the lighter flame.

'How's Ginny?' Alice felt a sting of irritation that he should make his indifference to her so obvious.

'She's fine,' she said.

'Where is she?'

'In the living-room. Look, Joe.' She caught hold of his arm as he began to open the living-room door. 'Stop here a minute. We need to talk.'

'Can't it wait?' he said, an edge to his voice. 'I've not slept, and I'm not up to talking much yet. You know what I'm like in the mornings.'

'I'm worried about Ginny.'

'Why? I thought you said she was OK.'

'It depends what you mean,' said Alice. 'Do you know she takes drugs? I found some syringes in her cupboard.'

Joe stiffened slightly, then shrugged. 'She went through a phase,' he said. 'So what?'

'I think it's more than a phase,' said Alice. 'Last night she didn't come back till five. The night before she—'

'Don't try to get me worked up. Just tell me what you're getting at.' He took a drag from his cigarette. She forced herself to sound calm.

'I think Ginny's in with the wrong crowd. Two

208

friends of hers came by here last night, asking for her, and they were . . .' She paused. 'They frightened me. I went out and followed them to an old house near Grantchester, a kind of squat. They were at the concert, too, and Ginny was with them all the time.'

Joe frowned. 'You've been very active on Ginny's behalf. I'd better talk to her, hadn't I?' He pushed past Alice into the front room. She followed.

Ginny was standing by the window looking out into the street, but she turned when she heard Joe come in. Her face lit up like a child's, and she ran up to him and threw her arms around his neck.

'Hey Gin. You're not too tired?' His voice had softened for Ginny, Alice noticed, but there was still a hard line between his eyes, as if the sunlight hurt him.

Ginny shook her head. 'Did they keep you long last night?'

Joe shrugged. 'Too long. The thing is that the bloke they picked up and took off in the ambulance decided to snuff it on the way to the hospital. They don't know who he was yet, and no one seems to have seen what happened to him. There was too much confusion, people fighting and trying to get through the door, people thinking there was a fire and freaking out. By the time the police got there most of the people who could have witnessed something were gone, and the guy bled to death before anyone got organized. So what they did was to grab the nearest bass guitarist and say, "Hey man, you were there, you must have seen something." You didn't get close enough to spot what happened, did you?'

209

Once more Ginny shook her head.

Alice, remembering the group of Ginny's friends at the door, frowned, and in spite of herself, spoke up. 'Maybe your friends saw something,' she said.

Ginny looked blank. 'What friends?'

'Rafe and Java, and the others who were there last night. You were standing with them at the back of the room.'

Ginny shook her head, a puzzled expression on her face. 'There was only you and Joe,' she said. 'I don't have any other friends.'

'But they were with you last night,' said Alice. 'Come off it, Ginny, don't be silly. You have to tell us about it sometime. You went to a house by the river. You can't have come back before five, at least, because—'

'I didn't go anywhere last night,' said Ginny to Joe. 'I went to bed.'

'You didn't come back from the concert! I waited for you, but you never came. Then your friends turned up looking for you; the same ones I saw you with at the concert. They said they were called Rafe and Java. Don't lie to us, there isn't any point. We just want to know . . .'

But Joe had stepped forward, all the softness gone from his face.

'Look,' he said. 'Leave off, will you? I can do without all this right now. What does it matter who she was with?'

Alice tried to keep calm. The last thing she wanted was a row with Joe. 'It matters that for some reason Ginny won't tell us where she's been going at night.'

'Don't start that. We'll talk about it later.' Joe

was wearing his stubborn look. A look that Alice knew of old. For a moment he looked very like Ginny.

'Later?' she said.

'Just *leave* it, Alice!'

The northern accent had intensified as he raised his voice.

Alice found she was trembling. 'Don't you see you're being made a fool of?' she said. 'Don't let her lie to you! I tell you, I can prove it. I can take you to the house.' She turned to Ginny. 'Tell him the truth!'

Tears had come to Ginny's eyes, and she turned away, hiding her face. Alice grabbed her by the arm.

'Stop it!' Joe's intervention was as rapid as her own. 'Let her alone! I said, get your fucking hands off her!' His hand was lifted, as if to strike; the high frequency of his emotion palpable. He was shaking, his eyes almost closed, then he gave a cry and hit the wall with all his strength, knocking plaster from a patch the size of a beer-mat.

With a sick feeling, Alice realized that only a tremendous effort of will had prevented him from actually hitting *her*. The thought was so ugly, so uncharacteristic, that she stepped back from Ginny, tears of reaction in her eyes.

'Oh, that's very mature,' she said. 'I hope you're feeling better now.'

Joe was cradling his hurt hand. 'I think I've cracked my knuckles.'

'Good.'

Now his voice was quiet again, the shuttered look back behind his eyes. 'I thought you might have changed,' he said. 'But you're still the same spiteful bitch. Going on and on, never letting up about anything. I was well rid of you.' And he took Ginny's hand and turned towards the door.

'Joe . . .' Alice tried to put her hand on his arm to calm him; he shook it away with a violent gesture.

'Get the fuck off me!'

Then Ginny stepped in. 'Please,' she said, tugging at his sleeve so that he turned back to face her. 'Please don't make a fuss,' she went on. 'I'm sure all this was a mistake. Maybe someone did call by, from the past that I'm trying to forget. Maybe that's who Alice saw. Please don't quarrel over me.'

Now Joe looked shamefaced, the anger submerging once again.

'Look, Alice . . .' He tried to smile. 'I think we're all a bit freaked out today. I haven't slept at all, and we've all been through quite a lot, and we both overreacted, right? Perhaps you did see someone last night. Perhaps it was even some friend of Ginny's. She used to have some pretty weird friends.'

'Don't be afraid to say it,' said Ginny looking into Joe's eyes. 'I want Alice to know everything. She has to know all about me before she can trust me and be my friend.'

Her eyes flicked to Alice's face for an instant; Alice caught the neon flash of a carnival wheel turning.

'I used to know all kinds of people,' she said. 'Pimps, addicts, prostitutes, most of them half-crazy.' She smiled. 'Joe changed all that. Joe was my white knight,' she said.

He tried to speak but she stilled him with a

212

gesture, something which Alice, in all those years, had never managed to do.

'I've really tried to forget those times,' said Ginny, looking at Alice now. 'But sometimes I still remember—'

And she looked straight into Alice's eyes and the word 'remember' echoed in the spaces between them, and Alice was seized by the peculiar feeling that she was being given a message, a very important message which she could not understand, and the understanding of which might change the world.

*   *   *

Alice waited for a long time after Ginny and Joe left the house, then she went into her workroom where she had left Daniel Holmes's manuscript. She put the papers carefully back into the box, hid the box in a cupboard in her workroom, and went back into her living-room to think.

Daniel Holmes was mad, of course.

And yet, some part of her wanted to believe his tale. Maybe the scene with Joe had finally decided her; or maybe the feelings which had assailed her since that first evening with Ginny, the dizziness, the odd scents she had associated with her; sugar, peanuts, candy-floss, the low, hot reek of the animal-house . . . Daniel had mentioned those too. The suspicion, the hatred Alice had felt for Ginny, the alien sense of dread. Rafe and Java, perfectly described. Ginny's face on paintings over a hundred years old. Ginny's face in the Corn Exchange hall. The Reverend Holmes, Daniel's nephew, in the church. Doctor Pryce, Daniel's

213

doctor, Ginny's doctor, dead in Fulbourn. Ginny's denials in front of Joe. Crazy Daniel might be, she thought, but she was almost beginning to believe him.

*   *   *

'Hello? Fulbourn Hospital. Can I help you?'

'I'd like to speak to Doctor Menezies, please.'

'Just hang on a moment, I'll see if he's here.'

Again, the soothing music, as Alice was put on hold. Tapping her fingers irritably on the side of the receiver, she waited, all the while keeping her eyes on the box in which she had filed all Daniel Holmes's writings.

'Hello. Menezies speaking.'

'Good morning. It's Alice Farrell; maybe you remember speaking to me the other day.'

'Yes, I remember.'

Alice hesitated. 'I'd like to arrange for us to meet. I have a problem I'd like to discuss.'

'I see. Perhaps you'd like to give me some idea of the nature of your problem before we meet?'

'I'd rather make an appointment.'

'I have a slot at half past twelve.'

'Fine.' Alice was relieved. 'That'll be fine.'

'Right. Well, if that's all . . .'

'Wait.' Alice took a deep breath, marshalling her energy. 'Who did you say was the doctor who died recently? Doctor Pryce?' A long silence from the other end of the phone.

'Hello?'

Menezies' voice, sharp and maybe wary. 'If you're from the press, you're wasting your time. I don't give interviews.'

214

'I'm not from the press. I just want some help,' said Alice firmly. 'Why? Is there any problem? Is it something to do with Doctor Pryce?'

Another long pause. Then his voice, cool and remote. 'I'll see you at twelve-thirty,' he said.

One

I could not remain in my lodgings any longer, for fear that Mrs Brown, who knew me too well, might comment on my changed manner, and so as soon as I arrived home I locked myself in my room and began to plan my escape. First, I bathed thoroughly and burned my bloodstained shirt; an expensive habit, no doubt, but my sense of self-preservation took over and planned, coldly, my new life with all the precision of a man born to the ways of Cain.

By now I was beginning to feel light-headed again; remember, I had hardly slept, I had seen more in twenty-four hours than I ever imagined in all of Heaven and Hell; and the knowledge I acquired on the way was written across my face. Looking at myself in my old mirror, I saw a half-stranger, unshaven and hollow-cheeked, eyes brimming with the light of power, frightening and . . . yes, oddly beautiful. I smiled at myself, noting a hitherto undiscovered sensuality about my mouth, a savage carelessness which had not been there before. I remembered Rafe, and how like an angel he had appeared to me under the bridge. Did I look like him now? I thought. Now that I was chosen? I turned away from the mirror, went to

215

the cupboard, found the bottle of whisky and a mug. I poured myself a good two inches of undiluted whisky, drank it in one draught, like medicine, and set about my packing.

There was not very much of this; a trunk of clothes and books was everything I needed to take, but my problem was really to make good my departure without having to meet Mrs Brown. I was afraid that if my landlady confronted me with my bizarre behaviour I might weaken; fortunately for me, she was out, and I contrived easily enough to have a cab remove my belongings to another part of town in her absence. I left a note for her, as well as two five-pound notes in an envelope in thanks for everything she had done for me; and by the late afternoon I was already settled in my new apartment by the Cam, a suite of three rooms on the top floor of a three-storey house. There were three other lodgers there besides myself, as the surly landlord vouchsafed. Having set eyes on the man I guessed, rightly, that as long as my rent was on time, and I did not disturb the peace, any strange habits of mine would pass unnoticed. I settled down on my bed and slept.

My rest was poor; I was troubled by dreams and memories worse than dreams, and though my eyelids were heavy with lack of sleep, it hurt to close my eyes, as if the memories which resided behind them had turned to broken glass beneath the flesh. In my moments of wakefulness my eyes were sore and crusted, and when, in the early evening, I rose and turned on the light, the brightness of it was more than I could bear, and I had to sit in near-darkness for almost half an hour before the discomfort abated.

By this time, I was hungry, and knowing that there would be nothing available for me to eat at that hour, I prepared to go out.

Having dressed with care, and shaved, I made my way to a small restaurant I knew on King's Parade. I chose it particularly because my friends rarely frequented it. I ordered drinks, followed by a rare steak, and sat back in a comfortable chair and looked around. Despite the bland normality of the place, I had an odd sensation of unreality, as if the little restaurant were simply a theatrical set, with sinister engineers working behind the scenes; I imagined wheels turning behind closed doors, the familiar sounds and smells and sights of the Cambridge evening outside a cover for the machinery of another, darker world. I sipped my drink quietly, waited for the world to return to focus, but the sensation intensified . . . not an altogether unpleasant sensation, and yet it disturbed me. Two people passed the window—a young man and a girl, faces pallid in the greenish light of the street-lamps. I saw them for a moment only, but their image remained fixed in my mind for several moments after they had passed; the young man turned towards the girl, she fixing her gaze demurely on the ground. For an instant, I seemed to see, with this newly acquired vision, the bone and muscle beneath their skin, the movement of the machinery of their bodies, occult and silent capsules of sinew and blood.

The thought chilled me; suddenly I was appalled at myself. I told you I had never been fanciful; these thoughts seemed not to be my own, but those of someone else, some incubus with a sense of humour. I turned my thoughts to the arrival of my steak, red and steaming in a pool of rich juices; the waiter set the plate down in front of me, smiled in the absent way waiters do, and left me to my meal. I set to eating with a hearty appetite, inhaling the rich subtleties of the meat as I cut and swallowed without even chewing, feeling the power return to my weakened body and my traumatized mind. That was all I needed, I thought to myself in satisfaction, just a good meal to set me to rights again. Rosemary and the others seemed very far away now, very unreal. Inconceivable that I had seen so much, suffered and experienced more than a normal man may in a whole life. I even began to doubt the happenings of that night; suspecting that the powerful hallucinogen administered to me by Rafe might have been responsible for those bloody, joyful visions.

The world sideslipped again with a lurch. I looked down at my plate, at the meat, the blood, and suddenly the sight of that blood sickened me. I remembered that other blood, so fragrant and lavish, how it had pulsed, how it had sprayed wantonly, generously—the acidic, metallic taste of the open wound. Human flesh was whiter than beef, I thought inconsequentially, but still there was a kindred among cattle.

Strange, that my horror should not be of the crimes I had committed; maybe they were too much for my scrambled mind to understand. The fact that I had fed on the murdered body of a woman before she was cold seemed unreal, distant; I felt only the vague dislocated guilt I might have felt on remembering a perversely sexual dream. No, what frightened me more than I can say, what still frightens me, was the fact that such things exist, behind the still façade of humdrum life. There was a whole world of scurrying life behind the scenes, once glimpsed, never forgotten, and I was a part of it now, inescapably caught in its busy machinery. I felt as if, in the middle of a ride on the big wheel of a fairground, I had happened to look downwards, and had seen the exposed organs of the mechanism which bore me, or as if I had seen the painted sky peeled back to reveal God, like a giant puppet-master, surrounded by the wheels and pulleys which keep the stars in place, grinning down at the Earth and holding the sun in place like a sleeping yo-yo.

I pushed my plate away, unable to eat any more. My heightened awareness taunted me with new and horrific sensations; I felt the warmth of the meat on my plate calling to the warmth of my belly where, even now, the unseen machinery was converting what I had eaten into faeces. I felt, for a loathsome instant, the boiling of bacteria in my intestines, the death of millions of cells in my brain even as I thought. And I saw myself, as if through a grotesquely magnifying lens: one moment infinitely large, the atoms of my body rushing away through space at the speed of light to the vast dark forges at entropy's end, the next, infinitely tiny, endlessly dying, a mote on a mote in darkness, helpless and lost, infinitely far from God.

I reeled, disorientated, and in that moment everything returned to normal once more: the restaurant, the dim light of the candle in front of me, the fragrance of the meat, the red wine in the glass. A moment of limbo, and I could hardly even remember my previous unease, as I cut into my steak once more and ate with satisfyingly primitive joy. I was chosen.

I ordered fruit and cake and more wine, then coffee and brandy to finish. I asked the waiter for a paper, and read the *Evening Post* for a quarter of an hour or so, noticing with some satisfaction that the body in the crypt had not yet been discovered. Even the 'Body in the Weir' case had been relegated to third-page status, with no new developments except that Scotland Yard were still at work investigating the cause of death. I scanned the rest of the paper for news of the previous night's activities in the tavern, and eventually located the report, half a dozen lines on the fourth page entitled BLAZE KILLS TWO. Obviously the fire the others had lit to cover their traces had fooled the police, at least temporarily. Feeling very much more master of myself, I paid my bill, took my coat and hat, and began to walk back to my new rooms, taking the path along the river, enjoying the carelessness of the moment, the quiet sounds of the Cam and the darkness of the path. I was not at all tired, though by now it was late, and I was not usually given to late nights, and I think that as I opened the door of my room I might have been planning to do some of my research while I waited for sleep, but as soon as I stepped through the doorway, all thoughts of books fled my mind. Even as I reached for the light, the voice stopped me, a voice shockingly feeble and hoarse, but still uncannily familiar.

'Danny. Don't put the light on . . . it's me.'

I squinted in the darkness, took off my glasses to see more clearly, made out a pale, unformed shape to my left.

'Robert?'

No answer, but a kind of creaking, choking sigh.

'Robert, are you all right?'

That ghastly sound again, accompanied by a scraping, shuffling sound from the direction of the bed. I was unused to the room, in addition, I had drunk far more than I was accustomed to; I struck a table in the gloom as I tried to move towards my friend, lost my balance and almost fell over a fold in the carpet.

'How did you find me? Are you in trouble?'

Something like a sob in the dark.

I reached him at last; from what I could feel, he was half lying on the bed, fully clothed. He reached for my hand. He was very cold. A faint medicinal smell clung to his clothes, mingled with a much stronger reek of whisky. I put my arms around him and held him like a child; all the while wondering desperately what Rosemary had told him. That this was somehow her doing, I did not doubt; only she could have reduced him to this state. Robert was a light-hearted, practical man with a firm hold on reality and on himself; but I had long since realized that he was not strong. One glimpse of what I had been allowed to see in those past twenty-four hours would have been enough to annihilate him; somehow, I had adapted, and for the first time in all our acquaintance, our roles were reversed. He clung to me, his breath jerking painfully, and I rocked him like a child, trying to think of some way to calm and reassure him. Whatever happened, I told myself, he must not suspect the truth; he must not learn about Rosemary, though whether I wished to protect him or her, I did not yet know.

221

I rocked him until the rigidity left his body, whispered inanities while all the time I planned and calculated my approach.

'Had a bit to drink, eh? That's better. Hold on. I'll make us a pot of coffee.' I stood up without difficulty (my eyes had by now acclimatized to the darkness), went to the sink, lit a small lamp there. I ran some water into the kettle, opened the door again to go to the kitchenette.

'Don't go!' Robert's voice was trembling.

'It's all right, old chap, I'll be back in a tick,' I said. 'I'll bring us a pot of coffee, you'll see, that'll make you feel better.'

When I returned I found him slightly more under control. He was sitting in one of my armchairs, his back to the light. His hat was lying on the floor beside him. He looked as if he had been crying; even in that dim light his face was blotchy, and his hands, clasped on his lap, were restless.

'Thanks, old chap,' he said, with an effort. 'Good of you to salvage the wreck. I'm all right now.' I turned to light the fire, which had gone out in my absence. In the piling of coal and paper, the striking of matches, the fanning of the flames with the bellows, and the final deft poker-work which set the flames crackling merrily, Robert had time to collect himself still more, and when I turned to him again he was sitting upright in his chair, and his face, though drawn and rather pale, was almost back to normal again. I poured coffee for both of us, knowing that this sequence of normal, everyday gestures—lighting the fire, spooning out sugar and passing milk—was reassuring my friend better than any words I could have spoken.

222

'Now then,' I said, when I had judged that the coffee and the warm fire had begun to take effect, 'why don't you tell me what's wrong?' I smiled, and passed a tin of biscuits. 'Help yourself.'

Robert shook his head. 'Thanks.' He took another sip of the strong coffee (he drank it black, with a lot of sugar), then set the cup down. 'I'm sorry, Dan,' he said, in a more normal tone. 'I've been a fool. I've behaved very badly to you over all this, and I hope you'll accept my apology.'

'Nonsense,' I said. 'There's no need. Now why don't you tell me what's wrong?'

He nodded, began to speak, paused. 'I don't know where to begin,' he said, 'or whether you'll believe me when I've told you. It all sounds completely mad.'

'You'd be surprised at what I can believe,' I said.

'All right,' said Robert, and as the fire died down, I heard his tale in snatches, incoherently but only too familiar. I listened in silence, only prompting occasionally and it was then, listening to that tragic little story, that I reached a decision which was to influence all my later actions, and may still cost me my life. Chosen or not, I had a loyalty to my friend, and I would keep faith with him. I would protect him, even from her. Even from Rosemary. Though at that moment, I still had no idea of where that decision would lead me, and into what fateful realms I would have to travel before I could call my soul my own again.

From the very first moment, Robert said, Rosemary had bewitched him. Robert was very much a 'man's man'; with his public-school, army and university background he had had little contact with women, and revealed himself to be

223

surprisingly innocent, an ideally susceptible candidate for Rosemary's special kind of seduction. He had never been in love before, nor had he ever thought he was the type, but he realized immediately that Rosemary was the woman he would love for ever, and though he was torn at the thought of stealing her from me (for he knew how much I had been dazzled by her), he hoped that I would not bear him a grudge. In her taunting way, she had led him to believe that she could love him, and there had followed a few weeks of idyllic happiness. He had forgotten everything but Rosemary, working at the university with growing reluctance, ceasing to write, neglecting his friends. I guessed how cleverly she had contrived to isolate him from the world, to make him wholly dependent on her; that was how she worked, eliminating everything which might interfere with her domination of his life, setting herself up as his witch and his icon. Her mystery tantalized him; sometimes she failed to arrive at their meetings, and when he demanded an explanation for this, she would simply look at him from her bruise-coloured eyes and say, 'There are things in my life that you will never imagine or know.'

Sometimes, as their intimacy deepened, he began to glimpse new facets of her. On certain days she would not leave her rooms, refusing to see even him, and occasionally, when he came to see her regardless and would not go away until he had seen her, her face was unaccountably pale and drawn, as if she had not slept, and her movements were sluggish, almost drunken. She never gave any reason for her strange behaviour or her mysterious illnesses, but looked at him with those sad, steady eyes, and told him that he would never understand.

He grew jealous—then angry. He made promises and broke them immediately, was tormented by jealousy and the fear of losing her. When he glimpsed her one evening in the company of two men, his jealousy knew no bounds: he challenged her to deny that she had a lover. She ordered him out of her house. For a whole week, he was racked by guilt and shame at what he had told her; he tried to find her, but was told by her landlady that she had moved away.

Robert began to feel afraid; he became convinced that Rosemary had committed suicide in her despair at his rejection. He began to haunt the river, he drank far more than he ought, both in public houses and at home, advertised in the papers for information concerning her—all without success. Six weeks had passed already, and Robert was in a state of near-breakdown. He was afraid to come and see me in case I blamed him for his treatment of Rosemary; such was his sense of guilt that when he saw me on the bridge, and later, when I found him in the tavern, he was unable to tell me anything. He slept little, ate less, and was willing to do anything to ensure her return.

She knew it, of course.

He found her late one night in a cheap drinking-house, looking ill and dazed. Her glorious hair was loose and tangled, her face thinner and paler than ever. Her dress was grey, enhancing her frailty and her wraithlike appearance, her head thrown back against the greasy wall and her eyes closed. Robert felt his heart turn to water, and for a moment he was paralysed, scarcely able to believe that he had found her at last. His next reaction was panic; she looked so ill, so wretched. He took her back to his rooms; she was unresponsive, as if she had suffered a shock, or taken an overdose of some hallucinogen. She was barely able even to walk, and he half-carried her up the stairs, laid her on the bed, and forced hot coffee between her white lips until she seemed to recover a little.

I always knew Rosemary was a marvellous actress; her story was superb, and Robert, susceptible as he was, believed it absolutely. She told him that she was a drug addict; that she had been one for several years, since, in fact, she had left home at the age of sixteen. It was this, and not her affair with the married man, that had driven her to attempt suicide, and though she had tried many times to rid herself of this pernicious habit, she had always failed, either due to a lack of willpower on her part, or, more likely, a lack of friendly support. Her few friends were all in the same situation; they had derived, in the past, a little comfort in being together, but it was a dangerous comfort, which sapped the willpower even more, and which made outcasts of all of them.

She had begun to take drugs under the influence of her first landlady and her husband, who had given her pills to combat her sleepless nights. Then she had progressed to stronger doses, and had finally discovered that she could no longer manage without them. The landlord and landlady, who had at first provided the drugs free of charge, began to demand larger and larger sums of money for their services, until Rosemary was giving them all the money she earned. She began to take on other work, to make more money. At first she was selective, taking sewing and knitting jobs or helping in public houses, then less selective, accepting cleaning and scrubbing jobs in disreputable bars. She was noticed, of course; it was impossible for a girl of Rosemary's looks not to be noticed, and, several times, she was solicited. She rebuffed these offers with proper disgust, but the two people who had once been her protectors began to pressurize her into being 'agreeable' to various guests who frequented the house: uncouth types for the most part, who drank heavily and played cards for money late into the night. Rosemary found out that her landlord and his wife were running a private gambling parlour under cover of their boarding house, and her presence at their parties was considered an asset and a lure. From that point to accepting to offer her favours for money, there was a terrifyingly small step, which Rosemary, nevertheless, quite properly shrank from taking, and the poor child was reduced to a state of almost perpetual wretchedness and nervous prostration, harried from all sides, and never with enough money to make ends meet. On the scene then appeared the married man of whom she had previously spoken, giving her, for the first time in her life, hope that she might once and for all escape the fate which seemed to threaten her; and when even this hope was denied her, she saw no other solution than the river to end all persecution for ever. Enter the god from the machine: myself, who at the eleventh hour saved her life and gave her the hope of a better world, and then, in the person of Robert, the unhoped-for dream of true love, at which she clutched like the drowning infant she was.

But fear had chilled her idyll for her before it even began; she was tormented by fear that if Robert ever found out what she had been, he would leave her, as the other had left her. She had tried to combat her addiction in solitude, afraid to ask for Robert's support, and, predictably, she had failed. She had sought out her erstwhile friends in secret, and paid them to procure supplies for her, and when she had been caught out in their company by Robert, she had not known what to say to convince him of her innocence. Terrified that, if told the truth, Robert's love might turn to disgust, Rosemary had gathered her pride and told him to leave her house, hoping that he would come back and promise to trust her; but he left, in his rage and jealousy, and Rosemary, believing him to be lost to her for ever, had succumbed to despair, and returned to the only source of comfort she had ever known. She had sold the jewellery which Robert had given her, grieving bitterly for every trinket, but unable to help herself, each day which passed a new link in the chain which drew her closer to the abyss. The friends, all people of ill-repute, pimps and prostitutes and other addicts and the like, became all the more necessary to her in her isolation. She became involved in strange dealings, hinted that members of her circle might have turned to crime to finance and protect each other and, though not directly involved, seemed afraid of the police; afraid that she might be accused of being in league with criminals.

It was at this point that I had encountered them

again, Rosemary looking ill and drained, and Robert in fine fettle, their roles seemingly reversed. But this state of affairs had not lasted for long. Rosemary had become less careful with Robert; knowing that whatever she did he could no longer make any move to challenge her, she began to show the underlying cruelty of her nature. She introduced him to Rafe and Java and Zach, insisting that as her friends they should always be welcome in his house. Sometimes they openly spent the night at her rooms. At this point I don't suppose Rosemary could have known whether Robert was infatuated enough to accept this, but I don't think it mattered to her. Perhaps the cruelty of it alone was enough to afford her the entertainment she craved.

Robert was unable to deal with the situation. He tried on several occasions to leave her, but never managed; her personality changed by the hour, childlike one moment, perverse the next. He attributed this to the drugs she was taking. But even he could not help feeling suspicious of the large amounts of money Rosemary was spending; he himself had been giving her a small allowance from his own savings and his study grant, neither of which were particularly vast, but it soon became obvious that she was receiving large amounts of money from elsewhere. She had already hinted that her friends were involved in some kind of crime, and Robert became convinced that she knew more than she admitted to. And tonight, when he had finally come in search of me, drunk and panic-stricken, he had seen something. At this point his story became so garbled that I could only conjecture as to what he had actually seen, but he mentioned blood on Rosemary's clothes; lots of blood, he kept saying. Even then he refused to admit that he believed Rosemary to be implicated; she was innocent, he maintained, a victim of circumstances. He knew it.

Oh, yes, she had told him a fine story. I knew Rosemary's stories of old, had been fooled by them once before, and I knew what an actress she was. I knew her, you see; not as my poor friend believed he knew her, not as Robert believed in her tales of persecuted innocence, the doomed maiden crying for love. And I loved her too, loved the darkness and the danger of her, loved her hate and her destruction and her promises of death. I was insane with love of her; but it was then, despite all of that, that I knew I would kill her.

Poor Robert, to be so much in love, and never to have seen her face. All he ever saw were the stars in her hair; he never felt the heat of her or tasted blood against her lips, he never knew her, the dread of her, had never taken the fruit from her hand. He never loved her enough to know that the only solution was indeed to kill her, to bury her deep under stone where she would be for ever trapped, unseen and unguessed-at.

As I listened I grieved for his folly, but there was something in me which laughed too, scorned his childish sentiments. After all, I was chosen, and he was one of the cattle. I pitied him, but with no tenderness. Rosemary had bled me dry. I wish it had been love which prompted me; I wish it had been loyalty. I do not think it was either. If it had been Robert in that bar, where I had fed not twenty-four hours earlier, if it had been his blood spraying, I do not think it would have made any difference to the greed with which I fed; the chosen have no loyalties. There was coldness in me now. I was not afraid. I knew then that I would not be like Robert, would not be the deluded fool feeding from her hand. She had opened chasms all around me, had dazed me with her glamour, but somehow, I, the bumbling fool, had shown another face too. Do not mistake me, I never acted out of remorse or loyalty. I accepted the gift she had given me—the appetites. I am still not certain why I acted; maybe it is that each man kills the thing he loves. The truth is, I wanted power. To be free of her, so that I could taste the cup she had offered me.

So that *I* could be Rosemary.

One

I left him sleeping; curled up in the middle of my crumpled eiderdown, face pressed childishly against his hands. My poor friend. I watched over his sleep for a while, not ungently, but with my new contempt, and at about half past three, as the night ticked away, I went out, locking the door behind me. The night was still, the silence filled with hallucinations. My breath was a genie coming from my mouth and hovering nimbus-like around my head. I walked the deserted streets like a lord, relishing the cold, the darkness. As I left the town, automatically veering towards Grantchester, in the absence of street-lamps I glimpsed the dawn hitherto only guessed-at, a thin line of pale phosphorescence at the edges of the horizon.

231

A black cat crossed my path. It paused for a moment, one paw raised, then I saw its jaws open in a soundless hiss, and it was off into the bushes. My stomach grinned, and I realized that I was hungry again. Oh, not with the desperate, stabbing sickness of that first time, but with a clenched anticipation which began at the root of my groin and spread, with a quick burst of warmth, to my stomach. *Appetites*, she had said.

I cursed myself for having waited so long. I should have left at midnight, when the bars closed; I might have found a drunk on a bench, alone, a waitress coming home from work. My mind recoiled from the thought, but my stomach kept on grinning as I quickened my step. Suddenly, I needed Rosemary, I needed the touch of her cool lips, her absence of passion, her purity. I wondered that not half an hour earlier I had actually considered killing her . . . and for what? I could have no loyalties, no jealousies; I sneered at myself and my bourgeois values; she belonged to all of us, we belonged to each other. From my earlier state of elation I was plunged into a sudden blackness. My hunger was no longer pleasant; my grinning stomach twisted and cramped. My erection felt knotted, cancerous. Tears of repentance clouded my eyes; I had betrayed her in my thoughts, and she had turned away from me. I felt like Judas.

Later I began to recognize this frame of mind, and I took measures to avoid it, but at that time I really had very little knowledge of what had happened to me, and I became very frightened. I suppose that users of certain kinds of drug must have experienced this kind of reversal, but until I met Rosemary I had really been very sheltered,

232

and I had not been prepared in any way for the hurricane of conflicting passions into which she had swept me.

It was then that I felt a touch at my elbow, and my nostrils caught a sudden, half-pleasant odour of weeds and damp. Someone whispered my name, and I turned, with a joyful terror. It was Elaine, one of my companions of the previous night, the waiflike, wan girl with the child.

'Don't be afraid,' said Elaine softly, 'I've been looking for you.'

'Why?'

'I knew you'd be like this.'

'Like what?'

'We call it "the little death",' she explained. She had the gentlest voice I had ever heard. 'You get used to it after a while.'

'I don't understand,' I said.

'I don't expect you do,' said Elaine, 'but you will. You have to eat, you know.' She gave the word 'eat' a bizarre inflexion which made me shudder; it was as if she had said: 'You have to die.'

I looked up, my face wet, and noticed her for the first time. She was not especially beautiful, and when Rosemary had been there, I had not spared her a glance. My first impression had been one of long, tangled hair like that of a storybook witch, and giant, dark eyes in a smudgy face. Looking at her again, I saw that she did have a kind of passive beauty, not the beauty of Rosemary, but something deep in the bones of her face. Starved, I thought; she looks starved.

'How old are you?' I asked.

She laughed, softly, without joy. In the shadows,

her face was paper-white, and seemed to hover, disembodied, above the collar of the black coat she wore. She looked terribly young.

'Seventeen? Twenty?'

Elaine turned her face away with a tiny sound, and I realized she was crying.

'How old are you?' I cried, realizing as I did that my meaning was different from the first time I asked.

'I don't know.'

'Who are you?' Suddenly my need to *know* was very urgent. 'Where do you come from?'

She stared at me, as if she did not understand my question, or as if the whole concept was ludicrous. 'No one. Nowhere.'

'You have to eat,' she repeated. It was the uppermost thought in her mind, and from the pocket of the coat which dwarfed her, she drew out a package, wrapped in cellophane paper. It was warm and loathsome to touch. I slipped it into my pocket.

'Thanks.'

Elaine stared at me, and smiled, looking like a frightened child.

'You don't understand, do you?' she said.

'You love her. We all love her.' She looked unhappy, as if repeating a truth in which she had long since ceased to believe.

'I love her.' It was nearly true.

'I was a model. People painted me. At first I used to work in a milliner's shop, you know, serving customers . . . I helped to make the hats, too; I used to be good at that . . . then some men came one day, and they saw me. They said I was a stunner. They paid me really well, just to sit, with a

234

book or a harp, while they painted me. I was sixteen. Then I met Rosemary. She wasn't called Rosemary then, she was called Maria. But that wasn't her real name either.'

'When?'

Elaine ignored me. 'She was a model, too,' she went on. 'The most beautiful thing I ever saw. She was engaged to be married to a young man; another painter, William. I liked him. She was seeing a married man, too. She called him Ned. He was crazy about her as well, but he wouldn't leave his wife. She didn't care about either of them, really; she would create scenes you can't imagine, threaten suicide, but inside she was just playing games. She told me, made friends with me, taught me.'

'She chose you.' I was beginning to understand.

'The young man, William,' Elaine looked at me pleadingly. 'He went mad. He burned all his paintings. He went for her with a knife.'

'Yes?'

'Then he killed himself.' Elaine looked at me bleakly. 'He thought he was free of her,' she said. 'But she came back. She always comes back.' Elaine turned away, and I knew that she was crying again.

'Elaine,' I began clumsily.

She did not look at me; her face was lost in the rags of her hair. Despair emanated from her like a darkness. I was helpless in the face of it; she was like a damned soul, and the keening sounds which came from her mouth were bleak as winter wind.

'Elaine.' I turned her, forcibly, to face me; pushed back her hair. Streaked with dirt and tears, her face looked unmistakably erotic, and I began to see the beauty there, which had caused men to call her a 'stunner'. I opened up my arms and held her; light and thin as a child, she was, huddled up in that man's coat, and the new appetites which Rosemary had awakened in me stirred greedily. I almost expected her to draw away from me; but as I unbuttoned her coat, drawing my own around her body so that she should not be cold, then her dress, leaving her standing in only a torn and dirty shift, she melted towards me with a sigh and a sob. Her white skin was smooth as ivory, and her limbs were like ice, but there was warmth there too, warmth upon which I gorged myself, there on the road, heedless of who might see us. She remained passive throughout our lovemaking, childlike, without passion, but I sensed her despair abate a little and when I had finished, my face flushed, she leaned towards me and kissed me, very gently, on the cheek.

'I was beautiful once,' she said.

'You're beautiful now.' I said it because she wanted me to, but she ignored me.

'Please,' she said. 'Help me.'

'How?'

She looked at me. 'Kill her.'

I stared.

'Kill her. Please. I can't bear it, every night the same. Do it while you still can. God! It's been such a long time. I was glad he killed her. I thought I'd be free. But she came back. She found me again. Since then—' Her voice broke, and I felt despair flood from her again. 'So long and she won't let me die . . . so long with nothing but blackness and blood. She won't let it end. Oh, kill her, please . . .'

I shrugged, once more in control. My meeting

236

with Elaine, as well as the presence of the parcel of food in my pocket, had restored my feeling of power, my ambition. I might kill Rosemary, I thought. But not for Elaine. She would be mine, then, as she was Rosemary's now; she and the others with her.

I looked down at her, but she was crying again, her face hidden in her hair. Without a second glance, I turned and walked away down the road to Cambridge, my shadow, faint in the greenish dawn, spindling before me. My hand crept to check that the package in my pocket was still there; it was, and despite the cellophane wrapping I thought I caught the ripe and dizzying scent of meat. I quickened my pace, instinctively. I didn't want to be on the road when the sun came up.

One

When I returned, Robert was still asleep, sprawled helplessly across my bed. Behind his eyelids, the blur of his eyes moved restlessly from side to side. I latched the door behind me, feeling light-headed from hunger and lack of sleep, and made myself comfortable in the chair, keeping my eyes on Robert.

Elaine's package was still warm in my pocket, and I drew it out, feeling queasy with hunger. It was easier the second time; the meat was rich and flavoursome, its texture at the same time appealing and repellent. I ate it quickly, watching Robert all the time. A few times, he twitched, cat-like, his eyes moved, but did not open, and I finished the meat, cleaned the cellophane wrapping with my fingers, and licked them like a greedy child. I waited for him to awaken, refreshed and strengthened by the food, and once again perfectly certain of what I was going to do, and as I watched and waited, my thoughts turned again, compellingly, to Rosemary.

What Robert had seen the night before, whatever it was that had distressed him so much that it had sent him running to me to be comforted, he had not been able to tell me, except in broken, breathless phrases. He thought he had seen Rosemary having some kind of an attack, he had said, had thought he had seen her *change* somehow, had glimpsed—or thought he had glimpsed—blood. I had heard enough to guess, however, that whatever it was, he had no proof, no certainties which might endanger either Rosemary or any of the rest of us. But I could not let him go without knowing that for sure. Strange, the ease with which I slipped into my new role; strange, how easy it was for *us* to become *them*. As I looked at my sleeping friend, I felt nothing of friendship. I looked into the face of the stranger who had been my best friend, and all I saw was Rosemary.

What had he seen?

'Dan . . . ?' The voice rose, waveringly; my eyes caught the gleam of his in the shadows.

'Dan,' he said again.

'I'm here.'

'I'm sorry about last night,' he said. 'You must have thought me a damn fool.' He smiled at me appealingly. 'I can hardly remember what I said,' he went on. 'You must have guessed I wasn't quite sober. All the upset about Rosemary, you know. I

238

wasn't myself, you understand.'

I listened as Robert retold the tale more rationally, in the light of day.

I nodded when it seemed expected of me, hardly able to mask my contempt. I was relieved that he suspected nothing, of course, but at the same time I felt disappointment in him. To think that Robert, whom I had always thought of as being so shrewd, could have been face to face with that terrible glamour and not seen it; that he could have held it in his arms, and not seen it for what it was . . .

He had even managed to convince himself that he had been drunk the night before; better to believe that than to be forced into believing that the world is a wheel within a wheel, and that a beloved red-haired girl may walk the night with monsters. After coffee, I managed to persuade him to leave. By this time I was feeling very tired; bright motes danced behind my eyes, and besides, I had my own truths to confront, alone, in the privacy of my room. I was supportive, comforting, sympathetic, and between my comfort, my sympathy and my support, I managed to manoeuvre him to the door at last. I closed it with a sigh of relief, moved to my armchair, sat down. I stuck my hands in my pockets, and my fingers encountered the rolled-up cellophane package in which Elaine had wrapped her present. For a second, I was reminded of my schooldays, of the neat little packets of sandwiches with which my mother always crammed my pockets—ham, cheese, pickle and onion, and sometimes a thick slice of plum cake, to be opened and eaten with great care, under the lid of a school desk, in the dim yellow light of the winter schoolroom—the memory was so unexpected and so incongruous that I gave a shocked snort of mirth.

Suddenly, someone knocked on the door.

I stopped, all hilarity gone. Silence. Not a sound.

'Who's there?' No answer. Only that eerie silence.

I opened the door, bracing myself for horrors. For a split second, I actually *saw* them; the shambling Freudian beasts of my imaginings; a monster's monsters. Then the shapes coalesced into one shape: neither small nor tall, a neat and felt-hatted shape, features sharp and hard, cynical blue-grey eyes like broken glass.

It was Inspector Turner.

Two

Doctor Menezies was older than Alice had expected: a big, fat man of about fifty, with thick, black hair and a full beard, who wore his blue pinstriped suit with reluctance and unease, as if he would have been more at home in a lumberjack shirt and jeans. His voice seemed less sharp than it had sounded on the phone, and Alice noticed that he moved his legs with difficulty, as if the joints were painful. Sharp, colourless eyes caught her glance as she preceded him into the office, and he smiled.

'Polio,' he explained shortly, manoeuvring himself into an armchair by the window. 'Do take a seat.'

He gestured towards a couple of chairs by the

side of a desk; Alice sat down. Her eyes flicked over the room, liking it. Green plants in front of a wide, sunny window, a Thai sculpture on a stand, some Indian abstract prints.

'Nice room,' she said, pausing a moment to marshal her thoughts, and fidgeting nervously with the handle of her raffia bag.

'Take your time,' said Menezies, turning a paperweight over in his large sunburned hand.

His colourless eyes gave nothing away; his body language carefully studied to give the impression of quiet interest. He asked no questions, simply allowing Alice to talk, and when she finally stopped, he waited for a long time before he said anything in reply. When he spoke, it was to ask a question.

'Have you been to the police?'

Alice shook her head. 'I didn't think they'd believe me,' she said. 'Besides, I don't have proof of anything. It all sounds crazy.' She shrugged. 'But somehow it seems to make sense. That's why I wanted to find out about Ginny . . . I needed an explanation.'

Menezies watched her for a moment, then his eyes hardened and left hers.

'I'm sorry, Ms Farrell,' he said. 'I can't deal with your problem. However, I'd be happy to recommend a colleague who . . .'

'Why?' Alice was completely thrown. 'I . . . I want *you* to help. Why can't you?'

He shook his head. 'I don't feel qualified,' he said. 'I'm too much involved already. I'm sorry, but I don't want to have anything more to do with this.'

'What do you mean?' Alice was dismayed. 'How can you say that? At least give me a chance. Read

241

the manuscript. Daniel's manuscript. I tell you, it all makes sense. Read it!'

Menezies gave a sigh and ran his hands through his thick hair.

'Ms Farrell,' he said. 'I don't have to read his manuscript.'

Alice opened her mouth to say something.

'Please don't interrupt,' he said irritably. 'I don't have to read it because I already know what's in it.'

Alice looked at him questioningly, but he continued in his new, weary voice, as if every word was a little too heavy for him to enunciate.

'I used to share a room with Jeff Pryce,' he began, 'back in the days when we were young doctors and didn't have very much money. We were still training; we were each assigned an "incurable" patient at the hospital to write part of our thesis on. Jeff got Daniel Holmes.'

He swallowed, almost painfully. 'For three years he worked with Holmes, night and day. It began as professional interest, and developed into a real friendship. He used to go to libraries all around the country to try and find the books Holmes was always asking for. In a way, I think he loved that old chap. I met him a few times, but most of the time Jeff and I discussed him. He was casebook schizophrenic, intelligent, erudite; and Jeff always claimed he was non-violent, despite his fixation with violence. He was a chronic alcoholic and he was taking a lot of heavy medication, but it never seemed to do much good. Jeff and he used to talk psychology together, and he would show Jeff the chapters of his book. In turn, Jeff showed me.'

He paused for a moment, reminiscing. 'The arguments we used to have about Daniel Holmes!

I used to twit Jeff all the time about how much effort he wasted on the man. I wrote the whole of my thesis on the basis of a few preliminary visits to my "incurable", but Jeff . . . there was no stopping him. I think he would have gone on seeing Daniel Holmes for ever, if he'd lived. What was worse, I'm not sure Holmes hadn't convinced him, in some odd way, that what he believed was true.'

Absently, Menezies traced the lines on one worn palm.

'He'd been talking about dying long before his suicide,' he continued. 'Making arrangements and the like. He seemed to think that the people he was afraid of were getting closer, that they wouldn't let him live much longer. I took that for a typical paranoid delusion, and if Jeff had had any sense, he would have too, and taken steps to protect Holmes from himself. But by that time Jeff was nearly as bad as he was. Out of bloody-mindedness he wouldn't give the case to anyone else, so it was too late before anyone got an inkling of the old boy's deterioration. Then one day Holmes cracked and hanged himself, and the whole thing came out. It nearly ended Jeff's career.'

For the first time since he had begun to speak, Menezies looked at Alice and smiled. 'For years after, Jeff Pryce was a man consumed by guilt,' he told her. 'He blamed himself for Holmes's suicide, kept saying that he should have looked after him better. I think the reason for his being such a good doctor was something to do with the fact that he never forgot about Daniel Holmes, and spent his life trying to make up for that first mistake.'

'But I don't understand,' said Alice. 'If you

243

already know about Daniel, why can't you help me? You're probably the only person who might . . .'

'No,' Menezies shook his head. 'Because that isn't the end of the story.' He pulled at his tie to loosen it, and went on. 'Because when you phoned me about Virginia Ashley the other day, and I said I didn't know her, I lied.'

Alice's eyes widened.

'She was Jeff's patient,' said Menezies. 'I told you the truth about that. She was admitted for a few months only. She had been taking drugs, amphetamines mostly, but some hallucinogens too, things like belladonna and muscarine. She was in a state of emaciation, she was addicted to the amphetamines, and she had had experiences while under the influence of hallucinogenic toxins which she could no longer distinguish from reality. Jeff and I had been good friends for a long time; he used to tell me about the most interesting of his cases. Nothing unprofessional, you understand, but enough for me to see that he was really quite excited about this girl. I never saw her, but I think he was quite taken by her. Then one day he came to my house to see me. He looked terrible. He was shaking. I thought he was going to have a stroke. I tried to calm him down, but I really couldn't get much sense out of him, except that he'd seen something or someone who had disturbed him. I gathered that it was something to do with Ginny, or some friends of Ginny's, but on top of that he was also ranting about Daniel Holmes and some things he had read in his manuscript. It didn't help that he was more than a little drunk.

'I did the only thing I could. I gave him a Valium

244

and put him to bed. The next day when I tried to talk to him, he wouldn't tell me anything, and pretended he didn't remember. That night he took an overdose.'

Alice stared at Menezies for a moment.

'He saw Rafe and Java,' she said.

'I don't know what he saw,' said Menezies. 'But maybe now you see why I won't help you.'

He shook his head. 'That damned manuscript.'

'Look,' said Alice desperately. 'Don't you see? No one else *can* help me! You're the only one who will believe me. You knew Daniel, you knew Doctor Pryce. You have to help me. If Daniel is right, then Ginny *is* Rosemary.'

'I don't want to know.' His voice was flat. 'I'm a doctor. I do my job, and I'm good at it. But I do know my limitations, and this is where my involvement ends. I'm not interested in finding out any more about this case, and I wouldn't be any good to you if I was.'

'But she may have killed Daniel,' Alice said. 'And probably Jeff Pryce, too. Who knows what else she might do?'

'I don't know!' His voice was strained, almost cracked. 'I don't want to know!'

'If she went to the trouble of finding Jeff Pryce,' went on Alice, 'how do you know you won't be next?'

Menezies was silent for a long time. 'I won't promise anything,' he said eventually.

'You'll think about it?'

He shrugged. 'Just leave the manuscript with me. I'd like to read it all the way through. But don't expect anything more; any help I can give you will be for my own interest, and nothing to do with my personal practice. OK?'

Alice nodded.

'OK.' She drew the manuscript out of her bag, took it out of the box she had carried it in. 'I'll ring you up tomorrow. Is that all right?'

He nodded.

'Don't get your hopes up,' he warned. 'You'll probably find that I can't help you.' Then he seemed to reach a decision. He reached up to a shelf above his desk where a number of old books were stacked.

'You might as well have this,' he said. 'I'm sure you'll find it interesting.' Alice looked at the spine of the book, and smiled. It was Daniel's book, *The Blessed Damozel, a Study of Pre-Raphaelite Archetypes.* Glancing at it briefly, she saw that it had no illustrations except for the black-and-white reproduction on the cover (a rough-looking sketch by Burne-Jones of his own Blessed Damozel, Maria Zambaco), but she held it tightly, her eyes bright, impelled by the sense of *rightness* she felt at having it.

'Thank you,' she said. 'Thank you so much.'

Menezies gave a twisted smile. 'I'll take the manuscript. Nothing more. No promises,' he told her. And though Alice smiled and nodded agreement as he stood up, carefully placing the manuscript into a big post office envelope, and though she kept her features carefully indifferent while she shook hands with him and left his office, she still felt a tiny lifting of tension within her ribcage, as if a small bird imprisoned there had just begun to sing.

One

I cannot believe that he did not see the guilt written so clearly on my face; it seemed to me that for an endless moment we stood there, speechless, in the little circle of the knowledge we shared. My head spun as his cold eyes held me, appraisingly. Then I recognized my paranoia for what it was and slipped into my artless role. There. I was committed. I had declared war against the light.

'Inspector Turner!' I said. 'Do forgive me; I really wasn't expecting you. For a moment I even found myself forgetting your name.'

The Inspector raised his hat with meticulous politeness. I recognized the technique; he wanted me to speak too much, thereby giving something away. I smiled at him.

'Do come in. I've just made some coffee; would you like a cup?'

'I wouldn't refuse one,' said Turner. As I showed him in, I noticed his eyes flick over the room, taking in the unmade bed, the cold grate, the rows of books on the shelves by the fireside.

'Please take a seat,' I said. 'In fact, I'm rather glad you've come.'

He gave me a mildly questioning look.

'I've been wanting to thank you for your support last time we met,' I said, with a mixture of openness and slight embarrassment in my voice.

'I wasn't myself, you know,' I said. 'I'd had a bad shock, as well as having just recovered from a severe illness at the time, and I'll always appreciate the way you put me at ease.' I wondered if I were overdoing the act; turned, rinsed him a coffee-cup in the sink, and began to fiddle with the coffee-pot, waiting for him to state his business. He did not. I poured, set the cup on a saucer, offered the biscuit tin, watched him help himself to two iced rings. He dipped them, methodically, in his coffee, with the same serious watchfulness, and I began to wonder whether my earlier awe of him had not been the product of my imagination. Then I realized that the biscuit dipping was an act; he was watching me from beneath his eyelashes, waiting to see if I would break.

'Anything I can do to help?' I said. 'Have you found out anything new about that poor woman?'

'No,' said Turner.

'There's been another murder?' I said. It wouldn't do for me to seem too obtuse.

Turner shrugged. 'It's rather early to say,' he said. 'So far, there's no reason for anyone to think that the deaths are even related.'

'So there *has* been another death?'

The Inspector nodded.

'Two,' he said. 'A waitress and a bartender of the Swan public house late the night before last.'

I frowned.

'Wasn't that the place that burned down? I read about it in the paper.'

Turner nodded. 'That's right. But the pathologist's report seems to suggest that the two victims hadn't been killed in the blaze, as we first thought. The bodies weren't badly charred, you know. It takes quite a big fire to destroy bodies.'

'So the criminal tried to hide his tracks by setting the place on fire?' I said, pouring another cup of coffee. 'It's amazing what modern science

248

can discover, isn't it?'

'Certainly.'

'Do you think it's the same man?' I kept my voice interested, though inside I was reeling with panic. *He knows, my God! He knows.*

'I don't think anything.' His tone was final. 'I'm not in charge of the case; Scotland Yard are better equipped to deal with that. It's just that, well, I do like to keep a professional interest in these things.'

'Ah.' His face was unreadable, but I thought I was beginning to understand a little. Turner had struck me from the beginning as being a forceful character. He had questioned me himself instead of asking someone else. His manner was understated, efficient. And this had been his case, the body in the weir had been 'his' body; quite natural, in fact, that he might feel some resentment at the way his case had been taken in hand, so publicly, by the Yard.

The Inspector changed the subject abruptly. 'I see you've changed your lodgings,' he said. 'Was there a reason for that change? Your landlady tells me it was very sudden. You left without even saying goodbye.'

'Ah, yes. There was a reason for that.'

Turner waited patiently.

'I was beginning to be . . . intimate . . . with a young lady,' I said. I did not need to feign embarrassment; my unease was real enough. 'There are reasons, for which the young lady and I—'

'Of course,' said the Inspector. 'Please don't feel that I am prying into your private life. Everything you say will remain confidential, naturally.'

I nodded. 'Thank you,' I said.

249

'I wonder,' he continued, 'whether you could recall whether you were in the company of this young lady the night before last, Mr Holmes?'

He saw my change of expression. 'A routine question, I assure you,' he said.

I frowned, as if I were trying to remember.

'No, I was on my own that night, and I really didn't do very much,' I said. 'I went for a walk around the town, as I usually do on a fine evening, then I worked on my thesis.' I caught his glance. 'I'm writing a book.'

'Fiction?'

'Oh, no.' I shook my head. 'Another stuffy academic tome, I'm afraid. A study in Pre-Raphaelite archetypes. It's a bit of a hobby-horse of mine.'

Turner nodded as if he understood.

'And the Swan Inn? Have you ever been there?'

I shook my head. 'I don't go out very much,' I explained. 'And when I do, I tend to go to restaurants or the theatre, not to inns. I don't have a good head for alcohol.'

I saw his quick glance at the open whisky bottle on the bedstand, and cursed myself for being too talkative. 'For a friend,' I explained quickly.

The Inspector lingered for another few minutes, endless minutes they seemed to me, then he left, raising his hat to me with a polite: 'Thank you for your time, Mr Holmes.' And as soon as he was safely behind that door again, I gave myself up to the outpouring of my tension. I was certain that he knew; how, I could not tell, for I was equally certain that he had no proof.

When I began to think rationally again, I considered what dangers he might present to me.

He was a policeman, he was trained to detect guilt; but I was inclined to think that the advantage was nevertheless on my side. The truth was so incredible that it would take him longer than a lifetime to discover it; and now that I suspected that he was watching me, I could prepare myself. But what if he had me followed? I thought.

The immediacy of my mind's reply stunned me for a moment; unhesitatingly, it flung back, not a thought, but an image of such stark intensity that it overwhelmed me momentarily. It was the image of myself striking, leaping as an animal leaps, my knife held facing upwards, a flicker of light in the shadows. I imagined myself striking, blood spraying across my face precious as the fount of life; saw the man beneath me fall, drowning, disbelieving. I felt the day's meal clench inside me like a fist, and I retched, dry, sharp bursts of nausea which turned into a recurrence of my hacking cough.

Not yet, my mind whimpered, as I clutched my stomach, doubled up on my bed; but the knowledge, untouched by remorse or nausea, stayed with me all the same. *Thought made flesh*, I thought to myself, with a hysterical cackle of laughter; and though a part of me still whimpered and wept, it was that thought, the knowledge that if I had to I would kill him, yes, and feed on his corpse, that followed me, relentlessly, into the unconsciousness of sleep, and the cryptic convolutions of my labyrinthine dreams.

Two

Alice could no more have passed a fair by than she could have ignored a packet of biscuits in her food cupboard. It was not that she particularly liked fairs; rather, she liked the *idea* of them, the memories of childhood that they recreated, better than the reality. Popcorn stands, coconut shies, candy-floss—pink sugar-sticky nests for wasps— tall men with loud voices and cold travelling eyes, the roundabouts and the big wheels and the hot dogs and the litter and the smells; wagons with gilt doorways and exotic secret signs. Pushing and shoving, children jostling for pockets in the crowd . . . doughnuts, spending all her pocket money on the shooting range only to win a single yellow balloon which burst on the way home, the high reek of animals in tiny cages, flying high on the big wheel, walking through the fair late at night with Joe. Joe winning a coconut on the stand, laughing. Joe eating pizza from a greasy paper plate, watching the stars both electric and real. A maelstrom of conflicting memories, like confetti, showered her from every side. For a moment, she looked at the worn, faded sign, gilt and red: FAIR! BIGGEST IN THE SOUTH! BIG RIDES!! Remembered, reached for her purse, and walked in.

Voices, music, voices, noises; beginning-of-summer British at play. And in the background, the lovely spires and turrets of the colleges, incongruous and timeless above the crowd. Alice smiled, tucked her shopping bag under one arm and began to move towards a toffee-apple stall, bought the biggest, stickiest-looking apple she could see, and moved away, taking her little circle of tranquillity with her. Aimlessly, happily, she wandered through the field, occasionally pausing to watch the roundabout with its thin, wild-eyed horses rushing past, the people at the stalls. (A father of three trying to win a teddy bear at the shooting-range: 'Go on Dad!'; a wide-eyed schoolboy staring enviously at the hoopla, twenty-pound notes taped enticingly on to wooden blocks, the caption RING IT RICH; a tall, thin boy of sixteen at the dartboard, grinning, lifting a giant pink rabbit into the arms of a laughing girl.)

A man pushed past her, one hand stuck in the pocket of his coat, the other holding a can of beer, he was almost close enough to Alice for his swatch of dyed black hair to brush her face. For an instant, he seemed fleetingly familiar, and she strained to see his face, but he disappeared into the amusements arcade before she could know for sure. She bit into her apple again; it was a good one, tart and pink inside, the deep-red toffee still slightly warm from the steaming vat of sugar on the stand, outer shell just beginning to go hard. She wondered why toffee-apples always turned out to be so difficult to eat: too wide to bite into, too sticky to get a firm hold on to. She had to take tiny, tiny bites, delicately working at the outer shell with the tip of her tongue. A man with tattoos on his face was selling rides on the roundabout; for a moment Alice was tempted, but decided against it. Fairground rides are only fun when you're not alone, she thought (doggedly shaking the memory of another Alice, hand-in-hand with another Joe, endlessly neck-to-neck in an interminable roundabout race between two horses, dappled grey and pink with cornsilk manes, while the roundabout played 'Camptown Races' and the world spun to a different tempo), and moved on.

He was standing by the main gate, unmistakable this time, stranger in the sunlight than he ever was at night. Even the crowds of students seemed to skirt him, so that he stood alone in a little pocket of isolation. Despite the warmth of the day, he was wearing his coat buttoned and turned up at the collar, and beneath it, at his ankles, she caught the gleam of sunlight on the chains of his motorcycle boots. Impossible to know whether he had seen her; surrounded by people as she was, there was no cause to be stricken with panic, but she was.

He seemed to be waiting.

She turned, mingling with the crowd again. Suddenly, her eyes were everywhere, testing, measuring the crowd with a new insight. 'If Java is there, then maybe Rafe is, too,' she thought; and on the tail of that, 'If Rafe is there . . . maybe the others . . . Elaine, Zach, Anton.' Maybe other ones she had not yet seen. Perhaps they were watching her in the crowd. Perhaps they were waiting for her.

Once again she quickened her pace. The smells of the fairground were much stronger now, dizzying; the crowd parted to allow her to pass, and she felt singled out, too noticeable. She began to jog towards the far end of the field, where the caravans and the animals were, where she could slip out unseen, in safety. A face snapped up out of the mill of people to look at her; a man with red hair tied back, black crosses dangling from his

254

ears. Alice met his eyes for a moment . . . saw the bird tattoo on his face. He flashed an insolent, disturbing grin at her, blurred again into the crowd. A woman brushed by her with a touch as light as snow; she started, looked around, but the woman was gone. From the corner of her eye, she glimpsed a thin figure standing beside a hot-dog stand, flaxen hair shocking in the bright sunlight . . . she wheeled round, convinced that this time, she knew it . . . she saw a girl, eyes hidden under a spray-mask of black make-up, bleached hair puffed out from her head. She ran in slow motion to the end of the field, slipped in between two caravans, washing hanging from a guy-rope between them, looked for the way out. A goat, tethered to a railing, interrupted its grazing for a moment to fix her with a long, glassy stare. She skirted round a sleeping dog, muzzle in its paws, and rounded the caravan.

'Hello, Alice.' It was the girl from the hot-dog stand; for a moment, Alice felt no panic. Then, as she took in the face, the features behind the make-up, the hair coarsely sprayed white showing traces of red still at the roots, she froze. Stupidly, she stood there, her eyes wide, her hands dangling absurdly, the only motion in a world of stillness.

Ginny took a step forwards.

Alice dodged in-between the caravans, heedless now of the dog, which looked up and started a loud, aggressive barking. She was a long way from the crowd of holidaymakers now, isolated at the end of the field. Her feet were heavy on the baked ground; the world juddered and jolted as she ran. There was a man coming towards her; red hair and earrings, a bird tattooed on one cheekbone.

He smiled, the sunlight snickering off his gold tooth. He pulled something from his pocket, something which flicked the sunlight into Alice's eyes in a long ribbon of polished steel. With a gasp, she changed course abruptly and dashed off across the field towards the people.

Behind her, Ginny made a tiny sign to Zach and Rafe, and the three of them fanned out, walking purposefully towards the other end of the field. Beneath the sprayed mask Ginny was smiling, and in her hand she carried a fat post office envelope.

Two

Joe quickened his step, eyes flicking left, right, left into the side-streets as he moved. His pace was elastic, half-running, half-walking, hands deep in his pockets, shoulders slightly hunched. He might have been an eccentric poet, on his way to some mysterious rendezvous, some crazed bespectacled inventor racing towards a new discovery.

For an instant, he stopped in mid-stride, thinking he saw her, then moved on. He saw her in a dozen places after that . . . but when he turned, Ginny was never there. It was past two now; she should have been home. She should have left a message, at least. He slowed his pace fractionally, trying to analyse the sense of urgency which had motivated him. He remembered Alice telling him how Ginny had gone out that night, telling him how two men had come looking for her, two men who were her friends. A vision of Ginny sitting in some JCR, some public lavatory, maybe a bus shelter or a bandstand in the park . . . Ginny smiling . . . nodding . . . Ginny shooting a long needle into her arm while the friends looked on, smiling.

He began to run, checking every little passageway, every shop window, every archway, railing or gate. She should never have gone without telling him, he thought. The world was full of bloodsuckers, profit-merchants eager to take advantage of someone as innocent as Ginny. How she had managed to get this far without going under he didn't know, especially after what she had told him the other night, strangely childlike, strangely untouched, sitting in his armchair, hugging her knees. She had told him everything. The drugs, the dirt, the men . . . with a little smile and a wistfulness in her eyes. By all rights the bloodsuckers should have got her.

Strange little girl . . . but she had guts enough not to let the bastards grind her down. She had gone right back to the edge and had come back all on her own, and that made her stronger than he was, stronger and braver.

With increasing anxiety Joe continued his search of the streets of Cambridge. Figures milled around him. The primitive rhythm of the crowd intensified the throbbing of his headache; the distant music of the fairground tunnelled into his brain.

Joe didn't like fairs much. There was something sinister about them, he thought, about the people who came and went, carrying the promise of returned childhood under those faded canvases, under that well-oiled and hidden machinery. Once, when he was a child, his father had taken him to the fair; like all little boys, he had loved it, had eaten candy-floss and baked potatoes, ridden on the roundabout, bought a balloon from an old woman with a scarf round her head and the warmest, most twinkling eyes he had ever seen . . . and right at the end, when his father had suggested that maybe they might get going home now, he had insisted on having one last ride on the roundabout.

'OK, Joey.' Joey's dad had always been the most tolerant of fathers; half a child himself, he had had just as good a time as Joey himself that day, and he had sat Joey comfortably down on the jewelled saddle of the big fairground horse and had turned away to look at the arcade.

'Hi-ho, Silver!' Joey had whispered. 'I'm the Lone Ranger.' Liking the sound of the phrase, he had repeated it: 'I'm the Lone Ranger!' As if in agreement, the roundabout had begun to move. Being six, Joey had momentarily felt the ripple of Silver's muscles beneath the hard pink hide; the horse had bucked, and the Lone Ranger had fought bravely to keep on. 'Hi-ho, Silver, awayyy!' he had cried, and the roundabout had sped up, the horses spinning and bucking, black horses and white horses and exotic red and blue and yellow horses, their manes flying, their glass eyes wild and frenzied. Joey had been ecstatic. He had felt as if all eyes were turned towards him, the brave boy on the wild horse. He had gripped the jingling reins with fierce joy, faces blurring around him with the speed of the ride. Suddenly, a face had swum up towards him out of the half-gloom; neon-lit and almost ghostly in the changed light, he had recognized the balloon-woman, earrings glinting exotically in a million refracted undersea colours.

'Heyyy!' Joey had shouted, recognizing a friend,

258

but the roundabout had moved on, spinning like a sun. I'll call to her when I get round the other side, Joey had thought, grinning in anticipation, holding his breath for the biggest shout he could give, loosing his left hand from the reins to wave . . . but when he had reached the other side, the shout had died in his throat, the grin from his face; the sight of the balloon-woman had been etched into his memory long after the roundabout moved away, long after it had stopped. She had been standing at the edge of a little group of people, a family, perhaps, though there might have been two families: a round, balding, red-faced man, a younger man with a beard, two women, one with a baby, and some other children.

The one who caught Joey's eye was a little boy, maybe his age or maybe a little older, a round, sturdy little boy wearing dungarees and holding a blue balloon in one hand and a half-finished candy-floss in the other. His eyes had been round and very serious. Joey liked to think that the boy had been watching *him*, the brave boy on horseback, and had made sure he looked especially big and reckless every time he passed him. There had been a purse sticking out of the little boy's pocket, at the back, the kind of purse you don't miss in a hurry, yellow and with a picture of Donald Duck on the front . . . but this time when Joey passed them, the purse had been missing. He had known it was missing because he had seen it, for just one instant, in the hand of the cheerful old balloon-woman, before she had noticed him noticing and stuffed it into her pocket. And that was why little Joey had ridden for the rest of his roundabout-trip without shouting, without jigging on the horse and shaking its mane, without doing anything but going over and over what he had just seen.

In a way, Joey had known that in that moment part of his childhood was over. He had got off the roundabout as stiff and straight as a little soldier, suddenly desperate to leave . . . but she had been there and waiting for him, and Joey had been smitten with terror that she might touch him, that she might *curse* him like those princes who were turned into swans, and he had begun to run towards the arcade where Daddy was . . . but not before the witch had caught hold of his shoulder with a brown old hand like a claw, not before he had looked into her eyes and she had whispered, with all of her venom and ancient rage: 'You never saw nothin', did you boy? Never saw *nothin'*!'

And Joey had nodded, going white, backing away like a cornered cat, because if he hadn't, he had been certain that this witch-woman would have killed him. And suddenly here was Daddy, Daddy coming out of the arcade, calling in his loud and cheerful voice, and in that moment Joey had wrenched himself free from the old witch's claw and run away towards the light. He had dreamed of her later, but he had never told.

And it was on the tail of that half-submerged memory that the thought struck him—no, not the thought, the *knowledge*. Of course! That was where he should look for Ginny. If she was in trouble, it would come from the fair. He did not know why, but the knowledge was suddenly real enough.

She was there.

He quickened his step.

Two

Alice realized soon enough that there was nowhere to go. Behind her, there was Rafe and Zach and Ginny, and, at the exit, Java waited, with that air of steady confidence. The envelope in Ginny's hand had paralysed Alice's ability to think; her mind raced in circles, fragments of thoughts chasing each other around her brain. How had she found the manuscript that Alice had left with Menezies? The post office envelope filled the world, bore down upon her like the Juggernaut. Then she was running, holding her shoes as she sprinted barefoot across the field.

As she reached the main part of the fairground, she glanced briefly over her shoulder, and she caught Ginny's gaze across the crowd, and Alice knew that she was *not* safe, that the crowd could afford no more protection to her than a herd of cattle. The only realities were here, between the cold lavender eyes of the nightwalker-thing (all vestiges of the human stripped from her face, unmasked in all her hatred) and the knowledge in Alice's own eyes, the knowledge which enabled her to *see* what no one else could see, the monster behind the lovely face.

Maybe that was what stopped her. Maybe it was that look above the black spray-mask, the triumph in the cold gaze . . . she held it, like a bridge of ice, held the gaze and returned it, with all the hate which she was capable of conveying.

She could see that Ginny understood her. She smiled, showing her teeth. Now, as if her anger

261

had cleansed her of fear, Alice felt suddenly cool and controlled. From the corner of her eye she saw someone moving towards her, and instead of moving back, she moved forward, smiling fiercely all the time.

She felt rather than saw the figure stop. Someone must have known that this was no place for a confrontation. Someone was afraid of the risk. Somewhere between here and there they had locked in combat, she and Ginny. No more fear, she thought. They understood each other too well for that. Round one began.

Alice turned and began to walk towards the exit, making sure to replace her shoes. The others hung back on the periphery of her vision, but made no attempt to come any nearer.

Ginny's gaze froze the back of her head, and Alice glanced back, almost casually, and kept on walking. The exit was twenty yards away.

But maybe they'll just kill Joe instead.

The thought struck her like a jet of cold water, so that she faltered, almost losing her poise. And then she was out of the gate, and into the safe, open street, and the game—whatever it had been—was over. After a while she began to shake.

Two

This time, he was sure it was her. Joe craned his neck above the crowd, oblivious to stares and irritation.

'Ginny!'

The figure turned, and it was not Ginny;

262

disappointment sleeted through him, and for an instant he wondered how on earth he could have mistaken that girl for Ginny. Then it *was* Ginny again, Ginny almost grotesquely changed. And, calling her name, thrusting with his elbows, he began to bludgeon his way through the mass of bodies.

'Ginny! Wait!'

The girl turned to face him, standing alone by the side of a shooting-range, pale face, pale hair, pale hands, looking frail and thin in her black clothes, ghostly against the glare of the lights. As he reached for her she shrank a little, and he smelled the acetone scent of the white spray in her hair above a sharper, smoky smell like burnt paper.

'You came,' she said.

He held her close. It was not the time for questions, he thought. She was so clearly vulnerable.

'What're you doing out here?' he said, forcing a little laugh. 'You certainly got me going for a while, you and your disappearing act. I thought you'd walked out on me.' He smiled, looking for needle-tracks and trying not to make it too obvious.

Ginny stared at him blankly, and Joe knew he had to get her home. She didn't look like someone who'd OD'd and there weren't any needle marks on her arms. But she did look ill, and he'd had enough experience to know what some pushers cut their dope with; it wasn't called 'shit' for nothing.

'What're you on?' he whispered, putting his arm round her shoulders.

Ginny looked at him, hesitating.

'Have you got any more?' he said. She'd have to ditch it, of course, he thought; the last thing he wanted was another barney with the police. He kept his voice quiet and patient.

'Have you?'

Ginny shook her head. Good. That was something. Now all he had to do was to take her home and to hope that she hadn't been taking strychnine or arsenic or washing powder or anything else in her China white. Christ, what a mess. And where had she got the money? The last he knew of it she had been broke, just eligible for the lowest of social security payments. He swore softly under his breath as he took Ginny by the shoulders and led her, like a blind child, out of the gates and into the street.

If he'd had any sense, he thought, he'd have ditched her as soon as he found out. He had enough hassle looking after himself without taking on a screwed-up junkie girlfriend. He'd seen enough of them when he was on the road with the band to know that the bad trips and the cold turkey and the overdoses weren't all you got, no: sometimes you hit the jackpot and you got the collapsed veins, the brain damage and the nasty diseases from dirty needles. That was why he'd never really bothered with much more than the odd bag of grass. Joe didn't mess with junkies; it was a rule for happy living.

But this was Ginny.

Fairground noise faded behind them, their steps real once more against the cobbles of the alley. She followed him, head bent, one hand tucked confidingly into his, the other clutching a fold of his coat. His heart did a quirky little off-beat at the

264

sight of her, the mask of paint leaving her skin oddly, touchingly vulnerable, and at that moment, he knew that he would have done anything for her, he would have died for her, like a folk-song hero, her name on his bloody lips. The violence of his longing almost stunned him; lost in thought, he remained silent until they reached the flat. They crept in aware of the watchful presence of Joe's landlady. Then he said, as he opened the door: 'There's nothing you haven't told me, is there?'

She centred her dark gaze upon him, almost aimlessly, shook her head.

'You've got to trust me,' Joe went on. 'I love you. I want to help you. You're too smart to be into that kind of thing. You know that, don't you?'

Ginny smiled, almost imperceptibly, nodded.

'Right. Come on in, then.'

Again, the almost imperceptible nod.

'So why do a runner on me like that? Who'd you go running to?'

Her response was inaudible, a fluttering of breath, like paper. Joe took her hands again, trying not to crush them in his hot grasp.

'I can't hear.'

'I was frightened . . .' It was hardly more than a whisper. 'After what Alice told you . . . You'd go away . . .'

'No chance.' It was almost beyond him to refrain from grasping her there and then, crushing her to him. Fear stayed him. She was too small, too slender. He wondered if he would ever dare to seize her in passion.

'No way. I'm here for the duration, Gin. You and me against the world. Forget Alice. We don't need her.' The words came rushing out, all the

265

words he had never found for Alice, words he had dreamed, whispered, imagined in the night, words unspoken, hidden away. Never had Joe spoken words like that before; but now, somehow, he found them, and the veils across Ginny's eyes were lifted, despair changing into something approaching hope. And in his wonder and the joy of that breakthrough, Joe was still conscious that at some point in that outburst, the details of which were already misting over in his thoughts, he had made a promise, only half-realized, less than half-remembered. There would be no regrets, that he knew. Whatever he had pledged was hers now. Only looking into Ginny's eyes, he knew that. But as he put his arms around her and gently led her inside, he was still able to wonder what it was he had promised her.

Two

There was no time for euphoria. She had not escaped, but had won for herself instead a kind of reprieve. No time to glory in that, she thought, but yes, time, a little, to prepare herself for the attack that was certain to come. Glancing through the window at the street, she picked up the phone, dialled the Fulbourn number, let it ring.

'I'd like to speak to Doctor Menezies, please. It's very important.'

'I'm sorry, the doctor isn't available. Who is this, please?'

'I'm Alice Farrell. I saw the doctor this morning. Please, when will he be back?'

'I'm afraid the doctor is ill. Doctor Lowrey is dealing with all his cases for the moment.'

'But he was fine when I saw him this morning!' said Alice.

'There was an accident, just after lunch.'

'What kind of accident?'

'I'm afraid I can't—'

'What kind of an accident?' Alice heard her voice rise. 'Please!'

The receptionist hesitated.

'The doctor was hit by a car, Mrs Farrell. A hit-and-run. The police were called. They're looking into it.'

Alice hung up in silence, feeling numb and slightly sick as she faced the truth which had stalked her since she first set eyes on Ginny.

There was no escape from them now, she thought. The timelessness which Alice loved so much had made Cambridge a prison for her, a stronghold for the nightwalkers; a nomad town where nearly two-thirds of the population came and went at intervals of three years apiece, a town of rented rooms and stolen intimacies. They walked the same cobbled streets, stood in the same archways, heard the same hymns from the chapels over the river from decade to decade, their faces mingling with those of their prey in the stream of memory.

They passed unnoticed as they lingered on the edge of that river of humankind, choosing their victims carefully: here a tramp, to be found in a pool of blood and wine, there a tourist travelling alone, elsewhere a student with needle-tracks on his arms and a reputation for dangerous living. Cambridge has a high suicide rate; statisticians tend to blame this on stress or drugs. Easy to find reasons; so easy to ignore the evidence.

How they must have laughed, she thought, revelled in their youth and power! How like angels they must have felt! How many dreams must they have haunted? How many chosen men remained with Rosemary in their hearts and memories? Oh yes, they must have laughed, as they slipped invisibly through the crowds, touching flesh in a million ways, scenting the thrill of trapped blood.

Alice shivered, almost glimpsing for an instant the fatal glamour. Then she stood up deliberately. No more, she told herself. Time had finally run out.

She wondered whether she would be sick. The panic was almost unbearable, with a momentum of its own, like spinning, like vertigo, like the biggest roller-coaster in the world with grinning Death at the controls and nothing but spangled black horror all around.

'Oh shit,' said Alice, and began reluctantly, with the drums of panic still hammering, to plan her attack.

One

Rosemary had been right; I was ill for the next few days, and the light hurt my eyes, but in time, even that symptom faded. I lay low in the warehouse, never alone; sometimes it was Rafe who stayed with me, sometimes Elaine, sometimes Zach. I ran a low fever for close to two weeks, eating little, but drinking much, for it seemed to me that I would never quench my thirst. I saw Rosemary only briefly, and then, never alone; she would appear for a few minutes to check on my progress, or show me the newspapers to keep up with Scotland Yard's manhunt. It seemed that the 'Body in the Weir' had been shelved for the time being, to be replaced by the 'Swan Inn', an unrelated case of murder and arson, thought by the Yard to be a cover for burglary. Two bodies had been found, too badly charred to be recognizable, but dental records showed them to be those of the bartender and the waitress. 'A man is being questioned by the police,' blared the newspaper in self-satisfied tones, a pronouncement which afforded sly amusement to my companions.

Rosemary would read these accounts to me, then she would be on her way again with a smile and I would be left to grind my teeth in helpless love and hate. She looked radiant on those visits; her face vivid, her hair like clouds. She wore dresses of flowered crêpe and silk chiffon and white linen with rose borders; every time I saw her, something different, exotic almost to indecency in that austere post-war decade, dancing through life like a fever dream. She radiated power on those visits, power and purity. The very touch of her cool fingers on my neck was enough to leave me sweating with desire; unstable as I was, I am always amazed that I never blurted out my revolt, stupidly, in my fever. Perhaps I did, and my wardens never thought anything of it. I suppose that, in that respect, we of those warehouse days and red nights were all brothers.

It was on one of these occasions, as I was nearing recovery, that she told me she was married. I was sitting by a window, looking on to the bare land at the back of the building. I had been reading a book, but had laid it aside when she came in, pulling back the blanket to stand up and greet her. Java was waiting at the door, his shoulder against the door-jamb. She was lovely that day, her hair all windblown against a dress of drab green, her eyes sparkling with youth and life.

'Danny, congratulate me!' Her voice was breathless from the wind, her hands stretched out impulsively.

'I'm married!'

I hesitated for a long moment, aware, in the preternatural stillness, of a pulse just below my left ear, ticking away my blood's time.

'Who to?' I managed to stammer.

Rosemary frowned.

'Well, Robert, of course. Who else could it be?'

Robert. I had hardly even thought of him for all the time I had been there. It was not that the news came as any surprise; no, I had already in my heart given him up as lost, but now that it was a certainty, the feeling of guilt (yes, and jealousy, too), came upon me with such heaviness that I was forced to slump back on to my chair to avoid collapse.

'Why, Danny.' Her voice was petulant now. 'I do believe you're cross.'

I found my voice, not without an effort. 'Of course not. I'm very happy. I'm just not quite well yet.'

'Poor Daniel.' She leaned forwards, her hands cupping my face. A faint scent of lavender reached me from her skin, like a memory. 'Better?'

I nodded, not trusting words.

'Robert . . . Is he, will he be, I mean?'

She laughed, enchantingly. 'Oh, Danny,' she said. 'You're so sweet. Is *that* why you looked so cross? You thought he'd be one of us? Oh no. I never mix business with pleasure.' She kissed me lightly on the cheek. Her kiss was like a tiny sting. 'He's nothing. Protection.'

'I don't understand.'

She sighed.

'Robert *loves* me,' she said. 'He loves me now to the point of unreason. He's a man; he needs something to protect. It makes him happy; it makes him feel strong. Not every man gets the chance to die for what he loves, Danny; in a way, he's one of the lucky ones. Your Robert would never be strong enough to face the way things really are; I have given him the dream.'

Something must have shown on my face; she smiled, touched my hand with the briefest, chastest of kisses.

'Don't worry, Danny. He's happy.'

'Why?' My voice was almost a wail.

Rosemary sat on the arm of my chair, and touched my face with her fingertips.

'No one said it was going to be easy,' she said. 'Being chosen isn't easy. We stand out in crowds. The cattle smell us, envy and fear us. They know that they are natural prey. That's why we need a protector. Someone to lie for us, to shield us, to die for us if he has to. Do you think that the hunt for us will die down? The police are stupid, but some day one of them will get too close. They are slow and dogged; eventually some accident will lead them unwittingly to our door. We have to feed; we can travel, we can hide, but one day they

271

will catch up with us. And when that time comes, when the search comes too close, we need to give them a sacrifice. Someone to take our place.'

'Robert.'

'He's the ideal choice, Dan. He provides impeccable cover for me, for the others, even you . . .'

'Me?'

'Of course. When he's caught, you can come out of hiding. What better reason for you to disappear than if you think your best friend is a murderer? You didn't want to betray him, so you ran away. At the very worst, all they can charge you with is shielding a suspect, and you know as well as I do that they wouldn't put you in prison for that. And after that? Well, you can find your own protectress then, your Roberta, if you wish. Just let your killer instinct take over.'

I thought that over for a few moments, though not, I am afraid to admit, with the horror I should have felt. I had done too much by then to show a normal human response, and I had betrayed my friend too many times already to feel squeamish about doing it again. Be content in knowing that I made the right choice, though for the wrong reasons. I think it very likely you too might have done the same thing. But at that time I really considered what she gave me: that enticing poison draught. I wanted it. I needed it with all the longing of my killer instincts. I reached for her, clasped her like a dream in my arms; I felt chiffon, air, smelt the perfume of lavender, but her substance eluded me as it always did, and it was so gentle that I hardly felt it that she pulled away from me.

'Later,' she said softly. 'When you're whole again. Ask me again.'

'One kiss,' I said.

Rosemary smiled.

'Flesh,' she said, with a smile. 'You're still so human, Danny. Later, you'll understand, later, when you're with us for ever, that blood is power. Blood.'

'I love you,' I said (it was almost true).

'Then love me,' she answered, holding out her wrist, its deltas under her blue skin.

I did as she said, power flooding my mouth, running down my chin, drowning my veins in the secret music of its flowing. Great thoughts filled my inspired brain, thoughts which I never quite remembered later, but which flowered there in the darkness as I fed upon her and she upon me, thoughts of creation and infinities, each unfurling in the red darkness like hearts in flower, longings and ecstasies undreamed of, pleasures of the blood more monstrous and sublime than were ever any pleasure of the flesh. For an instant I was void, a wailing infant in the eternal absence of myself, then I was creator, galaxies in my mind's eye, then annihilator, blood at my fingertips, blood in my voice, blood filling my giant footprints as I walked. Afterwards, I could never recapture that fleeting moment of absolute power, but, God forgive me, I lusted after it evermore, though all I can remember with any clarity now is the taste, so like the taste of tears.

One

Summer grew hot; the crowds came that year after all, and we endured the heat as best we could.

We came out at night, not that the days could hurt us, but because it was our time. The warehouse was airy and dry, like a hospital ward, and we were comfortable. I say, 'we'. Zach and Elaine, with the little boy Anton, shared my exile—maybe to keep an eye on me. Rosemary lived with Robert in a house close by, in Grantchester. Where Rafe and Java lived, I never knew. I suspected that they kept close to Rosemary, to guard her, but could not know for sure. The days passed uneasily, but with a kind of harmony, like the long summer holidays of my childhood, but the nights were sharp-focused, full of the glamour of the chase, intensified all the more by the police presence in the town which was constant, but as discreet as could be managed. We were careful, however, choosing our victims carefully among the vagrant population, singling out a tramp, a tourist travelling alone, someone who would not be missed until much later. I did not see Turner for a long while, nor did I read his name in the papers; the Scotland Yard investigation was headed by a Superintendent Lamb, who, as far as we could guess, seemed to be wasting his time and resources in dragging the Cam for more bodies. The investigation had veered away from us.

Rosemary had money, stolen in part from earlier victims, some of it given to her by her previous benefactor, and sometimes we bought wine and cigarettes from the late-night off-licence, and drank and smoked in our borrowed lodging like dilettante students discussing art and poetry. I saw her every night; she came late, after midnight, and I often wondered to myself how she managed to come so regularly without having to explain herself to Robert. Maybe she drugged him, I thought. Even if she did not, he was enough under her spell to let her do anything she wanted.

I kept on the fringes of events; believe me or not, I killed no one, but I did feed, ravenously. I rode the carnival-wheel all that time, in nights beyond dreaming or description. We drank whisky and wine mingled with blood. We fed from each other. We loved one another in ways which transcended the purely physical, though my appetites called for that kind of loving, too. And still, behind the curtain of that past glamour, there was the hidden canker of my hate, the culmination of my love and my hunger. At present, it seems that my descriptive powers are forsaking me; I can hardly even visualize the glory of that time, as if the memory of what happened after that has cast a darkness over the images there. I remember happiness, without knowing what form it took, remember the words, power, joy, rapture, without being able to visualize even the simplest memory.

At times such as these, I can almost delude myself into thinking that she is really dead; it takes a great effort of will to continue my story at times such as these. My young doctor thinks that the writing itself is perpetuating my delusions; that as an academic, I have been too much involved in reading my truths from books, and seek to make my fabrication true by writing it. Others disagree, seeing my work as an effort from my subconscious to exorcize the sickness within my psyche.

I tell this to my young friend to cheer him up; he really does seem very depressed about my case nowadays, even when I let him beat me at chess. I tell him it isn't good for him to become emotionally involved with his patients. He smiles, sadly, knowing that my seeming rationality is no indication of any improvement in my condition; sometimes I hint to him, in the words of my namesake, that when he has eliminated the impossible, whatever remains, however improbable, must be the truth—that what he fears might yet be true. Sometimes, when I say these things, he looks so wretched, feeling, perhaps, that he has failed me, that I fabricate some insane remark, simply to justify his beliefs, and he rewards me with his smiles, and maybe a game or two of chess. He tries to feed my interest in psychology by telling me about some of his other cases: the girl next door is a schizophrenic, sixteen years old and wracked with personality disorders. He feels confident that she will make a full recovery, however, as she responds well to treatment. Responds well to *him*, more likely. I want to tell him to be careful . . . Rosemary was just another such young innocent. Suddenly I feel very uneasy about that girl. I want to tell him to keep away from her, but I have teased him too much today. He humours me, but does not listen.

Time, I must try to remember how short it is; but the pills they give me stretch time, so that wasted days melt into wasted days. I was telling you about the summer before I killed her. Most of all, I have to tell you *how* I killed her, so that you too can do the same, when your time comes. And you must not be as weak as I.

You must kill the thing you love, as I, in the end, was not wholly able to do.

They can be killed. I know they can, and the action is as simple and dreadful as the taking of any life. Any hand can do the deed, any mind formulate the desire. But this is not enough. Their strange life can be taken, but not kept. It re-emerges like some deadly transparent thing of the sea, beckoned by the rays of the moon. They are not immortal, though their kind has lived almost for ever.

Their seed is everywhere, dormant, like a poison tree under the orchard, their roots quartering the earth and spreading like maggots into the minds of men. The evil seed may lie sleeping for a hundred years, before it wakes, shaking the snow of winter from its face and looking up into the sunlight. The ancient priesthood knew how to stamp out the seed of the night; they burnt it and buried it in stone and lime, but still it lived, in memories, in tales, in song. Every child who has longed to be Cinderella or the Wolf Boy, every young man who has dreamed of raising a dead princess with his kiss has sown the night's seed, Proserpine's underworld seed which grows the blood-red fruit.

Desire.

It takes a certain kind of desire, but all it needs is one person, one soul, to call her back, and willing or not, she will return. A single soul. That's all it takes.

And, oh—to be Rosemary. To burn bright as

277

Rosemary . . . to wield that power for myself. What would I give for that? What have I already given?

August . . . die she must. September, I remember. If only I did. But my mind wanders so. She had control over my mind that summer, as surely as she possessed my body. It was a sweet possession, feeding me, feeding from me. I didn't think about Robert at all; Rosemary was ours, mine.

How long it might have gone on, I do not know. I was comfortable in the warehouse; Elaine washed my clothes and brought me food. She even gave comfort to my other appetites when Rosemary was not available. Her only wish was to die, and there were many things in those days that I did not understand, one of those being how Rosemary could keep Elaine alive against her will. I had come to accept that all my companions, except, perhaps, Rafe, had died once before; Elaine had (or at least, believed she had) been dead for about fifty years, Java more than that. Zach had died in France during the First World War, but remembered little about it. That, or he was unwilling to speak of it. Anton had been killed by Elaine; from what I could understand, his presence gave Rosemary some kind of a hold on her. Perhaps he was her brother; I could never make her tell me. Perhaps—who knows?—he was her son.

All Elaine could tell me was that Rosemary had called them all back, though she knew nothing of how. I supposed (wrongly, I see now) that she had used some kind of necromancy; I had already steeped myself in dubious magic and ritual, and fancied I knew something about the subject; perhaps I even had some notion of trying it for

278

myself some day. I never had the chance to try, but it happened that I did see it in action, quite unexpectedly, late that August. The day Elaine finally achieved her heart's desire.

One

Do not think that Inspector Turner had given up the search for the Cambridge murderer so easily. He had not. I was not accused, but one tentacle of the search had begun to move once again in my direction; or so Rosemary told me.

Maybe in our hunting we had become complacent; maybe Turner had been observing us for some time, and we had not been aware of it. Maybe he had had Robert watched, and Rosemary had led him to us unawares. Whatever the reason, we were in the warehouse, all of us, one night, drinking and playing cards, when I was suddenly conscious of an unaccountable sense of unease. Maybe there was a stronger psychic link between Turner and myself than I knew at the time.

It was perhaps two o'clock in the morning; we had had to wait longer than usual for Rosemary, and we had hunted among the destitutes of Cambridge for our prey, wary of the late-night bars and the occasional lights in the windows of the colleges. Passers-by were infrequent after the police scare; people were wary of going out late, and we were all the more noticeable for the lack of other folk in the town, but it was always possible to find a tramp or vagrant lurking around the river or passed out in the doorway of a shop. We had even acquired a taste for such victims, as the alcohol in their veins gave the blood an extra piquancy.

We were all of us glutted and somnolent, drinking wine brought by Java and Zach, and smoking, and the room in which I slept was already littered with the empty bottles. I often drank on those nights; I think it helped me to distance myself, to taste the thrill of the hunt without the pangs of mind or conscience. The light was dim, coming as it did from a couple of candles stuck into empty wine bottles; the windows were covered with sacking. No one could have stumbled upon us by accident.

At first, I attributed the sensation of being watched to paranoia; I drank another glass of wine to still my nerves, but that did not allay my fears. In fact, the wine only seemed to attune my new sensitivity even more.

At last, I could not bear it. I turned to Rosemary.

'Are you sure no one followed us here?' I asked.

She looked at me. 'Poor Daniel,' she said. 'Do you think I care? There are plenty of us to deal with them if they did.'

In some ways, she was very innocent.

'I think there's someone outside,' I said. 'Watching the warehouse.'

Zach made a gesture of dismissal; he had been out at about midnight, and had seen nothing.

No one seemed to want to take my suspicions seriously, except Elaine, who looked up, her eyes huge in her shadowy face.

'I think Daniel is right,' she said. 'I've been feeling uneasy, too. I think the police have been watching us. I've heard odd sounds. I've seen people in the street.'

Zach shrugged.

'Send the kid out to see. No one will suspect a kid.'

Everyone agreed, except, strangely, Elaine.

'I'll go with him,' she said. 'It isn't fair he should be sent out on his own.'

'Afraid the bogeyman'll get him?' said Zach. 'What is he, scared of the dark?' But Elaine, in some ways, was as untouchable as Rosemary herself. A soft movement of material from the shapeless coat she was wearing, a scuffling of feet, and she and Anton were already gone. I followed them, at a distance, feeling unsteady because of all the wine I had drunk. I heard the sounds of their footsteps on the cement floor. I was just beginning to believe that I had imagined everything when I suddenly heard a cry.

Elaine screamed, and I heard her footsteps and Anton's, suddenly much louder, running through the building. Instinctively, I hid. A light flashed on close by me, and three figures ran past. I heard a voice, shouting: 'Stop! Police! Stop!'

The three men rushed past me, dwarfing me, monstrous against the white wall. Sounds behind me, from the room I had just left; I guessed it to be the others, finding their own way out of the building, scuffling, shoving, pushing away from the light. I knew that Zach and Java had a considerable armoury of weapons (stolen or otherwise acquired) hidden in the building. I was inclined to believe that the police might be in for a nasty surprise.

There was a large window in the passage, which was loosely boarded up. Thinking quickly in my panic, I yanked the boarding away and looked out. The drop was not high; I measured it in my mind, then pulled myself through the uneven gap, looking around for more police. I saw no one; the moonlight was veiled, shadowy. I ran out across the yard and into the bushes and long grass at the back. I lay on my stomach in the undergrowth, the smell of growing grass and cool earth in my nostrils. Across the flat ground, I could hear raised voices. Two shots were fired in rapid succession. I pressed my face against the ground.

When I happened to look up a few seconds later, I saw three shadows; I guessed them to be Rafe, Java and Rosemary, moving at speed across the yard. In a moment, they were out of the gate and out of sight down the road. I dared to raise myself higher, and as I did Elaine came running silently round the angle of the building, the tail of her greatcoat flapping stiffly out behind her. I could hear her breath, sharp in the quiet night air. She was crying, repeating something to herself which I could not hear. As she reached the path to the gate, I saw her clearly, in the faint moonlight, and realized that all was not well. She was limping, holding her dark coat around her as if for protection. In her hand I could see that she carried a knife, a long straight blade which flicked the light back at me like a mirror. I think she saw me, as I crouched in the shadows, but she did not betray me by as much as a glance. Instead, she turned to face the men who were following her, with a cry of challenge or despair.

One of the officers called to her: 'Here! You! Stay where you are! Drop the knife!'

Elaine drew back a little, holding the weapon in

front of her. She knew how to use it; had done so often enough already. The officer began to move towards her, while the other two fanned out to take her from either side.

'It's no good,' he said. 'Put down the knife.'

Elaine took a step back, away from me. For some reason, I felt that she was trying to lure the men away from me, and I shrank back into the dark.

The man was not more than a dozen feet away from her now; as he spoke, he had been edging gradually closer, one hand in his pocket. Now, he lunged at Elaine. One hand brushed her coat, but Elaine was too quick for him. The light arced from the knife she was carrying, then the man was on his knees. His expression was one of stupid surprise as his belly released its contents, then he began to scream, and I cheered Elaine inwardly from where I was hiding. But almost as soon as it happened, the second officer fired his gun, and she fell.

Now it was my turn to stare; I kept expecting her to get up.

The two other officers approached—I was not surprised to see Turner there. The other man went to his fallen companion, who was still very noisily alive. Turner went to Elaine, touched her with the toe of his shoe, knelt down to feel her heart. I saw her face for a moment, still and very white, lips parted to show bared teeth. Then I heard his voice, quiet and with a quaver in it which belied his apparent calm.

'It's a woman,' he said. 'She's dead.' Then, with sudden viciousness: 'Shit!'

He hesitated for a moment, then regained some of his momentum. Addressing the other officer,

283

who was trying to move his injured companion into the car, he snapped: 'Don't waste time. Call an ambulance. Hurry!' He was obviously shaken; even though gun regulations in those days were rather more lax than now, perhaps it was the first time he had ever shot someone in the line of duty, and the man's coat Elaine had been wearing had probably deceived the officers as to her size and the danger she might present. I almost sympathized with him, although the shock of Elaine's death had hit me hard. You see, I had really thought that we were immortal.

For maybe ten minutes, as I watched the ambulance arrive, the sound of its bell shockingly strident in the quiet night, I waited for Elaine to come back to life. For that time I was half-convinced that she would. It was only when she was loaded on to the stretcher on a polythene sheet that I began to think that there would be no resurrection. Even as the ambulance set off at full speed, its bell ringing, I felt an absurd stab of hope: surely there would be no need for the bell to be rung unless she were still alive? Cursing my stupidity, I realized that I was forgetting the injured officer.

'I really thought he was here this time,' said Turner in his quiet, intense way. 'I smelt him, damn it. We should have brought more men. Damn the Yard, I warned them there was something going on here. What's the good of bringing in three hundred men to investigate if they're going to waste their time fooling about the river? They don't know this town.' For a moment, he brooded. 'Who the hell was she?' he said. 'Was she with him?' The other shrugged.

'Maybe we're on the wrong track altogether,' he suggested. 'Maybe Holmes isn't our man.'

Turner shook his head. 'He's our man. And he was here. I *know* he was.'

The second man seemed less certain. 'What about those others?' he said. 'I'm sure I saw at least two more, but they must have got clean away. Where do they fit in?'

'I don't know.' Turner paused. 'But if we find who the dead woman is, then we'll find Holmes. I'm sure of it.'

Their voices drifted, and remotely, I considered my situation, still anaesthetised by wine, blood and shock. For a moment, I wondered how they would react if I just stepped out of hiding and said hello. Then the humour of the thought shifted, became something poignant; suddenly I *wanted* to be able to step out, into their light, like a child ending a game. I wanted to see their faces, to touch them, to run to them to be comforted. It was more than just a desire to confess. I choose to see what I felt then as the essential humanity in me in revolt, the thing which, through everything I have undergone, has never quite abandoned me. I stood up.

'Inspector.' His expression was almost hilarious. I found myself smiling, an absurdly wide, boyish grin. Turner brought out his pistol and pointed it at me.

'Put your hands up, Holmes,' he said. 'I want you to put your hands on your head and turn round. On the count of three. One. Two. Three.'

I shrugged and did as he asked.

'There isn't any need to be so careful,' I said. 'I haven't got a gun.'

He ignored that, and I sensed rather than saw

285

him bring out his card from his breast pocket. He read my rights quickly, without expression, like a little boy reciting grace before his birthday dinner.

'Take off your coat.'

I did so, watching as he searched the pockets by feel, still looking at me from the eye of his gun. He threw the coat back to me, keeping out of range of my hands.

'Put it on.'

'You needn't have worried,' I said. 'I wasn't going to hurt you.' That was true enough; what I had felt as I hid in the yard of the warehouse, that kind of love, invaded me again. I wanted to touch him, to make him real in my mind. I wanted to talk to him, to hear his voice. I wanted his wife, his children, his memories, his secrets, his bad habits. I wanted the cigarettes he smoked, the food he ate, the dreams he dreamed.

'You can turn round now,' he told me as his companion moved towards me to fasten the handcuffs around my wrists. To my mind, the situation was unreal, and I an observer, watching with a kind of detached interest, like a man who knows himself to be dreaming.

'Thank you.' As I turned I saw his face with great clarity. Thin light sketched his features in graveyard grey, highlighting the outline of the gun in his hand. I know nothing about guns; I couldn't even guess if it was loaded.

'You killed Elaine,' I told him as we walked towards the Wolseley. 'That was her name. Elaine.'

'Who was she, Holmes? Your lady friend?'

'No.'

'Where does she fit into all this, then?'

'She was a victim,' I said. 'Like me.'

286

Suddenly, I realized how tired I was. Like a dreamer awakening from a nightmare, I felt drained of everything. Perhaps it was the fact that Rosemary was beyond my grasp, possibly for ever, perhaps it was remembering Elaine's face as she died.

At that instant I gave it all up, the glamour, the promise of eternity, the power and the beauty. It hurt to give it up, but the giving was a deliverance.

'I'll tell you everything,' I said.

Two

He had left Ginny asleep on the sofa, and as he opened the door quietly to let himself out, he glanced back and saw her curled up, her face tucked into the crook of her arm. A sensation of utter protectiveness overwhelmed him. Joe, who was normally as jumpy and ill at ease as an adolescent, whose life was a constant roller-coaster of highs and lows, had experienced only a very few moments of true stability. Asked to define his life, the word 'comfortable' wouldn't even have had a mention. And yet now it seemed to him that all his insecurities had been bled away, that some miraculous transfusion had taken place so that suddenly he felt in control, all tension drained from his body. He went down into the street, the new sense of well-being inside him. He was smiling.

Two girls in jeans and T-shirts looked at him strangely, almost drawing away, despite the hour and the bright sunlight . . . one of them, trying later to explain why the memory of the man remained with her even though Cambridge was full of strange people, could only vaguely remember why.

'His eyes were creepy,' she said at ten o'clock in the Union Bar that evening, voice charmingly slurred after five gin and tonics. In a novel, she might have been able to say: *'His eyes were like a doorway into another world.'* But in real life she simply got drunk, went to bed with a young man from another college who she didn't even like, and woke up the next day with a depressive hangover and a vague sense of something lost.

Joe went on his way without even noticing her, riding the carousel of his thoughts. Absently he rubbed his knuckles, noticing as he looked down that the back of his left hand was dark with bruising.

It was Alice's fault. Experimentally he flexed the hand. Damn, it hurt. He wondered whether he had broken any bones. It was his left hand, the one he needed most when he was playing. If Alice had made him bust his left hand . . . Come to think of it, he hadn't seen her show much sympathy. In fact, he wasn't at all sure she hadn't been glad. Well, he'd get that straight when he saw her, too. He'd promised Ginny he'd square things with Alice, and he would. She'd done enough damage as it was. He might as well square it with her now. Still smiling, he quickened his step.

*   *   *

Alice picked up the knife, testing its weight. It was a long carving-knife from her kitchen, wooden-

288

handled and singing with sharpness. It made Alice feel almost faint to even think of using it on a person, but by now the worst of the sickness and the shaking had dissipated, to be replaced by a sense of unreality, as if true logic had been replaced by the strange surrealist logic of dreams. Just follow, thought Alice to herself. The knife knew where it was going far better than she did. Like the point of a compass it showed the way, implacably, back to the house in Grantchester.

Alice swallowed with difficulty, wondering if she dared eat anything, but even at the thought she felt herself gag in nausea, and turned towards the door. There could be no more delaying it, she knew. She had to be in Grantchester before night, when the nightwalkers came.

She had taken two steps towards the door, was taking a third, when someone knocked.

Alice froze.

'Dammit, she's out.' Joe kicked angrily at the door, twice, but only managed to hurt his foot. He looked at his watch; almost six. Ginny would be waiting for him at home, counting on him; he didn't want her to be alone in the house when night fell. She was so afraid of the dark.

But it rankled, it really did, to let Alice win, to go home to Ginny without having done what he promised. Maybe if he . . . He looked round, saw no one in the street except an old man with a dog. He turned, walked fifty yards or so down the street, then turned into the alley which led round the back of the houses. He was certain she was in there.

Alice's garden was quite large, long and overgrown with weeds and trees allowed to run wild. It was easy enough to cut across the neighbour's garden into hers, easier still to make his way through the tangle of bushes and flowers until he reached her back porch. Joe looked over his shoulder again, and idly tried the back door. It was locked, but he had expected that. He looked at the lock, decided that it was too strong to force. But there was a window. Forcing himself to be calm, he picked up a stone from the path. He lifted it to shoulder height, then tapped it—a tap was all it needed—against the corner of the glass. The window cracked. Gently, so as not to cut himself, he pushed the glass, pressed it until a corner of it loosened. Then he worked at the loose part until it came out of the frame altogether. He laid the piece of glass on the path beside him, began to work on another piece. It came easily this time, and bit by bit he soon managed to free the whole of the pane. One pane was all he needed; it was enough for him to be able to push his arm through the door and unlatch it.

He looked inside. 'Alice?' he called softly. 'Alice?'

One

In 1948 the police station in Cambridge was much smaller than it is today; there was one officer on duty that night, and he blinked stupidly as he saw the Inspector and I come in. I suppose that he had heard all about the excitement earlier that night; there was a morgue too, annexed to that little station, and maybe he had seen them bring in

290

Elaine from the ambulance. I imagined her lying, somewhere behind one of those doors, her hair spread out like a mermaid's on the white enamel. With my new, all-encompassing affection for humans and their world, I smiled at the duty officer.

'Don't be worried,' I said. 'I'm not going to hurt you.'

'Be quiet,' snapped Turner. Then, addressing the other man: 'Have you contacted the Yard yet?'

The officer nodded. 'Yes, sir. Someone'll be here in about an hour.'

'Good,' said Turner. 'Hold the fort for a while. I'm going to take a statement from the suspect.'

For a lazy instant, I wondered what he meant, then I realized that the suspect was me. The thought made me laugh again. It felt good.

'This way, please,' said Turner, directing me to the far end of the police station. I was absurdly pleased by his polite tone; everything about him pleased me then. I turned and smiled.

'In here,' he said. He was near enough for me to see his eyes, cold and grey as nails hammered into his face.

A little square room, tiled in white, as I had imagined the morgue, with a little table, two chairs and a latrine bucket in the corner. A strong smell of disinfectant hung in the air, reminding me, comically, of the boys' toilets in the junior school I had attended as a child.

'Sit down.'

I chose the chair next to the wall, took off my coat and sat on it. Turner sat on the table, looking down at me, his eyes unreadable. The PC who had been with him when he came in had joined us, and

291

was sitting opposite, pen poised over a little pad of paper to write down what I said.

We waited like that, in silence, for a long time. After a few minutes, I recognized Turner's technique of allowing the criminal to incriminate himself and, despite myself, I grinned. I *wanted* to incriminate myself, wanted to rejoin society, even at its lowest level; I had no desire to escape. I felt almost light-headed; there were no more choices to be made, no more decisions, nothing. It had all been done, though, decided for me.

'So, what do you want to know?' I said.

'Why you did it,' said Turner. 'The vagrant woman in the weir. Those people in the pub. And what about the body we found in Grantchester churchyard, all cut up into pieces? Was that you, too?'

I shook my head.

'It wasn't me, but I was there. It was the others. Rosemary.'

Turner nodded, although I could not tell by anything he said or any movement he made whether he believed me or not.

'Rosemary?'

I told him.

I told him everything I knew or had conjectured about her, exposed her utterly. I betrayed them all. I cleansed myself of them. Inspector Turner showed no sign of reaction at all; he simply listened politely, nodding from time to time as if I were simply corroborating something he already knew. When I had finished, he stood up, and I looked at him expectantly.

'Are you going to arrest them?' I asked.

'I'm going to get some coffee,' he said. 'I think

it's going to be a long night. Maybe by the time I get back, you'll have thought up a better story than that. I can wait. I like stories.'

And at that he and his companion left the room, shutting the door behind them.

I waited, knowing that he would come back soon. After a while, thinking about the coffee, and while I still had some privacy, I went and used the latrine bucket.

*   *   *

I must have dozed for half an hour or so, when I was awoken by the sound of footsteps. Someone was walking down the passage, their feet making a light pattering sound on the tiles. I remember thinking what a light tread the Inspector had. The footsteps stopped outside the door of the cell; I heard someone fumbling with keys, pulling the latch. I looked idly towards the door as it opened, then froze.

It was Elaine.

She was barefoot, her toes blue with cold against the tiles, and she was wearing a kind of hospital robe, stiff white linen, tied at the sides with white ribbons. Her face was even paler than usual. There was blood at the side of her mouth, as if she had fed too greedily, and blood had trickled down the inside of her leg, leaving a broad track of dark-red going up from her ankle out of sight into the robe. Her hair was like seaweed, her eyes brimming. With a shock, I realized that what she was wearing was not a hospital robe at all.

My system must have shielded me against the shock; it is one thing to believe, academically, in eternal life, and another entirely to watch a dead woman come back from the dead. I gaped, my head reeling, thinking: another ride on Rosemary's ghost train.

Elaine beckoned, wordlessly, and until the same happens to you, you will never understand the compulsion of that gesture, its not-to-be-disobeyed power. In a similar way does the statue of the dead commander beckon Don Juan to his last meal. There was no refusing her. I stood up, feeling faint, though by then I was used to horrors, and followed her, without a word, into the corridor. The door leading to the morgue was half-open, and as I passed, I glanced in. It was how I had imagined it: the tiles white in a crude electric light, half a dozen bare slabs for the bodies, the tiny sound of running water, trickling down the gutters by the sides of the room. I followed her into the front of the station, rubbing my eyes. Dark flowers blossomed behind my eyelids.

The station was a butcher's shop. Two men lay face-down on the floor in pools of tacky blood; someone, in his struggles, had struck the wall as he fell, stricken, and had left the prints of his hands and his body against the white paint, like grisly negatives. A third was slumped across the desk, his head twisted at an unnatural angle; Anton was sitting on the desk beside him, using a scalpel to cut pieces from his face, as absorbed as a child doing a jigsaw. Stunned as I was, I managed to see all the bodies well enough to realize that none of them was Turner. Somehow, the thought gave me an obscure satisfaction; but I said nothing.

They were all there, Rafe and Java standing on either side of Rosemary; I noticed that Rafe's face was bloody, and so was his hair, as if it had dipped in blood as he fed. Zach was standing at the door, keeping watch. Rosemary was at the window, looking out into the night; she turned as I came in, and her lovely face was suffused with triumph.

'Are you still afraid?' she said. 'Look . . .' and she made a sweeping, ballet-like gesture to indicate the carnage around her. Her eyes were limpid, pitiless; so must Helen have looked upon the wreckage of Troy. 'Is there a limit to what we can do?'

'You raised Elaine.' It was all I could say.

'Of course,' she said. 'I look after my own.' I heard a sob from behind me, as Elaine's breath caught in her throat.

'But Elaine is a romantic,' said Rosemary. 'She imagines the peace of sleeping underground. She wants the unsullied purity of death. The innocence of the grave.' She laughed. 'You make your choice, and so do I. And the chosen stay chosen. For ever.'

'But how?' I sounded foolish, a child seeking to comprehend miracles.

She shrugged.

'It's childishly simple,' she said. 'Even Christ did it, when he said to Lazarus, "Come forth." All you have to do is to call, and the chosen will come. Desire invokes, Danny, and we are the children of desire.'

I didn't understand what she meant at the time, I was numb with the aftermath of despair. I simply accepted what she said as I had accepted everything.

But now, after years of thought, I think I understand what she meant. Too late to help myself, but not too late for you, I hope. She was

295

the child of my desire, my dream-lady, my Blessed Damozel. I thought that after Robert's death I would be safe from her; I thought myself strong enough to withstand her call, but here, at the end of everything, I know better. *I* was the one who wished her back. I think I recalled her, as she raised Elaine, as she knew I would. In remembering, I recalled her; what is 'remember', except another word for the same thing?

Two

'Dammit, Joe, you gave me a shock. What the hell were you playing at?' Alice had stopped half-way down the stairs, and was looking at him incredulously. Why had he come in through the back door? she thought. And hadn't that door been locked?

Joe simply looked at her without a word, and Alice recalled with sudden unease the look on his face earlier that day as he'd crunched his knuckles against the wall. And the back door *had* been locked, she knew that, remembered checking the garden before she drew the bolt.

'Come over here a minute, Al.' His voice was eerily normal. 'I want to talk to you.'

'Just a minute.' She looked around, unease accelerating into panic now, for a means of escape. Somehow she *knew* that the man at the door wasn't quite Joe, the way that when she had painted the Ophelia pictures she hadn't quite been Alice. Alice felt her hands begin to tremble again, stilled them with an angry gesture. The panic was forced deeper, became a dull, controlled ache in the pit of her stomach.

'I was having a shower,' she called brightly. 'I heard you knock. Just sit down, and I'll be there in a min.'

'Take your time.' To her new sensitivity, his voice was a shade too bright. She saw him, suddenly, in her mind's eye, standing at the fairground gate like a garish sentinel, a toffee-apple in one hand, his brown hair sprayed red, and with a band of shadow over his eyes.

Urgently, she scanned the landing. The windows were too high to jump from. She would have to use the stairs, she decided; she would have to talk her way past him. She checked the weight of the knife, wrapped in a piece of cloth and pushed awkwardly up her sleeve, and went downstairs to join him.

He was waiting, sitting in Alice's armchair, idling with a paperweight, a fist-sized knuckle of white marble shaped like a surrealist cat. A swatch of hair had fallen over his eyes, hiding his expression, but he looked up when he heard Alice's footsteps. She looked sick, he thought as he took in her pale face, her thin lips, then the alien rhythm took over again, compellingly, forcing the alien thoughts into his mind. Joe didn't try to combat them; to tell the truth it was a good kind of feeling, a natural high, so to speak. He let the rhythm direct him.

Alice looked at his upturned face, half-expecting to see the face of the nightwalker behind his round, academic glasses. For a moment the lenses flashed light from the window into her eyes, then he grinned, a peculiarly Joe-like expression, at the same time endearing and rueful.

'Joe,' she began in a shaky voice, 'I'm in trouble. I . . . I can't tell you what it's all about, but I need you to promise me something.'

Joe shrugged. 'Well, that depends—'

'No!' said Alice. 'You have to promise. You have to keep away from Ginny tonight. Make some excuse. Say you're ill. Just keep away from her, just for tonight. Please.'

Joe frowned uncertainly. He remembered that he had wanted to talk to Alice about Ginny, but didn't quite remember what he had wanted to say.

'Why?' he said. 'Is there something wrong?'

Alice sighed. 'I'm not sure,' she said. 'There's so much I can't prove, and so much that sounds crazy. I can't expect you to believe it all. But I know that Ginny's friends are involved. I know that at least one man is dead, and that they had something to do with it . . .' She looked at Joe. 'I know you don't want to hear this,' she said.

'Go on,' said Joe.

And Alice, encouraged by the fact that he had not lost his temper or refused to hear her story, began to tell him everything, even more than she had intended to say. She told him about the paintings, the dream which wasn't a dream, Daniel's diary.

'At first I thought it must all be a coincidence,' she said, finding the pace of her narrative now. 'I thought I was going crazy, twisting events to suit myself. I *was* jealous of her, you know, that's what made me think that what I was finding out couldn't be true, but there are just too many things all pointing to the same conclusion. I have to find out her involvement in this.'

Joe looked at her in silence for a moment, then

he nodded.

'I see.' His expression was blank for a moment, then he let his shoulders sag and took his glasses off to wipe them.

'I've been a bastard, haven't I?' he said in a subdued tone. 'I blew up at you this morning, I even made a hole in your wall. I behaved like a complete prat, and the stupid thing is, I already knew you were right about those two blokes. I'd seen them before, and I saw them again today with Ginny. I knew they were selling dope as well, and she was taking it. Shit, you can't know somebody like that and not . . .' He pushed his hair out of his eyes. 'I just hoped that it wasn't true, I hoped I could stop it being true by bawling you out and not listening. I just couldn't take the idea that I was being taken for a ride again.' He paused. 'I'm sorry, Al.' He made an angry little gesture and rubbed his eyes with the back of his hand.

'Poor Joe.' Alice sat on the arm of the chair and put her arms round him, smelling tobacco from his coat and the clean smell of his hair. Nostalgia overwhelmed her.

Quietly Joe shifted the white marble paperweight to his right hand. The rhythm grew stronger inside him.

Alice saw the movement of his right hand, and she twisted, instinctively, to the side. The paperweight missed her head, and smashed into her shoulder. Joe was taken off-balance as the momentum pitched him out of the chair, and Alice had the time to leap back, to try and get something in-between them.

She had time to think: *That's not Joe.*

When suddenly he sprang, raking at Alice's face

with the hand which held the paperweight. She jumped back, at the same time kicking out at him with her right foot to keep him at a distance. She wobbled, almost lost her balance, and in the time it took for her to regain it he was on her, grabbing her by the hair and lifting the paperweight to smash her face. Alice kicked again, reaching his shins squarely this time, taking him by surprise. He loosened his grip and fell backwards, hitting his head on the angle of the table.

A second later Alice had scrambled to her feet and was at the door, unlatching it with trembling fingers.

'Alice! Come back! Alice!'

But his voice was already distant—a jumble of words on a rushing wind.

Her eyes were stinging as the wind rushed her down the streets and alleys towards Grantchester. And maybe it was Alice's imagination, but as she made her way across the river to Rosemary's house it seemed to her that, with every step she took, that fairground reek grew stronger: smoke and sweat and roasting peanuts, burnt sugar and petrol fumes and animals.

PART FOUR

Beata Virginia

One

She found a place for us to hide; in the apartment she had used before she married Robert. It was quite large, with two bedrooms, a bathroom, a little kitchen and a living-room, and she had continued to pay the rent because it was a good place for her to stay when she didn't want to be seen by him.

Not that poor Robert ever asked any questions; when she went out she told him she was going to see a friend, almost challenging him to make something of it, but he accepted what she said without a word.

Rosemary left us in the flat, gave one of the spare keys to me, and the other to Zach, and went home. It had been a long night, and she meant to go and get a shower, and sleep. For myself, sleep was beyond me. I tried for an hour or so to persuade Elaine to talk, but she would do nothing but cry, curled up on the sofa with her face hidden in her hands. I abandoned hope of ever getting a clear account of what had happened from her, so I indulged in a solitary game of chess (left hand against right), drank most of a bottle of red wine Zach had left me, and tried to make sense of what had happened that night.

Perhaps even then, I had some hope of proving to myself that there was a logical explanation for everything. Elaine had not been dead, merely stunned. Inspector Turner had missed her heartbeat as he felt in the thick coat she had been wearing. It must seem strange to you that I tried to disbelieve it, I the man who had witnessed so many dark miracles that by now I must have been immune to them. But I was not. Perhaps even then, I hoped to awaken from the nightmare, to prove to the ever-optimistic doubter within me that there was an explanation for all of the past few months. I was insane. I was ill, perhaps terminally so; maybe I had a brain tumour which gave me delusions. Somehow, the thought of death did not alarm me as once it might have done. It was the thought of life, yes, of *that* kind of life, which made me shudder.

The thing which convinced me of the reality of what I had seen was its very simplicity. If I had had to invent a resurrection my mind would have formulated something complicated; there would have been rituals, invocations, magic, science, anything but the bleak simplicity of this monstrous act. If there had been something there for me to analyse I would have felt secure; I could have believed in Mary Shelley's Frankenstein monster, brought to life by science, I could believe in secret amulets and magical potions, in words of power and holy signs, but not in this. My mind rebelled.

Despairing at last of either sleep or quietude, I decided to go for a short walk, thinking the night air might calm my thoughts. Even the knowledge that by now the carnage at the police station must have been discovered did not deter me; I found that I really did not care whether I was arrested or not. I took my coat and hat, opened the door to the apartment and locked it again behind me. I saw no one as I went down the stairs and into the street; although the dawn was beginning to show, threadlike, on the horizon, it was still too early for any idle passers-by to be abroad. I was about to cross the street, making my way to the river, when a small movement caught my eye, from the alcove at the side of the building, where the dustbins were kept. My heart jumped, but I told myself that it could only be a dog, nosing for scraps among the rubbish.

The movement came again, a kind of fitful scrabbling among the bins, too big to be a dog. I took three steps forwards, blinking into the darkness. The figure pressed itself further into the shadows, as if it were trying to sink into the brick wall of the alcove. It was a man.

'Hey, you,' I called. 'Who are you? Come out.'

The man did not reply, but I caught a little sound from his lips, a kind of wordless plea.

'Come out!' I stepped forwards again, overcome by curiosity, and saw him lift grimy hands towards me in supplication.

'Leave me alone.' His voice was little more than a whisper. There was something in it that I recognized, and I squinted at the man with a new interest.

'Who are you?'

He turned his face towards me, pale above the crumpled suit. For a minute I blinked, unable to put a name to the familiar face, then I recoiled, even though the man was in no condition to do me harm.

'Turner!' I said, and he cringed away. The man's icy poise was broken for ever, his face a mass of tics and twitches. He was evidently in deep shock.

'I won't hurt you,' I said, reaching out a hand. He pulled away with a little cry but I followed him into the alcove.

305

'I won't hurt you,' I repeated, pulling my flask from my coat pocket. I shook it, guessed it to be about half-full.

'Here, drink this,' I said, 'it's whisky.' A grimy hand struck mine, knocking the flask aside. But I forced it against his mouth. Some of it went in. I heard him swallow, noisily, like a dog, and then I heard the sound of him sobbing.

'I followed you,' he said, almost inaudibly. 'I didn't know where else to go.' He was silent for a minute; I used his own technique on him, waiting for him to say more.

'What did you see?' I said at last.

'I was in the lavatory. Someone came to the door. Higgins answered. It was a girl. He asked her in . . . Oh God!'

'You saw her,' I said. 'You saw Rosemary.'

'Rosemary . . . I never thought . . .'

'What else did you see?'

'She came in,' he said, in his whispering voice. 'And those others came in behind her. I hid . . .' He whimpered, a pitiful sound.

'What else did you see?' I hated to torture him, but I had to know.

'She went into the morgue . . . and I heard her say: "Elaine". Just that.'

'Is that all she said? Just her name?' I could hardly believe it had been so easy. And yet, thus had Christ raised Lazarus. 'Come forth.' Some miracles should never be performed.

'Turner. I want you to listen,' I said. 'I need to talk to you.'

He looked at me, his eyes wide. 'You know, I didn't believe you,' he said. 'I thought you were lying, or mad. I was so sure of everything.'

'Listen,' I said. 'I know a place. It's safe. I'm going to take you there. I want to talk to you.' I lowered my tone. 'I need your help.'

He turned his gaze towards me.

'Help?'

'That's right,' I said. 'It's safe where we're going. You can sleep there.' I hesitated, thinking that in his condition, he might not be in a state to help anyone. Yet, I thought, if he was mad he might still be of some use. I had no use for sanity on my side. What I needed was madness.

'You're going to help me,' I told him. I put my arms around his shoulders and half-lifted him to his feet.

'We're going to kill Rosemary.'

*   *   *

I looked after Turner for three days, in the first of a deserted row of houses just outside Grantchester. He was shocked and terrified at first, but began to recover as time passed. I developed a kind of friendship with him, spending as long as I could with him while the others were sleeping. I brought him food, clothes, bottles of wine. Most of all, I talked to him. I told him what I planned to do, no longer for my own sake, but to salvage the little humanity left in me. He had moments of sanity interspersed with long periods of mania, reminding me forcibly of myself in those first dark days of the hunger.

When the little death came upon me, I went out and hunted on my own, or I went to Elaine for scraps of the night's hunt, but I did not run with the others again. For one, I was too afraid of the police, who had now launched a national inquiry into what they called the 'Cambridge Police Station Tragedy'. Hundreds of extra police had been sent for from London, and policemen patrolled the night from ten o'clock onwards, questioning any passer-by. A semi-official curfew had been established, although Lamb of the Yard had proclaimed that the killings had probably been the work of a lunatic. So while the police chased rumours and false trails through the town Turner and I talked, feverishly, like two lunatics ourselves. I went over my findings and my theories, sharing every thought with him.

Rosemary permeated all our conversations. Rosemary at her most beguiling and her most deadly. I shared her with him like a lover; the sweetness of her and the poison. With him, I exorcized her, invoked her, murdered her a thousand times in thought and intention. For three days we contemplated murder, then we struck.

It was the last day of August.

Two

She was not certain what she would have done if anyone had been in the house; but they were not. It was boarded up and deserted, as were the houses all around, and she knew, with sudden certainty, that this was where the creatures met.

Looking at the place for the first time in daylight, she saw that the roof had partially collapsed, the slates stripped off to reveal the blackened beams. All but the very highest windows were broken, half-shielded from the rain by boards, but at one glass-fanged window the rags of a scorched curtain still remained, flapping in the wind like a black flag. Cautiously, she came closer, until she was facing the door. This too was broken, the wood rotten and the hinges half-torn away so that it stood ajar, almost invitingly, like a door in a fairy tale. Behind a cracked glass panel to her left, Alice could still read the names of the erstwhile tenants:

S . . PPER 1
. . SHLEY 2
. . KIN 3
KEN . . . Y 4

The house had stood empty for decades. Alice looked around, but the street was deserted. Then, taking a deep breath, she pushed the door and stepped forwards into the darkness.

The house was damp and stank of urine, mould and an under-smell of the circus. The nightwalkers were not the only ones to have used it as a hiding-place: on the ground floor Alice found traces of other visitors, sweet-wrappers and silver paper and plastic bags and empty tubes of glue. A box of broken toys had been dumped in one corner of the room, but dust covered it in a thick veil. Alice found herself wondering what had happened to those young trespassers, and she shivered.

The house was so silent and deserted that until she reached Rosemary's apartment she had almost begun to believe that she had been wrong, and that the nightwalkers had found some other place to hide; but as soon as she pushed the door to apartment 2 ASHLEY she knew that her instincts had been right.

There was a mattress in one corner, piled with blankets, and a table, and some chairs lined up against one of the smoke-blackened walls. Wine bottles littered the floor; a pack of cards had been left spilled across the rotten boards. A shoe-box containing syringes and silver paper on the window-ledge. Candles in empty wine bottles. Tied to the door-handle, a white rag, marked with bloody hieroglyphs.

The atmosphere and the sense of predestination almost paralysed Alice. It seemed to her that there were ghosts in the very air she breathed, ghosts like fumes invading her mind so that before long she was the one who felt unreal. Her sense of scale temporarily eluded her; here she was infinitely tiny, helplessly huge, suspended in limbo, racing faster than light. She was a puppet, jerking here and there on a cherry-coloured twist of string, dancing, spinning, struggling to breathe . . .

Alice tore herself from the paralysis and ran to the window, gasping air. The ghosts and illusions dissipated, and she forced calm upon her fraught spirit, learning to breathe again, reassembling her fractured thoughts.

There could be no more cowardice, she thought. No more hope of evading this commitment she had somehow accepted. When she had escaped from Joe, a hot stitch biting into her side as she ran down alleys and dodged under archways, she had somehow shed most of the burden of fear which had paralysed her. How it had happened she did not know; she simply knew that somewhere between Cambridge and Grantchester she had decided to *survive*, and that however ill-equipped she might appear to bring down Rosemary and her friends, she would give whatever she had to do it.

A sound jolted Alice out of her reverie, and she turned, the roots of her hair beginning to stiffen. In a single movement she had pulled out the knife and had turned to face the slight, grey figure which had detached itself from the shadows to speak to her.

'So you're here at last.'

Alice, the knife held out in front of her, adrenalin-charged blood singing in her ears, recognized the sparse grey hair, stubbly face, rheumy eyes and pink muffler; it was the tramp she had met the previous night. For a moment she hesitated, but, remembering Joe, held on to the knife.

The old man nodded, almost covertly. He seemed sober now; maybe it was still too early in the evening for him to be really far gone.

'What are you doing here?' Her lips were dry.

The old man nodded again.

'Same as you,' he said. 'Just about. I reckoned you'd be here sooner or later.' His critical glance took in the knife, her pallor, the stubborn look behind her fear. Scared, he thought, but behind all that, there was an underlying toughness of which even she herself was not aware.

'Remember me?'

Alice nodded, still wary.

The old man smiled, not pleasantly.

'I'm not what you think,' he said. 'It's just a good way of getting people to leave me alone.'

Alice narrowed her eyes at him, re-assessing her earlier opinion.

'I remember you from the other night. Had a look to you, like you were planning something.'

The voice had changed subtly, had sharpened, the back was straighter, the eyes less rheumy.

'I'm not sure I know what you're talking about,' said Alice.

'Of course you know. I know what you saw in Grantchester that night, and I know you've read Daniel Holmes's book.' He took a step towards her, as if to punctuate what he was saying.

'Don't move.' Her eyes fixed his with a hard light, and the point of the knife rose a little. 'How did you know about that?'

The man shook his head with a little gesture of irritation.

'Put that down, girl, we don't have time.'

'Not a chance,' said Alice. 'I've had that trick pulled on me once today already. Now if you want to talk—'

Suddenly, the old man's hand snaked out towards Alice. Before she had time to lash out, he had grabbed the hand which was carrying the knife and twisted it sharply. His fingers jabbed stiffly into the back of her hand. Alice jerked backwards instinctively, and found that he was holding the knife half an inch from her throat, his other hand locking her left arm firmly and agonizingly at the elbow and shoulder, the pain of the lock forcing her on to her toes. He held her for a couple of seconds longer, then released the hold.

'Here's your knife back,' he said, holding it out by the handle. 'Next time you have to pull it on someone, use it to cover your body and keep them at arm's length. Don't just poke it at them like that.' His voice was amused. 'Now, will you please

312

put it away?'

Alice pocketed the knife, still rubbing her aching shoulder.

'What do you want?'

'You'll want to hole up in the house for a while. If you go right up to the roof, you'll find there's a little room there with a stash of stuff, couple blankets, chocolate, flask of tea, all that. You can take what you want. You wait there till night comes. I've got some cans of petrol piled up there, too, you'll know what they're for later. You—'

'Wait a minute,' said Alice, recovering from her astonishment. 'Who are you? What the hell are you doing here, anyway?'

'I might well ask you the same thing,' he said. 'I've been watching you.'

'Why?'

'Because it's time you realized what you were up against,' he replied. 'Time you let an old man tell you what he knows.' She looked at him, wondering for an instant whether he was as sober as he seemed. His red-rimmed eyes were crazy as broken glass. He nodded.

'You're a bright girl. You know who I am.'

Suddenly, Alice thought she did.

'You're Inspector Turner,' she said.

He smiled, showing a broken tooth.

'A lot of water under the bridge since there was any Inspector,' he said. 'The Inspector died when that girl came back from the dead. What's left is what you see. I'm Alec now, Alice, my girl, just Alec.' He shrugged. 'It's not so bad, you know,' he added.

'I thought . . .' Alice's voice cracked. 'I thought maybe . . .'

'You thought I was an undercover policeman come to save all at the last minute?' He rasped a phlegmy chuckle. 'No. There was a time . . .' His voice trailed away. 'But that's all over. She killed me, like she killed Daniel Holmes. It's just taken a little longer, that's all.'

He sat down on the window-ledge, his back to the fading greenish light. 'He told me about the diary, you know,' he said. 'Before he went into Fulbourn. About leaving it in the church wall. He reckoned that if Rosemary ever came back, that would be where she would go. He wanted to be cremated, so that she wouldn't be able to raise him. But he wanted the diary kept safe. Because he'd got it right, you see. Right for the first time yet, and too late for it to do him any good, but right enough for someone else to finish her off for good, for ever. What we did in the flat, he and I—' Here he broke off and spat, raspingly. 'But he did have the right idea. She can be killed, and kept buried, so long as no one gets left to raise her. That was it. It was that simple. I knew soon as I saw you that you were going to be the one . . . you had that look on you. But now . . .' He stopped again, clenched his fists in their fingerless gloves. 'You're not ready to deal with them, yet,' he said. 'You think they're going to come like lambs? You've seen them; she'll come with the others, the ones Holmes called nightwalkers. You've never seen them at work. I came with you; came ready. You think you'll do anything against all of them at once?'

'I'm ready,' said Alice, not quite steadily. 'As ready as I can be.'

'With that baby knife? Do you really think you'll

314

use it?'

'I thought . . .'

'You didn't think. There's more important things for you to do than to get yourself killed. You have to do what the old man missed; only you can do that right. Leave me out there, in the alley between the houses. I'll deal with the ones that come.'

He saw Alice's stare.

'You think I can't? You think that I'm an old drunk with nothing left?' He reached into one of his pockets, pulled something out.

'See this?' he said, holding the gun out to her. It looked old to Alice, almost antique, but it was polished, the wood of the butt oiled like a beloved cricket bat, and the light filtering through the narrow window touched its smooth burnished surface with a cool grey glow.

'I kept this all through the bad time,' he said, with pride. 'When everything got sold, and my wife left me, and they tried to make out that I was crazy. While I got drunk and went on the wagon again. I kept it all the time. I knew that one day I might need it.' He gestured to her with the gun, grinning his broken, half-senile grin. 'Go back,' he said. 'I'll watch the street. No one suspects a wino, not in Cambridge, nowhere. I'll see them come. I'll stop them. You, just do what you have to do. You'll know what it is.' Then, as Alice hesitated, 'Go on! Time for talk later. I've known for years it would come to this; for years, and I've been waiting all this time, waiting and wondering whether I might get to die in peace before . . . but that doesn't matter much now. What matters is you and me doing the job in hand. Just be careful. The thing

315

wants doing properly this time around. You don't want to leave anyone to bring her back. Not anyone.'

*   *   *

When Alice was upstairs in the little room Turner had told her about, she looked out of the window, and thought she saw him, hidden in the shadows, a darker smudge against the stone of the alley, imagined him keeping watch against what might come.

She was a little way beneath the roof, in what must once have been an attic, and there was a tiny unbroken window through which she could see most of the street. It was cold by now, and she had taken one of Turner's blankets to wrap around her legs as she waited, because half the roof was open to the grey evening sky. She had found a flask of tea, and several bars of chocolate. When she had finished the food and drink she began to feel warmer, and by about ten o'clock she was beginning to feel drowsy.

Suddenly, as she drifted, her eye caught a movement below her, and instinctively she drew back. Very carefully, she came to the window again, and peered through the dusty pane. There. A kind of flicker in the shadows, as of a pale face turned furtively upwards to the light. Someone was watching the house.

Alice felt sick, adrenalin rushing to her head. Not now, she thought frantically; she wasn't ready. The reality of where she was flooded her; she was alone, unknown, in the nightwalkers' den, with only what she had brought to protect her. No one would know what had happened to her if she disappeared.

Mentally she shook herself. At least, she had the advantage of surprise over them, she thought. She would be ready for them before they even knew she was there. Daniel had done it, and in the same house. They could not know she was there. She was safe.

On the other hand, Ginny had her friends to help her, the very thought of which turned Alice to ice. She forced herself to look again. Yes, there it was, only visible to her searching, panic-sharpened gaze. It was watching.

She reached for the knife, felt its weight, ridiculously like a studio prop, in her hand. Despite everything, the weight was comforting, and the sick feeling abated, just a little. Alice forced herself to move.

Very quietly, holding the knife before her, she began to creep down the stairs, her eyes straining against the dark. Inch by inch, she crept down the stairs, her shoes making no sound against the rotten floorboards, her blood a double-bass drum in her throat. She forced herself to breathe, though the temptation to listen, to stop breathing so as not to miss the slightest sound, was very great. One . . . Two . . . In . . . Out . . . Avoiding the steps which were unsafe, she concentrated on the breathing, on the pounding of her blood, and with those preoccupations uppermost in her mind, managed to reach the bottom of the stairs. There was no one else in the house.

Outside, then, thought Alice. She had seen one figure only, but there might be more. Should she go out to meet them? Every sense screamed no, but Alice knew that to delay would only be to give the others a greater advantage when the final meeting came. If she could just creep out . . . Maybe she would catch them unawares. And Turner was there too, Turner with his gun. The thought that he was there, with his old service revolver tucked carefully under his woolly pink scarf partly reassured her and partly filled her with a kind of hysteria; what could they do, he and Alice, against Rosemary and her friends? A drunken, half-mad old man and a crazy painter, with no real faith in her own sanity?

She tried to hang on to the thought of Turner waiting in the shadows, tried not to think how old and frail he looked, concentrated on breathing. The knife felt slippery in her hand, but in her head there was a sudden coldness as she stepped out into the alley.

The alley, just two feet or so wide, ran alongside the house. Originally it might have been a passage between the front and back of the terrace or a place to leave dustbins, but now it was partially blocked with old cans, pieces of charred wood and other rubbish. She stumbled as she made her way to the mouth of the alley, heard her feet crunch on some piece of debris and froze. Pressing her back against the greasy wall she looked around her in a broad arc, the knife held out stiffly in front of her.

There was nobody there.

She moved closer to the alley's mouth, partly blocked by a parked car, dared herself to look into the street . . . braced herself for the sight of them, the night-walkers, waiting for her, but she saw nothing. What now?

Carefully, she looked around again, the knife

raking the air.

'Be quiet!' hissed Turner. 'Do you want them to hear you? Get down!' They both ducked back down beside the car.

'I saw someone,' whispered Alice.

Turner nodded. 'Stay here and be quiet. Don't let them see you. I'll be all right.' And at that he turned and went back to the mouth of the alleyway and stepped out into the light of the street-lamp. Alice counted to ten and went back to the shelter of the parked car, looked carefully out into the street from beneath its rusty undercarriage. Her field of vision was limited and for a minute she saw nothing, but she was none the less certain that, this time, they were there. She felt them there, in the soles of her feet, in the dirt under her hands, the smell of old rubbish and corruption. She knew they were there.

Somehow, the sight of them was not even a shock. Just a jolt from her heart as it revved up, that droning in her ears which always accompanied the adrenalin-boost. An unexpected voice in her head laughed and muttered—*time, gentlemen, please*—then Alice took over again, the cool, practical Alice she had encountered in the fairground. No time for panic, she thought, it's far too late for that now—and she watched for maybe a whole minute through the space under the car, as the nightwalkers came into sight.

They were all there except Ginny. Of course, Ginny would have stayed with Joe; only her minions would stay in the flat. She recognized Rafe by his fair hair, Java by his height and the little sounds she could hear from his motorcycle boots on the pavement. Sounds seemed to be magically amplified in the still night, and Alice thought she could hear all their footsteps, distinctly, individually, as she listened. Still watching she saw Elaine hanging back in the shadows, Anton at her side. The nightwalkers came closer, the light from the street-lamp touching their faces and their forms with a dull, uterine light. Java glanced around him, almost idly, and Alice flinched, certain that he had seen her.

Then she saw his gaze stop, snag abruptly as he saw something. Turner? She heard the old man's footsteps, audible now, in the street, and she pulled herself a few inches further under the car to watch. A furtive glance around one of the thick rubber-smelling tyres was all she dared try, but she retained an impression of a group of figures crowded around the street-lamp, not three feet from the house, discussing something.

Turner moved towards them with a drunkard's shambling gait, muttering, seemingly to himself. Then he spoke more clearly, in his 'street' voice, 'Hey! Spare change fr'a cuppa tea? Hey!'

Alice heard the nightwalkers react, heard the sounds of movement as they turned to see who was coming. She recognized Java's voice.

'Old man,' he said quietly. 'Get on your way without delay.'

'Wassamatter?' complained Turner. 'Jussa copper fr'a cuppa tea. Ten pence. Jus' ten pence.'

'Look,' the voice was sharper now. 'Get out of the way.'

Alice guessed that Turner was nearer to them now, perhaps almost close enough to touch. She could hear him complaining wordlessly.

'I'm warning you . . .' began Java, now out of Alice's field of vision. There was a scuffle, as of someone pushing someone else. A scrape of feet on the flagstones. Then she heard a shot. Someone screamed. Then Turner fired again. More sounds, shuffling, running feet, two more shots in rapid succession. Cries. A crashing sound, a breaking of glass. In a couple of seconds, without stopping to think about the danger, she was on her feet, out of the alley and in the street, the knife ready. In the dim orange light she could not see far, but retained the impression of Turner slumping beside the parked car, the pistol skidding out of his hands. Against the side of the car, Rafe was trying to stop himself from falling, his bloody hands printing smeary pentagrams on the glass. A sound at her left and Alice slashed out almost blindly with a cry and felt the blade snag cloth. She leaped forwards at the figure she had touched, and at the edge of the light she glimpsed Anton and Zach, crouching back into the shadows, and she felt a brief exhilaration. Their eyes mirrored, like cats'; Anton hissed, showing his teeth. Then they were gone. A clink of metal from her right, across the road. Java was almost invisible against the night, but she felt his eyes, saw a gleam of buckles and chains as he fled.

Silence.

Alice endured the silence for a minute or so. The street was derelict, and there was no one to come and investigate. Dizzy and drained by the surge of adrenalin, she forced herself to think, to assess and to gather the fragments of what had happened. For a moment, the world spun like a magic-lantern show.

Then she remembered Turner. She called out to him.

'Here.' The whisper was almost inaudible, coming from a patch of shadow beside the car. Alice sprinted towards him.

'Turner?' For a moment his face was a pale, unfocused blur in the sharp light of the street lamp, then she noticed the blood on his scarf, the side of his face. His hands went up to her face.

'Got two of the bastards,' he breathed. 'That woman. The blond kid. Think I hit the tall bastard. The others got away.' His breath was a terrible croaking sound in his throat, where the blood bubbled out of the cut flesh.

'Don't worry,' she said. 'I'll call the police. We'll get you to a hospital. Hang on. Here, let me put this scarf—'

He interrupted her with a gesture.

'No time.' He reached for the gun, which had been lost as he fell and was lying beside him on the road. 'Here. Take it before the others come back. Go on.'

Alice looked around; despite everything, the feeling of victory remained.

'I don't think they'll come back just yet.'

'Go *on!*'

But Alice had already grabbed him under his arms, and was pulling him into the alley.

'It'll be all right,' she said. 'Just hang on.'

*　　　*　　　*

In the semi-darkness of the house, Alice managed to light a candle, taken from the upstairs flat, and in its glow she inspected the damage. Turner was

322

still conscious, but had lost blood; his body was shaking with cold and his eyes were bloodshot. The cut was not as deep as it had first seemed, and the knife (if it had been a knife) had missed the windpipe and the main artery.

Alice, whose knowledge of first-aid was rudimentary, could only try to staunch the flow of blood, and pile blankets on the old man to keep him from the cold. The kitchen seemed like the warmest place; there was an old mattress on which Turner could lie, wrapped up in blankets, and the windows were boarded up, so it wouldn't be too cold. She helped him to walk into the little room and settled him in. When she had done that, she went back into the street and picked up his gun, then, cautiously, she brought the bodies into the alley out of sight. Elaine, with a bullet through the head, pale and almost beautiful; Rafe with three or four bullets in his chest, his thin arms spread, a splash of blood across his angelic child's face. They must have been killed almost instantly.

Back in the house, with their blood splashed on her arms and face, she began to review the situation. So far, Alice thought, things weren't looking good. The death of Elaine and Rafe still left her to deal with Java, Zach, Anton, and, of course, Rosemary. They would be forewarned, dangerous and hungry for revenge, Turner was still bleeding—for all she knew bleeding to death, and with no possibility of calling for help—and she had lost her element of surprise.

Alice did what she could; she brought the rest of the flask of tea, and some chocolate from Turner's hideout, took the gun from his shaking hand, and went into the wrecked lobby of the house to wait.

If it was any comfort, she thought bleakly, she was certain they wouldn't be long.

Two

Ginny seemed half asleep, her head tucked into the crook of his arm. The lamplight flickered on to her face and lit her hair like fireworks. The curve of her jaw was white, flawless, the baby hair at the back of her neck giving her pallor a golden bloom. She was wearing one of Joe's pullovers, a dark maroon, and the colour should not have suited her, but somehow it did, emphasizing her air of frailty, the clarity of her child's complexion. He shifted, carefully, not wanting to disturb her, but she opened her eyes and smiled up at him.

'Is it nearly time?' she asked.

Joe nodded. 'Nearly time. Do you want something to drink? Some chocolate? Something to eat?'

'I'm not hungry,' she said.

'Do you want to listen to the radio? I feel like some . . . rhythm.' His hands were nervous, moving to a quick complicated beat of their own against the arm of the chair. Ginny nodded and Joe flipped the switch to FM.

'I like this song,' said Ginny, and began to sing softly along to it in a clear voice: ' . . . Na na na . . . Love Street, da-da-da-da. Love Street . . .' Her eyes were closed and she was bobbing her head to and fro to the rhythm, completely absorbed.

Joe smiled.

'I'm surprised you even know it,' he said. 'Don't

324

suppose you were even born when this song came out. It takes an old fart like me to remember that far back.'

'I'm not that young.'

Joe tried to smile, but his head was aching.

'What's wrong, Joe?'

'Headache. Don't worry, it'll go away. I've taken some aspirin.' For a moment he thought he remembered something . . . something about Alice. Had he blown his top again? Had she . . . ? He shook his head. He couldn't remember. Suddenly the headache intensified. He felt dizzy, his vision jumbled to a thousand points of light, jiving and spinning before his eyes.

'Joe? Are you OK?' Ginny's voice was all distorted syllables. His own voice, endlessly remote, on a wind of white noise.

'Here. Take this,' she said, pressing a tablet into his hand.

'What is it?'

'Trust me. You'll feel better.'

Joe dry-swallowed the pill. It tasted faintly bitter, but almost instantly the sickness receded and the world came into focus again.

Joe took a deep breath.

'Are you all right?'

Joe nodded. 'I think so.'

He took another deep breath, and suddenly he *was* all right, with an abrupt surge of well-being and confidence. Energy exploded through him, and he stood up and picked Ginny right up from the floor and hugged her.

'Hey, that was pretty quick work, doc. Good thing you were here.' He grinned again. 'This ought to happen more often; I feel great!' Then his face dropped, became older somehow, his eyes narrowing. 'It must have been that scene with Alice that set me off,' he decided. 'I was all right till that happened. She . . .' He broke off, his fingers beginning to tap the arm of the chair again.

'She got me so pissed off, saying all that stuff about you that I lost my rag completely. I should have . . .' (*finished her off*) '. . . tried to reason with her but by the time I realized that she'd already made a run for it.' He blinked and rubbed his eyes, thinking for a moment that maybe he didn't feel quite so good after all. 'She needs help, Gin,' he went on, 'because from what she said to me, your ex-friends have got a hold on her already. She's swallowed their story, hook, line and sinker. God knows what else they've told her.'

Ginny nodded.

'I know,' she said. 'There's no saying what hold they've got on her if she's at that house; you must get her out, by force if you have to. Reason with her later, when she's out of there. Get her out of there, the sooner the better.'

Joe frowned, a memory chasing its tail in his mind, just out of reach of conscious recall.

—don't remember. Did I want to hurt you Alice?—

—shh don't worry—

—but was I did I?—

'I don't want to do anything to hurt Alice,' he said pensively. 'Perhaps we should just call the police. She—'

Ginny's voice was suddenly sharp. 'She'll thank you for getting her involved in that, will she? I told you before, those people are selling drugs, they're making money from all kinds of petty crime. Do you think that the police will believe that Alice isn't involved? You have to get her away first, or you might as well report her for trafficking yourself.'

Joe sighed. 'I suppose you're right, Gin,' he said wearily. 'By now they'll be asleep, and it might be easier to take her unawares; but what if she won't come? I can't just . . .' His voice trailed off uncertainly and he looked at Ginny for reassurance. For a moment her image swam before his eyes, her bright hair a spray of sparks. His vision blurred, the after-image of her hair printed on his retinas like neon. He shook his head to clear it, hearing his voice from a distance, muted, toneless.

'I really don't feel too good,' he said. 'Maybe I should see a doctor. I don't think I'm in good enough shape—'

'Trust me.'

She smiled up at him. 'We have to find Alice, remember? And it will be easy, I promise.' From her shoulder-bag she pulled out a little pouch, unzipped it and showed what was inside to Joe. A syringe, and four little ampoules of something straw-coloured.

Ginny saw Joe's expression and squeezed his hand reassuringly.

'It's all right,' she said. 'The hospital gave them to me when I got out. They're tranquillizers, that's all. Not big doses, either. One should make her sleepy and suggestible. Two should knock her out completely.'

'I don't think—' began Joe, but she interrupted him again.

'It would only be a last resort. They won't hurt

her, I promise you that. Otherwise, you might find that she's hostile and she won't come with you. All she has to do is to yell once and all the rest of the crowd will come running. Unless you want to face them all . . .'

Joe paused. 'All right,' he said. 'Just as a last resort, though. If nothing else works.'

Ginny smiled up at him. Her eyes were clear and innocent. She handed him the little pouch, carefully zipping it shut again.

'Here, Joe,' she told him. 'You take these.'

One

They were all there, in the flat: Rafe, Java, Anton, Zach, Elaine, all except Rosemary. I had told the others I wanted to hunt on my own, that they should not wait for me. They did not question my decision; they were used to my solitary habits by now, and Elaine, the only person who might have shown interest or suspicion, had ceased to talk since Rosemary had recalled her, and would only sit, dry-eyed in her corner, rocking herself like a frightened child. It was just after midnight. Since ten Turner and I had been hiding in the alley watching, making certain that everything was going according to plan. At eleven Rosemary had come, and had gone again, passing so close to me that I had caught a breath of her scent in the still air, and I had reeled with the closeness of her. But I had held fast, Turner's arm trembling beneath my touch as he had seen her, and I had known he felt something, too.

He was eager that night, infused with an excitement I knew was born not only of the wine we had both drunk to give us courage. For the first and last time, we were not alone. That night, I was happy.

At midnight, we crept up the stairs to the flat. I was calm, Turner was twitching with anticipation. I went to the door, opened it with my key and went in. I found them, as I had thought, in the bedroom, drinking wine. They had hunted, and they were drowsy, glutted and unsuspecting. Elaine was lying on the bed, her hair spread out on to the pillow like a mermaid's.

Tick . . . tick . . . tick . . .

I forced myself to sound normal, though my mouth was dry as salt, and my nerves like wires.

'Sorry I was so long,' I said. 'Is there any of that wine left for me?'

Zach held out the bottle by the neck, grinning sleepily. He looked very young to me then, very alien. His beauty was almost more than I could bear, sublimated, too, by the fact that I knew I was going to kill him.

'I'll get a glass,' I said then, and went into the kitchen.

In the kitchen, I found the glass, and put it by the side of the sink. Then I disconnected the stove from the pipe in the wall and turned the mains on full, jamming the gas-tap on. From my pocket I took a little wrench and removed the tap, so that it could not be turned off again. Then, I left the tap in the sink on full so that it would sound as if there were still someone in the kitchen. I can't even say

329

it was very hard to carry out; we had rehearsed it all every day that week. There was a jangling coldness in my mind as I forced myself to check that the window was shut. Very quietly, I left the flat, and with my key I locked it from the outside, plugging the keyhole so that the door could not be opened. With bated breath we listened at the door, but heard only the muted sound of voices from the bedroom, where I knew the others were waiting, drinking wine and wondering vaguely why I did not come. Then, I took from my pocket a large roll of masking tape, of the kind you use for lagging pipes, and I taped all round the door. I cut the lengths of tape carefully, with a craft knife, trimming it neatly at the edges. I went round the door-frame twice, making sure no air could get in. Then we waited.

This was the critical point: the five minutes or so before the gas began to permeate every part of the flat. If someone had followed me into the kitchen and heard the gas hissing . . . We listened, Turner shaking silently, his eyes round as an owl's. No one came. The voices in the background sounded lethargic, casual; a meeting of nineteenth-century British poets discussing art.

I held my breath and waited.

I could hear the ticking of my watch in my pocket, amplified as if under water, every second a step nearer to my salvation.

Tick . . . tick . . . tick . . .

One/Two

Alice stirred, then opened her eyes as the torchlight touched her face. Cold and the cramped posture in which she had eventually dropped off to sleep had almost paralysed her, and she twisted round, trying to shake the cold from her limbs.

Joe caught himself thinking, irrelevantly, cloudily—*cat's eyes you've got cat's eyes*—of the fairground, of walking hand-in-hand with a younger Alice, neon stars in her eyes.

She stiffened as she saw Joe, sitting up abruptly.

'What're you doing here?' Her voice, still blurred by sleep, was wary; Joe thought he knew why. His gaze travelled to the corners of the room, taking in the bloodstained blankets, the filth, the silver paper and used syringes on the mouldy floorboards. Yes, he thought he understood.

'Don't worry, Alice,' he said, forcing his voice to retain its gentleness.

Alice gave a sharp, dry bark of laughter. Her own quick glance around the room had taken in the silhouette of Ginny, standing still and passive at the door; she spoke to Joe, but without taking her eyes off the girl.

'It's happened before, Joe,' she told him. 'The hard-luck stories, the little girl lost. She uses it as a cover, so that even if she's found out, some other poor sap will pay in her place. She's been doing it just about for ever. Feeding on people, taking their love and their life, making victims of some, monsters of the rest. Can't you see, Joe? Just look at her. It's in her face. There's destruction in her face. If you don't believe me, there are two dead bodies in the alley out there, and an old man next door who might be dead.' Cautiously she was beginning to shift her weight on to her feet, ready to spring. Her hand was trembling on the butt of the pistol.

There was a silence, cold and blank as outer space.

Then Joe took a step forwards.

His face was unreadable, his hands, somehow threateningly, in his pockets. 'Alice,' he said. 'You're ill. I don't know what bullshit these people have been giving you, or what you've been taking, but you're ill and it shows. I want you to come back home with me. I want you to see a doctor. Get some therapy.'

He took another step, and suddenly he was holding something in his hand—a needle? thought Alice, pulling away.

'What's in there?' she said sharply. 'Who gave you that syringe?'

'It's just something to make you feel better,' he said. 'I wouldn't hurt you, would I?'

His voice was infuriatingly calm, like someone talking to a wild animal.

Alice kept her eye on him. She jerked her chin towards Ginny.

'Did *she* give you that?'

'I'm not having you accuse her—'

'And you believe her,' said Alice, backing towards the door, and at the same time gently lifting out the old service pistol. 'Yes, it's real,' she said, and stifled a ridiculous urge to laugh. Alice, still not taking her eyes from Joe and the girl, began to turn the door-handle. The laughter was barely restrained now, shaking her at the seams. It was so comic, her with her antique gun, and Joe with that expression on his face, staring . . . despite herself, she grinned, but even the hysteria felt good.

Suddenly she froze. The laughter died. There were footsteps in the alley.

Alice backed away from the door, fumbling now with the pistol, trying to work out how to fire it. Surely, there must be a safety-catch somewhere . . . hell, she didn't even know if there were any bullets in it.

She was still fumbling when the door swung open, and the nightwalkers came in.

Alice was able to look at them coldly, and was conscious of a savage glee as she remembered why Rafe and Elaine were missing.

'Joe,' she said. 'Be careful.'

Java gave her a single glance and turned to Ginny. 'The other two are dead,' he told her. 'Shot by the old man.' He aimed another glance at Alice. 'I slit the old fool's throat,' he said. 'He won't bother us again.'

Alice felt rather than saw Joe flinch by her side in the darkness as she backed away. She was aware of the three figures blocking her exit, and the slight form of Ginny standing at the door behind her. She moved towards the inner door, easing her steps over the broken glass, cans and rubbish scattered everywhere. To get to the back of the room Alice had to pass Joe, so close that she almost touched him; and remembering his attack on her in the house, and the fact that he still had a syringe which certainly didn't contain Lucozade, she edged past him with wary caution. But Joe was

333

uncertain; she could feel his confusion as she brushed by him in the semi-darkness. He had dropped the torch, which now shone in a narrow arc against the doorway, lighting Java's boots and making giant shadowplay of the nightwalkers on the ceiling.

'Alice?' His voice rose waveringly. 'What old man? Alice!' For an instant he reverted to the old Joe as he took a step forwards and half-fell on some slippery debris. 'Shit! What the hell is all this?'

But no one was paying any attention to him. As he spoke, Alice made a dash for the inner door, pushing past Ginny to disappear into the passage. Java and Zach followed her, but not too quickly, their boots crunching the debris underfoot.

'She won't get very far,' said Java. 'Anton, watch the door. Zach, with me.'

Joe's voice, faint and thin, 'Alice?'

A tunnel of blackness, a fathom deep, as Alice crashed her way through darkness to the stairs. Panic surged through her, as she fled up them. For a moment she could almost have believed herself to be flying against that wind, a wild witch with her hair in her eyes and a magic at her fingertips which could at one gesture harness the wind.

'Dammit, what the hell was that?'

Alice slipped back into the jerky motion of panic with a conscious jolt. What had she been thinking? She seemed to remember, with an elusive visionary quality, a sensation of . . .

—destiny
　—rapture
　　—space, speed.

It was a feeling of being so much more than Alice, that for an instant she had been beyond fear. She turned a corner of the staircase, the palms of her hands slick around the butt of the pistol, pushed open a door at her back and stepped backwards into the dark. She had no power; all she had was her intelligence and the gun. Those feelings were just illusions to confuse her. Suddenly the room seemed much bigger than she had expected; in the gloom Alice found that she could make out an unbroken window, the curtains drawn back to reveal a lighted square of window, moonlight reflections on a table, a candlestick, a pack of cards spilled across a patch of light as she pulled the door closed behind her. There were footsteps on the stairs by now; she could hear the sound of boots on the hollow wood, of voices remote, tinny, like the soundtrack of an old film. A snatch of music, half imagined on the rushing of the black wind, the wild jangle of a merry-go-round. A wheel turn—against the sky; a wheel turn—the sky under the façade of blue.

Footsteps on the landing; Alice levels the pistol. A slash of light underneath the door, bisected by the shadows of someone's feet.

Tick ...
      tick ...
           'Gas leak! Gas leak!'

Turner's voice had sufficient authority, even after what had happened, to rouse the few other residents from their beds; the smell of gas was enough to do the rest, and in a few minutes we had cleared the building, Turner making certain that no would-be heroes joined us in the house as I took the petrol-can and sprayed the third floor with its contents. I was taking no risks; there would be no recalling those charred bodies. No sound from the room, only a rushing emptiness, like a black wind, from behind the door, like the sea heard through a shell. I mopped my handkerchief in the petrol, took out my lighter and turned to go down the stairs, my heart ticking away my frozen thoughts like a razor against stone.

The black wind intensifies, a whisper of ice-cold music in a deserted gallery, a long-dead minstrel with a lute of hair and bone sings songs of hate under a black moon. I knew she was there before I even saw her, felt her breath in my ears as I spun to her measure and saw her face.

God, her face!

Rapture.
　　Tick . . .
　　　　tick . . .

Joe staggers and puts his hand to the wall to steady himself, his night-vision slowly reasserting itself above the glimmer of his mind's eye. For a moment he is still, allowing the world to stabilize, trying to think rationally. Java's words keep returning.

I slit the old fool's throat.

The silhouette of a beggar-child against the door, like a thin goblin sentinel, pale refracted light shining on his white face. Ginny, her hair incandescent in the dimness, staring into the dark with eyes like tunnels. To Joe she seems without

336

substance, a statue of glass and smoke. He brushes her hand in the dark, but she does not respond. He understands dimly that wherever she is, she is not there.

'Ginny?' His cry is almost inaudible. Ginny remains motionless, intent. With a terrible effort he forces his frozen body into motion again, the dark pressing on him like stone. A spike of panic drives through the soles of his feet as he passes the threshold and feels the cold breath of the beggar-child on his neck; but it has been left to guard the door, and though its hunger grins and gibbers at him it stays, obedient. The kitchen is cauldron-black, and he strains his eyes against the dark as he feels his way between obstacles towards the huddle of blankets underneath the window. There is a fetid smell of old dust and mould and sickness, horrible sickness, sickness like the smell of the hospital where his grandpa died, like the smell of the old balloon-lady at the fair. An old terror, half-buried from childhood, takes him by the throat; he gags with the fear of it, begins to feel his throat tighten. A dream, or the memory of a dream, comes back to him so clearly that for a moment he forgets who he is and where he is.

Tick . . .
tick . . .
t—

The door opens and Alice lifts the pistol, pausing only because she thinks it might be Joe. Light floods the room, a carnival light in a dozen bright colours, pink, blue, yellow, green. A sharp hot scent in the air like peanuts and roasting

337

apples and the slick sugary scent of candy-floss. For a second she forgets where she is, almost who she is; looks down at herself and sees (dirty jeans torn at the knees, blood in the creases in her palms, sweatshirt grimed with soot, the gun held uneasily in a shaking hand) her clean Indian skirt, the ends of her flowing dark hair brushing her shoulders. The disorientation intensifies for a moment; Alice frowns, trying to remember—a hand falls on her shoulder, a kindly voice speaks.

'Come on now, Alice. It's all right, you just freaked out for a minute.'

'Joe?'

He grins, pushing long hair out of his eyes.

'Who d'you think it is? Are you OK now? You were having your fortune told, and you must have passed out, or something. It must be the heat. Come on out here and I'll buy you an ice-cream.'

Alice frowns.

'Fortune?'

'Yes, don't you remember?'

She shakes her head. 'I . . .'

'You'll be all right in a moment or two,' the gipsy woman smiles, oddly young-looking in the bright light, the neon flickering on to her red hair. Odd, that she should have red hair, thinks Alice vaguely; she thought that all gipsies were dark. A bird tattoo is etched starkly on to her left cheekbone, eerily lifelike.

'OK?' Joe's voice is concerned. 'Do you want to go home now?'

Alice shakes her head, forcing her eyes back into focus, manages a smile.

'No, it's all right,' she says, but even as she speaks she looks at Joe and wonders how, in the damp and muggy heat of this hot summer night, he can still be wearing that greatcoat.

Tick...
    tick...

Turner shifts uneasily under the filthy blanket, tasting the tinniness and slickness of his blood in his throat. His dreams fall away from him like snakeskin.

In his dreams he has heard the nightwalkers come and go, for a moment he almost touched Joe's hands as he reached out to him, but Joe is snatched away again into bright ether, and Turner smiles thinly through blood-crusted lips and drifts back.

Tick...
    tick...
        t...

She makes children of us all, I told you; children in the face of her, the glory of her. She revels in our fears, the scent of our childish terrors, and she feeds on them, on all of us—she is the witch in the gingerbread house, the ogress, the wicked queen, the ravening wolf, the monster in the cellar, in the heart. This is her defence, this one rapture, shrinking us into children, wracked by children's fears, children's certainties.

As I face her, the Blessed Damozel, essence of every dream and fairy story and legend and fear, I am filled with a rapture I cannot analyse; I am diminished and at the same time increased. She laughs as she turns the wheel of the spinning-top

339

but at last I know that I am ready for her. I run
across the painted skyline, a perfect circle,
spinning for me. All around me rise the painted
trees, the houses with windows painted on their
bland red façades, the painted railway track
humming as I hear the sound of the train, that
hungry dragon from under the painted earth. I
hear it, its voice like the apotheosis of all monsters,
Rosemary at the wheel, bearing down on me. And
suddenly realize that we too have *power*, power
enough to break hers. We are children; we believe.
And with belief, with faith, we can destroy her.
Children have the only true faith, not the
stumbling faith of religions, those dim adult fairy
tales, but faith in magic, belief in rapture. Join
hands with me and chant the spell—

> *Tick* . . .
> *tick* . . .

Alice starts; for a moment she thought she was
somewhere else, feels the breath of the night on
her cheek. She looks at Joe as he grins, wolflike,
and draws a long black knife from the pocket of his
greatcoat. Somewhere in the background, a merry-
go-round the size of a spinning-top is playing; as
she watches, the bird on the gipsy's face spreads its
wings and flies away.

> *Tick* . . .
> *tick* . . .

As she is taken off-balance he strikes, the knife
reaching her at a clumsy angle, slicing through the
palm of her hand. She screams, the sound a clear

bright lance in the air. The fairground dances around her like a carousel ride, scents assail her nostrils; blood and peanuts and the rank stink of animals. Zach claws at her, one earring swinging; she feels his fingers jab into the side of her neck, almost paralysing her. She kicks out at him sideways, taking him off-balance, her mind a cold rushing emptiness. Her hands are someone else's hands as she finally lifts the pistol and fires.

For a moment time is suspended.

The shot surprises her even more than it does Zach. It seems as if the gun has gone off entirely on its own, wrenching her shoulder as it does, leaping in her grasp like an angry cat. A second before the shock even registers, Alice sees the hole appear in Zach's chest, sees him stagger and fall back, sees him jerk again in mid-fall, and then the world is nothing but sound, sound and blackness, and Zach on the floor. There are clouds in her eyes, and in slow motion and silently Java approaches, the knife a slice of shadow in his hand.

*   *   *

Rapture. The word is alien, like someone else's thought beamed by accident into Joe's mind. For a second he isn't even certain what it means, but as he hears its psychic echo the world snaps back into place with a sound like a breaking bone. The figure in front of him is nebulous, giant one moment and small the next, the knife a blade of shadow slicing the air before him. His eyes drop to the needle in his hand; he has kept it all this time without even knowing that he had it, and a certainty invades him. For a startling moment he is Joe again, flying, riding the storm on a wave of chords, a sorcerer's apprentice conducting an orchestra of howling, screaming fantasies. He leaps forwards into the wave with the syringe held high above his head.

*   *   *

The world comes back into sharp focus, but too late; Java is on her, crushing her windpipe. She swings her fist at him, still weighted with the pistol it strikes him on the side of the head, a messy blow which nevertheless loosens his grasp from her throat. The knife has fallen to the floor, and Alice is almost sure she can feel the hilt of it under her ribs, digging into her back, but she cannot reach it. She feels Java's hand come back to her throat and twists to bite him, feeling her teeth against his wrist. Almost gagging, she struggles to raise the pistol, but her hand is numb from loss of blood, her arm gloved in blood to the elbow. Slick with blood and sweat, the pistol slides from her hand and falls by her side where she cannot reach it. She guesses Java's grin as he closes both hands around her throat and begins to tighten his grip.

*   *   *

With a cry of (rapture) elation I (he) fall upon her, fragments of her illusory glamour showering me (him) like glass. I (we) have broken out of the spinning-top at last, like a dragon eating himself up tail first. She can have no more power over me (us), I tell myself; I am free. We are free. I reach

342

out to them over the years, to you, to him, to my figure reflected back over time like faces in a hall of mirrors. We are Daniel, you are Daniel, Daniel, young and old, legions marching across the years, marching across the painted blue sky. In this moment I can see you. I know you. I reach for your hand, here where all possibilities are true; I take your hand and give you the power I know we have, the power of light, the light of all things which die and suffer, all things which love and yearn for the unattainable. God help me, in this endless, sacred moment I feel redeemed, I feel *blessed* with all the brave certainty for which I will grieve in vain in later, darker years. Maybe it is the gas, the hunger, shock, or maybe, as I choose to believe, the divine re-asserting itself in my soul, but for a brief longed-for instant, I feel that despite Rosemary I have at last glimpsed God. As I struggle with the nightwalker, my glasses fall to the floor, my heel grinds the glass to dust. I feel (the needle in my hand) her bones beneath my hands, the hollow of her throat give way under the pressure (the syringe empties, I can feel its response). Her flesh yields reluctantly; for a moment all illusions are stripped away, and we see her face as it really is, the childish features cut away to reveal the nightwalker unmasked. In that instant she speaks to me, promises worlds and lifetimes. But she is weakened, ebbing like a bloodtide, waning, shrinking. The face of the demon becomes a burning rose, the cup passes over.

*   *   *

The pressure is unbearable, a single degree away

from death. Alice's nose is bleeding and her vision is darkening fast. Her right arm is almost completely paralysed now, and both she and Java are struggling in a growing puddle of sludge made of blood and dust. Her thoughts are terrifying, simple patterns, unaware even that they are thoughts. Suddenly she feels him flinch, his thoughts assailing her with a blast of unexplained panic, his hands going from her throat. For a second she fears that she will not be able to move, but she finds that she can. She grabs his knife, and hits him cleanly once, just below the ribs . . .

*   *   *

Joe's mind circles in a broken loop as he stares in shock at the red-haired girl. In the faint glow from the broken window she is a jumble of light and shade, hair the faintest nimbus of rose in a stark and violent monochrome. The syringe is planted in her neck, just below the jugular, and as he reaches to draw it out, the girl twists round to bite him, hissing, her eyes rabid crescents of white. She thrashes, snakelike, in his arms, she rakes his face with her fingernails, hissing in a deep, choked voice. He falls to his knees with his hands shielding his face.

God the light!!

Something is happening to Ginny; her face twists and shifts, her image like breaking crystal in the sunlight.

Joe reels before the force of the vision, cringing back against the wall. Half-obscured by the shiftings of the light against his retinas, he is still aware of the figure of Ginny kneeling on the floor, hissing and raking at the air with her fingernails, and though he can hardly see her real body, he seems to see behind the veils of flesh a formless thing, tearing at its own face to reveal something lightless and pitiless, reaching out its fingers to touch despair into his heart. He retreats to a foetal position, eyes closed like the door to his mind. Black flowers bloom behind his eyes, all sensation receding mercifully at the end of a tunnel of light. Going back to a soundless world, world beyond memory.

(Bye bye.)

(Wait.)

(No no no.)

(I said wait.)

The voice has authority, and automatically he obeys, turning in confusion as the accents coalesce into a figure, a face he does not recognize; a young man about his age with thin, academic features and old-fashioned half-moon glasses.

(Who are you?)

(Don't worry about that, you've got to listen to me. I haven't very much time.)

(What do you want?)

(You have to set fire to the house, make sure it's completely destroyed, then you have to burn the bodies.)

(Ginny, oh Gin—)

(Don't say her name, don't mention her. You have to forget her, no grave no funeral, nothing. Do you understand?)

(I—)

(It's terribly important. You have to forget her. If you don't do as I say you'll call her back.)

(. . . I)

Alice stumbled and almost fell and in the strange flickering light she thought she saw a figure standing in the room, a young man in an overcoat, grey eyes obscured by thick glasses, thinning hair hidden by a brown felt hat, but when she regained her balance he had gone, and there was only Joe, lying on the floor beside Ginny's body. The broken syringe lay beside her, but she could see the mark it had made, the bruise and the single drop of blood on the white throat. She took Ginny's wrist in trembling fingers, searched for the pulse, but found nothing. Just the rushing nothingness of the sea in an empty shell.

Beside her, something moved slightly, and she heard a sound, half-sigh, half-groan.

'Ginnyyyy . . .'

In an instant she was on her knees beside him, pulling him up. 'Joe? Are you OK?'

'Al?' He sat up abruptly, and Alice thought she could *feel* the fever in his body through his clothes. She guessed that he might be in shock.

'Where's Gin?' He stood up, still with that false briskness, and Alice wondered at how strangely *normal* his voice seemed. She supposed that she too was in shock, but for now the sensation was almost pleasant. Even the blood, which was still trickling sluggishly down her arm and the whole of her left side, seemed to belong to someone else.

'Ginny's dead.' Her voice felt remote, as if she had just come out of anaesthetic.

'What?' He was hardly paying attention. He patted the dead girl's face gently. 'Gin. Wake up. Come on, Gin. She's fainted. There was something in the air. Drugged incense or something. I passed out, too. Ginny!'

'She's dead,' said Alice quietly.

'Gin? Wake up, Gin.'

'Joe. I said she's dead. You injected her with the syringe she gave you for me. She meant you to kill me all along.'

'No!' He shook her, more violently this time. 'Ginny!' He turned to Alice. 'She's not breathing. We need an ambulance. Ginny!' He began to try to pump air into the girl's lifeless body by force, almost sobbing with the effort.

'Ginny! Wake up!'

'It's no good. Whatever was in that syringe wasn't a tranquillizer. She wanted me out of the way.'

'*No!*' He was crying now, still pumping at the girl's body. 'Wait! Ginny! I love you!'

And it wasn't the blood, or the shock, or even the relief of thinking it was all over. It was hearing him say that to Ginny, to Rosemary, even after everything that had happened, that made her lose control. Everything strong in her collapsed, and with that last 'I love you' in her memory's ear (so much sharper than reality), Alice began to throw up.

*   *   *

Some time later she found Turner's petrol and guessed its use. For all its damp, the house burned fairly well.

One

The radio's on somewhere in the building; I can hear it playing weird dream-notes through the walls, some kind of modern music, I suppose. I don't much like the modern scene; I expect it's because I'm too much of a purist. I never even liked jazz. But somehow, these notes, odd, semi-discordant resonances rarefied into almost nothing through the thickness of the walls . . . they compel me, somehow, I can hear the voice of the singer, low, almost atonal, a kind of lament; I can even hear the words:

Remember me, for I am not gone away.
I am in the air you breathe—
I am in every part of you.

No, I never heard that. I must be making that up.

Remember me when shines the sun;
I am glass—
The sun shines through me.

How strange, that my subconscious should speak to me through rock music.

Remember me when comes the night;
I'll haunt your dreams.

Two

It is raining, and the tiny sounds of the rain against the window tick against the glass like time going by. Alice remembers the cup of tea by her elbow and tastes it; it is cold. Moggy is sitting on her knee, paws tucked neatly under her body. Alice forces her eyes back into focus and re-reads the letter, crumpled by the weight of the cat. There are cat hairs clinging to the smooth paper. The hairs are brindled, like the cat. For a minute or two, the hairs are more clear than the writing.

A phrase catches her eye, holds it almost magically;

'*Something inside me still remembers . . .*'

'*and I'll never forget her.*'

'*Never.*'

She brushes the paper, absently, begins to read again; she knows the words almost by heart, but still she re-reads them, as if to discover some undisclosed secret in the close-written lines.

Dear Alice,

I have arranged the funeral in Grantchester for the 21 May. Nothing elaborate, but I wanted to make sure that she wasn't just forgotten.

I'd like you to come. First, I think it would do you good, and would get you to see things in a proper perspective. Second, I need to talk to you. I can't believe what you told me last time; I can't and won't believe it of her. I love Ginny and she loved me. I think she was disturbed; I'm willing to believe she was an addict, and after the result of the inquest I believe you are right in thinking that she intended to give you a drug overdose. Perhaps she even knew it was an overdose. At least none of that had to come out in court; they all assumed that she'd done it herself. In as much as I can feel gratitude in any of this rotten business, I'm grateful for that; because I know she was innocent. As for the rest, I'm convinced that what I thought I saw in the house was an hallucination caused by drugs; it's the only explanation I can accept. It would be better for you if you'd accept it, too.

I don't know what I'll do without her; I'm writing this to you and wondering when I'll start feeling the pain—in a way, the most terrible grief would be better than this. I've left the band; I found I couldn't take any interest in what was going on any more, and I didn't think it was fair on the others to drag them down just when they were beginning to get somewhere. Maybe I'll get going again some day; I don't know, but every time I pick up my guitar I just keep remembering Ginny.

I need you, Alice. You're the only person who knew her that I can talk to. I need to know all about her, to make her live again for me. Don't try to make me forget her; I can't. Something inside me still remembers and I'll never forget her. Never. She can live again, in me, in my thoughts and dreams. God, sometimes I feel her so close that I can almost touch her. Please come to the funeral; no one else will. I've ordered white flowers.

Alice stops reading.

In her mind's eye she sees a carnival wheel, still and black against the white sky. She walks across the deserted fairground towards it, as it looms dragonlike above her. For a moment she glimpses the intricacies of its inner workings, red with rust and black with oil, hears the voices of birds calling in the still pale air. Then a sound, faint and whispery at first, then beginning to gather momentum . . . the sound of the beast's intestines at work. A grating, creaking sound, a grinding of metal on rust, metal on metal. A sound like the machinery that turns the world on its axis like a roundabout, keeps the blue sky's circle in place. Slowly, but with the inevitability of Fate, or Faith, the wheels begin to turn.

Epilogue

I held out for as long as I could; it took me this long to realize that after all, this was where I needed to be. It's quiet here, tranquil; every day a new kind of serenity. I sit at the window and comb my hair into the sunlight, like Mariana, and I wonder whether death will come today. It comes to me in the mornings, almost gently, with the sun, and somehow with its coming I begin to understand Daniel better than ever before. We remember, Daniel and I: we remember and we know that it's only a question of waiting. A wheel turns, a clock ticks, a girl rides a roundabout through a carousel of dreams to come full circle again under the same sky which turned for Daniel's little train in his spinning-top all those years ago.

I haven't seen Joe in a long time; now that I come to think about it, didn't I see something in his eyes, that last visit, something bright and desperate. Something almost like hope?

Poor Joe. Of course he recalled her; I remember him at the funeral (yes, I was there, trying to prove to myself that we had won), dry-eyed and somehow unfocused, his little bunch of lily of the valley clutched so tightly in his hands that the knuckles showed white under the skin; and sometimes his hands shifted slightly, nervously, and I saw the marks his fingers had left on the delicate leaves, bruising them into transparency. No one else came; no friends, not the family she had said she had; no one, and yet all Grantchester

353

seemed to welcome her back, mutely, with the ease of long understanding.

Yes, it must have been then that he called her; perhaps when he dropped the crushed flowers into the grave and felt the fragrant call of the earth; perhaps he saw her standing by the hawthorn tree all in white, like a novice. Sometimes I wonder whether he saw her looking at me. But he called her, I'm sure of it; as sure as I know the air I breathe. The wheel has come round again, and she is coming. *April, come she will* . . . This morning I thought I saw her in my mirror, looking out from her haunted underwater eyes. Did I see her? Or did Joe? Was she holding a noose? *April . . . come she will*. It almost sounds like a promise. Something inside her remembers . . . and come she will. I don't think I can be like Daniel; I don't have the strength to hold out for as long as he did; and for what? For all our efforts, she still came back.

Something inside me remembers . . .

We remember, don't we? Yes, Daniel, and Robert, and Joe and Alice. We all remember, and we keep the faith while we can, alone, like children in the dark. That's what she did to us. To all of us.

April, come she will.

I think she's almost due.